DESPERATE UNDERTAKING

Also by Lindsey Davis

The Course of Honour
Rebels and Traitors
Master and God
A Cruel Fate
The Spook Who Spoke Again
Vesuvius by Night
Invitation to Die

THE FALCO SERIES

The Silver Pigs
Shadows in Bronze
Venus in Copper
The Iron Hand of Mars
Poseidon's Gold
Last Act in Palmyra
Time to Depart
A Dying Light in Corduba
Three Hands in the Fountain
Two for the Lions
One Virgin Too Many
Ode to a Banker
A Body in the Bath House
The Jupiter Myth
The Accusers
Scandal Takes a Holiday
See Delphi and Die
Saturnalia
Alexandria
Nemesis
Falco: The Official Companion

THE FLAVIA ALBIA SERIES

The Ides of April
Enemies at Home
Deadly Election
The Graveyard of the Hesperides
The Third Nero
Pandora's Boy
A Capitol Death
The Grove of the Caesars

DESPERATE UNDERTAKING

Lindsey Davis

HODDER &
STOUGHTON

First published in Great Britain in 2022 by Hodder & Stoughton
An Hachette UK company

1

Maps by Rosie Collins.

Part titles by Ginny Lindzey.

A CIP catalogue record for this title is available from the British Library

Hardback ISBN 978 1 529 35468 3
Trade Paperback ISBN 978 1 529 35469 0
eBook ISBN 978 1 529 35471 3

Typeset in Plantin Light by Hewer Text UK Ltd, Edinburgh
Printed and bound in Great Britain by Clays Ltd, Elcograf S.p.A.

Hodder & Stoughton policy is to use papers that are natural, renewable and recyclable products and made from wood grown in sustainable forests. The logging and manufacturing processes are expected to conform to the environmental regulations of the country of origin.

Hodder & Stoughton Ltd
Carmelite House
50 Victoria Embankment
London EC4Y 0DZ

www.hodder.co.uk

DESPERATE UNDERTAKING

The Campus Martius

1. Stadium Domitiani
2. Odeum Domitiani
3. Thermae Neronis
4. Pantheon
5. Stagnum Agrippae
6. Saepta Julia

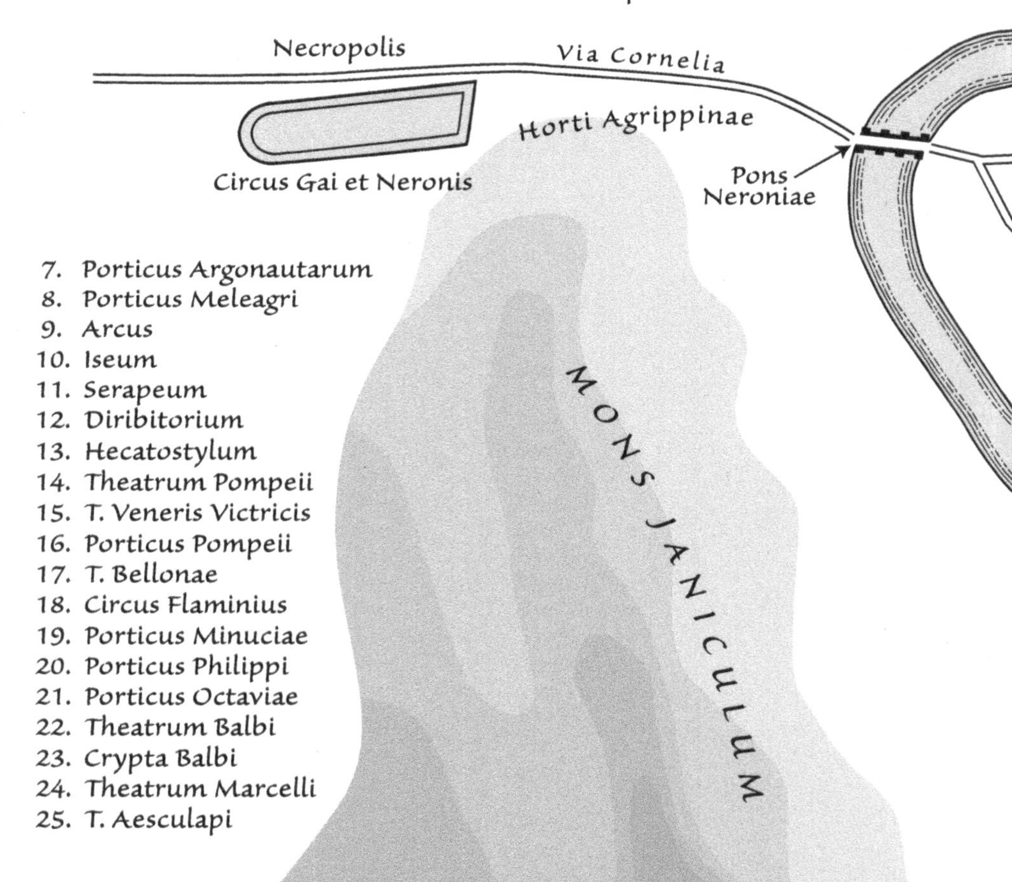

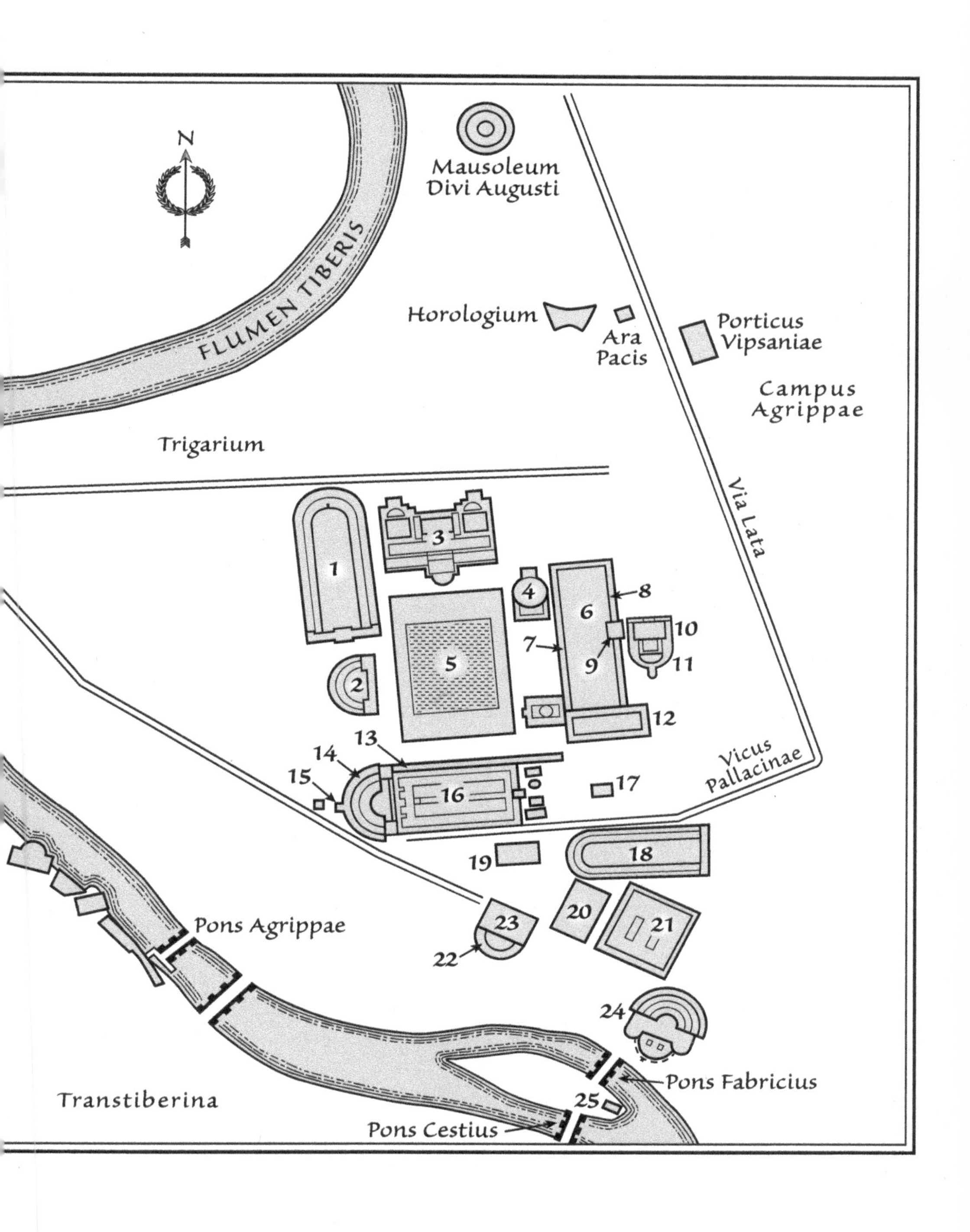
N
Mausoleum Divi Augusti
FLUMEN TIBERIS
Horologium
Ara Pacis
Porticus Vipsaniae
Campus Agrippae
Trigarium
Via Lata
1
2
3
4
5
6
7
8
9
10
11
12
13
14
15
16
17
Vicus Pallacinae
18
19
20
21
22
23
24
25
Pons Agrippae
Pons Fabricius
Pons Cestius
Transtiberina

Rome, AD 89: the Campus Martius

The Playlist

In drama and myth

Laureolus and Selurus (Bandit Kings), Minos and Pasiphaë (a couple from Crete), Daedalus (an inventor), Theseus and Jason (heartless heroes), Orpheus (a tragic tunesmith), Oedipus (a complex person), Ariadne, Phaedra, Atalanta and Medea (unhappy women)

Family

Falco and Helena	not in the plot
Albia	our leading lady
Tiberius	her leading man
Suza, Dromo, Paris, Fornix, Gratus	their chorus of staff
Gaius and Lucius	their dear little fosterlings
Gornia, Cornelius, Galanthus, Lappius	Falco's auction staff

Professional entertainers

Davos	a face from the past
Thalia	his on-off companion
Jason the python	off the scene, but unforgettable
Chremes and Phrygia	actor-managers: final curtain?
Byrria and Sophrona	a long-lost daughter or two
Atticus, Ariminius, Pardicus, Simo, Porrus, Philotera, Crispa	on cue, the acting company
Philocrates	simply a star
Plotinus	a musician with a broken string

In the Farcicals

Ambrosia, Gnaeus/Maccus, Septimus/Pappus, Megalo/Centunculus and Questus/Dosennus	am-dram, not even understudies
Lana	Ambrosia's mother

In civic life

Scribonius Attica	a very ambitious politician
Sabina Gallitta	his wife, a very keen patron
Mucius	investigating officer of the VII Cohort of Vigiles
Caunus the tribune	an idiot of dubious parentage
Hyro and Milo	intellectual firefighters
Corvinus	a praetor, another idiot
Lusius	his scribe, discovered to be still alive

Lower orders

Suedius, Sorgius, gravedigger	the wrong undertakers
Eucolpus; Naia Nerania; Assia	a landlord; his mother; her maid
Fugax	the strongest butcher in the world
Cintugnatus	a theatrical agent, trust him
Crispinus	a waiter, don't believe him
Barmen and waitresses, stallholders, lictors, the Urban Cohorts, a peeing man	
Spiffy	a soloist
[Three fishermen]	cut!

Animals, trained or untrainable

Barley	a brave pet
Buculus	the famous aurochs
Caprininus	a toyboy goat
Cleopatra	played by Rheon; Rhubarb, Rhubarb
Patursus, Matursa and Ursulinus	the three bears
Anethum	a lost treasure
Nux	a happy ghost

LAUREOLUS

I

'Who did this to you?'

'The undertaker!'

The dying woman made no sense. We were too late to save her. She had been clinging on, but she gave up on life as we tried to help her. The way she had been killed was as desperate as anything I had ever encountered. I was an investigator who had seen foul play before, but nothing as troubling, and never before with a victim who left behind such a puzzle.

Why did she blame the undertaker? Who meets their undertaker while they are still alive? People expect a proper sequence of events. Bodies are entrusted to a funeral firm only after someone dies; *then* they may be handed over for hygienic plugs, pre-cremation cosmetic work, convenient storage until relatives cough up for dusty urn space or clear a plinth in that showy mausoleum of theirs.

I am a reasonable woman, at least when I cannot avoid it, so I concede that errors can be made. All right: it may sometimes happen that an incompetent doctor or a money-grubbing heir is too quick off the mark. They despatch their hapless cadaver for processing just a smidgeon too soon. Then, in the quiet gloom where the body has been carried, something changes. The 'corpse' suddenly sits up. Determined not to go yet, it has snuffled back to life. Finding itself laid on a cushioned bier, or at least slammed down on a trestle, it probably yells. Anybody

– any body – would do. In that case, a black-hearted undertaker with a pressing need for cash *might* swiftly apply pressure to a windpipe to make sure of his fees.

Most would surely take more pleasure in announcing a miracle revival, if only to gain a free mention for their business in the *Daily Gazette*: 'Corpse stuns observers, asks for dinner and a warmer tunic . . .' Suedius, the sinister mortician in the Field of Mars, claimed to me later that corpses revived all the time; he assured me they would chase him around his premises, hilariously trying to kill *him*.

Who could blame them for going after him? I certainly wanted to. He was an idiot. He had no soul. He gave me a lot of trouble on this inquiry.

At the theatre, it seemed he and the dead woman were previously unacquainted. When Suedius turned up he winced stagily and asked us, 'Bloody hell! Who is she?' It did not occur to anyone that he might be lying.

He had been summoned in the ordinary way by the vigiles – except that he was told to come at top speed. The authorities wanted him to whisk away this tortured body before she, and the abominable manner in which she had been killed, attracted public notice.

Keeping it quiet would be impossible. The public had already seen the group of us rushing to the theatre. Gawkers all over the Field of Mars expected a sensation, because people knew a killer was at large. They cannot have guessed what was coming this time. We got wind of it, however, as soon as we entered: we could smell the dung and hear the giant wild aurochs scraping its hoofs and furiously bellowing. An amphitheatre battle bull, weighing fifteen hundred pounds, is terrifying.

He was famous. His name was Buculus. He would not stand dribbling in a stall while people fed him grass. He preferred to trash the stall.

We already knew this poor woman had been deliberately lured there by someone who intended her to suffer. She had not come teetering into the auditorium, dreaming of some acting role she coveted, then wandered onstage where she had a cruel face-to-face encounter with a primeval bull.

It was certainly cruel. But not face-to-face.

Nor was it accidental. A highly inventive madman, with at least one accomplice, had prepared the scene we had found at the Theatre of Balbus. It was meant to be a truly dreadful punishment. Merely to have the victim trampled or gored to death would have been too easy – and not theatrical enough – for the undertaker killer.

2

Curious? Then hold on while I begin at the beginning. Phrygia's was the second inexplicable death on the Campus Martius that morning. By the time her ghastly murder was discovered, I was already investigating the previous one, a case I had snitched from my father while he was away.

A couple of days of entertaining relatives during a festival were enough for my parents. Falco and Helena had rustled up a carriage from someone who had more sense than to go anywhere at the end of December. Then the dizzy pair took my three siblings rattling off down the misty Via Ostiensis to their coastal villa. The youngsters were now gathering driftwood on its storm-battered beach to warm up the draughty holiday home, while the parents pretended that seaside life was fun. I had been dragged along before, so I was having none of it. I stayed cosily in Rome with my own family.

I was not expecting interesting work for Falco – though we both knew I would steal anything that turned up. He had always been a private informer, and still kept his hand in, except when I managed to poach his clients: *Dearest Father, I hope you and Mother enjoy a relaxing break. Have checked at the office. All extremely quiet, no need to rush home …*

My family owned an auction house. Whenever my eccentric parents swanned off somewhere else, the staff were in charge, with me nominally supervising them. I was the eldest daughter, and fully trusted. An aunt did creative work on the accounts, but bills and receipts were taken to her at home; Maia could never be bothered to traipse all the way down from the Aventine and out to the Saepta Julia on the Field of Mars. It was my job to trundle across the city, banter with the porters and sweet-talk any customers.

The Saepta Julia was a huge two-storeyed gallery used by sellers of precious wares, or in our case mixed goods, some desirable, some less so. We had no control over what people chose to sell, though we cheerily auctioned anything.

There were no sales during the holiday. I knew how to run a sale and could even wield the gavel, but nothing was booked until well into New Year. I only came for a gossip. I had brought my dog and my husband, to give them both a walk. It was understood that Barley must not chew furniture and that Tiberius Manlius was allowed to rootle through caskets of waiting lots, still desperately trying to find a Saturnalia present for me. He had promised a necklace but then found himself stuck at the goldsmith's behind a long queue of forlorn husbands. Hieronymus would fulfil his orders at a leisurely pace through January. Instead, Tiberius now hoped to find me something antique.

I explained what this meant. 'It will cost you twice as much and the clasp won't work. If you take it to be mended, Hieronymus will put you right back at the end of his queue – but maybe it will be ready for my birthday.' My birthday was four months away. Tiberius knew, because he first met me in April.

He unfolded the X-frame of a battered old Egyptian stool, then dropped cautiously onto its rope seat. Barley the dog sat alongside, happy to have us together in one pack. 'I'm hopeless,' he conceded, scratching the dog's ears. 'Why did you marry me?'

'I believed your sales patter. Didn't you promise me a life of luxury?'

'I thought you were living on salt fish and pomegranates. Anything else would seem good by comparison.' His grey eyes were penitent. It was a tease, but I liked him making the effort.

Since I was a typical informer, there was truth in what he said. Both our lives took a jolt after we met. His reputation wavered because of his marriage to me, though oddly enough our union had made me half respectable. Now he was trying to establish himself in a building firm, while I put my salt-fish funds into provisions for our growing household. Builders take a long holiday over New Year. So, with festival bills to cover and mine the only income this month, when a man turned up asking for Father while we were at the Saepta, I went straight away onto the alert. Tiberius mooched back to rootling.

Barley gave one woof at the visitor, to establish that she could sink her teeth into him if she wasn't the nerviest dog in Rome. After that, she hid behind me. I was afraid of no one. I certainly saw nothing to worry about in the new arrival. He had a workaday cloak over a dull tunic. He looked more like a traveller passing through than someone wanting an auction. Still, he might have inherited a house from a rich patron. In our world, you never judge by appearance. Punters tend to skulk behind pillars like runaway financiers, while most professional dealers look like rat-catchers. You can never be sure.

I asked for a name, but he took no notice. 'Falco about?' His voice attracted attention, an easy, resonant baritone that carried around the Saepta's near-deserted upper gallery. Barley put out her snout and woofed again, though quietly.

'Gone on holiday. I am a daughter. Can I help?'

'How do I contact him?'

'Oh, he'll be back when he's ready. If it's about a sale that's already pegged on the calendar, see the head porter. He's the old soul who looks half dead. If it's new work, talk to me.'

The man had a square face, once handsome, with grey hair, and a confident manner. His frame must have been sturdy in younger years, though he now had stiffer bones and feebler flesh on him. He gave me a stare, then tried another ploy: 'Is Helena Justina with Falco?'

'He took her to carry the luggage.' I stared back. It was unusual that he had come here if he knew my parents socially but of course if he had been to their townhouse, there was no one at home. 'Falco and Helena will be together until they are taken up in the same cloud of mist to dance among the stars.'

The jokes and my romancing seemed to convince him that *I* knew them. Even so, he was desperate for some authority figure he could relate to. 'That your husband?' He nodded at Tiberius, who waved a hand to say he refused responsibility. He was burrowing despondently in a chest at the other end of the balcony. He kept holding up objects for my approval, so while I talked to the stranger, I was shaking my head and rejecting them. Who wants a dormouse pot? No one. That was why they regularly came to auction.

'So, you are in charge?' the visitor accepted gruffly.

'Afraid so.' I was close to thirty, well-dressed, wearing a wedding ring, self-assured. If he really knew my parents, he ought to know what quality of person they would leave behind to speak for them. None of these reliable traits had impressed the man, but I was still wondering whether there might be work for me here. I hid my impatience. 'I am the eldest, next generation. You don't say when you saw Falco and Helena last, but they have us three girls now, plus Alexander Postumus.'

He gave a start. 'Thalia's strange nipper?' I lifted my chin. He twigged that I wouldn't let him insult my adopted brother. 'Sorry. He seems an interesting boy! I met him with Thalia last month.'

Not many people would validate themselves by reference to Postumus, let alone mentioning his birth-mother, who happened to be an exotic snake dancer. Such things happen in our family, though perhaps not in yours.

'With Thalia?' I warmed up enough to smile. 'That would have been when Postumus caused a man to be suffocated by a python, then set an arena on fire?' I let myself reminisce mildly enough. 'Our darling does have a few accidents, though he never intends to be bad. Thalia sent him back to us, so he is away with the parents. I'm sorry but I really cannot say when they are all coming home.' I folded my arms, the gesture of a woman who would give no more until provided with references.

The man grudgingly accepted he was stuck with me. 'I am Davos.'

It meant nothing.

'I know Falco and Helena – met them must be nearly twenty years ago. You were not in the picture then!' he declared, almost accusingly.

'I am now,' I answered, staying calm. The parents must have met him on an adventure before they found and adopted me. They would have been newlyweds twenty years ago, while I was still a lonely street child in Britain. I had never imagined two slightly eccentric Roman people would one day pluck me out of misery and bring me here. Still, I reckoned I had settled in. I could hold my own against local attitudes. 'If you need something, Davos, I am the woman to ask.'

Davos was bridling again. 'Look, I have an emergency on my hands.'

'Try me!' I challenged. This was hard work. As a woman running a business in imperial Rome, fortunately I was used to it.

Tiberius had noticed the change in our voices, so he wandered over. He was holding a flying-phallus lamp. With most of my attention still on the visitor, I gave it a mischievous gleam of approval. The male organ turned up at a good angle to its hanging chain, though to my mind its feathery wings were not cute enough. We had little boys at home who would think it screamingly funny, but this was supposed to be a present for me. Tiberius conceded the point, grinning.

Breaking in on our silent exchange, Davos became agitated. 'I came to see Falco – and I can't wait. I shall tell you what has happened, but you will need a strong stomach. A couple are in trouble – names your parents used to know. The man has died – murdered, cruelly. Falco and Helena would remember him, Chremes, and his wife. We all met up in Syria—'

'Oh! Falco's playwriting period.' Still not absorbing the real situation, I was smiling. Both my parents talked of their eastern adventures fondly; a play Falco had adapted for performance had even been recently revived. 'So, Davos, you were in the theatre company they travelled about with?'

Davos looked grim. 'Yes, but I manage my own outfit now, joint venture with Thalia. We're all back in Italy, so the old troupe and mine often follow each other around on the circuit, or we even work in parallel for festivals . . .' He was talking to delay explaining why I needed a strong stomach. 'People know me. They know Chremes and Phrygia are my oldest friends. His actors are desperate and have asked me what to do—'

Tiberius cut in: 'What happened?'

Davos straightened up. 'Chremes was found this morning in Domitian's Stadium. He must have been there all night. Jupiter knows when he actually died. He could not escape – he couldn't move. Nobody heard him, if he cried out.' Davos choked. 'It's shocking. He was an old man, a man of refinement. He would have been mortified—'

'How?' I pressed him gently.

'He had been stripped naked and hung up to die on a cross.'

3

Crucified? Some genial fellow-traveller my parents once knew? A friend from their long-ago romp around Syria, when they were living in tents and acting on wooden stages? We all took a moment to breathe.

Crucifixion: a criminal's death. It was the time-honoured punishment for slaves who had killed their masters or for rebels, pirates, disgraced soldiers, political blasphemers, anyone too low to be shown human respect. Cynics might say anybody poor. No one who can afford a lawyer dies in that way.

To the Roman mind, crucifixion is a perfect method of execution, since it makes the convict suffer unbearable pain and humiliation, while witnessing such agony may deter others from committing the same crimes. Unlike death in the amphitheatre, no one needs to scour remote provinces for expensive lions. It is embedded in the Roman psyche, most famously since Crassus had thousands of Spartacus's followers hauled up to rot on crosses all along the Via Appia from Capua to Rome. Schoolboys who are thrilled by that episode are not always told that Crassus, a byword for greed, later died horribly himself when molten gold was poured down his throat by Parthiams. Crassus's head was then used as a football in a performance of *The Bacchae*.

I come from Britain. I wish I could say the wood and water tribes are less barbaric than the iron-clad masters of Rome's 'civilised' Empire, but truth is never so simple. During the Boudiccan Rebellion the luckiest dead had their heads hacked off and deposited as gifts to the river gods; unluckier Romans of both sexes were suspended bloodily from trees, after mutilations that suggested British forest gods are seriously sick spirits. I cannot bear to think what may have befallen my lost birth-parents.

The world is cruel. Victims of terrible crimes and their devastated relatives may welcome crucifixion. If it really deters crimes and prevents other victims having to suffer, so be it.

I had heard that, when conducted properly, this punishment should be supervised by an officer of at least centurion rank, using specialist troops. Cynics will say those soldiers are trained in how to prolong the agony yet, to be fair, the ritual scourging, with severe loss of blood and other fluids, may actually hasten the end for a victim. The soldiers must remain on site until the criminal is dead so, being anxious to return to their barracks, they will naturally help things along by breaking large bones, battering the chest, lighting asphyxiating fires and spearing the heart. None of this is necessarily done from cruel motives. A soldier who risks death in battle may perhaps feel considerate of another's pain.

Without help, death on the cross can take many hours or even days. There will be cardiac arrest, organ failure, severe respiratory distress and mental torment. In Rome, the Esquiline Gate had once been the official site for executions – an outside place, to avoid polluting the sacred city.

Unofficial crucifixion was murder; murder was a crime with a special court and judiciary. It would certainly go down very badly with the Emperor if killing was being carried out in such a gruesome manner inside a jewel of his civic building programme, his spanking new stadium on the Field of Mars. Domitian loved his stadium, where he staged high-flown Greek-style athletics contests. These, our paranoid Emperor thought, gave polish to his image as a generous, civilised ruler.

It was a weird place for a killer to choose, though the location was only part of the mystery.

Tiberius had gone indoors to fetch a portable chair from the office. We seated Davos so he could recover a little. He leaned his elbows on the chair arms, head lowered. Tiberius resumed his wonky pharaonic stool. Barley lay down by him. I propped myself against the balustrade around the upper balcony.

With our premises on two levels, we stored heavy goods downstairs. Up here, Falco had corralled a small area where he passed off pre-sale 'bargains' on private buyers. I fetched out Father's wine-flagon, with the very small cups he gave these special customers. It was good strong stuff, as he wanted to enjoy it himself, to give added conviction. Davos tried it, then raised his cup to the absent Falco. We all gulped, then put down our empties on the ground.

Still frowning, Davos supplied more details. Chremes and his wife had led a touring theatre troupe, which, though Davos called it tattered, had managed to survive for years. Now back in the home country, they regularly performed in southern Italy, occasionally went north towards the Alps, and once a year visited Rome. Chremes no longer acted, but he remained a passionate company manager, supported by his equally strong wife. He had presence, which he needed to gain official approval to take part in major festivals – most recently he had secured a place at the Plebeian Games. They mainly took place in the Circus Maximus, with a ceremony dedicated to Jupiter on the Ides of November, plus chariot races, all preceded by five days of theatrical performance.

Tiberius interjected, 'I had some involvement in that, Davos. Selecting plays.' Because he was modest about his role as a magistrate, I supplied the detail that he was a plebeian aedile. They organised those games, so last month he had viewed rather a lot of rehearsals while he chose the official programme. 'So, did I see Chremes?' he wondered. I knew he was aching to check his notes (Tiberius took careful meeting memos, the full stylus-and-wax-tablet works, then kept them for months afterwards). He very much wanted to pinpoint this troupe in his mind.

'You must have vetted them, and my own group too. We were both chosen – different plays, different days, obviously. That meant,' said Davos, with regret, 'I was too busy with my own production to mingle socially. We all stayed on afterwards, wintering in Rome, hoping for more work at Saturnalia and New Year, but I still missed my chance to greet my old friend. I've been spending time with Thalia—'

'You know Thalia?' asked Tiberius, being careful not to give any verdict on her startling physique and character.

'Know her? Rather more than that! You've met her? What a cracker! We call ourselves a couple. Mind you, Thalia bonds more closely with her bloody snake.'

'Jason,' I said. We all honoured Jason the python with a respectful pause.

'Don't tangle with him!' agreed Davos. I knew Jason was a big boy nowadays, full of reptilian mischief. 'I shall never know how the woman does it . . . Anyway, she and I were catching up, which is an exhausting process – not least because of having to wrestle the bloody python into his basket, or he gets jealous – so I failed to come over the river to visit Chremes. Now he is lost for ever.'

'And in a horrible way,' I hinted, to bring Davos back to the story.

He took the cue. Chremes and his troupe had been renting rooms around the Field of Mars, attracted by the Saturnalia trinket stalls and the merry atmosphere. Actors and their support teams enjoy wine and all that goes with it during a festival. Yesterday Chremes suddenly went missing. It was odd. He and his wife were in decent lodgings, a treat they always gave themselves even if the actors and musicians grumbled. He went out and never came home. She kicked up a fuss. She was so agitated that their company members were persuaded to leave their lower-class rooming-houses and go out searching.

Somebody spotted a fake play notice. Scrawled on a wall outside Domitian's Stadium, it claimed Chremes was due to act there, though he had not mentioned this to anyone. The stadium was never used for plays: there was only a running track and no stage for drama.

Immediately they went inside, the searchers saw their missing man, his naked corpse dangling from a large wooden cross.

With foreboding, I asked Davos, 'What was the play? The play they saw advertised outside the stadium?'

He could see I had guessed it. Tiberius had realised too, for he was already shaking his head in disgust. '*Laureolus*,' confirmed Davos. His voice was grim. Like us, he despised the piece. *Laureolus* was always one of the most popular plays in Rome, but after Domitian gave it at the opening of the Flavian Amphitheatre, it acquired an added twist. Nowadays its appeal is loathsome.

Laureolus, the lead character, is a bandit. This colourful anti-hero has lively adventures, makes wisecracks to the audience, robs other characters with gusto, then is pursued, caught and punished. As an outlaw, he suffers crucifixion. Sometimes in performance his death is speeded up by bringing on a savage bear. An audience won't sit on hard stone seats for days: they want sudden horror to scream at, then smartly off home for their dinners. A bear does the trick.

Why is this needed? What now makes this play so very, very popular is that the lead actor doesn't simply nip down a trapdoor or slide into the wings to die. Directors force a willing criminal to play the main part. Doomed to the arena anyway, the condemned man has a moment of acting glory, then perishes to wild applause: Laureolus really dies onstage.

4

'Has this all been reported?' Tiberius was bound to ask that. He had only a week left as a magistrate, but he would not waste a day of it.

'Useless!' Davos growled. 'I wasn't present when the body was found, but apparently some turd in a toga, a praetor, rushed along in a panic—'

'A praetor! That's over the top.' Praetors ran the legal system. These lofty judiciaries tended to keep aloof, lest they be contaminated by experience of real life.

'Presumably called in because the locus is so prestigious,' Davos growled.

'Know his name?' demanded my husband.

'Corvinus. Minimal interest, once he'd taken a squint. So long as Chremes is speedily removed, and the stadium made to look as if nothing ever happened, he'll dump any work on the local vigiles.'

'Are they being helpful?' Tiberius asked. I knew better than to bother. The vigiles would hate dealing with a very public, sordid crime like this.

'A joke!' scoffed Davos. 'That was why the lad from Chremes's company was sent running to me. You must know the attitude. Actors don't count. Bunch of noisy nuisances, terrible dress code, foul habits, bound to be drunk . . . The official take says this is a stunt that went wrong.'

'Oh, what stupidity!' scoffed Tiberius.

'Just ducking a problem,' I told him.

'Right,' said Davos. 'The red-tunics are asking a few questions in the neighbourhood – did anyone see anything? No? Oh, it's persons unknown, then! End of story.'

I glanced at Tiberius. 'Seventh Cohort,' I commented, without enthusiasm.

'Ursus?'

'No, the Seventh cover both the Circus Flaminius and the Transtiberina. Ursus is out-stationed in the Transtib. It will be his senior putting his feet up here.'

'Pity.' Tiberius meant that we knew Ursus. The investigator-in-chief on this side of the Tiber was bound to be hostile: he would not want to work with an informer, especially one he did not know. In any case, the Seventh were routinely derided as the worst of all the vigiles cohorts. Prejudiced slackers. History of bending rules.

Davos was being realistic about his own profession. Actors ranked with gladiators and brothel-workers – social outlaws. A dead actor barely counted as a loss of human life. Still, the involvement of Domitian's Stadium meant the Seventh would have to close the case somehow. A report would be required. I assumed that, like most of his colleagues, their man in charge of investigations was perfectly capable of inventing some story for his tribune, especially when it was likely to be passed on to the Emperor. He would have to do better than 'a stunt that went wrong', though.

Davos grumbled, 'We want to find out what happened. We need a decent investigator, not somebody who looks the other way.'

Tiberius nodded understandingly. 'So you came to see Falco.'

'I've seen Falco solve knotty mysteries. But it's no use if he's not here.'

'Hold on! You have an excellent alternative. Marcus Didius trained Flavia Albia,' my husband argued. 'She uses his methods, she is highly intelligent, people respond well. You can trust her.' Ever the best of marketeers, he added demurely, 'And at reasonable rates!'

I gave Davos a smile. 'As you see, Tiberius Manlius receives no dinner at home unless he lathers on flattery.'

'Might you take an interest yourself, Aedile?' Davos asked him, sounding hopeful, but Tiberius demurred: at New Year he would be too busy arranging his replacement's official handover. In addition, he pointed out, this district was not his; he had best not interfere in another aedile's patch. I noticed he made no offer to speak to his colleague about the problem. That might have been because Tiberius Manlius thought the other three men who shared his role were place-holding incompetents. Besides, with a new intake taking office next week, his current colleagues would have laid down their styluses and sloped off to their rural villas.

We were different. Hell, we were different in many things! At this point in early married life, we were barely holding together one new home, let alone a string of holiday estates, like most officials.

Reluctantly, no doubt, Davos returned to me. 'So, Falco taught you?'

'Everything he knows, or so he maintains.' To prove it, I produced a scowl like his. My father did not believe in toadying to clients, using earnest claims of thoroughness and skill. He was himself, take it or leave it. If he liked your job, he would do it. Thank him and pay up. The method suited me, too. I gave examples for Davos: 'Poking your nose in without being asked. Upsetting the authorities, offending victims' relatives – all while sticking to a fixed belief that everything anyone tells you will be lies.'

'Sounds like him!'

'We worked as a team briefly, while I was starting out,' I said patiently, 'but you must know, Davos, the only partner Marcus Didius ever really likes is Helena Justina.'

'I remember! I am willing to put in cash,' Davos offered. 'I haven't asked Phrygia whether she wants an investigation, but I guess she will. How can she not? They had been together a long time – she'll be distraught and won't let him go without an explanation. She will hate what's been done to him and will need to understand. I came straight here – I haven't seen her yet. Thalia will be prepared to club in something. She knew Chremes. Hades, who in the business didn't? Your work will be funded.'

I said frankly that we needed the money. I suspected my parents might help out for free, if these were old friends. Davos might have expected that. But I had a living to earn, and since he seemed willing, I offered him a discounted rate, with a promise to minimise expenses. We shared a joke that Falco had certainly not taught me considerate cost-control. Father's idea was to charge as much as possible.

Then, with no time to waste before any clues disappeared, I began at once.

Davos and Tiberius came with me, curious to see the scene. My dog Barley circled ahead of us, pretending she knew the way. The new stadium was close enough. All we needed was to walk across the back of the Pantheon Baths. It would have been easy, but for having to skirt around Agrippa's Lake. On the far side of this notable sheet of water, silvered beneath the winter sky, lay both the long Stadium and the neater semi-circle of the Odeum. These gorgeous buildings were laid out parallel to the Saepta Julia and at right angles to the extensive, much older, Theatre of Pompey, with its big complex of colonnades and temples. Once occupied by a muddle of workshops and even by poor housing, this whole area had been burned out by the huge city fire during Titus's reign that we all still remembered anxiously. After Titus died everything was rebuilt by Domitian, much more formally.

As we walked, tightening cloaks around us, I mentally prepared questions. I would have written the list in a note-tablet, but anyone who has ever tried to write while on the move will know why I did not.

- How was the victim lured or brought here?
- Did he know his killer?
- If the place was locked up for Saturnalia, how did they get in?
- Why the stadium?
- How many people were involved in erecting the crucifix, and putting him onto it?
- Where did they get the cross? How was it fetched here?
- Why did no one nearby see or hear anything (or did they?)
- Then, why, for Heaven's sake? What was the motive?

A couple of bored vigiles, hard ex-slaves in red tunics, were guarding the grand entrance on the straight end of the stadium.

'Who is your officer?'

'Mucius.' The name was unfamiliar. We had been right: no chance of leverage.

I let the men debate getting permission, while I slipped past and went straight in. Falco had taught me to seize opportunities. He reckoned you can achieve a lot by simply behaving as if you have the right to be somewhere.

I knew he sometimes brought my young brother to the foot-races – it was easy to obtain last-minute tickets since Father worked at the Saepta. He knew the gate-keepers, of course; Father knew everyone. I never came. The prudish Emperor Augustus had barred women from watching athletics – we could see arena bloodshed, but nude running might excite our passions so this was my first visit.

The place was striking: the largest stadium outside the Circus Maximus, which has a cruder presence that reflects its great antiquity. Completed only about three years ago, this was much more elegant. Its expensive marble style matched the Flavian Amphitheatre, created by Vespasian; Domitian probably used the same workforce and materials. His father's financial acumen had certainly supplied the funds. Rabirius, the talented designer of imperial palaces, had also built this. Like all his projects, it was a beauty.

A classic Greek shape but with Flavian design elements, two layers of barrel vaulting supported the seat tiers. Exterior ornament was clean travertine stone, with two orders of engaged columns, simple and stylish. Service corridors ran beneath, where scruffy stalls and ambulant prostitutes had already established themselves, but commerce was politely hidden from sight. We had approached at the flat end, which was topped by gilded victory statues.

Inside, too, everything was exquisitely faced with pure, elegant marble. In the enormous space, it took me a few moments to identify various clusters of activity. The two steep banks of seats began at a height of about fifteen feet and must have risen to a hundred at their highest, so all views of the track were perfect, unless a giant with a big hat was seated in front of you. A few silent men I guessed were from the theatre company were squatting at ground level; they were slumped in attitudes that suggested they had found the body, shocked and grief-stricken. I could let them wait. They were not going anywhere.

Grand architectural features marked entrances halfway down each side and at the far-off hemispherical end. Near the entrance I had used loafed a couple more vigiles, rough-and-ready bare-armed men in red, like the ones outside. They had been left ostensibly on guard; they had a civilian with them, a weedy, shifty man who I guessed was the custodian. They had already lost interest in the crime scene. While I got my bearings, I could hear them discussing a completely different incident in which a local mother whose husband had left her could not cope with his desertion: she suffocated their two children and then killed herself. Engrossed in their blame for the woman, the gossiping men took no notice of me. I walked in past them and paused.

There were starting-blocks on one side at this end. The wide track ran away impressively, up and around the distant U-bend before returning. In the distance I made out a small group of dedicated runners. Amazingly, they were at practice as if it was a normal day for them. To get there they must have walked in like me, right at the scene of tragedy. Clearly it had not deterred them.

In the middle lay a long empty area. On this open ground, I could see where the crucifix must have stood, though it had now been taken down. It would have been a dramatic sight. Anyone who entered the stadium was meant to stop dead. A statement killing, absolutely. I visualised it, then hunched in my cloak, depressed.

Workers – ragged public slaves with shovels – were already filling in the hole where the cross had been set up. Rome has its priorities. Were it not for all the coming and going on restitution, those obsessive runners at the far end would probably have been completing full laps. I scoffed to myself grimly that they could have practised how to avoid a fellow athlete who stumbled and fell: they could have dodged their way around the stiffening corpse. That was because he was still there, lying on the track.

Chremes had been moved from his original place, though he remained on the cross. That shocked me. The big wooden construction must have been hauled out of the hole, then carried away piecemeal, leaving drag marks that one slave was sweeping over. Despite adding to the weight, the victim had been left fastened there. Did the slaves not want to touch him – or had they not cared?

I walked over to where his corpse waited for attention. Alongside, a big-wheeled cart with an open back, all painted black, clearly belonged to local morticians. Its donkey twitched his tail at flies as Barley went to say hello. It looked a heavy vehicle: deep wheel ruts had scarred the athletics track. A slave was tutting over that, getting no reaction.

A man with a boy assistant was taking a professional interest in the corpse. They had a stretcher ready on the ground but so far they were just maundering. I did not interrupt. Since the body remained fixed in position, I was able to make an assessment in situ.

The way the cross lay on the ground, Chremes was now staring up at the sky. He must have been over seventy, if not older, as Davos had implied. He would have been a tall man.

He had the belly of someone who had enjoyed life, though his elderly limbs were bony, their skin blotched by poor circulation, a long-term condition, not a product of recent assault. The head that lolled on his scrawny neck would have been called noble if he was some old togate Republican, though his straggling grey hair was artistically long, curling at the ends. He had not bothered to shave during the five-day holiday – I could make that out from his visible neck and chin. Part of his face was hidden. He was gagged, with what looked like a loincloth, presumably his own.

Where were his other clothes? Nowhere visible.

Prior to death he had been beaten. Somebody had put passion into that; it implied a deep personal motive for this crime. There was dried blood, apparently from flaying wounds on his back and sides, though I would need to see the body turned over to be certain. Perhaps he had been dead or unconscious when he arrived. Perhaps, when I discovered more about how the crime was carried out, I would feel glad that he had lost any awareness of events.

Preparations to fasten him up could have been made with the fully-formed cross lying on the ground, though at official execution sites uprights are left standing in pre-dug holes, ready for future use. Crosspieces are brought along for each new punishment. Criminals can be hoisted aloft, already fixed to the crosspieces, or lifted on afterwards. Either way, setting up must have taken at least two other people, plus ropes and stepladders. This cannot have been a single-perpetrator murder.

Whatever the order in which it was organised, Chremes's arms had been fastened to the crosspiece. Tight binding around his wrists continued to near the elbows. I assumed that wrists alone would not bear the full weight of a body. It was neat, serious ropework, by people who were used to fixing things.

The dead man's feet had been immobilised on either side of the sturdy wooden upright: what looked like long military nails were hammered in through each ankle. As I stood silently noting details for myself, the undertaker was explaining to his apprentice: 'Nailing the feet stops their legs kicking. It's not needed for the process. I've seen them use a small support for the feet.'

'To help him stay up?'

'Drags things out longer. Death happens because the bodyweight is pulling down on the arms. He can't breathe. His chest muscles will not work, so he has to heave himself up on his stretched arms, for as long as he can manage it. He will try to snatch gulps of air, but pretty soon he's dying from no breath and exhaustion.'

The snub-nosed boy listened as if he was used to grisly lectures. He was just waiting patiently so they could get on. He looked a smart little biscuit: he was turned out in a neatly belted tunic, with a clean face and his dark hair combed. I expect his family was pleased he had a steady job. He was about ten.

His master, a solid lump of nearer forty, boasted a paunch as hard as a wine barrel, piggy eyes, a puffy face, and the swagger of a man who openly enjoyed the putrid side of his trade. Myself, I would never place a child in his care, however much I might need extra income for my family. 'In many forms of unnatural death, you have to consider accident or suicide. In crucifixion that can be ruled out. Look how well he's roped on. He never did that to himself.'

'Somebody put him up there?' The boy took an interest obediently.

The undertaker now deigned to notice me, so he could roll his eyes at the boy's dumb questions.

'Yes, this poor man has been murdered,' I said. 'I am Flavia Albia,' I explained quietly. 'I have been hired to ascertain the facts for the victim's wife and associates.'

'Oho!' exclaimed the undertaker. He leaped back with his hands aloft, as if this news astonished him. 'A woman enquirer?' He stopped posturing and commented, 'I suppose another female will be a comfort to the widow.'

'Having her questions answered properly may give her most relief!' I flashed back.

He deduced that I was trouble. I had already decided that he was going to hamper my investigation.

Hey-ho. A good business relationship is useful – but for an informer it is often a forlorn hope.

5

I squared up to him. 'Let's set the boundaries, then you can get on – and so can I. You are the vigiles' duty mortician, I take it? I'm looking for answers so if you spot anything helpful, please pass on details. On the city west side, I regularly deal with a colleague of yours called Fundanus. What's your name?'

'Suedius. Let me explain, I don't expect you know this, we're in the full glare of public interest. The troops want to go slow but they have to show willing. A praetor has been to inspect the scene.'

'Corvinus,' I said, to irritate the patronising swine with my prior knowledge. 'Poked his nose in, sodded off. The vigiles will cope in their own way – he left them to it. I expect he doesn't want to attach his illustrious name to anything that looks difficult.'

Suedius sniffed. 'In view of the special location, I have to clear away the remains. It's needed for public decency.' He applied fake humility, while he whined, 'As the deceased is coming to me, I expect to organise his send-off – normal procedure. No objections? I assume someone will be paying for any private ceremonials?'

'Someone will let you know.' I could feel myself being boot-faced.

'You cannot sign off on it yourself?' he insinuated hopefully.

'Not my role, I'm afraid.' I might end up helping, though I first had to confirm with the widow that she wanted me involved. Until I had met her, I would never take decisions or incur bills. Especially for a funeral: every element can cause discord. Unhappy people find reasons to flare up: cremation versus interment, urn versus memorial plaque, ask the aunt from Caere or snub the brother with the drink habit . . . I do like to observe who falls out with whom during the bereavement period, but the burial process is their business.

'Who will be mourning the deceased?' Suedius still meant, who could he charge for the rites?

I accepted that he had a job to do. 'He leaves a widow and many friends. There may be interest from the actors' guild. His name is Chremes. Assume that everyone he knew will be distraught, and please treat him as a respected member of the community.' Suedius pulled a face. He was crude, but I had to continue sounding reasonable. 'I will need to know where you are taking him, please. Apart from informing his associates where he is lying, a check on the corpse by eye in the open air may not answer all necessary questions.' I unbent somewhat: 'I can mention your involvement. I'll do it when I'm talking to his nearest, as soon as the moment seems right.'

'Ah! Very courteous.' Don't push it, slimeball! 'The boy will tell you our business premises.'

The boy spotted my note-tablet, so he seized it from me of his own accord and wrote down an address: by a crossroads on the Vicus Pallacinae.

Barley went up to sniff this boy, apparently an interesting experience. I watched. He had careful, rounded handwriting and managed without needing to draw lines first. I deduced Suedius must be illiterate. Though not unknown, a man in his position ought to have been able to read and write. I could see this child must have been to school for a year or two; now his job was to take down information. However long ago he started, the little lad was now confident and seemed to enjoy his responsibility.

'Thank you. What's your name?'

He looked surprised to be asked. 'Sorgius.' Young Sorgius shoved the tablet back at me, nervous of social interaction.

At this point Tiberius and Davos arrived. They glanced at the corpse, wincing.

'Show some respect!' Davos snatched a cloth that was lying on the stretcher, throwing it across the victim's groin. Romans are not shy of nudity, but in crucifixion enforced nakedness adds to victims' shame.

Suedius crouched and began to remove the loincloth gag, as if he had intended to do this all along but had been held up by me. With his face uncovered, we could see Chremes had been struck in the mouth, losing teeth. There were no signs on his knuckles or elsewhere that he had fought back. I presumed being punched happened prior to death and I suspected someone else had been holding him immobile while it happened. The abuse confirmed that somebody had really hated him.

Standing up awkwardly, Suedius went to the cart for a clanking tool-caddy, from which he produced a long set of pincers; I dreaded to think what he generally used them for. He stooped over the corpse. With difficulty, he hauled out the big ankle nails. Suedius then carefully unwound the ropes, which he coiled with maddening deliberation. Without needing instructions, the boy heaved the heavy loops up onto the cart. He knew what to do with anything they could make useful.

Once freed, Chremes's body rolled sideways off the cross. I made Suedius pause while I glanced over the deep weals on the dead man's back and sides, now they were exposed by his new position. 'You haven't found his clothes?'

'What – are you saying I pinched them?'

I was not, though I felt he might have done. 'I hope you wouldn't be so crude. But where are his tunic and shoes? Was he stripped first, I wonder? These wounds don't really show it.' Some of the weals were too sharp-edged to have been inflicted through cloth, though others were less distinct, while a few had fibres visible in the dried blood.

As I made my inspection, I heard Davos sucking his teeth at the violence. 'Did this beating happen at the stadium?'

'Not here. No bloodstains or scuffling marks,' Suedius told him. 'At least the stadium boys haven't had to clear that up. Does it matter?'

'Everything matters.' I was terse. A crime scene somewhere else would give me a second chance of clues or witnesses.

'Oh, I wouldn't worry, if I was you,' he said complacently.

I managed not to snarl. I felt very aware of Davos, also on the edge of losing his cool, though out of the corner of my eye I could see Tiberius standing close, ready to discourage him. 'I have to worry. Was he dead when they raised him aloft, do you think?'

'Doubt it. If he was, why bother whacking him on his long bones?' Suedius bent and pulled up one leg of the corpse, to show where someone had struck below the knee and broken the tibia. 'The pain finishes off the business. Shock. Well, he would have been in a state beforehand, by the look of him, so *more* shock.' Broken skin had bled, trickling down his leg, so from my medical knowledge Chremes had indeed been living when this blow was inflicted. Hopefully, he had not lasted much longer.

Suedius let go of the leg. Davos flinched as it fell back. 'Steady,' I chastised the unfeeling mortician. He gave me a nasty look. I returned it, close to letting fly at him.

Suedius blanked me. To Davos, he said, 'He must have gone very quick once they smashed his leg. They haven't bothered to spear him. What I'm saying is, if they knew what they were doing, they would have come prepared for a good poke in the ribs. Sharp blade on a long pole. To finally do for him.'

Like me, Davos had to restrain himself. Set-faced, he pushed aside the boy and, with Tiberius to help, he lifted his old friend himself. That ensured the retrieval was conducted with some gentleness. After laying the corpse on the stretcher and placing that on the cart, Davos again gave the dead old man a covering, this time not just for modesty but spreading the cloth over him completely as if to blot out what had happened. He stood for a moment with his head down.

Oblivious, the heartless funeral director repeated, 'A good big whack to break his leg. Then they probably left him here on his own for a nice quiet passing in the dark.'

'In the dark?' I queried.

He nodded. 'All kicked off last night, if you ask me. From the state of the body—'

'Thank you. I understand!' I managed to stop him.

Tiberius had moved back to examine the cross, though he made no comment. He picked up the two huge nails, which he inspected. He looked like any foraging building contractor as he discarded the one that had been badly bent, seeming to keep a reusable item. But he gave me a nod: he was securing evidence. 'Military.'

'Relevant?'

'Probably not. Probably "fell off" a supply wagon. In the trade we come across ex-army components all the time – it's almost legitimate. Every chandler has buckets of grey-market goods in his storage shed.'

Suedius and his boy began bashing apart the two elements of the cross, then made as if to haul the heavy wooden parts onto their cart alongside Chremes. My husband stopped them while he inspected the timbers too. Both pieces had been rough-hewn but the work was competent: even widths, no splinters. 'What is happening about this timber, Suedius?' Barely giving the man a chance to reply, Tiberius carried on, 'Feel free to take the short baulk for pyres, if you can use it. That's badly split, but the longer piece is still serviceable. Drop it off at the Saepta for me, will you? Say it's for the aedile Faustus, Falco's son-in-law. I'll pick it up later.'

He had a way with him. It was no coincidence how he cunningly worked in his own title and made my father sound a well-known local character. Even Suedius silently complied. Once again Tiberius looked like a contractor pinching materials, yet I presumed a more respectable purpose.

It was nearly midday. The funeral director jauntily clucked up his donkey; the laden hearse jerked as the beast staggered and struggled. As it managed to move off, those runners came back from their exercise. Automatically, we split up: I apprehended the athletes, while Davos walked over to the group I assumed were his acting friends, and Tiberius went to talk to the vigiles.

The runners were sweating after their session. Barley gave them a woof on principle, then skulked with me in the face of their muscular bravado. Even at the end of December they had been exercising naked to show they were hardy professionals; some had yet to resume their tunics – not that they had much to hide. They were carrying a starting-block that they must have dug out from its proper position earlier. A public slave bustled up, tutting, and started banging it back into its running lane. Before the athletes sauntered away, I managed to talk to them.

They were dedicated to their life. I asked if this was their first return after the holiday. They grumbled that it had had to be. Even men as keen as them were obliged to observe Saturnalia. Once they were able to return here, nothing had stopped them. They admitted without shame that they had seen Chremes on the cross this morning. He was hanging there, looking dead already, when they came in. Members of his theatre troupe had just arrived and had found him. The tragic scene, in the runners' opinion, was nothing to do with them. They were only annoyed because the body's discovery meant too much was going on at this end of the stadium: they were prevented from using all the running track. They would have to practise full laps tomorrow.

I made myself sound neutral about their obsessiveness. 'You come every day?'

'Of course.'

'Did you see anyone else this morning, either in here or just outside? Anyone except the dead man's friends?'

'Nobody.' Would they have noticed? I wondered. Or were these hamstring heroes too preoccupied with times, muscles, breathing, cramps and competition?

Since they could not have anticipated finding a crime scene with an open gate, I asked how they had expected to gain entry to the stadium. Had they a prior arrangement with the custodian? Was he the man over there, the one I had noticed earlier with the vigiles?

They had no idea. They had never met any custodian in person, though their trainer had made an arrangement to allow them inside; this applied all the time, not only in a lull after a festival. Since running practice often began at dawn, one of the gates would be left looking closed by a heavy beam, but if people knew how and were strong enough, the security bar could be lifted off. The athletes would surreptitiously let themselves in. The public slaves usually turned up to work here later. Even if the slaves were still on holiday at the moment, the custodian had seen to it that they could come in when they wanted, which to these self-centred young men was all that mattered.

I guessed that until he was rousted out today because of the corpse, the custodian had awarded himself a holiday too. All through Saturnalia, the stadium had been left unlocked. I wondered who else knew that?

6

As I walked towards Davos and the theatre people, Tiberius came over to join me. One corner of his mouth was clenched, giving me the hint that his talk with the vigiles had been unfruitful. I nodded, being the soothing wife. His annoyance simmered down as we walked together.

'Vigiles, as we thought, are looking for quick closure, Albia. That limp twerp is the building manager. He doesn't know anything, he saw nothing. He wasn't here last night because he was still taking time off for Saturnalia – although when glared at hard, he does admit one of the gates may have been accessible. Claims it is a traditional service for genuine athletics practice, with absolutely no bribery involved.'

There were three men waiting, the finders, hunched in cloaks and looking sad as they stood up for us. All thin in body and in face, they were young, middling and old. One wore a woollen hat; one had long hair tied in a skinny tail at the back of his neck; one had patchily thinning hair. They were probably clean, though looked as if they might not be. If you had to pass them in the street, you might cross to the other side – yet as soon as they spoke they were likeable.

Davos must already have told them my role. Expressing sympathy, I introduced Tiberius and me, outlining what I would try to do for the widow. Davos named them as Atticus (the hat), Pardicus (the pigtail) and Ariminius (the alopecia).

In the theatre troupe they all mucked in, doing a bit of everything, but Atticus and Pardicus were primarily actors while Ariminius was a scene-shifter. If nobody else was available, he would run onstage to shout, 'There's a ship in harbour! It is our long-lost master!' He drew the line at girl-parts or wearing an animal suit. 'Pardicus is the cheeky one, though they're all feeling bruised at the moment, obviously. They will talk to you,' said Davos, 'but they've been stuck at the stadium all morning, so they're desperate to get out of here.'

'I shall be quick.'

Davos still looked over-protective, but Tiberius drew him off to one side. That spared me any unwanted interjections. I leaned against the wall around the track, putting on a friendly manner; I asked if the trio could provide character notes to start me off. The vigiles would have hammered them with questions about finding the body; I wanted to move forward. 'I know Chremes was your manager, with long years of experience. Can you describe what he was like? I didn't see him at his best today.'

It took them a moment to get going. They looked at each other nervously, but then Pardicus began: 'Tall. A commanding presence. He was always striding around and looking down his craggy nose.'

'He wasn't really arrogant. He could usually extract what he wanted from the authorities,' Atticus told me, as if he slightly disagreed. 'Permissions to perform. Jupiter knows how he persuaded some of the petty magistrates in provincial towns, let alone the snooty supremos in Rome.' I managed not to look over to see whether Tiberius Manlius had overheard himself being disparaged. 'He understood the rites involved, I mean, looking humble and honest and what size of sweetener to pay.'

'Yes, but he could be an innocent, in a world of his own. He loved to play dice.' Ariminius had squatted down to pet my dog as if he himself needed comfort. I hoped his hair problem wasn't catching. 'But he was absolutely no good at it.'

I sucked in air through pursed lips, reflecting on that. 'Had he been gambling? Running up debts?' Gambling in public was legal at Saturnalia, though even if Chremes owed enormous wager payments, crucifixion seemed a harsh response. Stupid too: as a dead man, he would never pay.

Fending off Barley from licking his face, Ariminius refuted it. 'No worse than usual. He and Phrygia had a bust-up over money, but nothing special. His wife, that is.' My gaze must have sharpened so Ariminius explained, 'They had blazing rows for fifty years. Famous for hating each other. Most of it was technical, theatrical stuff.'

'But money featured?' The actors all shrugged it off: money always matters.

Atticus weighed in insistently, wanting me to understand the relationship: 'You're going to ask us, did he have any enemies? Not Phrygia. Look, if Phrygia was going to top him, it would have happened decades ago. Fights were simply their way of life. Some couples constantly argue. They did it on a grand scale. Whatever one wanted for the group – where to travel, who to admit to the company, what play to put on – the other would always suggest the opposite. He would loathe any suggestion of hers, then he would prance around declaiming that she was a madwoman while she sucked in her cheeks bitterly.'

'Who was right?' I asked quickly. 'About choices?' The three men gave no answer, which suggested to me it was Phrygia who often knew best.

'She had a lot of wisdom?'

'Expert!' growled Pardicus.

'Chremes knew it really. But they never held back,' Atticus continued. 'They both had savage repartee – actors are words people. They enjoyed their wrangling. She will be devastated, losing that.'

'Probably drop dead from the silence,' Pardicus agreed. 'I hope she doesn't pick on us instead!'

'Will she continue running the company?' I asked.

'She knows nothing else.'

'Anyway, where might she go?' I pondered. 'People in your profession tend not to have homes, I suspect?'

'Chremes was a Tusculum man, he often said it – but I never knew him go back there,' said Pardicus. 'No idea where Phrygia came from originally. She may have forgotten herself. They met on the road, aeons ago.'

'Greece,' Ariminius put in. He sounded gloomy. 'But she was never Greek.'

'As they always described it, they got hitched by mistake. Even so, they stayed together year after year, despite all the bickering.'

'Sounds as if the couple lived out one long personal-retribution play,' I suggested. I'd like to say the actors looked impressed, but they clearly thought this was pretentious twaddle. 'All right, can we tackle the vital question a different way. Did Chremes have any *other* enemies? Somebody in the company, for example?'

They all agreed not. The group was happy, or as happy as any working partnership can be: not very, but that was Fate. Everyone relied on Chremes and Phrygia for their living; despite occasional tricky periods, the couple had always kept their dependants together, and just about in work. Ariminius joked that Chremes was probably intending to flit from their current lodgings without paying rent, though the landlord would not have realised yet.

'Chremes made a habit of defaulting?'

'He goes all weird and superior, then conveniently forgets that he owes someone. Sometimes, if they haven't been forced to pay in advance, Phrygia leaves behind money on a side table.'

'Not often enough!' snorted Pardicus. 'We've had to race away from quite a few towns, and not because audiences had complained about our talent.'

'Do they?'

'Often. No damned taste, audiences. With Chremes dead, Phrygia will pretend, oh dear, she cannot understand money and has none to offer. Even a landlord can't sue a ghost.'

'True! So I assume there is no big pot of gold that a killer hopes to be inheriting.' They all laughed derisively. I conceded the point. 'No treasure, then! But basic stock and perhaps goodwill? His wife is the heir?'

'The company, with all its props, costumes and transport is hers, if she still wants it.'

I asked again, to be sure: 'Even if she does, you're saying she would never arrange to have Chremes killed, to acquire a sole share?'

'No, she bloody wouldn't!' That came from Davos. Half-hidden glances passed between the others at his passion. I wondered whether, prior to Thalia, Phrygia had been an old flame of his. It would not have happened afterwards: the snake-dancer would have seen to that. 'Phrygia now owns everything, without any funny business,' he snarled. 'She did most of the management anyway. I acted with them for years – I can tell you. She knows the business inside out and she used to be a fine actress. But she and Chremes were a working partnership, one she will badly miss.'

'Routine question,' I assured him. I added carefully, 'I take it you know Phrygia quite well?'

'I knew her *very* well in past times.' Well, that was frank: it answered my question, 'I'll not stand by to hear her insulted.'

I shook my head at him. 'Nobody is insulting her, Davos. My father would have asked the same. An inquiry must be systematic. You don't want me being mimsy. That's how truth gets overlooked. All right, she is innocent. I accept it. Look, I assume someone has gone to tell poor Phrygia what has happened to her husband?'

Davos said the same messenger who had run to him at Thalia's camp had then come back to break the news and sit with the widow. 'If Phrygia knows what happened, I am only surprised she hasn't teetered along on those ridiculous shoes she always wears and thrown herself upon the body.'

'Not the hysterical type,' said Atticus. From his tone, I visualised someone austere. Someone patient enough, perhaps, to wait wherever the couple lodged until people bringing news converged on her.

'She has played enough flinty priestesses,' Pardicus agreed, although he then added, 'Too heartbroken. Believe it, she will be distraught.'

The widow must be next on my list to visit, but while we had the three who had found the body, I took advantage. We led them out of the stadium, saying, if we could find a bar open, they deserved a restorative.

7

As we were leaving, I wanted to look at the advertisement that announced *Laureolus*, starring Chremes. This good idea was thwarted: the stadium's public slaves had washed away the graffito. We arrived just as they wrung out their sponges and threw them into a bucket. All we could see was lovely wet travertine. Most of the stadium exterior consisted of recurring arches, a simple satisfying scheme, but the double entrance at the straight end had facings of plain marble slabs, crying out to be defaced. I asked the slaves what they had cleaned off, but none could read.

Pardicus tried to help. 'I'm reciting from memory, but it went something like: *See the cruel bandit Laureolus, with his famous punishment and death personified by that mighty king of the stage, Chremes, notable throughout the East and all of Italy.* "Laureolus" and "Chremes" were chalked in larger letters, so you couldn't miss them. There was a sketch of a cross.'

'All chalked, not painted?' I asked.

'Black charcoal, probably. Neat, not a scrawl. Similar to the posters we write up ourselves for all our plays.'

'*Notable throughout the East*,' mused Davos. 'Someone knows the group's acting history.'

'*Personified*,' said Tiberius. 'Not suggesting the full play, only a scene. The crucifixion itself was the message: this is punishment of Chremes.'

'So what had Chremes done? Who had he upset so badly?' I asked. The three men from his group only shrugged, all helpless. To them, the actor-manager was a working professional, with his own quirks, yet someone who needed to get along with people. 'How was he during the recent festival? Was his mood normal?' They nodded. 'So he seemed himself, yet he vanished unexpectedly. Phrygia became concerned. You went out searching. When you finally found him, what had drawn you to this stadium?'

'Nothing,' said Atticus. 'We were just seeking him everywhere.'

If they had happened upon the stadium advert sooner, they might have found Chremes still alive. I tried not to think it. I did not want them to catch my thought and blame themselves.

When killers send messages, in whatever form, some lurk to watch how their signals are received. I could see no idlers gawping at us, however. 'Think back if you can, please. When you first arrived here, was anyone else about? Somebody waiting to see what happened, as the body was found?'

They all believed there had been no one. Their discovery happened very early in the morning. The streets were unusually deserted. It was barely light. The air felt chill, with a high dew content; the sky above was heavy with unshed rain. The few people whose paths they crossed on the Campus Martius were still sluggish after Saturnalia. Businesses remained tightly shut or were planning to open much later than usual. Their own footsteps had rung eerily on the pavement slabs; they had heard no others.

They had looked for Chremes all through the night so by the time they came here they were depressed and weary. The great double entrance at this end of the stadium had stood silent; its gilded statuary up above was twinkling with condensation after a night of Tiber mist. From the chilly street they walked in under a portico, hoping someone in the arcades had seen Chremes. No one was about. The corridor booths were all locked up. Then Pardicus noticed what was written up. Ariminius happened to see that one big entrance gate had its security beam grounded alongside. Walking across, they were able to push the gate wide enough to go inside. They found him. Chremes was directly opposite. He would have been staring straight at them, had his head not slumped sideways.

'We were too late. He was done for.'

'We went over the running track, right up to him. We called up, but there was no hope of him answering.'

'Those bastard athletes arrived straight after us but they ran off, not helping.'

'Had you heard them on the approach?'

'No!' growled Ariminius. 'They must have pounded up after we went in.'

'Warm-up,' I agreed, equally dry. 'Did they speak to you?'

'No, they ignored us. They seemed surprised the gate was already open. Once they followed us in, they stared, then all went along to the other end of the stadium. They behaved as if finding a dead man on a cross was perfectly normal.'

'But a damned nuisance to them!' scoffed Pardicus. 'Bunch of morons. All skin and sinew, nothing in their skulls. For all they know, the stadium is haunted by some maniac who will now write up a sign about a coming foot-race, then murder one of them. I hope it happens.'

'Jupiter! I can't bear to be here any longer. Let's go!' grumbled Davos, infuriated.

We set off to find a refreshment venue, with me considering what Pardicus had said. Were the killers acting on spec? Could they have lain in wait and taken the first victim who happened along? Might it as easily have been an athlete? I thought not. The crucifixion preparations – planning, materials and skills – ruled out a random murder. The notice naming Chremes was much too specific. These killers knew exactly who he was, his full history. It sounded to me as if 'that mighty king of the stage' contained some jeering insult. I felt sure I was looking for a motive with very deep roots. Long-term brooding could explain such a brutal punishment.

Everything in the area had warmed up now. At lunchtime on the Campus, bars were not only open, they hummed. We managed to squeeze up against a counter, street-side, where Davos ordered mulsum all round. There were hot fruit tarts. The bread was good. Everyone pitched in, not talking much. Once they settled, I apologised but I asked whether there was anything more to tell me about finding the body. When they had nothing to offer, I said I would go to visit Phrygia. Tiberius whistled: the dog chose to depart with him as he went on his own to see Mucius, the Seventh Cohort's lead investigator. Davos came with me.

8

Company members were slumming around the Campus Martius, but Chremes and Phrygia had hired a more refined room. Davos said this was their normal habit. Like most people who bragged that their troupe was a commune of equals, its leaders assumed special privileges: they always secured better accommodation, where they could keep themselves private. They were currently staying on the other side of the Via Lata, the great triumphal road, which cuts through all the personal aggrandisement of Augustus and Agrippa, now redeveloped by our own Domitian.

Marcus Vipsanius Agrippa, the bull-necked close friend of the first Emperor, Augustus, must have been an interesting man. Nicer to know, too. His advice had probably clinched the outcome of the crucial Battle of Actium where Antony and Cleopatra were defeated, but then he surged on, sharing a grip on power while loyally remaining second-in-command. Clearly not squeamish, he navigated city sewers in a bumboat and had the Great Drain cleansed; he even married Augustus's daughter Julia, a morally unhygienic piece of goods, as many men could attest.

Agrippa was an energetic builder and a seeker after knowledge. He bequeathed us monuments that have become rightly famous, stuffed with educational objects, mostly plundered. Rome owes him a lot. He wanted us to remember that. He had been given control of a huge area in the northern sector of the city. As well as the innovative Pantheon on the Campus Martius, alongside his baths with permanent free entry, on the further side of the Via Lata he created the Campus Agrippae, a big memorial park where people loved to stroll. It contained the Porticus Vipsaniae, a dramatic gallery of art that he had also made available to the public; it housed a Map of the Whole World, based on geographical facts that Agrippa had systematically collected. His sister finished the porticus after his death; I like to think that, by using the family name for it, Vipsania slyly called it after herself.

Many of Agrippa's collected facts were collated in Pliny's *Encyclopaedia.* My husband had been known to read aloud dense statistical matter from these scrolls, which fascinated him, though he would usually stop if distracted with a plate of smoked cheese.

When the terrible fire nine years ago obliterated much that had stood on the Field of Mars, some buildings were saved, thanks to Agrippa's aqueduct, the Virgo, which ran underground. The conflagration had somehow failed to cross the Via Lata. Cynics may feel that was due to the presence of the station-house of the First Cohort of Vigiles. They fought the city fire very bravely but must have protected their own barracks with special interest. It had meant the Porticus Vipsaniae also survived. The Map of the Whole World was saved. Davos and I walked through the gardens, too anxious to enjoy them, following directions he had for where his old friends had been lodging.

A few residential streets remained near Agrippa's Park. We were south of the Gardens of Sallust, facing the Quirinal Hill. A district organised by Augustus as a new part of Rome, it lay outside the ancient Servian Walls, where that battlement came down from the Capitol and ran northwards. Around here was all open and airy, different from the teeming habitations of the original ancient city. It was an inconvenient distance from the Forum, though handily placed for anyone wealthy who owned estates to the north of Rome. They could bundle up the Via Lata or the Via Salaria, then rush away to Etruria or the Sabine Hills.

Well-heeled locals were not above hiring out rooms during festivals. They could make a quick denarius, then push out their lodgers and be kings of their property again. You don't hear a lot about this, probably because the hirers 'forget' their casual income when they falsify their tax returns. [*Oh no we don't!*] [*Oh yes you do.*] One such entrepreneur was renting to Chremes and Phrygia. He might have thought he was taking advantage of innocent Saturnalia visitors, but from what I already knew, they would have outwitted him, like cheeky runabouts in comedy.

Davos had been told how to find the place by Simo, the actor who had first raised the alarm with him. Chremes and his wife had an upstairs room in a courtyard house. We found the trusty messenger waiting there, as he must have been for several hours. He was downhearted on a stool, all by himself.

Simo was older than I had expected from Davos calling him 'a lad'. A wiry man in his middle thirties, he had thin red hair, receding at the front, white skin and pale blue eyes, like a northern tribesman. He looked tense. He jumped up and told us he had not found Phrygia here; nor had she returned in all the time he had waited. When he had asked other people in the building, they had never seen her today. They knew her husband had vanished mysteriously, so assumed she was out looking for him.

'There's been a few jokes here, about him copping an earful when she finds him,' sighed Simo. 'I just smiled along. I haven't disillusioned any of them with the real story. They still don't know he's dead. Nor how.' He looked choked.

Phrygia's absence left us in limbo. I told Davos to take Simo out for a bite, while I would continue the vigil here. Since nothing could happen without the widow, we agreed that, once he had looked after Simo, Davos would go over the river to tell Thalia what had happened. Though her statuesque body and bawdy humour terrified people, the snake-dancer was instantly drawn to wounded creatures. Humans in trouble could rely on her. She was bound to come striding across to console Phrygia. I guessed she would help the rest of the troupe come to terms.

I stayed in the room alone. It was my private chance to get a feel for the stricken couple. They seemed to have brought plenty with them and had installed many home comforts they must have gathered on their travels. Being professional, I did wonder whether their more luxurious accommodation might have caused enough envy in the troupe to explain why Chremes was killed; however, it seemed unlikely. They led the company: they had some entitlement. Who kills their governor because he lives separately and lolls there on tasselled bolsters? Normally junior colleagues are glad to be left free from supervision.

If they were harbouring an oddball, he might perhaps have struck out crazily – but I was sure other company members would now be pointing out anyone like that. Nobody had told me to concentrate enquiries on their mean-spirited wardrobe-master or the muttering, mad-eyed chorus leader.

I had hardly begun to look around when I heard someone coming. A man bounced in.

The first impression was of a half-bald head, a neatly trimmed beard and extremely bright eyes. On his portly frame he wore a long brown tunic, which he accessorised with a pushy attitude. At fifty to sixty, he looked like a thriving imports negotiator, one with three mistresses and a socking great villa at Antium. He probably had a smaller house in the revitalised ash-fields around the Bay of Naples, where he parked his wife. He might convince himself she knew nothing about the mistresses, though I bet she did.

Finding me gave him a start. 'Oh! I didn't know anyone was here!'

I stopped fantasising. 'I am waiting,' I said, not even mentioning Phrygia.

'Are you one of the theatre people?'

'By no means. Are you?'

'Certainly not! I am the landlord,' he exclaimed in horror.

I smiled. Actors might be legal outcasts but, to my family, a landlord was even more of a bandit. My father used to rant that men of property were beyond insulting – though he had been quieter about it for some years, since he became one.

'Well, do come in,' I offered graciously. With a landlord, I like to establish that I am in charge, even when he thinks he is in his own home.

9

Calmly staying seated, I introduced myself, the easier to extract his details in return. 'I am Flavia Albia. I am the wife of a magistrate.' I might as well use this while it remained true. I would lose status soon, when Tiberius reverted to private life.

'Eucolpus.' A Greek name, though he looked properly western. I guessed either he or a recent ancestor was a freed slave. That would certainly not stop him becoming a man of substance. He now lived in a large house; the rented room had fine proportions. Though I guessed it was only basically furnished for visitors, it had been improved with the actors' well-chosen treasures: their cushions and large pots in sophisticated shapes and colours. 'Are you here to commiserate?' Eucolpus demanded. 'About the missing husband?'

'I am here to investigate.'

'Oh!' He was almost hopping, an agitated man whose sneaky mission I had interrupted. He had his eye fixed on a large woven saddle-bag, so he did not really absorb my words.

'Your house?' I asked, as if checking he had a right to be there.

'One of my properties. But I live here with family members.'

'If you came for some purpose, please don't let me prevent you.' I was hoping to find out what he was up to. He edged closer to the bag, a large square tough thing, in shades of crimson, black and yellow wool that was showing its age, especially in its ragged fringes. It looked as if it had once been slung on a camel. I knew this because my parents had similar, obtained on their trip to Syria.

'I was hoping to collect my rent for December. Phrygia had promised me for today. I won't want to bother her while she has troubles—'

'Her husband has been found. He is dead.' I sprang it on him, though I saw it was no surprise.

'Yes, I heard at the market. Word is running around.'

'With details?'

Eucolpus nodded. He seemed guarded, though, perhaps because I was a stranger. I do believe there are people who believe in discretion when tragedy occurs.

I avoided gossip about the crucifixion, telling him quietly, 'Phrygia may not know yet. If so, I am preparing to tell her.' He showed no sympathy for her: he kept staring at that bag. 'Go ahead,' I pronounced. 'Pick up your cash if the amount is already agreed. As you say, it will be kindest not to badger Phrygia. Luckily, I am here. I can see everything is done properly. You can leave a receipt, which I can witness.'

'Are you sure?'

'I am acting as Phrygia's agent.'

He looked startled, but the idea reassured him enough to have him immediately fingering the bag. I noticed he wore a couple of big signet rings. 'This is where they always keep their funds . . . They have stayed here before!' he came out with as justification. That meant he knew the couple could be a trial over money – not badly enough for him to have turned them away as tenants when they returned this year, yet worrying him now he had heard about the death.

I asked, under cover of general conversation, 'So, you all know each other well. How long have they been staying here this time?'

'Their second month. They paid me upfront for November, but December has been slower coming.' That fitted all I knew, including their visiting Rome for the Plebeian Games last month.

'Take what you are owed,' I urged the landlord again. 'Do it while you can. The poor lady is about to be hit with funeral bills and other costs.' Paying me, for instance. It would be crude to mention my fees to a stranger, especially since Phrygia still needed to have my role explained. I did have a better motive: I was keen to hurry Eucolpus, in case Phrygia came in and found him at it. She might be upset, and I wouldn't blame her. Also, I did not want the rent issue to get in the way of me breaking the bad news to her.

Eucolpus boldly dived into the saddle-bag; he drew out a purse containing coins, counted them as fast as a money-changer, then made a fuss about returning a clutch of other little purses to the bag. He had a rectangular pouch on his belt, containing note-tablets and a bone stylus, one of my clues that he was a businessman. While he wrote out a receipt efficiently, I murmured more innocent questions: 'My parents know Chremes and Phrygia but I have never met them. What are they like?'

'Decent tenants.' A landlord has his preoccupations. Eucolpus passed me the receipt to countersign; in possession of his money, he visibly relaxed. He became more willing to engage. 'I never had much to do with them. It was purely a short-term arrangement, maybe once a year. We never mingled socially – though I went to their plays.'

'Any good?' I asked, smiling.

'The theatre is not really my choice for a night out.'

'They obtained tickets for you?'

'Complimentaries.'

Well, free seat tokens would sway a man who otherwise preferred the races or gladiators. 'Nice! What have they been performing this year?'

'Plautus.'

'Oh, which one?'

Eucolpus looked vague. 'I'm not well up on drama – it had an old man with a son, and a slave-girl who had been abducted . . .' There are more comedies by Plautus than people generally reckon; this plot could be any one of them. The slave-girl has usually been extricated from a brothel, unless she is not really a slave at all but somebody's missing daughter, who was previously lost at sea. Either way, the feisty young woman ends up with the so-called young hero, who is usually a wilting weed. She would do better to grab the money-chest that often features, then run off with the fast-talking kitchen slave whose smart actions keep the plot moving.

'Happy ending?'

'All resolved.'

'That's the main thing.' I smiled reassuringly. So the abominable weed was given the feisty girl: that was typical. It so often happens in real life too, although not when I am around to thwart it. 'Do I gather you got on well with Chremes and Phrygia?'

'I always found them pleasant people.'

'No disagreements? Landlord and tenant strife?'

Eucolpus was cottoning on now. I watched him learn how it felt to be a suspect in a murder case. Although this was new to him, he had realised he should be careful. 'No disagreements,' he stated firmly. He looked sharp enough to be thinking up an alibi for last night, when Chremes was killed.

'Easy tenants? No disturbances?'

Eucolpus guessed I probably knew what kind of reputation his tenants had had. 'It is true they can be somewhat strident.'

'I have heard their life together described as a constant contest,' I said frankly. 'Loud quarrels, wounding insults.'

'Something like that. I always forgot from year to year, but they had been exactly the same before. Just their way. They keep their arguments to themselves . . . Kept,' he amended awkwardly.

'The rumpus didn't bother you?'

'It didn't matter. One next-door room happens to be empty most of the time. My mother is on this side, but she is elderly and extremely deaf.'

'Ah. That's a shame. Then she won't have overheard anything that might explain today's tragedy?' I attempted, privately cursing.

'No, she won't!' said Eucolpus, flatly. 'Please do not disturb my mother.'

'Of course not.' I was intrigued by his insistence. Meeting his mother immediately slid higher up my actions list.

I thought it time to broach his late tenant's grim fate. 'I imagine the market gossip you heard was about Chremes being crucified. That would spice up buying a cauliflower.'

'Right. I won't fancy today's purchases.' Ashamed of joking, Eucolpus abruptly dropped his voice in conventional respect. 'Horrible shock!'

'It seems a gruesome way to kill him.'

'Unbelievable,' Eucolpus agreed. 'This is a very quiet district. Nothing like murder happens around here normally. All very sordid,' he let himself say.

'And there must have been a reason,' I replied. 'In my experience there will have been previous trouble between

Chremes and whoever did it, trouble that could have been brewing for a long time. Would anything during this visit suggest what it was?'

'Nothing I am aware of.'

'No external quarrels?'

'Apparently not.'

'If the couple had visitors—'

'My door porter would have known. I have asked him already. He tells me no one came to see the actors recently.'

I would have liked to be first to quiz the doorman, but nothing is perfect.

When Davos and I arrived we had passed him, the usual thin runt who came nosing out when we knocked, but who easily let us into the house and allowed us upstairs on our own. He had *not* told us Phrygia was out: we only learned it from Simo. I suspected the porter was less diligent than his master believed, so he had never noticed her leaving. I had taken a poor view of him, normal with doormen. My father had taught me long ago that they simply live to frustrate honest visitors.

'My colleague and I entered via your porchway, of course,' I said. 'And your porter did check us.' That is, he never asked our names, he took no interest in our reason for coming, he merely told us he couldn't leave his post so we would have to find our own way up. This fitted my pa's definition. 'Is there another way into the property?'

'A back gate for deliveries.' Eucolpus brushed the fact aside. 'No one else uses it. Only tradesmen.'

I was beginning to realise how things worked here. He saw himself as extremely efficient, but I bet he was wrong about people using the back gate.

IO

Clutching his purse of rent money, Eucolpus wanted to leave. I waved him away. I could see him wondering whether he should let me remain in the actors' room, but my air of authority outweighed any care for his tenants' rights. Although his bumptiousness had reappeared, he was keener on fleeing with his cash than on having a confrontation.

After a few moments alone again, I looked inside the large saddle-bag. The other purses were lightweight. I assumed these were part of Phrygia's budgeting process; I pitied her lifetime struggle with a husband who gambled. At least that was over now.

Silence had fallen. Where was she?

I remembered a period, just after Tiberius and I were married, when he, too, had disappeared from home without an explanation. He was traumatised both physically and mentally, after being struck by lightning. People do not simply jump up and walk away from that, smoking slightly. I had researched the subject, desperate to help him. Doctors and textbooks said such events have a deeply troubling long-lasting effect. Apart from the initial pain, victims will be changed for life. Although Tiberius soon offered a reason for his vanishing act, I reckoned he had been overtaken by a fugue state, a condition that caused him complete bewilderment. I still kept an eye on him, in case it ever happened again.

The point is, when I could not find him, I had not sat at home waiting to see what happened. I'd like to say I went out and found him. That is the kind of woman I am – though after checking around locally, I had been baffled about where to search. Instead, I decided to supervise his workmen, which seemed a useful task. Near their site I did happen upon him. He claimed this was intentional and he had thought I would realise what he was up to.

Was something similar going on here? Some men don't need an accident as an excuse; they are prone to wandering off on their own interesting missions. My mother has a few stories about that. Falco would leave clues, though only if he had time, never if a suspect suddenly needed tailing or he had had an unexpected bright idea. The story about Phrygia did not fit this: unlike a wife whose husband regularly roamed, she became very quickly worried about Chremes. In fact, his disappearance was so uncharacteristic, the members of their company shared her anxiety and were soon persuaded to search for him, continuing all night.

The others thought Phrygia had stayed here, in case Chremes returned or other news was brought. While it was possible that waiting had become too much for her, so she had rushed out to search in person, surely she would have left a message to say where she had gone? Could she not stop to do it? Was this woman, who had been described as effectively controlling the company, as much of a madcap as me? (I admit this trait.) She was considerably older, by all accounts. Life had forced her to be the sensible partner in her marriage. She took good decisions. She had to.

I reached a point of serious anxiety for her. As I waited, surrounded by her clothes and personal comforts, I suddenly decided that Phrygia must have been lured away. Even at that point I became convinced her absence meant some danger was threatening her.

II

Picking up my cloak, I went out onto the balcony that ran around the interior of the house, above a courtyard. Down below there was a small fountain, currently dry, where a licheny cupid, who had lost his quiver, teetered on one leg. Battered chairs and a wooden table were parked in a corner for summer gatherings, the chairs currently tipped against the table-top so rain would run off their seats.

A watchdog on a long chain – heftier than my Barley, long snout like a wolf, spiky brown fur – was being petted by a boy slave, the kind of long-haired tot with half-unsewn tunic stripes that people use as a tray-carrier. The dog deigned to lick the boy's face, then went back to scratching his own rear end. Others who must belong to Eucolpus's household had been standing in the courtyard, gazing up towards Phrygia's room: a bent old man, a younger one leaning on a broom, and a girl who knew how to look as if she was extremely busy even though she carried no props to prove what she was supposedly doing. They were all thin and dressed in washed-out colours, but their clothing lacked the patches that our accident-prone slave at home, Dromo, always had.

As soon as I appeared, they moved indoors to their duties. I called out for them to wait, but they slipped away faster. I was left on the upstairs balcony, only able to listen to a few normal household sounds. The broom knocked. Somewhere a rug was being flapped. Then, luckily, I heard voices from the room where Eucolpus had said he stashed his deaf old mother: the one who was not to be disturbed. No chance! I went straight in.

'Hello!' she squawked.

'Hello!' I rapped back, pitching my voice so she would hear.

'There's no need to shout!'

'I'm sorry.'

'What?'

'Keep the noise down!' ordered a skinny maid from a stool in a corner where she was mending a hole in a tablecloth while eating a well-stuffed bread roll; it was greened-up chick-pea paste by the look of it. Her voice was muffled. 'Do you mind? I'm trying to concentrate on this.' I could see from the doorway that sewing was not her natural talent. Still, she was frowning hard as she poked a needle with some determination, while holding her bread between her teeth.

'Ignore her,' breezed the old lady. 'It's her time of the month again.'

The maid, who had dark hair pulled back painfully into a tight plait, removed the roll from her mouth the better to enunciate. 'That was last week.'

'My mistake!' her mistress retaliated. 'Don't pay attention to her. She's snarky all the time.'

'Oh dear,' I said sympathetically, already suspecting why the maid was liable to answer back. If she had any character at all she would need to deploy it with this difficult charge.

'I want to get rid of her, but they won't let me!' the old mistress carried on. Her maid merely munched more. This must have been a regular refrain. 'I'm locked up here in misery while they all enjoy themselves. Nobody cares.'

Someone cared enough to have supplied their tricky biddy with silken bolsters, plaster plaques with portraits of family members, and a singing finch in a cage. At her elbow stood a small marble-topped table on which were a little silver cup and an elegant glass wine-flagon, accompanied by almond biscuits. 'They just want me to go! I am all by myself here, waiting to die . . .' She implied her dying would not be far off, though I prophesied otherwise.

In my experience landlord's mothers who are given house-room tend to be embittered. They resent the fact that a son they once tyrannised now has all the power, because he has acquired the money. Personally, I don't blame them, though the adjustment must be hard on their sons too.

This one was a tiny, hunched figure, whose snappy attitude might result from genuine arthritic pain, though she clearly saw herself as a lively personality. They kept her by day in a long chair, like a disconsolate empress, covered with a slew of rugs, down which she liked to spill her dinner. I suspected she might do that on purpose, enjoying her chance to behave badly. I bet they never let her get her hands on a walking-stick to thrash people.

When her nose dripped, the maid jumped up and wiped it, then resumed sewing. The old dame braved it out, as if having your nose blown at ninety was only to be expected. Bright, challenging eyes peered at me over the topmost rug. Her voice was high-pitched and peremptory. 'Who are you? What do you want? Who let you in?'

'I am Flavia Albia. I am looking for Phrygia.'

'Who's she?'

'The tenant next door to you.'

'I don't know anything about her!'

'That's a pity.'

'I know nothing about anything!' she declared proudly. 'Everyone is waiting for me to die, you know.'

'So you said. I see you love keeping them in suspense.' Smiling, I went on, 'It's a shame you don't hear things, or while you were keeping everyone waiting for you to croak, you might have heard something useful about what's gone on.'

'What's that?'

'The husband has been murdered.'

'Was it gory?'

'No, but very shocking.'

'I want to know!'

'It's good value. I have seen the corpse. I'll tell you the details,' I offered, smiling calmly, 'after you tell me about any visitors who came, any strife they had with other people, and why Phrygia has bunked off somewhere unexpectedly today.'

'I am deaf. I never hear anything.'

'I know all about loss of hearing.' I had a cousin who had been deaf from birth. Junillus was a mischievous character. I knew about convenient senile deafness too. 'A variable affliction, is it? My grandma's hearing came and went depending on whether she was bored or agog for gossip.'

Without even needing to look where the cup was, the doughty dame grasped it and sipped her wine. 'You're a brazen piece.'

'Have to be. I deal with brazen witnesses,' I answered. 'Now, I reckon that you and I have a lot to get through. Don't go squiffy on me.'

When she gulped a large swig defiantly, I moved the small wine-table a foot beyond her reach. Then I captured the cup and put it on the table. The maid looked up to watch me, as if learning problem-management. This girl had the air of a downtrodden minion, yet I thought her perfectly capable. I hoped the mistress was leaving her a decent legacy. There was something in their attitude that spoke of mutual understanding. Gripes aside, they were a team.

'I am going to scream for help,' the old one tried.

'Scream away. They won't come. They'll just hope you're finally passing at last.'

'I need my commode.'

'Later.' I have been taught not to be cruel to old ladies but I had noticed that the maid, who must know when action was required, did not move.

'I'll wee everywhere.'

'Cross your legs, then. What's your name?'

'Naia Nerania.'

'What's hers?' I nodded at the maid.

'Bossy.'

'She seems mild enough.'

'Assia.'

'Assia, listen. Naia Nerania is going to talk to me now. I presume anything she has eavesdropped on you will have heard too, so you shout out to me if anything she says is barmy or untrue.'

Assia nodded. Although she had established a fixed care routine, she was adaptable.

We had a few riffles of annoyance first, but pretty soon Naia Nerania gave me what I needed. Chremes and Phrygia occasionally had visitors, usually members of their troupe who came on theatre business. Last week there had been none of that, presumably because during the Saturnalia holiday they were all too busy carousing in rougher parts of town. Chremes and Phrygia had gone out to join them for a big formal meal one evening, once they finished arguing with each other about what to take and what to wear.

'What to take?'

'Holiday bonuses. She spent all day filling purses for their people. He complained it was too much. She said it ought to have been more, and would be, if he hadn't wasted so much money playing dice.'

If any domestic matter involved an element of choice, this couple held opposing views. As I had been told, yammering away at each other was their way of life. Yet if anyone called on them, they smoothly put on a united front. They played the lord and lady, grandly holding court. Acting was their profession, and they could do it without any dramatist writing them lines.

In the couple of months they had been here, no ructions had occurred with their own troupe. Only right at the beginning was some difficulty mentioned, a question about which play of theirs would be accepted for the Plebeian Games. They had had no option, since it was a decision made by the authorities. Someone they spoke about as an old acquaintance had nevertheless nagged them over it, though nobody had come here.

At home, they had denounced him together. For once, they had both agreed: his complaints were unfair and ridiculous. Phrygia had scoffed, 'He never changes!' The trouble died down. They were then taken up with producing their play at the Games. It went well. Afterwards they stayed on here, routinely bickering.

Yesterday afternoon Chremes went out on his own. This was nothing unusual. He said he was going for a drink. She shouted, 'And the rest!' He told her she was unbearable; she said that was rich from him. He usually came back once he had lost all his money, which never took long. Not yesterday. By evening Phrygia was clucking with alarm, so she summoned her people, who thundered out in a herd to look for Chremes.

Phrygia had stayed here on her own. From time to time the actors sent messages that they had not found Chremes but would carry on looking. Night fell.

Very early this morning someone else came. His knocking woke Naia Nerania and Assia, though neither went to look. They could hear Phrygia speaking to him. He said her husband needed her to come at once to a place nearby. Phrygia croaked that Chremes must be in debt again; she sounded furious, but she rushed off with the messenger to rescue him.

Assia had stepped out onto the balcony to look. The hour was so early no one else was stirring; even the watchdog had stayed inside his kennel (well, he liked to keep office hours). Assia saw Phrygia and her male companion heading to the tradesmen's exit. The messenger could have got in at the back of the house because – of course it was wrong, but this was a quiet neighbourhood and everybody around here did it – the gate tended to be left open for laundry collection and household deliveries. It appeared to be locked but was accessible if you waggled it in a special way. All the local drivers knew the trick.

The maid had never seen this man before, she said. She had viewed him only from behind. His accent, when he brought his message, had been working-class Roman. He looked and walked like a tradesman. Not a waiter from the bar where Chremes was supposed to be, nor a child who had been given a copper to deliver a note. At a distance, he was short, stocky, not young, maybe in his fifties, his hair covered by a woollen cap, with bandy legs and a very wide belt with something like tools stuck into it. Assia would recognise him again if he was made to stand with his back to her. So she assured me.

She was a brilliant witness, and I was not surprised. Sometimes Fortune smiles on you.

Before I left, I fulfilled my promise to tell the doughty Naia Nerania what had happened to Chremes. She enjoyed herself, speculating gruesomely that the dubious messenger might have had a big hammer in his tool-belt and a pouch full of long nails for fastening feet to crosses.

But, as I would soon discover, what had happened to Phrygia involved a different kind of carpentry.

12

Promises should be honoured. Maybe not to your banker or that scoundrelly lover you know you ought to dump, but good witnesses deserve their reward. They may have more to tell you later. Keep them sweet.

I hoped this delay while I filled in Naia Nerania on how Chremes had been crucified would not be significant. A new search for his wife was now vital, even though Phrygia had left the house too long ago. If madmen had organised an attack on her, I was already too late to stop it.

I went down to the courtyard. As I reached ground level, Eucolpus shot out of a doorway from his private quarters. Someone must have snitched that I was in with his mother; I could see he was about to harangue me. I felt there would be nothing to gain from asking him whether anyone else in the household had been aware of Phrygia's messenger. Assia had said nobody else had been about; her word was good enough for me. So I called out gaily, 'You were so right! Your matriarch is deaf and useless!'

I scuttled past him, heading for the back gate. He was too surprised to follow. Out of the corner of my eye I saw him turn nervously towards the stairs that would take him up to see his mother. His attempts to shield her may have been well-meaning, yet nothing she told me had needed to be hidden and I knew she had enjoyed our talk. I entertained myself by imagining the coming clash. Eucolpus would groan that his mother was uncontrollable and Assia disloyal; I thought he needed to grasp that Naia Nerania would be much less trouble if he allowed her some social interaction instead of leaving her up there, waiting to die.

Today might shake him up. I had told Davos that my father reckoned an informer's role was to interfere. If nothing else came out of this case, I would have followed the code by leaving one old lady with a new lease of life.

This was not helping me track my client, however – the client I had not even managed to meet yet.

The tradesmen's gate opened from the inside without too much latch-waggling. Once I emerged onto the street behind the house, I realised there was no chance of finding witnesses. One pigeon sat on a roof, but he was asleep. Rome has many lively thoroughfares, awash with useful stalls and open-fronted shops whose staff like to keep an eye on comings and goings; they are interesting roads that will be wandered through constantly by inquisitive grandmothers, as those civic guardians patrol their neighbourhood to find things to complain about. This was another kind of place: a short, narrow, silent backstreet with only closed doors and shuttered windows. All the criss-crossing clothes-lines dangled empty, perhaps as a gesture to the holiday, but more likely because it was bad drying weather. No urchins played. Not so much as a rat or sniffing street-dog sauntered there, because no decayed detritus cluttered either of the gutters. The drains must work. Fly-tippers had failed to discover the place. The pigeon opened an eye briefly, then went back to sleep. This was a street where nothing ever happened.

Eucolpus maintained the whole district was quiet, a respectable haven where murders were unheard of. Normally that is nonsense, a claim made by social climbers who are lying to make their houses sound expensive, but today Eucolpus was right. If death by deliberate misadventure ever did occur, any bashing or throttling would be well-planned, competently carried out, and with a cover-up so perfect that no one would ever query the deed. The only exception might be if a thoroughly decent culprit was horrified by guilt. In such a nice district, killers were bound to leave behind polite regrets, an explanation of motive and a full confession, before they neatly committed suicide to save investigators any bother.

Still, there were plenty of other streets where knocking off your wife or obliterating a business partner served as local entertainment. When the vigiles cannot cope, or no one has any faith in them, that may bring business to informers.

I stood on a kerb, downhearted. Nobody was in this back-street even now in the afternoon, so at dawn it would definitely have been deserted. I had a perfectly useful description of Phrygia from the excellent Assia, which I could not use; there was nobody to run it past.

Assia had said the actress was extremely tall, taller even than her husband when she wore her highest heels – the ones she preferred. She always applied thick cosmetic paint, spread on with a wobbly hand, plus shoulder-scraper earrings that rattled; she chose stagey clothes, long, flowing layers in rare, bright colours. When Assia saw her leaving, Phrygia had been trailing two different stoles. From the front she would have been an exotic figure. From the back she looked half finished, like a statue that was intended to be placed in a niche so the sculptor did not waste effort.

If someone had noticed a woman as striking as that, teetering off in panic in the early hours, along with a stocky tradesman, who must have been an incongruous companion, they would remember. I prophesied that nobody had.

Despairing of other options, I walked slowly to the corner. I saw no one. I went into the side alley, also uninhabited, then along to the larger road onto which the Eucolpus house fronted. That, too, was desirably quiet for its invisible residents, though it did have an air, suggesting that if I waited an hour or so, perhaps a lone crow might fly over.

Otherwise, I could see no operating businesses, no waiting chair-carriers, and it was growing too cold for anyone to come out for a stroll. A few extremely well-kept homes dared me to knock with my desperate questions, but only so their door porters could tell me to get lost. I started to yearn for the drunks, thieves, escaped ducks and raving misfits who filled the streets on the Aventine. There, I could hardly move three strides without being hailed by somebody who went to my bath-house or knew one of my aunties. For any errand, I had to build in gossip-time.

Fortunately, my timing here was right. Being a successful informer needs a special knack: whenever you are stuck on your case, you must run into a coincidence. Don't try too hard or you will fail; worry bleakly over something else and it can happen. I had brought it off this afternoon. A dog I knew suddenly ran towards me, tail wagging. 'Barley, good girl! Where's Master?' Following her. Coming along the main street in one direction were my husband and another man I did not recognise, quickly introduced to me as Mucius from the local vigiles; a couple of troops in red tunics trailed behind their investigator. As I hailed these arrivals, almost at once the gingery actor called Simo arrived the other way, with some of his colleagues.

We probably made the largest group to have been on that spot since the street-party for Nero's death. Clustering eagerly with them all, I told what I had discovered. We started to organise a search party. Then, in order to show that this was his patch, with no room for waffling amateurs, Mucius became proactive.

Medium height and regular build, round-faced, not head-shaved, as the vigiles so often were, but with tight, light-coloured curls, Mucius looked more like a pastry-cook yet he had the usual military background. It gave him the usual attitude. He was job-worn but unfazed by life. He expected idiots, liars, bullies and busybodies who criticised how his cohort worked. He breathed cynicism and toughness. He knew how to act as if he was efficient, which no doubt carried him through most crises.

He listened to all I told him, which was a good start. Perhaps he sensed that if he dawdled too much on this case, I might pre-empt him. Not intending to stand for that, he had one advantage: he got out onto the streets in his area, so he knew the local wildlife.

He dug out a witness. He knew where to look. Soon we found out where we would be going next. Thank you, Mucius.

An extremely dirty vagrant was allowed to snooze by the local fountain so long as he never washed his feet in it. This loopy loon was completely away with the naiads. Still, he answered Mucius, rather than be beaten up at a station-house. He grumpily supplied what we wanted: yes, just after first light he had seen a woman who answered our description, plus a man with a tool-belt, walking quickly past. Phrygia was already known to me as someone with judgement; she had had the presence of mind to realise the filthy tramp lay by this fountain all the time, so she called out, 'If anyone asks for me, I'm at the Theatre of Balbus!'

Apparently she had sounded keyed-up, though not terrified – or not yet. She was unaware that her husband had already died, in pain and exhaustion, on a cross in the dark, before she was lured out from the house. She, too, was on her way to die, but cannot have realised.

By now, we felt horribly certain her hurried mission would have ended badly. Once we reached the theatre we knew for sure. Someone had planned for Phrygia to participate in a scene from the Cretan play.

PASIPHAE

13

I had never been to Crete. I had sailed past it, the year after Falco and Helena adopted me, on our way home from a tour of Greece. The next year we sailed south of Crete again, going in the opposite direction to visit Alexandria. It is a big island with a long history and a mad mythology. Helena Justina had been trying to educate me, her young British foundling, so while we travelled she told me colourful stories of the labyrinth, the Minotaur, Daedalus the inventor and his gormless son Icarus, who flew too near the sun.

She had to tell me twice because, as a gormless teen myself, by the second year I had forgotten everything she said the first time. I duly felt outraged that the princely Theseus, after being helped by Ariadne and her clue of thread so he could find his way back from the labyrinth, swiftly abandoned her on Naxos so he could marry her sister, Phaedra. All goes wrong for Phaedra: lusts for stepson, lies to husband (Theseus), stepson dies horribly, she tops herself. That was routine domesticity in historical Athens. Only to be expected, said Helena, given all that had been inflicted on Phaedra's mother back in Crete. Those princesses were probably glad to escape. They were a badly functioning family, worse even than the Didii. Still, Helena blamed Theseus for most of it, the twerp who had made his father jump off a cliff because he couldn't even put the right-coloured sails on his boat.

Theseus sneaking off from Naxos while Ariadne was asleep ought to have been a bitter warning to me, but of course I soon found myself being dropped with a thump by a flawed hero I happened to be mooning after in real life. He married someone else. *Io!* Does it sound familiar? It meant I could understand why, for Ariadne, a sozzled wine-god arriving in a happy carnival, his personal chariot pulled by panthers, might seem an acceptable substitute. Joining a Bacchic throng, with wine to hand, must be better than sobbing alone. I did some of the lonely sobbing and, frankly, it stinks. There were plenty of drunks on the Aventine, but none of them had godlike looks or exotic transport, so Ariadne might have been rescued by Dionysus but I ended up with an ex-legionary called Lentullus then, eventually, Tiberius Manlius. Both were, in their different ways, good men – and good for me.

The second time Helena talked to me about Cretan myths, to take our minds off sea-sickness while our vessel rolled and bucked towards Egypt, some of it did stick. To this day I know that Daedalus, the magical artificer, made statues so realistic they had to be chained to the wall to stop them wandering off. 'I ought to try that with Falco,' Helena would murmur.

Daedalus created something else too: a convincing device that had been reproduced on the Roman stage, where good taste never played much part. Theatre directors without consciences used it as a money-spinner for their utterly mindless audiences. Trust them. Never mind dramatic catharsis. If it's lurid, the public like it. And the public did like the Minotaur's mother.

The authorities would allow a representation of her gruesome fate, if a cash-strapped entrepreneur bribed them enough. If ever law-and-order troops caught a really disgusting murderess, another live re-enactment might occur. It was rare, because female killers are generally too smart to be caught, but Pasiphaë's experience in the Daedalus contraption would seem a suitable punishment – and the producers would make the scene fatal. The excuse was that this served instead of being sent to the beasts, even though arena beasts don't rape victims. Rape, to theatre managers, is good. In a drama, rape can be passed off as intellectual purging, mental refreshment for city-worn audiences. That's nuts. *Pasiphaë* was even more horrible than *Laureolus*.

Myths are so gruesome. My mother had put it in context: Pasiphaë was the daughter of the Sun and an Oceanic goddess; she had major status in her own right. Assigned in marriage to King Minos of Crete, she had given him eight children, so she was a respected matron and, as my mother stressed, quite blameless.

Nevertheless, tragedy occurred, the husband's fault as usual: the god Poseidon gave Minos a majestic white bull for sacrifice, the bull from the sea. Minos adored it. Dumb even by regal standards, he kept the present for himself and secretly sent another animal to the altar. Sharp-eyed Poseidon was not fooled. Minos was punished, but the gods picked on his wife to suffer. Pasiphaë was cursed with unbearable physical desire for the beautiful white bull.

Daedalus, the brilliant inventor, was earning a crust at the Cretan court. On request, he created a wooden frame on wheels, covered with cowhide, inside which the besotted queen positioned herself. Daedalus towed his model to a meadow where the white bull grazed; it eagerly mated with the fake cow and – good afternoon's work – it impregnated the queen. Pasiphaë gave birth to a monster. It had a human body but a bovine head and tail. It was the Minotaur. Though his mother did her best to nurture it, her freak creature grew up to eat human beings, so then Daedalus, who never stopped inventing, built the Cretan labyrinth as its prison.

For Roman entertainment, live re-enactment of Pasiphaë being mated with a bull was a sure-fire hit. Outside the Theatre of Balbus, we found that someone was advertising this lurid sensation here. As soon as we read the new-looking charcoal invitation, it was easy to guess what ghastliness might be waiting inside.

We had had to cross most of the Campus so were breathless and in a panic after a lengthy hike. We had hurried down the Via Lata, turned along the Vicus Pallacinae, rushed down the long length of the Circus Flaminius, then struggled past the substantial Porticus Minuciae where grain was distributed. Across the street from this porticus, the Theatre of Balbus was a small Augustan building, recently restored by Domitian after damage in the city fire. We approached halfway along its complex.

A general entrance was open. We piled through, gasping for breath, and came into a square vestibule, empty that day. To our left was a spacious outdoor area called the Crypta Balbi. There, between the acts of a play, audience members could stretch their legs in a large garden, with a shrine to Vulcan, or take refreshments in three covered colonnades; it also had one of the best public lavatories in Rome, such a rare treat at theatres. My dog ran into the garden, much too excited, so I went after her and tied Barley to a tree with the lead I always carried. This forethought probably saved her life, though she howled pitifully as I left her.

We approached the auditorium. To our right was access to the seats. The stage lay ahead. There would be dressing areas and scenery stores, both below and behind, reached by narrow steps; the public would normally be excluded. We took a ground-level doorway with a short pass into the orchestra. Someone called out, 'Muck alert!' We had to step around a significant slew of nearly liquid dung.

Already we could hear, smell and sense the rampaging presence of Buculus.

14

He was well-known to arena-goers. Though murder had never formed an official part of Saturnalia, for Buculus a one-bull riot must have felt appropriate. Festival behaviour was fine by him: brought to Rome from some peaceful European forest or water meadow, he had adapted to being part of the imperial entertainment industry. Rampaging was what he nowadays did. You could tell that he liked it. He mainly rollicked around an amphitheatre on the bloody sand, but being led to the more cultured Theatre of Balbus had not fazed him.

Buculus was an affectionate title: 'little bull'. It was ironic: a once-cute chestnut-coloured calf had grown up to champion size. We heard him before we saw him. The beefy beast hated humans and he was loudly informing the world of it; maddened by sexual frustration, the noise he created was appalling.

We had come in at ground level below the north end of the stage. To our right, tiers of empty seats rose in standard wedges that formed an elegant semi-circle. The open space called the orchestra lay ahead of us. The stage to our left was supported on a massy stone podium, head-height from our position; the wide performance area represented a street, with a three-storey carved marble *scaenae frons* towering behind. There we saw him.

Somehow, the aurochs had been taken right up onto the stage, no doubt with great effort. We would have to deal with him in order to reach Phrygia. My heart was banging. I had curious knowledge of those beasts. Lentullus, my first husband, had had the biggest adventure of his life on the banks of a river in Germany, where he swung on the tail of a gigantic wild bull that was trying to kill my father and their companions. Lentullus told me all about it. In contrast, Falco was terse: 'Terrifying. Never go near one!'

We had to.

The woman we were looking for could be seen onstage above us – or what was left of her. We had missed her big scene. The bull stood, still pawing the ground, alongside her.

'Oh, hell, it's an aurochs!' Tiberius Manlius had read his Caesar, so he knew the big fact about the ancient aurochs: they can never be tamed.

'It's Buculus.'

'I wasn't asking for an introduction!'

Phrygia lay motionless. No sound came from her. As I had dreaded, she was encapsulated in a large wooden frame. Trapped, she must have been at the bull's mercy. As he saw us arriving, Buculus returned to the wreckage. With one of his enormous horns, he tossed the whole bundle as lightly as a feather pillow. The fake cow, complete with its human contents, travelled a yard then crashed back onto the stage as it must already have done many times. Before we arrived, blood had been shed everywhere. A hide had been ripped off the device; it lay in a heap, angrily torn. Smashed and splintered wood was widely scattered.

'Stand back!' shouted Mucius, the vigiles investigator.

With steaming snorts, the celebrity bull stared down at him. We could see Buculus had great intelligence, wickedly intent on keeping us away from his victim. He was much larger than domestic cattle. Tall as a man at the shoulder, he had long speedy legs, which gave him a tight turning-circle. Despite his weight, when he decided to move he was able to canter as lightly as a sprite on a water bubble. He could outrun anyone. He knew it.

On his fattened winter body, his coat was glossy brown, with a pale eel-stripe atop his spine, running into a heavy tail that would stew up to feed half a cohort. His shiny muzzle was lighter, dripping long trails of slime. All his power was in his neck and huge shoulders, which supported massive horns that curved up and outwards dangerously: nearly three feet long, their tips pointed forwards and the horns' weight only helped Buculus to swing around more easily. His angry eyes watched us. He was bellowing for the hell of it.

In an amphitheatre, where savage beasts usually fight, there is a high safety wall surrounding the arena; theatre stages are not built for men to scramble away from danger. Feeling exposed, we all started to edge very cautiously forwards, closer to where the fake cow had been tossed. Buculus raucously expressed his rage again.

'I hope he's got a trainer,' muttered Mucius. He had the normal vigiles' sense of humour.

'Anybody brought a bit of rope?' asked Atticus, in an undertone.

'Don't let him smell your fear,' advised Tiberius, hollow-voiced.

'Why didn't I take a day off?' Though reluctant to shift his eyes from the bull, Mucius turned his head. He mouthed instructions to one of his men to race to the new amphitheatre and hope to find handlers. Some with the right experience might be down in the underground passages where the beast cages were kept ready for the arena.

'Let's hope the buggers aren't still drunk after Saturnalia.' Pardicus sniffed.

'We're all right,' I murmured, inching further towards the orchestra. 'There's an aedile on the premises. Their remit is capturing stray animals.'

'Stuff that!' answered Tiberius, like a ventriloquist, barely moving his lips. He had had to tackle a wolf once, but it was old and sick, and slunk away when politely told to shoo. It then hung around the meat market for weeks; schoolchildren called it Romulus. 'Run for your lives, if he jumps off the stage.' It would be very easy for this bull to do that.

Buculus nuzzled the smashed-up cow contraption, wondering whether to hurl it around again. His large, wide-set black eyes stayed on us.

Ariminius and Pardicus suddenly turned away towards the entrance we had come through. I had spotted them glancing at one another: they were peeling off to do something. Whether or not they had acted in this theatre, they would know where the steps up to the acting area were and how to negotiate hidden places backstage. The remaining vigilis followed them.

Mucius also took brave action. He ran right across in front of the stage, past all of the fancy marble frontage. He was waving his arms and yelling out to the bull, 'Hey, Buculus! Try somebody your own size!' We saw what he was trying to do. Phrygia was at our end of the stage; Mucius wanted to lure the bull away so we could reach her. 'Here, boy! Good boy – come and play with me.'

It failed to work.

Buculus was about to assault his victim again, but Ariminius, Pardicus and the vigilis had reached the stage. They popped out from behind, through the scaenae frons.

'Use all the doors!' Tiberius shouted up. 'Distract him. We have to move him away from her!' Every stage has three permanent scenic doorways across the back wall, though not normally employed for effect in such a real farce as this. 'If he charges, turn sideways to look smaller. His blind spot is behind him.'

Was all that lore in the aediles' handbook? Tiberius had spent his childhood in the country. I'd always imagined it as long walks through charming wheatfields and having a pet rabbit. Had he, a true boy, liked to mingle with sweaty cattle-wranglers?

'Ho, Buculus!'

Actors are masters of many types of entertainment – dance, acrobatics, musical instruments. Pardicus, with his pigtail, was middle-aged and looked experienced; Ariminius, with the thinning hair, was older but still agile. They might have done tricks with animals in their time, though never like this. It was more likely to be a mischievous donkey or a dog who could count. That did not deter them. Their producer's wife needed rescuing, and for her they plunged into a drastic action scene. They yelled instructions to the vigilis, who imitated what they did; he quickly got the hang of it.

They used the three doorways that normally represent characters' houses. Waving and calling, they took turns to goad Buculus, while nipping in and out of the tall doors. He responded eagerly, ready to take on this deadly game, threatening to kill them if they failed to dodge fast enough. He liked chasing people. One at a time they attracted him, then jumped out of sight hastily, while another man called out from a different doorway. From ground level, Mucius was shouting instructions. Buculus was just too large to pass easily through to the space behind. His hoofs struck sparks as he pirouetted, and his horns scraped the newly restored marble door-casings.

The base of the stage podium was decorated with niches and statues, all recently cleaned and refinished. While Buculus was kept busy, Simo and Atticus shinned up the fancy stonework to collect Phrygia. Tiberius gave them each a leg up, kicking marble gods and benefactors in the face as they went. The bull saw them coming; he wheezed angrily, swung around, put his head down and ran at Atticus. Simo pulled off his cloak and swept it in front of the animal, drawing him away. The vigilis ran forward and took over the cloak. Buculus wheeled around after him, while Simo and Atticus hastily put shoulders to the wooden shape. They propelled the fake cow to the edge of the stage, then heaved over the entire jumble, before hastily slithering down after it to escape the bull. Crashing the model cow down to ground level felt drastic, but I recognised that little more harm could come to Phrygia inside.

Simo bent double and Atticus squatted on the ground, as they both recovered. Tiberius and I, with the investigator Mucius, began frantically hauling at the contraption's splintered staves to extract the woman. She had been tied to it inside by her arms and legs. Mucius had a knife, so he sawed at the bindings, trying not to cut her. We could hear that Phrygia was still breathing.

'You're safe!'

She was done for.

We pulled the woman out of the broken contrivance as gently as possible. It was too late.

Members of her troupe were in hysterics. '*What happened? Who did this to you?*'

She left us. Pain, shame, shock and too much blood-loss took her. It was a blessing that she did not linger. I wanted answers, of course I wanted answers, but I saw she had been too badly hurt. No doctor could save her. I would not have had her suffer for one moment more.

Her faint voice gave a final response as she was dying: 'The undertaker . . .'

15

Even with my previous, often scatty clientele, this was the first time I had lost one without her even seeing me. I could tell she had indeed been a tall woman, far from young, a lover of dramatic eye paint and exotic garments. She might have made a fascinating client. Now all I would remember was her terrible death. The usual negotiations would not apply: with the corpse of Phrygia lying at my feet, my terms were set. Although we had never met in life, I felt bound to avenge her.

I had seen death. Natural, accidental, pointless, deliberate, and now wickedly contrived. This had to be the most horrible. In shock ourselves, none of us were going to discuss details, but it looked as if the sheer weight of the enormous bull had caused the wooden cow to collapse, perhaps as soon as he attempted his physical union. Whether he succeeded in mating was unclear. I hoped not. Phrygia's other wounds showed all too clearly how the maddened beast had broken into her prison then attacked her with his horns and hoofs. He had tossed around what remained of the framework, with her still tied inside it. The human wreckage we managed to retrieve was beyond saving.

Buculus was still marauding above us. To stop him jumping off the stage, Pardicus, Ariminius and the vigilis kept daringly taunting him. Robbed of his first victim, he was now chasing them ever more angrily. He was learning. They were tiring. Still they risked provoking him. Between the three scenery doors plinths were ornamented with tall slender pillars and carried large statues: the men were able to dart out onstage then leap up onto the bases to frustrate the bull. It was incredibly dangerous. Though he skidded as he twisted and turned, the galloping giant was faster than them.

Pardicus slipped. With a contemptuous swing of his mighty head, Buculus gored him. Yelling in pain and bleeding, Pardicus forced himself up onto a statue plinth out of harm's way. He needed help, but Buculus now pranced too close. Ariminius wanted to go to Pardicus but his feints only further enraged the triumphant bull. The vigilis managed to snatch up the cloak, making passes, which drew off Buculus to one side. Ariminius flew up onto the plinth. We heard tunic cloth ripping as he began to make a tourniquet or bandage.

Down in the orchestra, Mucius had freed Phrygia's corpse. We were about to try to carry her body to a safer place, when Buculus spotted us. He lost interest in the cloak. The vigilis yelled down from above.

'Look out!' shouted Tiberius. '*Run!*'

The vigilis above us threw himself headlong at the bull's shoulder. He cannot have considered what he was doing. Buculus shed him as easily as if brushing off a broken branch. The man fell, screaming because he was now a target, although luckily Buculus had other ideas. The vast animal made a flying leap to bring himself right down from the stage to the orchestra. His sturdy legs buckled awkwardly in landing, but with an impatient stagger he regained his feet. Now he was at our level, ready for new fun. He raised his tail contemptuously, ejecting a loud splatter of heavy liquid dung. Then he bucked once, shoulders up, rump up, tail up. Lowering his head, he charged.

Mucius, Tiberius and I went sprinting to the nearest exit. The aurochs galloped after us. Tiberius had an arm around my shoulders, hauling me along faster. Mucius was just ahead, scooting along like a sand crab racing the tide.

We crashed right through an anteroom and fell into the larger vestibule. From there we had choices: outside into the street, up into the seating tiers, out into the Crypta Balbi colonnades. The bull could only have followed in one direction; if we split, some of us would be safe.

Fate casually intervened. Thank you, loveliest of goddesses!

As Buculus was squeezing through the doorway behind us, a vigilis entered from the street ahead. He came in breathy at a trot, then stopped. His jaw dropped, seeing the snorting bull so close. I recognised the man Mucius had sent out in search of animal handlers. There had been no time for him to go to the Flavian Amphitheatre and back. He must have raced to the meat market, bringing someone we all recognised.

Twisting in through the doorway, this mighty figure had to duck below the lintel. A shadow fell across the room. He wore a ragged, sleeveless tunic even in the dead of winter, with a massive belt, and he carried in an odour of raw blood. He was an enormous size. Rampaging cattle did not faze him. Our vigilis had done the best thing possible: he had brought Fugax.

16

I had seen him before, many times. Anyone who had ever been to the Forum Boarium, whether passing along the riverbank or purchasing meat for sacrifice or dinner, would know this market-stall prodigy. His huge stature was unforgettable. I had once dared to buy a bone for my dog from him; it felt rashly heroic. His vast leather apron was covered with blood and his odour of raw meat would have made a gaping crocodile seem mint-fresh. I bet he was never invited to weddings. Nobody would risk him kissing a bride.

With bulging muscles held in by a wide leather belt and boots big enough to drown wolf cubs, Fugax must have been nearly seven feet tall. I never asked permission to measure him. All the women I knew were agreed they would not have wanted to be his birth-mother. Midwives winced.

Fugax had developed his physical build to match his height so, with a ready diet of meat from the market, he now looked like Hercules's scarier brother. He must go to a gym; I was glad it was not mine. Perhaps he acquired his ironic nickname of 'shy like a fleeting fawn' in adult life, or perhaps even as a massive new-born it had seemed a good joke. He carried it off, acting as if he was normal. Fugax fled from nothing.

The scene altered subtly. Now we had Fugax, who spent his life handling agitated cattle. Fugax, whom everyone in the meat market would yell for in a problem situation. Fugax: the strongest man in Rome. Quite likely the strongest in the Empire. I hoped he was.

Fugax and Buculus both stopped. They assessed each other briefly. Without a word, Fugax went straight in, face on, no fear.

Fugax took up a wrestler's split stance, feet apart but not level, back foot planted at ninety degrees. With his gigantic hands outstretched a yard, he reached, grasped the aurochs by the horns, then simply leaned. His hips, knees and ankles were flexed, his arms locked out. Buculus breathed frothily. He threw his own weight forwards as fighting cattle do, though made no impact. Both showed the strain. Neither budged. It could have been a new contest in the Olympian Games. Neither participant would give.

'Let's have you now,' Fugax encouraged. He had a voice that seemed to rumble from a cavern in Hades, though his tone was kindly. He might have been calming a misguided calf that had knocked over barriers in the market. His feet were constantly shifting slightly, as he maintained his purchase. His gaze was fixed on the bull's. 'All right now, boyo.'

'Jupiter!' croaked Mucius. 'Where's a herd of distracting heifers when you need them?'

Behind the bull, our companions appeared, Ariminius supporting Pardicus. 'It's Fugax – what's to do, Fugax?'

'Keep out of the way!' suggested the gigantic butcher. His strained tone showed he was engaged in something difficult, even for him.

Buculus shifted one leg. Fugax leaned in harder. He was engaging every muscle, but Buculus held his ground. Both breathed hoarsely.

The rest of us were sheltering tight in doorways, peering anxiously around architraves. We could give no help; this was hardly a beast to pen into a corner with a couple of flimsy theatre flats.

'No loud noises,' ordered Fugax, anxiously, through gritted teeth. 'No sudden movements. Don't shout. Let him calm down.' After a wait, while he and Buculus shoved against each other again with neither giving ground, he managed to gasp, 'I am going to need help.'

He could not mean from us. Everyone here was useless for his purposes: actors, a magistrate, a vigiles investigator with, dammit, a woman. Hopeless. Or so Fugax must have thought.

He reckoned without Manlius Faustus, aedile and maniac, my husband. Before I could stop him, he gave my hand a sudden squeeze then moved away from our doorstep refuge. Holy heroics! Tiberius walked quietly in a big wide arc around Buculus, making a short comment to Fugax. Terrified for him, I could hear my husband talking to the bull in a gentle, steady voice. It was how he soothed his nephews, the two little boys we had fostered, when they were crying for their dead mother.

'Cruddy hell, Flavia,' murmured Mucius. 'Get your fellow out of there, before he's done for.'

'He'll be fine.' Oh, really? Of course, he was a man of surprises. A cautious man, I told myself, a thoughtful man who liked to know the facts before he took sensible action. Never rash. Competent. This man had nerve: after all, he had married me. 'Trust him.' Juno. However had I ended up with such horrible wifely loyalty?

I nearly screeched. Tiberius, who had been standing quite still, now walked right up to the aurochs. Almost underneath that hairy belly, he put a hand on the bull's solid great flank, then pushed against Buculus with his bent arm. All the time he was lulling him with that quiet, strong voice. Buculus, of course, pushed back. He sank on his rear legs to do it, so I hoped that stopped him kicking, because I knew a bull could kick a man to death. Tiberius exclaimed at the weight that threatened to flatten him. Fugax grunted, dodging his feet around again now that Buculus had shifted. One slip, and a horn would pierce him fatally.

It looked as if they were trying to move the bull over, putting him against a wall, the better to control him. Buculus was having none of that. Simo and Atticus copied what Tiberius had done, gently approaching, softly speaking, lining up and helping to push. Buculus barely acknowledged their efforts.

Face to face, Fugax kept talking to the bull, keeping his voice low, soothing the animal. Buculus flicked his ears forward: he was listening. Tiberius and the others tried to lull him too. One of the vigiles sidled, very slowly, towards a street exit, perhaps going for more help.

The contest between men and beast had to be moving towards a finale. Fugax could no longer stop his legs shaking. Raised veins snaked over the massed muscle of his upper arms, which were beginning to show trembles. The great roll of his neck was forced high, the skin on the back of his shaved head creased with effort. His mighty chest must have been under such pressure he risked tearing muscle or bursting his lungs. His face set: squared pursed lips, forehead wrinkled with strain. He made no sound, but we could see: any moment he would release the pressure, step backwards and give in.

Buculus, under his own stress, suddenly conceded. He dropped his head, in submission. His tail lowered.

Unexpected voices. Men entered. Men with poles and clanking buckets, jaunty men with prods, staves, pronged tridents, coiled ropes. Men who knew Buculus. More important even than their equipment, one of the group came in leading a small brown goat. He released the knotted string so it could trot straight over to Buculus, who dropped his nose to greet his obvious stable-mate.

The keepers berated their lost charge as if he had just stepped out of a field to explore: 'Here you are, naughty boy! This is where you've got to. Who's been taking you out to play in the big city?'

'Not us!' snapped Tiberius, still leaning against the aurochs. His position was dangerous enough, without him chastising the handlers. I needed courage to live with Tiberius Manlius. Whatever the crisis, he would always argue a matter of principle. There was a constant risk that his stubbornness might cause an incident. 'Have him back as soon as you like. He's all yours.'

The keepers stared, sensed Tiberius was trouble, but knew they had the advantage. We needed them to remove their beast. They shoved Tiberius and the others aside, taking over Buculus, stroking him, cooing endearments, appearing to check him in case we had done him any damage.

'Just a big hairy baby, aren't you?'

'He killed a woman,' Tiberius informed them, his voice hard, 'but wicked people put him up to it.'

'Let's leave the experts to it,' I urged, playing peace-maker. I grabbed my husband by the hand, meeting initial resistance though he did give in. I could hear Barley barking. Although I had always been a city-dweller, I knew you should never let your little dog run around near cattle. Buculus ought to spook her with his size and weight, but there was more chance my poorly trained scamp would spook him. Then anything could happen.

Tiberius and I went out into the garden. The cold open air felt wonderful. We fell into each other's arms as we generally did after desperate danger. The dog tried to climb up us. He lifted her and clutched her. I brushed away tears. 'You are crazy. You could have been kicked to death!'

'You just have to get in close.'

'Dear gods. Don't do it again, please.'

'No, love,' said Tiberius, soothing me with his voice the same way he had calmed Buculus. I allowed it. The trauma we had just been through was beginning to affect me, or I would have been angrier. Even Tiberius was trembling. He was human too. He knew what he had done. In retrospect it terrified us both. We could not let go. We kept an ear out anxiously, in case Buculus burst free on a new rampage.

The actors and vigiles came outside with us, attending to Pardicus, after his goring. Only Fugax stayed behind in the vestibule, holding his role as a hero; I heard him boasting to the keepers as they concentrated on Buculus.

The handlers jeered, but mildly. It never developed into a contest. Everybody knew the score. A woman was dead; much worse might have happened. Nobody could relax until they had Buculus safely back in his stall.

A keeper came into the garden, to dangle his bucket in the long rectangular pool that formed part of the shrine to Vulcan. He skipped away jauntily, taking the bucket to water the bull, returning almost at once for a refill. I went over and asked how the aurochs' usual guardians had lost him. The man said somebody had secretly stolen him last night; the keepers had no clue who had done it. 'Someone brave!' The thieves had probably used his goaty friend to lure him; it was called Caprininus and was a right little character.

I asked how the handlers had known the bull was here. There had been panic when Buculus was found to be missing. They were certain to be blamed – and he was valuable. They had tried following his trail of dung through Rome, but people had given their pavements an early-morning wash-down. It took them all day to arrive here. They found Caprininus wandering loose outside, so they hurried into the theatre.

'It's bad what he's done to that woman, but he was set up for it on purpose. Don't you go thinking you can arrest Buculus for murder, Aedile!'

Tiberius answered gravely, 'I believe that under civil law no animal can be held culpable.' Give this man his due, he knew all the rules he administered.

'He will be relieved!'

'Play things down,' Tiberius warned the grinning keeper. 'Buculus cannot be blamed, but anyone who had charge of him could be sued for negligence – failure to control him. If his crime could not reasonably have been prevented, a judge might say compensation must be paid – or Buculus himself handed over to the injured party.'

'Lucky the injured party is dead, then!' was the keeper's uncaring riposte.

'Buculus was stolen,' Tiberius assured him. 'Whoever did that is the murderer.'

'And a cattle thief!'

'That too.'

Our ordeal was safely ending. Somehow they had managed to put ropes on Buculus – long ones, I noticed. As the bull was led out, seeming docile after his adventure, we all told them courteously how glad we were they had come to find him. The great butcher, Fugax, was going back to his market stall. Since he never normally left the Forum Boarium, Mucius was sending a vigilis to show him his way home.

Everyone thanked Fugax too. I hugged him. In repose, his face was rather sweetly dimpled and his manner subdued, yet my hug for that big butcher was, in my view, the bravest thing anybody did all day.

17

The aftermath seemed interminable.

More vigiles had arrived, a lot more: the night shift must have joined the day shift, with men curious enough to volunteer for extra duty. We could hear that crowds had gathered outside on both sides of the theatre, but the troops kept them back even though they themselves sauntered in for a look around. Pardicus was tended with more first aid, his blood staunched professionally by the red-tunics. Then he disappeared, sent somewhere for care and rest. Ariminius went to look after him.

Two of the new vigiles were staring at the stage, having a deep discussion. Never assume ex-slaves are all brawn, not even fire-fighters. 'It's in the *Book of Spectacles.*'

'Martialis? He's a nutter.'

'You could be right, my friend. He writes for money but he complains he never gets enough. It must be depressing. "This was vindicating the age-old myth. That unhappy Queen Pasiphaë coupled with the bull of Dicte. We have seen it," writes the nutter poet.'

'We would have seen it ourselves, if we had been here.'

'Splitting hairs, man. This is so rich – it goes beyond pathos. It's the classic theme of drama: humans must endure undeserved suffering, will of the gods, no fault of their own.'

'But *did* she deserve it? Our officer will say we have to find out whether this woman really had offended the gods. If so, what was her bad action? Was it fated, or a tragic flaw in her character? And the key question, could she have avoided it?'

'Wrong, you goons!' shouted Mucius, with spirit. 'Your officer is going to tell you wacky intellectuals to stop standing about, or your own suffering will be well deserved!' The philosophical critics raised their eyebrows in pity at his lack of culture, then wandered away out of his reach. 'Why do I get them?' he asked the ether.

My husband muttered to me that it was *his* undeserved suffering, but we both kept our heads down, like schoolchildren pretending not to have heard a question on some homework they had not finished.

Mucius shot a suspicious glance our way, but he was wary of criticising an aedile. He began creating a racket about needing the public slaves who looked after the theatre. His men listened considerately, then shook their heads at his agitation. Even so, a few slaves arrived and were admitted with their brooms. To thwart the public coming to stare at the body, a man had been despatched for Suedius. He quickly arrived. Apparently, he had hitched up his funeral cart as soon as he had seen us running down the Vicus Pallacinae, where his premises were, on our way here to find Phrygia. That seemed an age ago. I managed not to snarl that I was sorry if we had kept him waiting.

'Bloody hell! Who is she?' Suedius demanded, which seemed to prove he was not the undertaker she had mentioned. After peering at the tragic remains he added, as crass as ever, 'Something's made a monumental mess of this old bird!'

Simo, one of the actors who were still there, enlightened the mortician coldly that she was the wife of the crucified man he had attended earlier. Suedius only wanted to know from Mucius whether the Seventh would cover his call-out fee. Then he asked if he should organise two funerals jointly and, now there was no surviving spouse, who would pick up the tabs for burial?

'Just get on with it!' Mucius snapped nastily, as if he knew Suedius of old. 'Do your job, Suedius. I want her out of this theatre. I want her gone now, before the damned auditorium becomes a tourist site. Hide the woman in your shop as quick as you can and I'll talk terms later. As if that stadium nightmare wasn't enough!'

'Calm down, lad,' Tiberius murmured.

Mucius thumped his curly head in frustration, as he grappled with the problems of this second troubling crime scene. 'We're bound to be harassed with more high-level interest. Somebody get those bone-idle slaves moving! I need the stage prettied up and all this molten bullshit sluiced away. Any time now we'll have chalk-white togas mincing through, squawking complaints about the stinks.' He covered his nose as if, with the aurochs gone, he was suddenly aware himself how bad the smells were.

'I'm to get her out.' Suedius in humble mode made my teeth jar. 'Nice and quick. Understood, Tribune!'

'I'm not the bloody tribune! Just do it!'

The only point in favour of Suedius was that, for once, he told his attendant, Sorgius, to go out to the street to look after the donkey. It meant the youngster would not witness the ugly process of gathering up Phrygia's disjointed, bloody corpse.

During this interchange, Tiberius was crouching to inspect splintered planks from the fake cow.

'He's a one!' chuckled Suedius, stepping back from Phrygia. 'Show him some salvage, he's in there!'

Tiberius straightened up. 'That's right. Oven fuel.' His voice had a different steadiness from when he spoke to Buculus. A warning. At home, I would have signalled for everyone to leave him alone. Bending again, he wrenched the wood apart, though his ultimate aim was piecing the timbers back together. Mucius came to watch; he sent a man onstage to collect what was still up there, which included one of the fake cow's crude wooden legs.

Tiberius gave the shambling funeral director a long, straight glance. 'I am looking,' he explained, in a taut voice, 'for carpenter's marks. Any I find will be compared to the timbers from the cross this morning. Did the same man do both jobs? Find me that carpenter,' he told Mucius, in an easier tone. 'If you show me other work of his, I can identify his signature. But I wouldn't allow such a soulless brute to work on any site of mine.'

Rolling up his tunic sleeves, he had roughly reassembled the model cow. It was a box-like coffin almost five feet high, standing on four sturdy columns. I helped to hold it upright for him, as the damage had left it lop-sided. Unlike the legendary device made by Daedalus, this had no wheels, only heavy blocks for feet. The thing looked crude, but originally it had been covered with cowhide. That must have made it seem more life-like and even enticing to a randy bull.

'Collect up that cover,' Mucius ordered someone. 'You never know, a tanner may have had a burglary. Bound to be in our records,' he joked. That was unlikely.

Tiberius pointed out how each of the legs was numbered, with various alignment marks; he said they had been scratched with what he called a race. 'Someone definitely owns professional woodworking tools.' He decided the cow could have been made elsewhere, then brought here for onsite assembly. 'Somewhere there's a workshop.'

'Local,' decided Mucius. Now he had Tiberius as an intelligent associate, his stress was lessening. 'My lads can enquire.' He glanced over at the earlier pair. 'Once they've finished gabbing together about sodding plays.'

Helped by Mucius, Tiberius upturned the reconstituted cow to inspect its interior compartment. The frame had considerable weight, even after the bull's efforts had broken it.

I made myself look, too, trying not to envisage Phrygia trapped there. Inside were fixing points, big heavy-duty metal staples, which still contained fragments of the rope that had held the woman in position for her ordeal.

Tiberius picked off twisted fibres, with angry jabbing movements, though he removed any complete fragments more carefully. 'Suedius! I want that rope you pinched.' Suedius looked surly. 'The rope you took away from the crucifixion this morning.' Needing cooperation, Tiberius retracted a little. 'All right, I don't need all of it, only any ends. Cut each of them off with a few inches, then mark the cuts you make, so we can differentiate afterwards. It may be possible to show that the same rope was used in both murders.'

'I haven't got time to ponce about.'

'Neither have I! Do this, will you?'

Mucius intervened: he sent one of his troops to take the undertaker's boy to their premises. I had seen Sorgius load the coiled rope onto the cart, so we knew he would be able to identify it. 'Any trouble, strangle the little rascal with the rope,' commanded Mucius. 'See if it works. Call it weapon-testing.'

He was having a hard day. 'Suedius, jump to it! Scoop up that body, then clear off!'

Suedius grumbled, though he did begin casually flipping limbs straight. 'Someone might have warned me that she's dropping apart.'

Although I could accept that Phrygia had indicted someone else, I marched up to challenge him. 'She told us "the undertaker" did this. Was that you?' I was raging. He stepped back, looking nervous. 'You, Suedius? Or anyone you work with?'

'Me and my boy? Never met the woman.' That sounded like a classic lie, though it was probably just his normal way of speaking. Partway through edging her body onto his stretcher, he lifted Phrygia's head. Remaining fairly neutral for him, he surveyed her peach-painted elderly face. 'Not much of a looker! Horrible artwork. I'd remember all this clogged eye makeup. We can improve her,' he offered, 'if anybody wants her laid out for viewing.'

'Keep her covered.' I was terse.

'All right, if you want.'

'Whoever did this must be found. Suedius, if it wasn't you she accused, have you any idea who else in your business she might have known?'

'On the Campus?'

'I suppose so.'

Suedius probably enjoyed the idea of blaming somebody else. 'I'll have a think who there is. I can get Sorgius to write a little list for the vigiles.'

I nearly urged him to give the list to me instead, but if he sent it to the Seventh, Mucius would be the one who had to trek around interrogating other morticians.

'Since you pinched my lad,' Suedius called out to him, 'you'll have to lend me some muscle to haul this corpse to my vehicle. I can't carry her by myself. It will do in my bad back.'

Mucius ordered him to make sure the crowd outside could see nothing of the remains. Then subdued members of the vigiles removed Phrygia, widow of Chremes, from the scene of her appalling death.

I found myself badly shaken by what I had seen. Feeling queasy and distressed, I walked across to the nobles' seats around the outer edge of the orchestra. This had turned into a terrible day, and I had not even started a full investigation yet.

Tiberius was taken up with organising removal of the fake cow. He had sent to the Saepta Julia for auction staff to bring Father's delivery cart, along with the timber baulk he had already commandeered from the stadium death. Everything would go to the Aventine. All potential evidence would be stored in our yard at home. Mucius had agreed.

Throwing a last disgusted glance at the fake cow, the cohort investigator shook hands with my husband, then stomped after me to the marble seats. 'Gods, I need a breather!' He, too, seemed deeply affected by what had been done here. I guessed why: the vigiles have their own faults but are truly upset by violence against women. They despise the men who do it.

Emotionally exhausted, Mucius and I perched on the marble thrones that were provided for the great, good and unprincipled when they came to gossip loudly and pretend to watch plays. We sat in silence, both trying to recover our equilibrium. Mucius had instructed his troops to find any witnesses who had seen the bull being brought here last night or this morning. He expected that nobody had noticed anything unusual. An aurochs might be enormous, but in a district full of temples, people would always assume any fine-looking animal was being taken to an altar for sacrifice. It happened all the time. What's new?

As if I was some kind of accomplice, he admitted to me he could see no good approach to this impenetrable case. I crossed my arms under my cloak, slumped in similar despondency. We had no real leads.

Eventually, we rallied.

'Now then, Flavia Albia! I hear you enquire into things.'

'We haven't met before, but I know Ursus, your colleague. Also, Titus Morellus of the Fourth Cohort. Either will vouch for my methods. I won't get in your way.'

'Better bloody not! Ursus was given a medal last week. Two long-running killers arrested.'

'I know. If informers won medals, I'd have one as well. He's horrible but fair. He will confirm we shared the work on those.'

'It's no job for a woman. What do you do it for?'

'Fees. There was a grateful client in one of those cases. Wife murdered. I acted as intermediary. It reassured the family.'

'Really! Well, don't rely on cooperation here. I'm not having that soft swine Ursus sticking me with a precedent.'

'Honest, you'll end up glad I'm here. And don't you try blocking me!' I managed a grin to soften the situation. 'Calm down.'

'Who's twitchy? Is that aedile having a role in this?'

'Faustus? No. We decided this morning at the stadium. An extra death changes nothing. This business will be mine.'

'He's very fascinated by that fake heifer.'

'Yes. He will share his knowledge of carpentry, but Faustus won't work a case in the Campus. This is another magistrate's patch. Anyway, he needs to go home to our house. We're right up on the Aventine. No one was expecting us both to be out all day. We're looking after children and there's an invalid staying. One of us must see to things domestically.'

'Isn't that your job?'

'Only if I am not working.'

'So, you will be poking around here.' Mucius resigned himself.

'No option.' Tiberius and I had not even discussed the way forwards; he knew I would be committed to Phrygia. He would also realise the Campus Martius was the other side of Rome from home. Practically, I would have to stay over here to do my work.

Mucius kept muttering about me being involved. 'You come along, expecting my cohort to cooperate . . .' In truth it was not a rebuke. He might as well let me interfere. The case was already bad enough. An amateur tangling with these wild killings added nothing much to his own burdens. Even if we combined resourses, we stood little chance of solving anything. 'You knew this woman?'

'No.'

'Not even a connection?'

'My parents knew her and her husband.'

'Your parents! Isn't your father that Falco? Your fellow told me. I know him,' he muttered, as if it was no recommendation. Working at the Saepta, the Seventh were Father's local cohort. They would be the boys who barged in and turned over his warehouse, 'inspecting your premises for suspected stolen goods'. Falco must have bought this man drinks to improve relations.

Mucius loosened up some more, sharing his own grief: 'Damn woman croaked, "The undertaker did it." Pity me, Flavia Albia. I'll have to trot around every stinky funeral yard and ask whether any bloodthirsty attendants just happened to have put a woman in a box last night to attract a giant angry bull.'

'Good luck!' I said wanly. 'I'm sure if they did, they will tell you.'

'Of course! Own straight up – why not?'

'You'll manage.' My father and his old crony from the Fourth dismissed the Seventh as brutal and corrupt. Still, their district was filled with such highly visible national monuments that Mucius had to be competent. 'Ursus spoke very highly of you, Mucius.' Ursus had actually never mentioned him to me. 'You'll get around all the other undertakers as fast as you can, Officer. Unfortunately, they will give you no help and no one in the wider world will applaud your efforts.'

'Thanks for nothing.'

'I could help?' I ventured tentatively.

'Don't you bloody try. You're not my stinking optio. The whole point of having a trainee on your heels is to pick them yourself and get some gratitude back! Keep out of my way. I'll do the recce myself,' he grumbled on. 'It's not one for the boys.' Like most questions that the vigiles asked of the public, this would be pointless, but he still had to waste boot-leather and precious time on it. A dying statement cannot be ignored. I made a capitulating gesture, to show I was grateful I could avoid the task. 'The "undertaker"! Gods help me,' Mucius growled again unhappily.

I wiped away tears that I had not even realised I had shed for Phrygia. 'Some kind of mortician must have been involved, Mucius. Trust her. She was a sensible woman, by all accounts.'

We slumped into silence again.

'Review time!' Mucius sat up straight. He must be too depressed to argue any more. 'What's the score, Flavia Albia? What horrible plot have we got here?'

I pulled myself together, too. So, the vigilis and I started to compare notes.

18

These were not one-man crimes. More than one killer must have been involved, perhaps a group, though that would be unusual. Neither murder was spur of the moment. Someone had put in a lot of brooding first. They had planned everything, built specialist equipment, and on the day they had deployed clever management.

Whoever carried out these murders was daring, inventive and extremely violent. This undertaker character and his associate, or several together, must be harbouring some intense grudge. Chremes and Phrygia had committed an unforgivable offence, or these maniacs believed they had. Knowingly or not, the couple had made vicious enemies. In response, their killers had intended both to suffer. They were punished in two ways: first the fear from realising what was about to happen, then their final terror, shame and pain.

The two murders were discrete: though obviously linked, they were very different. This dissimilarity seemed intentional.

Each victim was abducted alone; each died alone. Keeping them separate must have made it easier to overcome and kill them, especially in such extraordinary ways. Neither had been required to see what happened to their spouse. Were they taunted with it? Perhaps they never knew.

They died in a stadium and a theatre: the locations presumably mattered, yet they were empty at the time. For Chremes and Phrygia, their reckoning was personal: they had performed their ghastly death scenes only in the presence of their killers. We presumed the killers stayed to watch as long as possible.

They wanted to shock us, the responders. These two murders had been staged to be visual, vile acts to give joy to their perpetrators first, then to disgust whoever found the bodies. The killers wanted their anger recognised. I wondered whether they were attacking the whole theatre group, killing its leaders to impose some revenge on everyone. Mucius complained that it was a hit at the vigiles, but he would think that.

Drama was key. Scenes from plays had been used as murder weapons. This was extraordinary. Mucius found it so baffling that he called the last couple of actors across to us.

Simo and Atticus, the redhead and the younger man in the hat, had been hanging about miserably. They confirmed a key fact: neither *Laureolus* nor the Pasiphaë story had ever been performed as a play by their company.

Simo suspected Chremes would have done it, if he could; Phrygia never allowed anything so salacious. Their repertoire was pretty sedate by comparison. All the company constantly dreamed of obtaining fame from serious tragedy, especially Phrygia; however, to attract decent audiences they invariably stuck with Roman adaptations of New Greek Comedy. That meant Plautus and Terentius, or occasionally Naevius, though of course everyone called him an arrogant Campanian . . . Their wider portfolio included a ragbag of unaltered Greek standards, headed up by Aristophanes and Menander. Phrygia liked the old classics. Chremes groaned; he favoured scripts they threw together themselves to fit whoever was currently in the company. *The Girl from Naxos, Paxos, Samos, or Some Other Vaguely Familiar Greek Island.* If they had two actresses, or female musicians, who would take their clothes off onstage, which was permitted in Italy, it would be *Two Naughty Girls from Lesbos.*

'Public taste. No one gets to do anything decent these days. Davos even had to give that farce *The Spook Who Spoke*!' uttered Atticus, in a hollow voice. My father's play. I made a gesture of asking forgiveness. Atticus patted my shoulder as if Falco's doings were not my fault. He said, 'I'd like to see Falco apply his mind to whatever in Hades has gone on today.'

Mucius muttered, 'Well, we'll have to rely on whatever he has taught his daughter!'

'He taught me enough!' I growled defensively.

Mucius now attempted to follow the only lead we had. 'For some mad reason the deceased here accused an undertaker. I don't suppose any of you acting laddies has been moonlighting?'

His phrasing was tame enough but they both took offence. 'You are looking at us for this?' demanded Atticus. 'Stuff you!'

Simo folded his arms and scoffed too. 'No way! Even for a fireman, you must be an idiot.'

Mucius must be used to bad reactions. Staring at the fiery redhead in the same way that Fugax, the big butcher, had glared eye-to-eye with Buculus, he rubbed his chin. 'Settle down. I always have to examine any people who knew a victim.'

'Start close' was his watchword, naturally. It often proved a good first move – in the trade we all used it. He was bound to view Chremes and Phrygia's own theatre group as a handy bunch of suspects. I would have done the same if I had only just met them.

I knew more about them than he did. 'Mucius, they are a travelling company.' You have to be fair or your case goes astray. 'They may knock on doors offering to pick fruit when they are short of money, but a sideline in funerals would never work. They never stay anywhere long enough. Oh, if somebody dies when they are on the road, I expect they roll the body into a ditch or at least dig a hole to leave them decent. But they can never run any fixed-location business, certainly not as undertakers.'

Simo backed this up. 'We make spare cash by serving in bars. At least we can pinch a drink or two. Forget burials. We have quite enough trouble with stiffs – but I mean star leads, corpsing their way through the principal roles. Tell him, Albia!' urged Simo. 'None of us holds any grudge against Chremes and Phrygia. None of us could ever have done anything to them – besides, we were all together last night, all out combing the Campus after Chremes disappeared.'

'That's true,' I soothed Mucius, who still wore a suspicious grimace. 'Known fact. Stop gurning, Officer – you'll crack your face. I already interviewed them. They don't have a motive and their alibis are solid.'

'They're alibiing each other,' Mucius complained, though his heart was not in it. He prepared to march off, after throwing the two actors that pathetic line 'Don't leave town!' He came back a few steps. 'Better still – as soon as I give you clearance, get out of town and don't come back!'

We watched his broad, unhappy figure retreat back across the orchestra. Rome placed its incidents of foul play in the hands of such men. Sometimes they caught a perpetrator, frequently they failed. At that moment, I was not sure that adding me into the mix would be any improvement.

It had started to rain. Not heavy, but spitting and spiteful. December is my least favourite month to take on something challenging.

The two vigiles who enjoyed culture had ambled up close to listen in. Their names, I found out eventually, were Hyro and Milo. Mucius eventually told me the Seventh's tribune kept them on because while they were deep in discussion together at fire scenes they would carry out acts of incredible courage. But otherwise, thought Mucius, they were idle buggers talking utter crap.

'This here today,' the first asserted now, 'was all wrong historically. Classical drama would forbid letting a bull appear right on the stage to kill somebody in full view. It would never have happened at Athens or Epidaurus.'

The second shook his head gravely in agreement. 'Any death is always heard behind the scaenae frons. It is absolutely unacceptable to show characters dying in view of the audience.'

I said I was sure they would mention that error in their theatre review for the *Daily Gazette*.

19

I had decided I must stay on the Campus that night. After two horrific deaths and the Buculus terror, I felt utterly drained. I longed for my own warm bed, but I needed an early start tomorrow. The auction staff had lent Tiberius their delivery cart, stroppily accessorised with Kicker the mule. He would have to drive it himself: Felix, the carter, was visiting his ex-wife for Saturnalia. They were estranged, but she made a good barley cake. He had left behind the two scrawny chickens, Piddle and Willikins, who habitually scratched around in the back to make the cart look as if it contained nothing worth stealing. 'You have to throw them corn, love, so they will stay there and not jump out. Don't let them end up in a pot in our kitchen.'

'I'll fend off Fornix.' Fornix was our cook. He snatched anything that would braise.

Twilight was closing in, yet the wheeled-vehicles ban had not quite ended; Tiberius would claim building contractor's dispensation because he had a load of timber. Barley jumped up eagerly beside him; she loved a ride on a cart. I kissed the dog and patted my husband, then waved them off.

I did consider claiming use of the room rented by Chremes and Phrygia, which, after all, was now empty and paid for. The idea felt creepy. Besides, because Phrygia had been collected from there to be murdered, Tiberius was anxious about security. So, I would camp out in the Saepta Julia. Gornia, the fragile old porter, always stayed in the warehouse on a truckle bed rather than be taken to his own bare lodgings. He would be company and there were always couches awaiting sale. I would just have to inspect them closely for insect life.

I left the theatre with Simo and Atticus. We walked via the Vicus Pallacinae; on our way we identified where Suedius worked, though without going in there. I had had enough of him.

The actors showed me where they were staying, in rooms above a couple of bars, on the lower end of the Via Lata, where the Vicus Pallacinae turned off. We could pretty well see the Saepta, so I left them there and went on alone. I said I would come down that evening to meet everyone. We all needed respite, but I knew there must be a chance that, having lost their leaders, the theatre group would disperse. I was keen to order my thoughts. I would rest on my own first, then go back to find them, armed with my most urgent questions.

'Are the rest of us in any danger?' Atticus asked me, as we parted.

Until I found out what had happened with Chremes and Phrygia, there was no way to be sure. I told him it seemed most likely the couple had made enemies together, but no one else was implicated. If any other actors really had attracted the killers' notice, I presumed they had some idea about why and who. None, Simo assured me.

Oh, really?

This would be something for later. I slightly distrusted the way they brushed it aside. I left Simo and Atticus looking like men who had an offering they were not yet ready to share.

Had I felt less weary, I might have picked at this pimple straight away. Still, some things are better left to mull.

I had an idea of my own about what I needed to investigate first, because identifying the undertaker struck me as critical. I had noticed something earlier, perhaps about him, that I had not even told Mucius of the Seventh. A canny informer is open when they have to be, yet keeps one step ahead.

'Was Faustus all right about driving?' Gornia asked, when he saw me at the Saepta. 'Felix has bunked off for the festival with his woman – well, he has two, really. So holidays take him longer than everybody else.'

'No need for Felix. Manlius Faustus is a man, Gornia. It is his heritage to believe himself a brilliant driver.'

'He'd better not damage the cart!'

'He won't.'

'And not lose the chucks.'

'I told him. He will take care of the chucks. He was born in the country. He helped people catch a giant bull today.' I still did not like thinking about it. I tried to distract myself. 'What's Felix up to, juggling women?'

'Oh, Felix is just an idiot. He has always been the same, Albia. He thinks it's a big secret. Everyone knows he has two on the go – your father even reckons there's a third hidden away somewhere. Still, Falco likes to exaggerate. I put a tall candelabrum on the cart,' Gornia told me. 'I thought your fellow might want it as that present he was looking for. He can have it on approval. Your pa will be all right about that.' Everyone knew Falco liked his new son-in-law. Father had told me this was a surprise, since he had expected I would turn up one day with some limp radish who couldn't open a door handle. 'Faustus can give the lamp stand back, if he doesn't like it.'

'It is a present for me. It should be me who decides whether I like it!'

The old man peered at me. He had known me since I was a slip of a girl, fresh in from Britain. 'Bad day? Well, you know where Falco keeps the decent wine.'

It seemed a very long time since that morning, when Tiberius and I had poured Davos a tot of the drinkable wine, gulping it down ourselves too, while he was telling us about Chremes.

Oh dear: Davos. Davos and Thalia still had to be told that their friend Phrygia was also dead, and the gruesome way in which she had been killed.

20

The actors were not at the Golden Cup, which was the bigger bar but very quiet since it had the highest prices. These were proudly listed, with pictures of lop-sided jugs, above a painting of some dead ducks, a bunch of spring onions and various untouched hams on hooks. Someone had convinced its landlord that catering was his way to a fortune; he needed a new financial adviser. Also, he ought to hire a defence lawyer because his chosen thermopolium name was a fraud: all his drinkware was basic pottery.

My group had taken over the Halcyon instead, which was friendlier and noisier since it was so small you had to snuggle your neighbour and keep shouting. This bar was advertised by a faded sign of a beaky bird floating on a twiggy nest at sea, a birdie who in myth was supposed to calm the waters and bring about a peaceful atmosphere – that was more dud marketing.

A few disgruntled regulars were squashed at a battered table indoors, finding it hard to catch the waiter's eye, while he looked after the actors who were crowding on the pavement; they had spread their elbows to stop anyone else accessing the counter. The waiter was a thin drip in a droopy apron, who had no idea how to escape when customers monopolised him. I was a woman, so he blanked me anyway. I could see remains of suppers and beakers, though I was glad Gornia had shared his bite at the Saepta since nobody asked whether I wanted anything. Fortunately, informers expect this. Anyone who offers one of us a drink and a saucer of mixed olives is bound to be as crooked as a rustic scythe.

Thalia and Davos were there. I could tell they had been told about Phrygia. Hands clasped around his cup, Davos was staring ahead, stunned. He, too, had produced a play for last November's Plebeian Games. Was he wondering, *Could this have been us?*

Thalia was the largest personality at the counter. She had not brought her snake, thank goodness, but was scowling at the filthiness of life, while she startled passers-by with an outfit that barely stretched over her fabulous frame. If her skirt had ever been long enough, it had shrunk at the laundry; the plunging top was never intended to hide her formidable bosom. Stunning as ever, Thalia favoured earrings like training weights, gold acrobat's boots and a bauble-trimmed stole, the ends of which she regularly hurled back over her mighty shoulders, threatening people's eyesight. I noticed that no one risked a protest.

Once I appeared, Thalia forcefully introduced me. 'Listen, people! This is Flavia Albia, my little boy's clever big sister.' Davos gave me a nod in greeting, while Simo, the wounded Pardicus, Ariminius and Atticus shifted slightly, all nervous of offending Thalia by pointing out they had met me. She careered on, as always seeming unaware of how embarrassing she was. 'Albia's from Britain, but I owe her mother a big favour for taking my boy, so ignore her ghastly origins and be nice. For a druid with a filthy temper, she's more or less passable – but don't stand within kicking rage when she gets in a strop.'

I smiled quietly. The woman was almost family. Of course, she claimed insult rights. If I was foolish enough to seem stressed by it, she would ask me out loud if I was having a painful period. I went with the banter. 'Good to see you, Thalia! I am sorry about the circumstances. How is Jason?' The python. Her terrifying dance-partner.

'Too big to bring out now. Just as well. He knew Chremes and Phrygia.' Thalia sighed. I had a close-up view of her bosom heaving. Something reminded me she was one of the few people who made my father nervous. 'I wouldn't want Jason to hear what has happened. He is so easily upset.'

People had made room for me at the counter. 'Pardicus!' I murmured, as I squeezed in. 'I thought you would be tucked up in bed recovering from that horn in your ribs.'

'Needed company. Thalia has given me a salve.'

'Lucky man!' the snake-dancer hooted, undaunted by the presence of Davos, who was loosely called her husband. She tapped a satchel slung around her to indicate that it held a trove of unguents. 'I even rubbed it in for him myself!'

Although Pardicus had originally been described to me as the cheeky one, he was looking subdued now – not, I suspected, because Buculus had gored him. Even his thin pigtail seemed to have lost lustre. But Thalia's medical knowledge was famous. She once saved my mother's life after a scorpion bite, which, when I thought of it, had happened on their incident-filled tour of Syria with Chremes and Phrygia.

I mentioned that I was surprised not to have found a bigger gathering. They told me all the stagehands and several actors had gone off to make family visits at Saturnalia. If word reached them that their leaders had died, they might never come back. It helped me somewhat. If they were in other parts of Italy, that limited my circle of suspects. Atticus told me Plotinus, whom he jokingly called their music director (guffaws all round), had gone to buy a new string for his lyre; that seemed to be a euphemism. Pardicus said a couple of girls who played instruments and 'danced' were busy tonight as they had secured temporary work as servers at the Golden Cup.

At this point, because of the noise and the squash, it was decided we would decamp there, to hold more relaxed discussions. None of them bothered to leave half-drunk beakers behind; they just carried them next door, along with all the drippy waiter's stale sesame sticks. I now had a feel for the group's general lifestyle. The Halcyon's waiter looked put out at us leaving, though he feebly allowed them to hijack his snacks. Then, as they noisily rearranged the Golden Cup's inside tables and benches so we could all sit together, the new landlord gave us his own filthy look. Our lot ignored him too. Simo and Atticus were renting his garret, so they were determined to use his leisure space, even when they brought in refreshments from elsewhere.

I was introduced to 'the girls', a pair who were older than me under their face-paint, called Philotera and Crispa. I gave these part-time waitresses a quick professional once-over. They were hardly wispy dryads but could not have hauled a dying man onto a wooden cross, I thought; nor could I see them guiding an aurochs through the streets and onto a stage. So, although they had never joined the men on the all-night search, I ruled them out as suspects.

Since they had nobody to serve, they sat down among us, ignoring the landlord's edginess. He was a mere employer; they overruled him blatantly. I could see why he had hired them. They were both seriously glamorised, even though their eye makeup trickled in sooty streaks when they cried over Chremes and Phrygia.

'This has been a terrible day,' I sympathised, as the tears flowed. 'Look, Davos had already asked me to find out what happened to Chremes, and now Phrygia has also been killed in a ghastly way. I shall be working on both. The murders happened in Rome, so I'm inclined to think something here in the city caused them. I came tonight hoping you good souls can help me work out what that was.'

'Chremes and Phrygia kept to themselves,' argued Philotera. She had big dark eyes and was proud of how she dressed, but her character was lacking. She had exclaimed at how awful today's events were, but she wanted to believe there was nothing anyone could do about the tragedy. Not my type.

'Maybe. Still, let's start with the vital clue. Phrygia made a dying accusation against someone she called an undertaker. Please, everybody, rack your brains. Who could she have meant? Has anyone died and had a funeral while you have been here? This time, or even on a previous occasion?'

'We never stay in Rome for long.' Philotera shrugged, rearranged her evil-eye pendant against the neck of her tunic, and rattled her three faux-gold bangles. You guessed: one was a glass-eyed, mock-Egyptian snake.

'But someone may have passed away,' I corrected her patiently. I noticed Crispa hid a smile, as if there was generally friction between them. Crispa was prettier and, from the way she sat and listened, I thought she might be more intelligent – Philotera must have been aware of it. 'I gather people come and go in the troupe, so whoever died may not have made much impression. Any ideas?'

Since they were all staring at the table blankly, I tried an easier question. 'Tell me something. What was that play your company performed at the Plebeian Games? Someone said a Plautus.'

'*Miles Gloriosus.*' Ariminius sounded gloomy.

'Oh, a classic!' I would have thought Eucolpus, the room-hire man who told me he had seen the play, would have remembered it was the famous one about the boasting soldier. I certainly knew I had seen it once. The title role can be played with gusto – which can be grim to sit through.

It seemed Ariminius disliked the play as much as I did, though I remembered his main job was as a scene-shifter. I let him moan, hoping for insights. '*Miles Bloody Gloriosus* – which has twelve characters, five of them with confusing long Greek names that start with Pi. Pyrgopolynices – I ask you! He is the self-glorifying braggart who gets tricked by an idiotically simple fraud. The other parts are bog-standard. Clever cook. Drunken slave—'

'Snide parasite,' put in Atticus, who must have been the company's youngest member, with least say in what part he was given. 'I had the task of putting some life into the parasite's lines.'

'Everyone has to start somewhere.' Simo grinned at him. 'Then of course there are captures by pirates. Flavia Albia, don't pirates have anything better to do than sail around capturing characters from plays?'

'And this farrago even has that crowd-pleaser, pretend twins!' Ariminius concluded his critique with a stage groan.

I applauded quietly. 'A cast of twelve? I don't count that many of you!'

'Some are off on holiday,' Simo reminded me. 'And the boasting soldier was played by a little fellow Phrygia brought in.'

'Not one of you?'

'*Not!*' several of them chorused.

I detected resentment; I made a mental note. 'A little fellow? Was he any good at filling the stage as the braggart?'

'His shrunken size made the boasts sound more ludicrous. It worked. He could shout and stomp all right. Nero complex,' Atticus told me, the analyst in the group. 'Nightmare. "*I am the best actor in the world. People rave about my mellifluous voice. I have a wonderful technique and the largest public following. Believe me, I attract all the women.*" Bah!'

I thought it best not to ask whether the man's conquests had included Phrygia. Did that explain why she brought him in? She was elderly and looked quite daffy even as a corpse, so it seemed unlikely – though perhaps when I became an old woman myself, I would call that prejudice. Instead, I shot a glance at Philotera and Crispa, who caught my drift: they pulled faces and winced. Not them. Or perhaps, I decided cynically, both of them. If they ever hooked up with the little fellow, they were not admitting it, not in public. Not with colleagues who would jeer at them.

'Did he have a good voice?'

'Bloody marvellous!' snarled Atticus, bitterly, scratching his head under the felted hat he always wore. His own voice was fine enough, though as he was still young it sounded light. He needed more grief and hard drinking. 'Phrygia was right about his basic talent. And he has a following in Rome.'

'He is not with you now?'

'No, thank you, charitable gods,' scoffed Simo. 'He lives in Rome, but he's gone off to some hillside hideaway.'

'With a woman?' I laughed. They all giggled with me. 'Sounds like an alibi!' I joked again. Up in the hills meant at least twenty miles away from Rome: the short actor had put himself in the clear. His ladyfriend with the lofty estate might even vouch for him.

Time for the clue I had picked up earlier that day: 'All right. I'm going to tell you something. Before we went to the Theatre of Balbus, I had heard about a possible motive. It may give a lead to the so-called undertaker. I haven't mentioned this, even to the vigiles.' We all snorted, deriding the law-and-order lads. 'Apparently Chremes and Phrygia were overheard arguing – I know, I know, what's new? A woman at their lodgings told me. Was there some trouble before the Plebeian Games, a problem over which play the company wanted to perform?'

Once again, everyone looked baffled. After a moment, Simo said, 'There is always discussion. What we offer is a matter for the producer. We mere players are barely involved. If they like one, they fix it. They fix it, we act it.'

I noticed Davos nodded in sympathy, though he actually said to me, 'If, as a company leader, you were coming to Rome to canvass for a festival, you would normally have a suitable project in mind.'

Thalia gave him a wifely shove that nearly flattened him on the table. She muttered, 'With Chremes and Phrygia, make that two projects, in two minds!'

Everyone ruefully agreed. Then it was Pardicus, the wounded man, who roused himself sleepily. 'We knew they were discussing scripts with an aedile.' Tiberius Manlius? By now I knew he would have looked through his note-tablets at home, so he would know whether or not he had been involved. If this had gone wrong somehow, I hoped he hadn't. 'It was sorted out quite early on,' said Pardicus. 'I got the manipulating slave part, with a lot of the action, so I wasn't arguing. We all counted ourselves lucky. We had a narrow escape. Instead of *Miles Gloriosus*, it could have been that crackpot jumble, *Rudens*.'

21

I said I knew I had seen *Rudens*. It means *The Rope*, though I could not remember any rope in it. They all laughed uproariously.

Davos contributed: 'That's the trouble, Albia. There is a mention of a rope that someone vaguely says he'll hang himself with, though he doesn't, which is typical. The chief prop is actually a chest. You know – some winsome fishermen land it, then the contents very conveniently prove who a long-lost daughter is. Load of nonsense. We used to perform the piece a lot in the old days out in Syria, but we had a version your father adapted. He inserted a big tug-of-war – lots of stage business, highly popular. At the time, we had a couple of boys who hammed it up handsomely. Tranio and Grumio, their stage names were, remember them?' he asked Thalia.

'Trouble.' She looked broody. 'I certainly won't forget that pair. I had to get rid of a very promising Egyptian cobra after it bit Grumio.'

'The tug-of-war was a riot,' Davos continued. 'Mind you, we were in a desert, where people lacked decent entertainment! We all used to pretend we thought Falco was a clown. The general view was that Helena Justina helped him write. Sadly, that script was left behind when the company decamped from Palmyra. Don't tell Falco!'

'More important, I won't tell Helena!' I chuckled. 'What is the problem with the play?'

They all chortled again. Never suppose actors view playwrights as sophisticated creatives.

'What's wrong? Apart from the plot, the setting, the characters and most of the lines? The title,' Davos explained. 'Being kind, you either have to take the rope as referring to a tug-of-war and write it in, or else you present it as some dubious metaphor. The second way, it only relates to a struggle for ownership of a girl—'

'Two girls,' put in Ariminius.

'Right! Two girls. Old Plautus chucks in everything and the washtub! Heroine and heroine's friend, I think. But, the real problem, Albia, is that this piece must have started life as two different Greek plays, which Plautus stitched together crudely. He did the same, better, with *Miles Gloriosus*, but he made a lousy job of this one. Scenes don't follow on properly. The first half has no logical connection with the second, so you can only hope the audience goes out in the interval, gets drunk, returns to their seats late and doesn't notice.'

I could see why this hodgepodge was rejected for the Plebeian Games. Tiberius, for certain, would have spotted poor joins. 'And why is it so well-known?'

'Two girls!' repeated Ariminius, heavily.

Philotera and Crispa groaned too. Since this was Italy not Greece, they, and not male actors with fake busts, would have played the pair.

'The lovelies take their clothes off?' I guessed in despair.

'Been shipwrecked, haven't they? They have to be ticked off by the priestess at the shrine,' Crispa confirmed, mimicking: '*Maidens, hail to you. But, prithee, whence am I to say that you are hither come with your wet garments, thus woefully arrayed?* See-through rags are always a popular costume. Later they get hauled to an altar where they are clinging for sanctuary, so extra wisps of drapery get pulled off them, of course. Juno, I hate those parts. Still, we didn't do it, so why am I complaining?'

I liked her attitude. 'So, who were you in *Miles Gloriosus*?'

'Who was I?' Crispa struck a pose. 'I was Philocomasium, a young Athenian maiden, intelligent and courageous, who has been abducted by the nasty braggart soldier, so she has to pretend to be her own twin sister to get away from him.'

'Her twin sister? Why?'

'Why? It's a play.'

'Right. Sorry I asked.'

'She must be crazy in any case, because her boyfriend isn't up to much. Atticus played him very nicely!' Crispa joked. He must have been used to teasing: he smirked obligingly. 'This is a one-heroine play so I had the action, while Philotera could only do a twirl as the good-time girl who is hired in another part of the plot to outwit the soldier.'

'Oh, I never mind being a good-time girl!' Philotera sniggered. Having met many professionally, I suspected it was all too true.

I managed to grab the last sesame stick from the Halcyon. 'Right! You did *Miles* instead, which I know is a romp if you like that stuff. Tell me, does it call for stage props or any other things that have to be made in a joiner's workshop?'

I watched them all working out why I asked. The men had been at the stadium and theatre today when Tiberius was examining the cross and the fake cow.

Davos answered, 'No, it's not like *Rudens*. That requires a chest of old treasures, a temple with an outside altar, a pile of big rocks and a cottage with its roof blown off. The set in *Miles* only has two houses side by side, though they do need a party-wall with a hole for the separated lovers to smooch through and a skylight for a slave to spy on them.'

'Yes, but we had no need for a carpenter,' Simo told him. 'Everything came off our own wagon. Big sword and shield for the soldier, then even portable doorways for the houses.' He saw me looking curious. 'We had no scaenae frons, no triple doors. We didn't perform in a theatre. We were in the Circus Flaminius.'

The Flaminius, which was paved and had neither a chariot racing track nor permanent seats, was most often an informal setting for markets. My family had held auctions there, though that meant pushing and shoving to seize space from the stallholders. While the main events of the Plebeian Games took place in the Circus Maximus, occasionally the programme had used the Flaminius, here on the Campus Martius, as an overflow venue.

'Performance in the bloody round. What a pig. Endless scenery shifting,' groaned Arminius. 'And I had to stand there, hidden, during half the scenes, holding the two houses up. When Pyrgo's slave, the discreditable Scelederus, was supposed to be looking through the skylight to see the lovers snogging, we put him up on a stepladder, which I had to cling on to in case it fell over – he's a big lad, I didn't want him crashing on my head.'

'Porrus. Nice fellow,' Simo told me. 'Plays minor parts. Gone to see his older sister. She'll fill him up with festival food and he'll come back to us bigger than ever.'

While they all shared jokes about Porrus the major-sized minor-parts man, I reviewed my leads. Failure: I had no clue to the undertaker's identity and no possible carpenter.

'We all have to be handy. I can knock a nail in myself, if I have to,' Ariminius said. 'But I could never do anything like that horrible fake cow.' He shuddered. We all did.

'You don't know anyone in Rome who makes stage scenery or props?' I tried. None of them responded. I tackled the issue one last time: 'Look, just suppose you had performed *Rudens*, where would you have acquired the cottage with its roof blown off and all those other things?'

'That would be one reason why they did a different play,' suggested Davos.

It was Crispa who at last gave me the lead I had been seeking. 'No, it would have been all right. I knew about Chremes wanting to do *Rudens*. He thought it was a good choice for the Circus Flaminius. It's not set in a city, like most comedies, but at a lonely spot on a beach. Without a fixed stage, everything would be easier.'

'What was he going to do?' jeered Philotera. 'Buy a big creel of seaweed?'

'Yes, well, I only know that I got groped because of his idea – not by Chremes,' Crispa added hastily. 'Don't speak ill of the dead. It was one of the extras he nearly admitted to pad out the cast. They came over to talk to Chremes at the Pickled Pig.'

'We stayed there first,' Simo explained to me. 'We were asked to move out after Plotinus caused a fight.' He spoke as if fisticuffs were a normal occurrence and being moved on was not unknown.

'Plotinus who's gone to buy a lyre string?'

'If he can cadge the money from his grandma,' Atticus confirmed. 'He's shameless.'

'Chremes met those other people secretly where we were lodging, so Phrygia wouldn't know he was up to something,'

Crispa said. 'She would have said they were unnecessary – and too inexperienced. Anyway, she had told Chremes right from the off that *Rudens* was a bad play.'

'So how did you come to meet those people?' asked Philotera, suspiciously, of Crispa.

'The rest of you had gone out to lunch. I had a belly-ache, so I stayed behind and was introduced.'

'Chremes always liked to parade his female talent whenever he was negotiating.' Davos sniffed.

'Too right! He never changed. There was one among the hopefuls who fancied me. Not bad-looking, but a jumper. You know. When he thought he'd jump on me, I had to fight him off. Chremes only looked away and let it happen.'

Crispa had lost herself in reminiscence. I asked quietly, 'Who exactly were these hopeful extras Chremes was talking to?'

'We didn't need them,' Crispa argued, so obsessive she had missed my point. 'The cast list of *Rudens* is thirteen, that's only one more than *Miles*, and three are only fishermen, singing about their miserable lives as they trot by – so, hell, we could easily have omitted them.'

Atticus stopped her rebelliously. 'Don't be daft, Crispa. You need the fishermen; they have to net the chest of valuables to prove who the long-lost daughter really is! It's the only real plot point, right at the end, so the poor bloody audience have waited hours for it.'

'Well, Atticus, you keep them in if you like, with their precious box of goodies,' Crispa scoffed. 'I still say we could have managed. I could play a loathsome fisherman myself, any day. You only need a trident and a thick accent. In most of the scenes there are just a few characters, so we would have doubled up parts, the same as always—'

'Never mind that,' I interrupted. 'Please tell me who these extras were!'

Crispa shrugged and tossed her hair. 'Oh, nobodies. Only some hopeful amateur group. They all thought acting along with us in the Games could be their ticket to fame.'

22

'Untrue,' commented Atticus, *sotto voce*. 'Otherwise we'd all be famous!'

'And rich,' yearned Philotera. 'Without having to sleep with town councillors.'

This bunch need a grounded playscript; keeping them to the point was hard. 'Just tell me,' I pleaded, 'where did Chremes find his potential extras?'

At least Simo, the youngest and keenest, could be relied on: 'One of them had approached him, Albia. Chremes and Phrygia were being shown around the Circus Flaminius by the aedile's staff, before finalising what they would offer. They wanted to see what performance spaces were going to be made available so they could judge which plays would work there. I suppose they looked a bit colourful. She always dressed unusually and he would fling his cloak back over his shoulders with a big gesture, as if he was casting away all the world's cares. Someone on a market stall was watching, came across and asked if they needed any more players.'

Davos guessed the outcome: 'Phrygia said no thank you straight away, but Chremes was too soft to reject the offer?'

'That's right. You get those amateur-dramatics types, always hanging around temples wanting to put on jolly scenes for the god's birthday.' They all groaned at the thought.

'A reason to spend evenings away from their wives, using "rehearsals" as a cover,' mocked Ariminius.

'Excuse to prat about like gods in fake beards!' Philotera snarled.

'All the men flirting with those sickly women hangers-on, who bring caraway biscuits and are hoping to get laid,' groaned Crispa.

'Atellan bloody Farces.' Atticus was referring to crude rustic dramas, the ancient street performances that high-minded people sneer at as obscene – which they intentionally are. 'I don't see why they need to rehearse. It's all improvised anyway.'

'Right!' exclaimed Crispa. 'They even call themselves the Farcicals.'

'The *Farcicals*?' It was my turn to groan. 'What kind of market stall?'

'Luggage. Passed off as leather. Told me at the Pickled Pig.'

'Thank you. Did anyone else ever meet these acting hopefuls,' I asked them all, 'or only Crispa?'

'Only Crispa.'

'Only me.'

'Right.' I was starting to feel exhausted. 'This is a good lead, thank you. Crispa, let me pick you up tomorrow morning. We shall go to the Circus Flaminius and you must point out any marketeer you recognise. I assume it was a man who made contact with Chremes?'

'I don't want to see that bastard who jumped me at the Pickled Pig.'

'Don't worry. You'll have me to protect you this time.'

'The grabby lech will say she was asking for it,' Philotera sneered, their relationship prickling again. 'I bet she was, too!'

Simo, who seemed to know what went on among his colleagues, told me Phrygia had also been present during the last face-off with the would-be acting group. 'Chremes had to take her along. By then her ladyship had twigged, so she wouldn't let him loose on his own. He made a lot of promises. Phrygia always ended up having to let people down again. He needed her when he had to tell them no thanks, lads. The first time he hadn't been vague enough.'

'Worse,' said Crispa, who had been there on the first occasion. She mimicked Chremes in a plummy voice: '*I am sure we can accommodate such dedicated enthusiasts!* The idiots must have believed he was agreeing to take them on.'

'Sounds like a classic brush-off to me!' I commented. 'But perhaps I am cynical.'

'Realistic! So Chremes took her along,' Simo reported. 'She told them straight: another play had been chosen, out of our hands since the programme was decreed by the authorities. Very sorry and all that, but the Farcicals were no longer needed.'

'Were they upset?' I demanded.

'Who knows? Only Chremes and Phrygia were there.'

'It was early days,' said Atticus. 'The Farcicals shouldn't have been sensitive. Negotiations happen. Never mind whether the amateurs were up to playing decent parts in written plays – which they never would be. During the programming, everyone was liable to get stuffed by the authorities. Chremes had to plead for a slot. No one in the real business would have been surprised. The amateurs should know the routine. After all, they live in Rome.'

'We have a saying.' Simo reinforced the point. '"Nothing is agreed until the trumpet sounds." You need to get a boot onstage before you truly know you're in.'

'Aediles' choice.' I felt slightly guilty on behalf of my husband, even though I knew Tiberius dealt with people fairly. 'So, at the time, I suppose you heard that these extras had been sent packing?'

'Phrygia knew we were annoyed. She told us straight away,' Atticus confirmed. '*I have axed the local dabblers, you will all be delighted to hear* . . . Same time she was announcing it was to be *Miles Gloriosus* for us.'

Again, Simo elaborated: 'She said never mind what idiocy Chremes wanted. The only cast addition would be the little fellow she knew, coming in to play the lead part. That, she made out, was only because the aedile had requested him.'

'Why? Was it his boyfriend?' I asked, joking.

'Boyfriend? Not according to the kind of flirt the star turned out to be!' scoffed Crispa, with feeling. 'He had no time for bum-boys, he was busy enough with his women.'

'I wonder how she knows that!' mouthed Philotera.

'Phrygia had worked with him in the past,' Atticus informed me, ignoring them.

I smiled gently. 'Worked? Are you sure he was not *her* boyfriend?'

'And why not?' At this point Thalia joined in. The snake-dancer had been sitting quiet, but now let out her raw laugh. 'Why shouldn't he be? Age is no barrier – at least, I hope it won't ever be for me! Phrygia had been a game girl in her day.' Exactly like Thalia, I thought wryly. There was no chance to ask whether Thalia herself had ever known the actor who played the braggart, because something else struck her: 'Oh, hell, Davos, we do need to tell her daughter what has happened.'

I noticed she said 'her' not 'their', as if this offspring belonged to Phrygia but not Chremes. 'Who is her daughter, Thalia?'

'Ah! The big pretence is it's that actress Byrria, who has made a name in Rome. She started out with Phrygia and the rest, in Syria. Davos knew her then, didn't you?' He nodded obediently.

'I've heard of her,' I said. 'One of my uncles had a crush on her some years ago – before he was reined in by marriage and fatherhood.' Well, he pretended to be reined in. 'I think it was all in his head. The gorgeous Byrria never noticed him.'

'That's Byrria,' Thalia agreed. 'Always a touch of the Vestals. She's beautiful, and she can act like hell, but she ignores all the men who flock around. They hate it. Purity is not what an actress is supposed to be for.' Crispa and Philotera bridled at that. Thalia played oblivious. 'I happen to know that Phrygia was never her mother. That was just an idea that suited everyone. Byrria gained a lot of help with her career, while Phrygia forgot that Sophrona, my own water organist, is a very tall girl about the right age that I fostered as a favour to Phrygia and am damn well hanging on to.'

It was interesting that Thalia could have taken in someone else's child, yet she had passed on her own baby to my parents. Then I remembered Thalia's interest in my grandfather's fortune, which she had hoped Postumus could inherit. 'I've heard Sophrona playing the big water organ, with your troupe, Thalia. She was wonderful.'

'Very precious. I'm not having her wander off to follow any fancy ideas about her "real" family,' said Thalia frankly. 'Her father was long gone from the start, gone before she even let out her first cry. Phrygia was well shot of the swine. But Sophrona does know who her mother was – so, Davos, young man, we had better get back over the river so we can break the bad news to her.'

As they stood up to leave, I asked whether Byrria or Sophrona might have been resentful of their situation. Would either young woman have been brooding about the past, brooding so much that they had now turned on Chremes and Phrygia?

'Don't even suggest it!' Thalia ordered me. 'Today is a tragedy for both those poor girls. They don't want you poking your nose into their affairs, as if you were your father and mother after too much hot sun and a dodgy amphora. Don't bother with Byrria or Sophrona. Believe me, Flavia Albia, whoever thought up today's horrors, your "undertaker" will be a man – one with a lunatic mentality.'

I thought she was right. After reminding Crispa about tomorrow, I too left the gathering.

23

I was so tired that night, I fell deeply asleep even though I was lying on a grocer's up-for-sale daybed under a rug Gornia had given me. The couch's upholstery suggested it had been battered by orgies, and the rug smelt like the one our driver, Felix, threw over the mule. Kicker must like to share it with the chickens. Bits of old bran stuck into me.

After I flopped there, the terrible deaths at the stadium and theatre crowded back into my brain. Once asleep, I had dreams like historical portents, even though I knew the events they seemed to prophesy had already happened. That was the end of satisfactory rest. I rose next morning, feeling like a sick hen, one with parasites and droop.

I realised actors were bound to emerge late, especially as I had left the group settled in for a long night of despondent drinking. Crispa and Philotera had even told the landlord he could leave the bar in their hands and toddle off to bed. Since there were no other customers, he snuffed a couple of oil lamps, whisked a sponge over a counter, then did slither away.

They were all in the grip of a ghastly bereavement. Last night they grieved. With their leaders gone, today they would have no reason to drag themselves into the misty morning light. They wouldn't want to think about what might happen to the troupe now. Would it even carry on?

Sitting thoughtful by myself, I spent time on the Saepta's interior balcony, with my hands wrapped around a beaker of mulsum, while I waited for street noise to grow loud enough to rouse Crispa naturally. Some informers will brutally pull a witness out of bed. It is a useful way to disorient a suspect, but she was being helpful. I wanted her alert and cooperative. I hung around until the auction staff strolled in, laughing and tossing bread rolls from hand to hand, then I sauntered along to fetch her.

That morning Rome was a grey place. It added to my feeling that this case would be difficult to crack.

The Circus Flaminius had existed first but now seemed crushed in between the Porticus of Octavia and the Theatre of Pompey. It was overlooked by the Capitol, though the Temple of Jupiter on that cold day was shrouded in grey haze. This monument was half the size of the Circus Maximus, slightly smaller than Domitian's Stadium. Never used for chariots, it was the home of ritual horse races with long-ago origins; they were rough affairs, run around rugged posts. Despite monumental arches, more recently built at each end, and a huge statue of Augustus showing off as a god, the circus retained an earthy knockabout feel. That was emphasised by its market clutter, though the stalls were temporary. Totters had to give way when required. Assemblies could be held there. The Flaminius had even been flooded once, for a sacrifice of crocodiles on the opening of the Forum of Augustus. At least that was less macabre than the time Sulla killed six thousand foreign prisoners, whose screams terrified senators cowering in the nearby Temple of Bellona. Rome might be the hub of civilisation, but it had reached its position by hard-hearted butcher-generals scrambling through blood.

Now you could buy food. A soggy flatbread for a late breakfast on the move. No filling that I could detect, just a smear of fish pickle. It summed up the Flaminius. At any decent market, workers and customers were able to obtain cracking good food but this was a slummy place.

Crispa and I walked slowly through the soulless stalls. Miserable offerings centred on second-hand fabric: clothes, mats or cushion covers. Even new items were thin, in despairing colours and nastily embroidered. Father used to claim he got his tunics from the Flaminius, when at his poorest, although I think his mother would never have allowed it. Items here pretended to be rag-men's finds, though many were probably stolen. Sickly garden plants, wilted by the cold weather, stood hopelessly below tables of vegetables that looked as if they had been picked out of rubbish buckets. There were strings of mismatched pebble necklaces, all in unappealing shades of grey, some nevertheless advertised as jet or amber. Finally, since the stalls tended to cluster by type, Crispa and I strolled past a short row of disheartened luggage-sellers.

It is a well-known fact, the bane of my profession, that you cannot trust a witness to identify a person of interest. How excitedly they assure you they will know the perpetrator again – yet they generally fail you. Witnesses are a hopeless resource. Although Crispa had sat with people throughout a long lunch, their features, voice, physique and manner had made no impact. So, the actress walked along a row of battered bags and sagging purses, without recognising any of the shabby scruffs hunched behind the stalls. One was a woman, though we paid little attention to her.

I might just as well have come alone. I had to fall back on my usual method: march up to a stall and ask. Did any of the luggage sellers take part in amateur drama? Oh, yes. Apparently the woman did.

'Crispa, for Heaven's sake! You never said one of the people who came to see Chremes was female!'

'Oh! Didn't I? Yes, one of them was.'

'Was it that one over there?'

'I can't remember . . . Yes, probably.'

I saw no point in pretending we wanted to inspect any faux-leather satchels, sad things with other people's old shopping lists scrunched in bottom corners. I told Crispa she could go home. Then I approached and demanded that the woman stop trying to sell something awful to a bystander. I wanted her to talk to me.

'Why not?' she replied, with a pleasant smile. She can't yet have realised I was a crack investigator and she was a suspect.

I had not entirely ruled her out as the undertaker killer. She might lack the strength for the physical effort needed, but in my view a woman was perfectly able to organise, and that meant she could organise men to help her. Any woman might possess the intellectual wickedness to devise two astonishing murders. I myself regularly planned hideous fates for people who had upset me.

Her name was Ambrosia. She was hardly a dish for the gods, but said it was her nickname with the Farcicals. She was stocky, broad-featured, rosy-cheeked and self-confident. In any other situation I might even have trusted her.

Yes, she took part in their little plays. She liked acting, though most often the others made her sing and dance; she didn't mind that – the lads she performed with were a lovely lot and this club was her social life, so she was easy. They found plenty of opportunities to perform. In Rome, temples were always having *lectisternia*, those outdoor rites where ceremonial couches were brought onto the pavement then spread for gods to lie on to dine. Since statues made dull spectacles, drama and musical performances would often occur at the same time, to give the public something lively to watch. Her amateur group had built up an annual events calendar; they also improvised shows at crossroads, short comic scenes in masks that were, as Atticus had groaned, in the ancient tradition of Atellan Fables. In between, they rehearsed, because even improvisation takes practice, or else they made costumes, gathered props, worked on ideas . . .

'Do you make scenery?' Could I visualise Ambrosia with a hammer and nails?

'No, it's more like, you know, street theatre. A character will announce where a scene is set, and he describes it. That's enough because, with the public, nobody really listens.'

The Farcicals comprised a regular core of five: Ambrosia, Gnaeus, Septimus, Megalo and Questus. All had attended both meetings with Chremes, the promising lunch and the brush-off.

All had day-jobs. Whenever they could, they met up once a week, though that could be a bit tight, because most of them were feeling the pinch so they did other work as well as their regular jobs.

'Anything special?'

'Anything we can get.'

'Does anyone have a second job as an undertaker?'

'Ugh! No fear!'

Was that reliable? Still, I could double-check with the others. I persuaded Ambrosia to send word to her four friends; she promised they would meet me later today, during their lunch-breaks. 'So, what is this about then, Flavia Albia?'

'Somebody died,' I answered obliquely. 'I offered help for the widow.'

'Is she coming to the meeting?'

'No. She can't, I'm afraid. She died as well.'

'Oh, the poor thing. That's a real tragedy.'

24

Onward!

At the Suedius funeral firm, slaves of both sexes who tended bodies and then followed processions to cemeteries were sitting around, shivering in a gated yard along with the black-painted cart and some beaten-up sarcophagi. Since their business relied on a supply of corpses, its workers were low beings in the public's eyes, as if they positively wished death upon people in order to make money. Polluted by constant contact with corpses, they were barred from anywhere respectable and even had to clean up at the baths during night-time hours when no one else would be there. They lived in their own world, halfway between life and death. Nevertheless, when I appeared, they waved me indoors charmingly. They were probably sniggering behind their hands about my expected recoil.

I was prepared for the smell. Bunches of dried herbs failed to make any impact upon the pervading miasma of dead flesh and decaying organs. Bodies on stretchers lined the walls of a gloomy interior. I could see why people who had any choice about it held their viewings at home in the atrium. In fact, I understood why any place as ghastly as this might have produced a madman who was capable of bizarre murders. A criminal undertaker seemed highly possible.

Flickering shadows from iron taper-holders showed up the ghoulish cadavers, among whom I spotted Chremes and Phrygia. He had a cloth across his middle. Her broken remains were better covered, but I recognised a platformed shoe on one visible foot.

A man of means was stiffening up with rigor while waiting to go to his cremation. He would be carried there on an expensive upholstered couch, sleeping his death sleep among fringed coverings and cushions. With its padded back and sides, it looked more comfortable than where I had lain with those bad dreams last night. Since personal discomfort no longer concerned the deceased, he had been picked off and dumped on the floor. In the customer's place, on his elegant put-you-up, Suedius currently lay snoring.

The boy Sorgius had drawn a draughtsboard down in the dust, beside a stone table where they carried out embalming. He was playing against himself. For each new move he scrambled around on his knees to the opposite side of the board. He mumbled exclamations and insults relating to his game, taking both parts in the conversation, with additional remarks from invisible onlookers. I recognised his kind of play: the child must have had no friends, though he seemed happy in his loneliness. One of his inventions was an intelligent player, the loser a complete dud. His spectators sounded a rough lot.

I shouted at Suedius to wake up. The sleeping figure's mouth dropped open. Without opening his gummy eyes, he rearranged a well-stuffed, gold-braided cushion under his foul head. A helpful child, Sorgius looked up and yelled his name too. Suedius grumbled back to life. He sat up, making no apology for pinching his rich customer's bier.

'Suedius! You've just ditched him on the floor. Are people never free from having their rest disturbed, not even after they are dead?'

'He was a brute, by all accounts. His family can't wait to see him going up in smoke.'

'They seem to have spent enough on his fancy furnishings! Do I spy gilding, Suedius?'

'They want the couch back afterwards. I have to burn him without it. They're a despicable crowd. They feel bad about not having spent more time with him. Too late! At least it means they cough up more silver for me,' Suedius pronounced. 'What do you want, Flavia? If it's about your two over there, some of those players came to see me an hour ago and I fixed them up for the Via Cornelia necropolis tomorrow evening. Wear your best. They say it will be a big affair with declamation and music.'

'Thanks for telling me, but it's not about that. Have you put together a list of other undertakers, as you were asked?'

'For that nightmare noodle, Mucius? I did it. He has it. Ask at their station-house.'

'I want to find him urgently. I know how the red-tunics work – if he is out pursuing enquiries, he won't have told anyone where he was going. He'll have left himself bar-time, for one thing. You tell me where you sent him off to so I can track him while he's plodding around.'

'If I were you,' suggested the lazy dog, 'I'd just go and wait at his barracks for Mucius to come home.'

'Can't do it. I need to find him before lunch.'

'Well, I don't remember who I suggested. Ask Sorgius.'

I should have done that in the first place.

* * *

I found Mucius. He was at the second place on the list that young Sorgius reconstructed for me. A bright child, with a good memory. The other premises and their inhabitants were as bad as where Suedius worked, so Mucius was not a happy man. I told him he could break off soon, because Ambrosia had summoned the farceurs to a bar called the Charybdis. I thought he should join forces with me to interview them. 'Make it official. Add some menace.' Afterwards, if they gave us alibis, as they were bound to unless they were idiots, Mucius could have his lads do a fact-check. Alibis have a tendency to be false. In fact, many people think that's the whole point of providing them.

'The Charybdis? That's a sty even pigs refuse to muck in.'

'Ambrosia said it has an area outside, where the landlord lets the drama club rehearse.'

'More fool them. We didn't have to round them up there. You should have told them to assemble at my station-house.'

'They wouldn't have come.'

Mucius belched obnoxiously, knowing I was right.

I met him again later at his favoured dive nearby, which was called the Abyss of Tartarus. I hate anaemic places with no character that are supposed to be suitable for women. It certainly had a polished counter, because nobody else ever went there, so the owner spent much free time housekeeping. Mucius bought me my second flatbread of the day, this one with a tolerable minced seafood mix. It was stuffed rather thinly but that saved bits dropping out as we made our way to interview the amateurs.

Their headquarters, the Charybdis, was even worse than Mucius had said: it had run out of wine. Regulars milled around outside in bewilderment. Across the street, a waiter at the Infant Hercules stood, his hairy arms folded, below a painting of a pot-bellied baby strangling sinister snakes. He was looking over the road with a satirical smile as if a supply crisis happened at the Charybdis every week. Next door at the Winkle, an aproned entrepreneur with greased-back hair tried to call customers over for a drink with him. He was offering free gherkins, though nobody took him up on it.

By the time we arrived, the would-be actors had learned somehow that Chremes and Phrygia were dead, and the ghastly ways it had happened. That was a pity. They seemed to have been in discussion, as if it really was fresh news, but they all clammed up as Mucius and I came through from the bar to the back. Their rehearsal area was a little enclosed yard with a couple of stone benches along the walls and a broken sundial. It had a gate that presumably led to the latrine, or at least to a street where men could pee in the gutter. Female customers could sit on the benches, discussing their horrible mothers-in-law, while they waited for the coast to be clear for them to use the alfresco facilities.

Naturally Mucius asked the questions, while I took the meeting notes. I saw his own memo afterwards. His crude list ran: *tasty, chancer, chancer, crook, chancer*. He reckoned that was all he needed because he could see I was being thorough, so if he wanted to check any points later, he would come and pinch my tablets.

Mine contained the following useful points, neatly set out:

- **Ambrosia**

Thirties, stocky, broad-featured, rosy-cheeked, self-confident

Real name not supplied. Stage name: 'Ambrosia', chosen herself (women never used to perform in farces, so have no character names). Acts a wife or daughter who easily deceives the old man

Work: luggage seller plus garland maker, occasional midwifery

Alibi for last night: home at her mother's (no husband)

Gnaeus

Late forties, skinny, bright eyes, ? bright mind, not much to say, annoying nervous giggle

Acts 'Maccus', most popular character in farces, the greedy fool, hooked nose, hunchback

Works as house painter, plus tray-carrier at the races

Alibi: at home with wife (second wife – NB this caused laughter, suddenly quashed. Is there a story?)

Septimus

Mid-thirties, overweight, drink problem? Acne scars, bruised soul he claimed, a poser

Acts 'Pappus', the old man deceived by wife or daughter

Work: baker's barrow boy plus odd jobs

Alibi: widower, at home with young children

Megalo

Sixties, done a lot of heavy work but getting creaky, surly but bold, bald, big beard

Acts 'Centunculus', a comic slave

Work: dock worker plus bar jobs when available, scraping out dolia (giant pots)

Alibi: at home with wife

Questus

Forties, tired, scrawny, bruises 'from work', jumpy about our enquiries

Acts 'Dosennus', an arrogant soldier, another humpbacked cheat

Work: ballast-loader on wharf, plus Emporium rat-catcher

Alibi: at home with wife, not his own but the lady would confirm. NB Make sure her husband's out, don't land him in it

Mucius took alibi addresses from each, while I began the serious discussion. I extracted more about the club's activities. They performed a mix of religious drama, rustic comedies, musical interludes and noisy dances. Anything, said Questus/Dosennus, with words and movement. Anything, quipped Ambrosia, that called for tambourines.

They had a regular clientele among temple administrators, who, they claimed, thought them a reliable hire. The Campus Martius was richly supplied with temples: by the Theatre of Pompey alone, in addition to Venus Victrix sited right above the stage, there were four small Republican-era shrines, plus Bellona on the main road. Further temples were dotted about the Campus. The group had been operating together for some years. They did it because they liked it. It gave them an interest.

Under further questioning, it became clear they were looking for more ambitious challenges. New or rebuilt religious sites, like Domitian's exotic sanctuary of Isis and Serapis, snootily refused to countenance them, so they wanted to build up a better profile in order to look attractive to the more snobbish caste of priests. They assured me their standards were good enough. Had Chremes agreed to let them participate, they would have been thrilled. Performing at the Plebeian Games would have provided the boost they needed.

'So, when Chremes – or our informants reckon it was Phrygia – did the dirty on you,' Mucius asked ponderously, 'when they came up with *no luck, bumbling amateurs, so get lost*, were you hugely disappointed? Did you go raving mad at them?'

'Not raving,' replied Gnaeus/Maccus quickly. It was the first time he had spoken. He had a light voice with a touch of inbuilt derision. 'We were just bitterly disappointed.'

Mucius kept going heavy-handedly. 'Which of you hopefuls knew Chremes and Phrygia, the unlucky victims? Who had met them previously?'

Nobody volunteered.

'Right. Now, own up: any of you do woodwork? Whittling? Second-hand cupboard restoration? Spare time concrete formwork?'

Silence.

'And who, when they must be bloody desperate, doubles up jobs as an undertaker?'

Again, silence.

Let us agree: these questions from Mucius were urgent and critical. They really did need answers. But I would have phrased them differently and used a subtler tone.

25

When the vigilis decided he had had enough of this, he left. I ran after him to express my doubts about his blunt interviewing. With a comradely wink, Mucius assured me that was all right. He would sort out some lads to check alibis then wait at the Abyss of Tartarus. Meanwhile I could scamper back and make friends with the Farcicals at the Charybdis, pretending to be nicer than him. Pull a girlie bluff: see what I could screw out of them through my kind of smarming.

A dumb plan is better than no plan, so I duly went back to smarm. The group were still there, heads together, discussing our interview.

'Oho, the mucus slimeball has sent us his glamorous assistant!' Gnaeus quirked his eyebrow up pretentiously. He and the hefty Megalo seemed to be cronies: Megalo posed in an attitude of surprise and sniggered with him. Gnaeus let out his irritating giggle. The others looked embarrassed.

'Let me set you straight,' I corrected them, which was not the smarm I had intended. 'I am the lead investigator. The mucilaginous officer is my run-around, whatever he thinks. I shall be in charge. I thought I ought to come back and apologise for him.'

'He was all right,' murmured Ambrosia. She was clearly a decent woman, though I must remember these people played parts for a hobby. Her good nature made me question why she liked being among this group, none of whom would be my choice to invite on a Campagna picnic. 'But thanks for apologising, Albia.'

'He's a clod. Aren't they always?' Although a professional troupe who travelled around would be more certain to have tricky law-and-order arisals from their work, these Farcicals lived in Rome. They had probably been moved on from street performances many times; besides, all citizens knew the vigiles. 'I just needed him to show me around the district, Ambrosia. I live and work on the Aventine normally.'

'You are a long way from home!' snickered Gnaeus. With Mucius gone, this one had come out of his shell. Seated on a stone bench, kicking his distressed sandals, he now became positively pushy. 'Are you expecting to be on the Campus Martius long? Will you be staying somewhere nice?'

It sounded like a chat-up line. Reluctant to reveal anything personal, I simply said I would be at Didius Falco's auction house.

'The Saepta is full of informers, so you should feel at home there!' His tone was so sneery that I decided Gnaeus had a bad attitude to women. Was he the one who had groped Crispa? I doubted it was significant. Misogyny was so common in Rome, it hardly meant he would have inflicted Buculus on Phrygia. That had taken extra cruelty. This man did not seem mad enough. 'Haven't I heard of someone called Falco? What's your connection?' he pressed.

His over-insistence made me all the more wary. I answered obliquely: 'I met him and his wife abroad, some years ago.'

'Is he working on this case?' asked Megalo, also sounding as if he knew something about my father.

'No, he is away on holiday. A friend of Chremes and Phrygia has offered the commission to me.'

'Who is the friend?' Gnaeus demanded at once, still much too inquisitive.

'A man called Davos. He has his own acting company. Why?' I retaliated, suddenly pushing back myself. 'Do you know him?'

'Not that I remember.' Gnaeus dropped his bullying as soon as I stood up to him. I felt that was typical.

Ignoring him and Megalo, I turned instead to Septimus and Questus who seemed less aggressive. To double-check, I asked them whether anyone else attended their club, anyone who was not here today: apparently not.

Septimus, though he only looked in his thirties, played grandfather characters in their farces, while Questus had the coarse-soldier parts. I discussed with Questus: might the Atellan Farce soldier, called Dosennus, be the original of the braggart in *Miles Gloriosus*? He agreed the character from farce must have been reimagined by the playwright Plautus. I asked if he had felt aggrieved when he heard the Plautus play was the eventual choice for the Plebeian Games, but he would not be acting the soldier. 'Didn't you feel you could have taken that part?'

Questus looked uneasy. Septimus immediately supported him. 'That's one for professionals, we have to admit it. To be honest, he was shitting bricks at the very idea of *Miles Gloriosus*, weren't you, our Questus?'

Questus, who always seemed jumpy, nodded confirmation. 'That's a big play. I never did any role with that many lines. Our farces are short. I thought I would never be able to learn the long script.'

'He's very good,' Ambrosia put in. She must be the

Farcicals' kindly mother hen. 'Albia, he could have done it, easy. People love him as Dosennus, don't they, Questus? And you adore doing it.'

'But, let's be honest,' said Septimus, 'we did not expect him to be chosen. That Chremes had never said any of us could have main roles.'

'We knew we would only pop on and off with a line or two, if we were lucky.' Ambrosia agreed. 'And in the end we didn't even get that.'

'Anyway, they brought in someone to play the soldier.' Questus might have the biggest reason to want revenge for disappointment, yet he seemed genuinely glad to be stepped over in the part.

'An out-of-towner?' I asked lightly, as if I knew nothing about it.

'No, he lives here. That woman in charge knows him,' Septimus added.

'Knew him!' giggled Ambrosia.

Blushing over Phrygia's death, Septimus subsided. I noticed Gnaeus and Megalo sniggered together. They were like the naughty boys on a school bench. Ambrosia looked sorry she had pointed out the gaffe.

'He is a huge name!' Questus seemed awestruck. 'Made a mint at it.'

'Rich as well?' I exclaimed. 'Do I know him? What huge name does he go by?'

'Philocrates.'

'Also known as the empty-headed wizzle-waver,' sneered Gnaeus, nastily.

I shot him a quick glance. 'Wasn't he quite good as the braggart? For a wizzle-waver?'

'Oh, he can act.'

I smiled. 'Yes, that's what the professionals told me. I gathered even they were none too pleased at having him dumped on them, but they did say he filled the role with style.'

'He could play a bamboozled fool!' agreed Septimus, with a bitter note. 'Could have been born to it.'

'You do sound miffed, if I may say so!'

'It wasn't very nice,' he complained. 'The way we were led on at first with jolly smiles, but then dropped down a big hole suddenly.'

'But we can take it!' Megalo, the oldest there, was looking at me rather carefully. I could feel him trying to put me off. He understood that loathing Philocrates gave the Farcicals a motive. 'You don't crucify a man or gore a woman to death because their attitude is "not very nice". Do you?' he demanded. His force was understandable. Presumably this group all knew that if they failed to stand up for themselves, they were obvious suspects and seriously in trouble.

I asked them once again, less crudely than Mucius had done, whether anyone had known Chremes or Phrygia before. As one, they still denied it. Septimus admitted he had seen the professional troupe perform here in Rome in previous years, but he had been too shy to make contact backstage. When Chremes came to meet them at the Pickled Pig, Septimus had muttered nervously that he admired their work. Chremes threw up his hands and growled, *Why, thanks, young man!* It was offhand and patronising, so afterwards Septimus only sat quiet and listened.

We held more conversation of a general kind, from which I gained nothing. I emphasised that Mucius was checking their alibis for last night, so if anything bad was likely to emerge, better own up to me in advance. But no dice.

Finally, I told them what Suedius had said about the funeral arrangements in case, as fellow actors, they wanted to attend. Really, it was for my own benefit: informers always hope for graveside revelations, even though it rarely happens.

Having apparently established better relations, I said my goodbyes. The Farcicals all had work to return to, so I was aware of them dispersing after I left the Charybdis. They went off in different directions, all separate (I watched). I returned to Mucius, at the still-empty Abyss of Tartarus.

His troops had not yet reported back, though he said that didn't matter since all the so-called alibis would have been fixed in advance.

'You have an expert grasp of public behaviour, Mucius!'

'I can scratch my arse. Got anything?' he asked, through a mouthful of a new flatbread.

'No. All as clear as Tiber silt. If any of them did it, no one is giving out. Some were aggressive but I couldn't spot proper signs of guilt.'

'Ah well,' Mucius replied, as if explaining something very obvious to someone who must be very dim, 'that's because there is nothing for a sweet informer to spot. They all sound the same, Flavia Albia, because they are all covering up for each other. None of them is innocent. Trust me, they were in it together. They all did it.'

26

I did not share this conspiracy theory. While some sour feelings had bubbled beneath the surface at the Charybdis, I felt that the Farcicals would never engage in extreme violence. They seemed too humdrum. They all did different work, and it looked as if outside their club they lived their own lives. I could not imagine them planning and executing two utterly grotesque crimes. After advising Mucius not to arrest them until he had more cause, I escaped from him and his raddled convictions as soon as I could.

We needed clues. I had a private idea of how to find one. It might be way off, but informers are used to hooking up material from murky millponds.

I did not need vigiles approval or backup. A woman could do this, solo. I returned to the Circus Flaminius. There I went to the second-hand clothes stalls, where I spent an hour rummaging among the rancid garments. Most smelt of sweat or worse. I saw a lot of rips, open seams and dubious stains. As little things jumped out of folds to bite my skin, I kept the dank tunics at arms' length. 'My brother needs a new outfit. He's sick of showing his ankles to the cold weather. We can never find anything to fit him – he's a beanpole, ridiculously tall. Have you got anything long?'

Tunic after tunic was shown to me. They came in all colours, mostly nothing special, with neck braid or with shoulder stripes running down the front. Many were wide enough for tubbies, but few were long and none exotic. 'No, he's too fussy, he drives us all mad with it. He wants a bit more style than this. We call him the King of Commagene.'

The invented beanpole brother almost became real to me. As I searched for something to kit out this figment, the stall-holders grew used to me while I became much bossier. I looked at every long tunic on sale that day. Then I poked into bundles that were not even being offered yet. 'What's in this hamper under the table? Anything good?'

'That only came in today. I haven't had time to price it up. I warn you, things may need cleaning.'

'Face it, my friend, not much at the Circus Flam is sent out for pre-sale laundering! Just a quick peek, may I? I'm sure you don't mind. I don't want to miss anything.'

'I've not even looked through the pile yet—'

'Oh, I'll just dive in . . .'

I had the hamper upended. As its contents spewed, I finally came upon what I wanted. First a long, heavy cloak in porphyry red dropped out of the tangle. Shaking it free, I held it up, raising my arms in order to test the length. Lifting it was almost beyond me; the last owner must have been a strong man, much taller than me, who would have moved with unusual gravitas, like a king in a costume. 'Oh, yes! This is good, nice and long, lovely nap – and it's even complete with shoulder fixings!'

The stallholder, who cannot have known about them, grabbed for the big shiny gongs, which were joined by a weighty three-strand chain. I jumped backwards to thwart him. 'Hold on!' The two disc brooches were a very passable alternative to gold, generously traced with botanical patterns and each set with a selection of coloured-glass shapes, square and triangular, in red, green and blue, one piece missing. The jewellery would have value but, more important to me, this cloak would be recognised by anyone who had ever seen it being worn.

I folded it over one arm, keeping tight hold while I foraged among the rest of the hamper contents. I knew I was finding my evidence. A belt – also likely to be familiar if I showed it to any witnesses. One male shoe, brown, laced sides, a long size, plenty of wear on it.

By now the stallholder was agitated. I kept dodging him. He might call for help from other stalls, but he was never going to whistle up the vigiles. Soon I had shaken out a long, long-sleeved graphite-coloured tunic with elaborate hem embroidery, then a grubby-white under-tunic, fraying at the cuffs.

'Hello, hello!' Both tunic and undergarment were heavily bloodstained. Even I recoiled.

The stallholder froze. Had he known? I, too, stopped pretending: if I had ever had a very tall brother, Junior ceased to be relevant. Somebody else, wearing these clothes, had been savagely attacked.

I gazed at the seller. We both knew why he had not called out for reinforcements. No one else in the market would want to be seen with these items. I now had him on the hop. He was wondering, feebly, whether to run away.

The blood was dry, though the stains looked fresh. Someone had worn these clothes quite recently, while he suffered a beating. I knew people who had known him, who could identify his clothing. I knew who he had been. And, of course, where his naked body was lying now in the Suedius mortuary.

'Stand still. You can own up. You are an honest merchandiser, as far as I'm concerned.' He was a thieves' middleman, their filthy fence, but I needed his input. There was no point in threatening an arrest. Besides, removing one seller from the Circus Flaminius would hardly change the slew of stolen goods that surged across these sad tables. 'I'm not after you. I am only interested in your supplier. Who brought them? Just tell me how you acquired these clothes.'

I could not tell whether the man had had any inkling of what that hamper contained, though clearly this was not the first time he had taken in goods with a bad history. He had no conscience about the bloodstains. Without my intervention, the soiled items would have been washed and sold on.

'I hope you haven't shelled out much,' I sympathised drily. 'You'll get no profit today. There's a Campus-wide hue and cry for whoever caused this bloodshed. A praetor is on it. You don't want that kind of trouble.'

The totter feigned nonchalance, though I could see he agreed. Unless you are a scholar, writing a three-volume history of Roman law edicts, praetors are bad news. 'What's going on?' he asked boldly.

'Haven't you heard about the atrocity at Domitian's Stadium last night? Dead man, crucified, right on the racetrack? Unless you can prove otherwise, these clothes came off that victim. They are going back to him too. Thanks to your kindly custody, the murdered soul can wear his own duds for his funeral.'

The stallholder gurgled a faint protest. It did no good. I was ruthless. I had seen Chremes nude and battered. I was determined to give him back some dignity.

In return for not reporting the salesman for his stolen goods, I extracted his source: he had obtained the clothes from a regular supplier, a hopeless vagrant by the name of Spiffy. The name was ironical. Spiffy was the opposite of smart: he could claim no noble ancestors and no fancy home address. He lived rough. I guessed he would die rough, too, if all he had to live on was what marketeers, themselves on the breadline, gave him in return for any filthy rags or dead men's effects that Spiffy picked out of gutters.

I rejected the no-fixed-abode excuse. The colourful threats I came up with extracted a pathetic whine that Spiffy was thought to sleep with one of the sphinxes of Isis and Serapis. I knew it well, since the sanctuary lay alongside the Saepta Julia. After giving the stallholder the Mucius imperative of *Don't leave town*, I took myself to the new Egyptian spread that Domitian had rebuilt. His elaborate expansion of these exotic temples and their environs was in gratitude for an event when his life had once been saved. Many of us wished that rescue had never happened.

I enjoyed the thought that filthy riff-raff had colonised the elite new shrines in Domitian's Isis cult. A weird one. Imagine finding your husband's body snipped into forty-two parts, piecing him back together and using the mummy for insemination.

Look, I am an immigrant. We need a target. People like me are always ready to despise other foreigners. Egyptian flummery is good for that.

On my way there, I went up to the Saepta Julia, where I dumped the clothes with Gornia; they were too heavy to lug around. I brought warehouse staff out with me. We found Spiffy. He was the shabbiest, grubbiest vagrant ever. His fleas were getting drunk on the odour of wine arising from him.

I explained to this sorry soul what I wanted; he denied all knowledge. The porters picked him up and swung him around as if they were about to throw him against one of the Egyptian obelisks. He howled. I told them to stop. They dropped him heavily onto the ground, but kept hold. He muttered that if I gave him a copper, he would show me where he found the clothes.

I showed him a copper, which I promised for later. He led me back down to a sad lane off the Vicus Pallacinae. The area felt familiar, though the lane was just a muddy entry, barely wide enough to walk down. Weeds tried to grow, but even weeds found the location unsocial. Spiffy pointed to where he had picked up the clothes bundle early that morning, next to a gatepost. The gate failed to open from outside, though I rattled it. Spiffy had nothing else to tell me so I handed over the coin and let him go. The air where he had been standing still stank after he left me.

I walked a little way along the lane. Spiffy's stink followed hopefully. I was still holding my nose and considering what to do, when the gate abruptly opened. A man I had never seen before came out, wedged the gate with a boulder that must be kept for the purpose, then boldly relieved himself. The whole lane served as an open-air latrine for premises alongside. He saw me but did what he had to do anyway.

He was obviously desperate. I am not a cruel woman, so I let him get on with it. He must have thought I was lurking with the same idea, so when he whistled off he politely left the boulder in position. Neither of us had spoken or acknowledged the other's existence.

This was Rome. The Golden City – at its basic level. At least he had pointed the other way and not wee-ed on my tunic hem. Best of all, he had helpfully left the gate open.

Silence fell. I walked back and went inside. I closed the gate behind me. I found myself in a small exterior yard. It had stone benches and a broken sundial. I had been there before.

I was at the Charybdis bar again, in the Farcicals' rehearsal space.

27

For Mucius, this might confirm his theory that the Farcicals were all guilty. It did not do the same for me. I was ready to believe at least some were involved in the killings, though I still could not believe in a collaborated attack by them all.

Was this bar where Chremes had been lured before his awful fate? The crime scene where he was set upon, held, beaten, and then stripped? Or did that happen elsewhere, with the perpetrators bringing his clothes back to their normal haunt some time afterwards?

If the initial assault did take place there, it was quite close to the river. The Campus Martius was supposed to be reserved for monuments, but behind the Tiber's bank sordid drinking shacks abounded, the Charybdis among them as a particularly scruffy one. From here there would have been a good walk up to the stadium, right around the Theatre of Pompey and past Domitian's Odeum. It was no distance normally, but when they made the trip it would have been dark on the Campus. Then they had the problem of dragging a naked man, an elderly man who had been severely knocked about but might still have been resisting. That, plus transporting the cross, was all highly risky.

They liked risk. That was obvious.

I looked carefully around the rehearsal yard; I found no evidence of bloodshed. The paving slabs and benches might have been cleaned last night or this morning, although that is difficult with age-worn rough stone. In fact, nowhere looked as if it had ever been washed. I doubted the Charybdis even had a cleaning slave; it was obvious no one degreased the streetside counter or swept the pavement. At least this outside area must be occasionally sluiced with rain. Last night had been wintry damp, though not enough to have naturally diluted the amount of blood Chremes must have shed when he was thrashed. I was sure now: the beating had happened elsewhere. If one or more of the Farcicals had done it, they could simply have tossed his clothes here later, probably after they left him on the cross.

If asked, they would say anyone could have dropped rags in the lane. I could never prove they were lying, or that discarded garments, found by a vagrant, outside the premises, were directly linked to any Farcicals' activity in the yard. I did walk into the bar area where I asked the proprietor if he had thrown out some old clothes or knew anything about them. He stared at me as if I was mad.

I should have known he would. That is how any low-grade, lacklustre bar owner stares at a woman with her own ideas. Especially a woman who has dared to venture on her own into the filthy hovel where he poisons his short-sighted, nose-blind, taste-lacking, self-demeaning regulars. I cursed him, then I cursed his horrible bar. Neither had helped me.

The find might be indicative, but it told me no more. I saw no need to report it to Mucius.

I left the bar and returned to the Saepta Julia. I walked via the Golden Cup and the Halcyon, where the actors confirmed that Chremes had recently been seen wearing a tunic and cloak that fitted my description. The garments were his.

I left them weeping once again. At the Saepta, one of the warehouse porters took the whole bundle to Suedius, with instructions to dress the corpse in his own clothes for the funeral tomorrow. I left Suedius to discover the bloodstains and decide what, if anything, to do about them.

'He wants to know, where's the other shoe?' I was told later.

If I ever found that, its location might be a clue, though I was not hopeful. 'No idea. Did Suedius say what he's planning to do about it being missing?'

'Sling a cypress bough over the bare foot. He's got some going spare, he told me. He pinched them from another funeral.'

'Remind me not to die in this district!'

'Oh, don't worry, Albia. Your pa never pays an undertaker. We'll cart you up to his place on the Janiculan and build a nice pyre in the garden. What do you want inscribed on your memorial?'

'*A decent woman, much put upon*. Make sure to carve, *Don't pee on my grave*. No, on second thoughts, leave that out. It only gives passers-by ideas.'

It was as well I returned to the Saepta early. Tiberius had sent back the warehouse cart, with its chickens, and loaded up with home comforts for me. A rug and cushions, a hamper from our chef, and spare clothes, which were in the care of Suza, my young maid. Apparently they had had words: Tiberius instructed that for work I would need plain clothes and no jewellery, so I could blend in unobtrusively. Suza always wanted to dress me up. She was only mollified because Tiberius and I had a dinner invitation tonight so she could deck me in splendour. It was my turn to groan.

However, I was not about to plead a headache and duck out. There might be leads. Tiberius would pick me up later. He had tracked down Scribonius Attica, who, according to my husband's laconic message, was his colleague who had dealt with Chremes over the Plebeian Games. Scribonius was the aedile who approved *Miles Gloriosus*. It was his wife who thought so highly of Philocrates that she recommended the famous actor for the main part.

'I dare say,' wrote Tiberius, 'you will think the worst of that, Albiola!'

Too right, knowing husband! He said that the wife had been away, but Scribonius would send word to her. So, to assess just how juicy her interest in the actor was, I hoped the woman would be our hostess that evening.

'Big earrings?' asked Suza hopefully.

'Absolutely! The biggest you have brought.'

28

Scribonius lived north of the Campus. He probably tried to pretend his address was on the Pincian, a hill that is covered with elegant gardens, much sought-after by owners of squillion-sesterces fortunes. He was on the edge, but close enough to make him feel good. From his upstairs windows, if he craned his neck, he might glimpse the Mausoleum of Augustus, looking like a rather large gazebo in his grounds.

The evening was bound to be a strain. I hate socialising with people who use meals as an excuse to impress their guests with their wealth. An immediate disappointment was that our host's theatre-loving wife was absent; he told us she had been on holiday at their villa in the Alban Hills – 'Tiberius Manlius, you must get one, you rogue. Anyone would think you cannot afford your own leisure estates!' Clearly this man was astute.

A message Scribonius had sent to tell his wife of the deaths and this intended dinner must have taken too long, so he had to apologise. 'She won't travel in the dark. But I still get a chance to meet your lady – I have heard so much about her!'

I managed to shift my flimsy blue stole along my shoulder, like a woman with nothing better to do, readjusted bangles, applied a meek look, said nothing. I had decided not to cause trouble, so I acted like a woman who stayed at home wearing face lotions. Thanks to Suza, I was beautifully turned out, which is all that men like Scribonius expect in a wife.

A tray of prawn bites was being brought around, though they took a long time to reach me. I had not even been offered a finger-tot of party wine. Tiberius passed me his, then seized another little dink for himself.

'What have you heard? All bad, I hope!' he joked, pretending to be a racy character.

'They say you picked a lively one!'

'Oh, no. I let her pick me.'

Scribonius might have felt nervous, but I had had a tiring day. I couldn't make the effort to be outspoken. Besides, I like to familiarise myself with my surroundings before I do anything unpredictable.

I gave him a discreet summing-up. He must have been the same age as Tiberius, who was thirty-six, the traditional age for aediles. Scribonius had swept-back darkish hair, beady brown eyes, a broad body, and an attitude I recognised. He thought too much of himself.

Products of lush living are not my type. I fell for Tiberius when he was disguised as a street scruff. Tonight he had omitted to brief me on our host, although I had heard him grumble about colleagues often, so I could guess. We would howl together with outrage or laughter, or both, after we went home.

Four aediles are elected annually, of whom two can be patrician: ambitious senators who climb the slippery ladder to high office, forcing their way through quaestorships (financial fiddles), praetorships (legal fiddles), consulships (political fiddles) and governorships (foreign fiddles). Scribonius was one of those noble brutes, whereas Tiberius was merely a plebeian who had discovered he enjoyed civic duty. By contrast, Scribonius told us all about the impressive posts he wanted to hold, while Tiberius kept quiet; he would now be abandoning politics to become a full-time building contractor. Scribonius would never understand.

The quality of the pre-meal bites, when I could get one, promised well for the banquet so I kept up the good behaviour. I had been well trained. My parents taught me many social rules for attending a free dinner, such as: take your own napkin, speak no treason, only fart when your host does, don't get thrown out until you have finished feeding and have sampled all the wines.

The number and the elegance of the wines Scribonius served that evening confirmed what his befrescoed near-Pincian home advertised: he was extremely rich.

Was it his wife's money? I thought he had probably owned plenty, then she brought him more. That would be very satisfactory to a man of his type. Otherwise, we could gauge their marriage by the fact that he now stayed in Rome while she spent Saturnalia somewhere else. Theirs must be a partnership of convenience, which neither Tiberius nor I would want, though as Scribonius said openly, 'You are an intriguing couple, according to word at the Temple of Ceres!'

He did not need to specify that his gossip had been extruded by Laia Gratiana, a temple hanger-on who happened to be the tight-tensioned ex-wife of my husband. I had him now, but she had obviously sprayed around her poison, so Scribonius implied we were in some way reprehensible. We smiled. We liked our ways. Coming from a man who owned a fine harpist he wasn't bothering to listen to and twenty beautiful Greek vases that he must have bought only because they fitted his salon shelves, a sneer was never going to shake us.

I looked at the shelves. His old Greek vases were new Italian. The outpouring of modern Campanian copies is fine, so long as you don't pass them off as Athenian. These were gorgeous and would have been deservedly expensive, but in praising his own good taste during most of the appetiser course (whole white truffles, herby fried anchovies), Scribonius showed himself up. There is another social rule that says, don't boast to the daughter of an auctioneer. Repro is repro in anybody's scroll. Listen, chuck: if your silent guest wasn't concentrating on eating your dainties, she could have thumpingly set you straight.

Tiberius, who knew exactly what I was thinking, enjoyed himself describing our genuinely ancient, genuinely Hellenic *pithos*, a huge globular vase with an octopus writhing over it, which we had been given as a housewarming present.

'You only married so recently!' boomed Scribonius. 'It's all new, all roses for you. Just wait a few years. Then disillusionment sets in.'

Tiberius and I looked sympathetic, both poised to probe. Unfortunately, that was when a rash of slaves marched in with main-course dishes, whipping off silver meat covers with a clatter, then flashing away with Spanish carving knives. Scribonius bragged that he had sent them on a specialist training course. As I discreetly glanced at old grey eyes, my husband began to work his way through partridge in almond sauce, while we managed not to counter with news that we had a celebrity chef at home. We would have felt bound to invite Scribonius and his missing wife to a dinner cooked by our own wonder, Fornix. Tiberius might not have been my husband for long, but he knew which colleagues he was allowed to bring home.

Switching subjects smartly, we tackled the reason Tiberius had got us invited. We wanted our host to tell us about his approval of the Plebeian Games play.

Scribonius Attica had enough grace to acknowledge that most of the work leading up to the Games had been dropped onto one willing work-donkey: Manlius Faustus. He admitted to me that the other three aediles had spent all last year using my husband as their prop. He did say it with admiration. 'The Plebeian Games are a case in point. Faustus must have sat through many tedious hours of rehearsal. The rest of us heartily thank him for sparing us. Some of the groups were ghastly, I believe.'

'A bit grim, but I'll live,' demurred Tiberius, ignoring worried servers as he handed me a tureen of leeks. They were extravagantly peppered, though swimming in oil. No leeks are ever as good as when my father hurls them into a hot skillet with goat's cheese and olives.

'You will live with honour, Aedile!' I meant it, although mumbling glib praise as the supportive wife was not my natural medium. He grinned at my discomfort. I smiled back an acknowledgement. 'But, tell us, Scribonius, you helped out with the Chremes group, didn't you?' I can screw a poser to a post.

'I do occasionally pull my weight!'

'Oh, well done!' I toyed with a meatball, while I looked admiring.

Tiberius was burrowing around an apparent lobster shell, though it was in fact pastry. The paste could have been lighter, I suspected, but its gingered ham innards must be tasty; he was being quite vigorous. I tapped his wrist, since Scribonius clearly supposed a wife would nag about manners. I would never have objected otherwise; I would simply have leaned in and spooned up what Tiberius had loosened. He, adorable man, would have scraped out more to share with me. We were a true working partnership: in the office, on a construction site, or around a dinner table.

Scribonius admitted that he had involved himself at his own wife's urging. Sabina Gallitta, as she was called, had wanted to promote someone Scribonius described as 'a friend', who 'happened to be an actor'.

'How interesting,' I breezed. I was not intending anyone to gloss over the fact that having an actor as a gigolo was scandalous; it was especially dangerous with Domitian as society's moral censor. 'Would this toyboy be the infamous Philocrates?'

'Oh, he seems pretty ordinary!' The husband was failing to convince himself; he looked jealous.

I was too discreet to blame his wife openly. I mopped my lips with my napkin, then straight away had another go. 'Oh, someone told me he has a ripe reputation – though obviously not with Sabina Gallitta. You wouldn't let her loose with a louse, would you?' Still innocent, I cooed sweetly, 'Is Philocrates up in the Alban hills with her?' To which Scribonius had to nod.

While Tiberius stripped the pastry claws, he had managed to appear merely tolerant of my sniping. Really he liked it. He wished he could be as rude as me.

There is a convention that the four aediles are a band of brothers; often that means squabbling ones. But he joined in, sounding friendly enough: 'What about your choice of play, then? What was the story there, if I may ask?'

Scribonius, who was either very good-natured or extremely dim, forgot my charge of playboy-screwing and obliged us: yes, he had plumped for *Miles Gloriosus*. It was his wife's idea, because the colourful braggart seemed an ideal role for her 'friend', a showcase for what she believed to be his stand-out talents. Chremes's group had originally suggested *Rudens*; they were planning a big new scene with a tug-of-war. However, the helpful 'friend' had scoffed. Philocrates had seen the play performed with a tug-of-war before, by the Chremes and Phrygia troupe – he had even acted in their version once. He thought little of the innovation.

'Careful,' warned Tiberius, teasingly. 'Flavia Albia knows the adapting playwright.'

'Oh, really?' Scribonius tolerated his wife's cultural connections but was indifferent to ours. This spared me from having to talk about my parents' adventures. Falco's memoirs were embargoed: they would require heavy redaction, not only to escape defamation suits but, under Domitian, a death sentence.

'I heard that the *Rudens* script with the tug-of-war was lost abroad,' I proffered. 'Presumably Philocrates was thrilled by the part he played instead. I am interested because I heard Chremes and Phrygia had been pestered by somebody about the choice of play. I suppose that wasn't him? Philocrates never had a falling-out with them?'

'Not at all.' Scribonius was definite. 'Philocrates was all-round delighted. There was no reason for him to pester anyone. He was *very* ready to take the lead role!' added our host, now openly snide.

'And he performed well in the part?'

'So people said.' Again, I noted jealousy. His attitude was too grudging, given that the other actors thought Philocrates had lived up to his reputation.

'I am sorry we haven't been able to meet him.' I made this a professional remark. I had no intention to gush over the actor's celebrity status.

'Well, I am expecting my wife to arrive for the funeral. I told her we ought to show respect to Chremes and his wife.' I wondered, had he given Sabina Gallitta an order – and, if so, how would she react? 'Philocrates must want to be there too, since he knew them. I suppose she will bring him back with her. Did you meet the actor-manager while he was alive?' Scribonius asked me, showing a glint of ghoulish curiosity.

'No. Nor his wife, I'm afraid. You did?'

'Only as far as I had to, dealing with the Games programme. Did you see the bodies?'

'Yes.'

'Grim sights?' When I left it unanswered, he filled in the silence. 'Well, I had to meet them, though I cannot say I remember much about either. They were in a profession I normally avoid, of course.'

I deplored his double standards. So, dallying with actors was fine for the wife, but taboo for the man who hoped to be a consul? I felt he would come to regret his forbearance towards Sabina Gallitta. Consuls' wives, like Caesar's, are supposed to be above suspicion. This man was a lazy planner, even of his own career. I prophesied he would be lucky to grab even a quaestorship now, and that would be his own fault. It was stupid, too, to have let it become public knowledge that he had approved a play so his wife's lover could star in it.

While I mused, Tiberius commented more directly on the murders. 'Someone clearly held a terrible grudge against both victims. As Albia mentioned, it seems to arise from the choice of *Miles Gloriosus*. How do you feel about that, Scribonius? Have you any fears, given your personal involvement?'

Our host looked tense. 'I was doing my job.'

'Should never be a cause for retribution,' agreed Tiberius. 'Who would volunteer for office otherwise?'

'Didn't you receive an unpleasant message yourself recently, Faustus?'

'Yes, and at home too.' Tiberius, almost subconsciously, took my hand as he mentioned the incident. 'Luckily, in the end, that was all it was – a message. We identified the senders and their motive. They have been dealt with.'

His colleague was frowning. 'People will always grumble! Still, you don't expect to suffer violence. Not in return for self-sacrifice in a public role. We must hope killing off Chremes and Phrygia will be enough to purge the grudge – whatever it was.' Despite that self-reassurance, Scribonius kept talking as if not entirely convinced. 'I am safe here. Plenty of staff, house secure, people always around. I consider myself well-guarded.'

He was leading up to something. Tiberius and I waited.

'Mind you,' breathed the man, as his blasé attitude suddenly slipped, 'I invited you tonight because I have something rather odd on which I would like your opinion. There was *this* . . .'

He signalled to a slave, who must have been primed to have the item handy. Tiberius read it, then handed the piece of papyrus to me. It had been neatly removed from the front of a written scroll – and not because someone wanted to use the back for a shopping list. A title page had been found fastened, with a long, military-style nail, to the aedile's elegant front door. None of his trusted staff had heard anyone doing it. While I absorbed the message's significance, Tiberius asked the slave to fetch the nail for comparison purposes.

This was the torn-away front page from one of the most famous Greek plays ever: that monumental tragic drama, *Oedipus Rex* by Sophocles.

ŒDIPUS REX

29

Oedipus? After Laureolus and Pasiphaë, we were moving up a long distance culturally!

The aedile Scribonius would never be on a play's cast list. With his high political hopes, the anonymous suggestion was crazy. Acting is an outlawed profession. It carries none of the glamour of becoming a gladiator, which occasionally patricians do even at the cost of their reputations. Nowadays the risks were worse than ever. Domitian had a habit of finding out, even years afterwards, and punishing such thrill-seekers.

Scribonius Attica would certainly not act in public; nevertheless, had he just been announced as the killer's next victim? We had hoped Chremes and Phrygia were the only people in the undertaker's sights. Was there a longer list, a list on which Scribonius came next?

Aediles are not provided with a unit of husky lictors because their role is religious in origin which, in theory, makes bodyguards unnecessary. As an aedile's wife, I regretted it: I wanted mine to stay in one piece. But these officials tend to be rich men, able to finance their own attendants. Tiberius sternly advised his colleague to keep permanent guards close around him. 'Live privately, at least until Flavia Albia and the vigiles have tracked down the killers.'

'I refuse to be housebound because of homicidal maniacs.'

'Quite right – but, my friend, do be sensible.'

I backed up Tiberius firmly: 'And, please, do not respond to any summons you are not expecting!' The case was tricky enough already. I did not want a stubborn magistrate increasing its difficulty. I would warn the Seventh Cohort to be vigilant on his behalf, yet I was sympathetic to their stretched resources.

Scribonius remained adamant: 'I intend to show myself at that funeral. I want to announce to the world that I will not be intimidated.' This noble declaration has brought tragedy to people from Julius Caesar on. It is the bane of hard-pressed law-and-order troops, not to mention a cause of anxiety for their loyal wives. I managed not to sigh. Abruptly, he demanded, 'Has something been said about the killer being an undertaker?'

'Yes. Phrygia, with her dying breath. She gasped a strange accusation. We don't really understand what it was about. She had suffered terribly and may have been confused.'

Scribonius must have been following events, because I had made no reference to this, yet he knew. Now he wanted more facts: 'What about the funeral for the actor-managers? Who is fixing that up?'

'A mortician called Suedius. You may have come across him; he operates on the Campus Martius. The vigiles associate with him when they have to.'

'I don't know him. We use someone else. Is he the man accused? Has he been investigated?'

'I checked, but it seemed Phrygia and he had never met. Suedius himself denies it.'

'He is to be trusted?'

'It seems certain that, even if Phrygia knew what she was saying as she died, Suedius cannot be the person she meant.'

'I'll be safe, then!' Scribonius announced. 'The ceremony is tomorrow? I shall give orders that no other funerals are to take place in the cemetery at the same time, and I shall use my full powers to ensure the decree is followed.' I saw Tiberius raise his eyebrows at this rash decision, though he thought there was no point in arguing. Scribonius tried to laugh off his own fears: 'Anyway, my wife will attend with me. She is enough to scare off any trouble!'

Tiberius could not quibble at that, because he knew his own scary wife would be going too. He tried to suggest we should all put in an appearance together, as a courtesy, yet not stay long. I said that was very sound (while making up my mind that, since I would be working, I would do as I chose).

'In any case' – Scribonius revealed he had in truth given nervous thought to the message – 'that notice about the play was no real death threat. It won't fit. Oedipus Rex commits sacrilegious acts, through no fault of his own, but he remains alive.'

True. In the Sophocles play, the sphinx who prophesies his doom is bumped off, but she has been eating the people of Thebes and setting cruel riddles. She clearly asked to be hurled off a cliff. The adopted Oedipus unwittingly kills his own father, Laius, and marries his mother, Jocasta, who can't bear this and hangs herself. When he discovers what he has done, Oedipus only tears off her shoulder brooches and gouges out his eyes with them – a curiously domestic touch. It leaves two more plays to follow, with the blind king tortured by his fate and wandering in exile, a frail soul whose various children will come to grief too. But he dies under the protection of Theseus of Athens (yes, the swinish Ariadne-duper, who also caused his own father's death, in the wrong-colour-sails episode). Somewhere offstage, the welcoming earth opens to receive Oedipus into a secret grave. No gods raise objections. He departs gladly, with his daughters present, supporting him. His time is up. Apart from mysterious earth movement, it is a natural release.

That may have seemed to Scribonius like nothing to worry about. I myself would have locked my bedroom door and stayed inside with a smoked ham and a good book, until somebody trustworthy promised me it was safe to come out.

30

It was late when we left the Scribonius house. There had been the usual never-ending tussle over our departure. First, he nagged us to stay the night as his guests. After Tiberius had wriggled out of that, debate followed about transport. We had arrived in a hired litter, but Scribonius insisted we take his carriage home. This was a big four-wheeled *carpentum*, the aristocrats' showpiece for travel. It would be a nightmare struggling through the streets, since all of Rome, a city of endless deliveries after dark, would be crammed with bulky carts, poorly driven by their fanatically irascible drivers.

'No, no, you must have something decent. I don't know why you ever came in public transport in the first place. And why no lantern slave?' Because, sir, ours was Dromo: we were better off without him. 'My fellows will take you all the way to the Aventine, if you are going there. Just give them directions, wherever you need them to go.'

It was kind of him, in fact. While his carriage was prepared (which took an age, of course), I made conversation, teasing that he had not allowed his wife to take the conveyance on holiday. Perhaps shamefaced, Scribonius confessed that Philocrates had driven her to the hilltop villa in his own. The actor owned a dizzy two-person *carruca*, with leather-strap suspension and bronze plating, a vehicle that was the envy of boy-racers all over Rome. Any celebrity of standing would need his own wheels to convince himself he mattered – and I guessed when Sabina Gallitta wasn't being taken around in it, the *carruca* was useful for impressing other women.

'Small men love their flash-and-dash!' remarked Scribonius, now openly bitter. He left unsaid that a *carruca* was a lavish travelling car, almost always fitted with a bed.

Small men? He was a good average height himself. Although I thought him an average personality too, I did feel a tinge of pity as we waved goodbye.

Trapped in the heavy *carpentum*, we endured its snail-pace for a while. Tiberius was fuming. He hated to be under an obligation. Our plan had been to stroll hand in hand to the Mausoleum of Augustus, then down towards the Altar of Peace and the marble solarium with its red granite gnomen sundial. On the way, if we saw a chair for hire we would summon it, but this area was quiet and comparatively safe. Tiberius would stay with me at the Saepta Julia, where we had left my maid. Last seen, Suza had been happily talking to Galanthus, a young boy who had briefly lived in our house. He was now learning from Gornia how to manhandle furniture and display the lots at auctions. With them was my cousin Cornelius, chubby and sweet-natured, a junior auctioneer who often dossed at the warehouse because, like most of the Didius family, his home life was terrible. Gornia had oversight. Tiberius could take Suza home tomorrow morning.

Forestalled, eventually Tiberius leaned out of the window – it was perfectly safe, as we were going so slowly. When his yelling failed, a passer-by caught the carriage-driver's attention. We asked that in view of the traffic, he should turn off past the Porticus Vipsaniae. We would invite ourselves to the house of Eucolpus and take the empty room that had been previously occupied by Chremes and Phrygia. At least it had a furnished bed, not a couch with a horse blanket.

We did that. The carriage left. The porter let us in without comment; we saw nobody else. As we crept past the room of Naia Nerania, we heard a harp being played for her, but no voices spoke behind the closed door, so we did not knock. The lullaby ceased, not long after we had made ourselves at home in our borrowed quarters. Later, I heard somebody moving about in the room on the other side of us, which was supposed to be unoccupied. If there was a new tenant, they quickly settled down.

Although Tiberius had previously not wanted me to stay there alone, I was safe with him – or so he said with a raffish grin. In fact we were so exhausted we just slept. It is a contradiction of marriage that although you can now make love whenever you want you are also free, when wined and dined and tired out in the aftermath of hideous crimes, not to bother.

We could have slept in next morning but, uneasy in a strange environment, we rose early. I would have introduced Tiberius to the old lady, but there was no sound at all from Naia Nerania's room, so we once more crept past without rousing her. The same porter let us out, again without comment. We strolled gently through quiet streets, stopping on the Via Lata to buy a takeaway breakfast, which we took along to the Saepta.

A shock awaited us. At the warehouse we were greeted by Suza, my maid, shrieking. She was a bouncing teenager who, unless I had to be tricked out for something special, normally preferred to snooze until halfway through the morning. Here she was, before most staff arrived, wide awake and over-excited. With her was Galanthus, around the same age, by origin a palace dancer and still effete with a kiss-curl. This morning Galanthus looked more stricken than Suza. However, Cornelius, unperturbed, had gone out for bread rolls.

'Calm down. What happened?'

'Somebody broke in and tried to kill Gornia!'

That was ominous. We ascertained quickly that Gornia had escaped harm, and though well over ninety, he was viewing the incident as merely a blip in the calendar. At his age, he said, an intruder was welcome to bop him; it would save him wondering continually when Pluto would claim him.

Whoever carried out the break-in cannot have expected to come upon Suza, Galanthus and Cornelius, still talking. They had been sitting behind a cupboard, so the light from their oil lamp would not keep Gornia awake. On hearing the intruder, the trio arose in the gloom. Galanthus, who had once survived a vicious attack himself, went crazy. He rammed the presumed burglar in the belly with a stiff roll of tapestry, choking him with dust and puzzled moths. Suza, though weaponless, gathered all her adolescent puppy fat to protect Galanthus, dealing the man a two-handed shoulder blow. As he staggered, Cornelius struck him from behind, with a huge mallet. All three yelled their heads off, with stout young lungs.

Woken by the noise, Gornia capered on his truckle bed; he jangled a long skein of cowbells that were kept beside him so that if he felt strange in the night he could summon help. In ran Lappius, our largest guard. His torch set fire to some baskets, but the young folk threw the tapestry over them. Once he saw the ancient porter was safe, Lappius chased the intruder. He lost him somewhere out in the unlit Saepta Julia colonnades.

The intruder had dropped a lump of stone. It was a two-foot-long piece of broken balustrade. I tried a cautious lift but found it heavier than the weights my gymnasium trainer made me use. No normal burglar lumbers himself with anything as cumbersome as that. But it would have crushed a skull.

Tiberius looked upset. I knew what he was thinking – the same as me.

That intruder had not visited last night to kill Gornia. He probably had no idea he might encounter staff. Instead, he was looking for an informer – and not one of the sleazy operatives who always hung around the Saepta Julia. He wanted me. He must have been hoping to stop my investigations into Chremes and Phrygia. He had reason to think I might be there. He wanted to kill me.

31

No escape: Tiberius Manlius not only escorted Suza home that morning, he dragged me along too. Without me, the warehouse workers took the precautions they normally used for a valuable sale. Now on full alert, Gornia and Lappius checked for theft; nothing seemed to be missing. Staff would trot around the gallery jewellers to ask whether anyone had seen anything last night, though it was unlikely. Cornelius was sent to the vigiles station-house to see Mucius, not only warning him about the threat aimed at Scribonius Attica but reporting this attack on me.

That was why I went home to the Aventine. I wanted to avoid Mucius. His priority today should be soothing words and official advice for the fancy Scribonius household, but he might follow up on our intruder too. I was nervous he would use the incident to ban me from investigating. While Tiberius had not suggested my backing out, I could not entirely rely on domestic support. I had a good husband, and he might line up with the vigiles. Tiberius always said he had faith in me, but I knew I was causing him anxiety.

As soon as we walked into our house, we saw that work had consequences. We were giving a home to two little nephews; they ran out to us, put their fists in their eyes and pointedly began crying. Only this month their mother had died; they needed stability. Instead, first I spent two nights away without warning, then Tiberius also left them yesterday. He was all morning at the Temple of Ceres, then came home and went into his study alone. Troubled by the death scenes we had witnessed, he must have kept his own counsel.

My cousin was staying with us with her invalid husband, but he was so ill they were preoccupied. Household staff, including their nurse, had been with the boys the whole time, yet Gaius and Lucius had picked up that a mystery was being concealed. This may have reminded them of scenes around their mother's dying – or else they were by nature mithery children. On our return they loudly protested.

Barley the dog came to see who had arrived; she turned around and stalked to her kennel.

Dromo didn't bother to descend from the upper balcony where he was sulking on his mat. He just shouted down, 'I am your lantern boy. Why didn't you take me last night? Everyone makes out I'm no good. What's the point of having a job around here, if nobody lets me do it?' There was more.

Tiberius and I glanced at each other ruefully. It had been too easy to assume that if casework claimed us, the home would continue to function. Other people's neediness was a big change for me, after working alone for years. Even Tiberius had not fully adapted to our new circumstances.

Fornix marched out from the kitchen. 'I had a quarrel with the butcher. No one has given any indication as to how far I am allowed to go with him. I really needed one of you here to adjudicate!'

'Oh, Fornix, you are a diplomat. You will sort him out.'

'For your information, he stomped off saying he was never coming here again. I told him that was fine by me.'

'Juno! Just keep in with the fishmonger, will you?'

'Ha!' exclaimed Gratus, my house steward darkly. He obviously knew something. I pretended not to notice.

I spent a morning at home engaged in routine tasks, making my presence visible for anyone who thought they owned me. I tried to reimpose a sense of calm. I organised laundry. I went to the stable and talked to the donkey. I told my cousin Marcia to take charge if I was absent.

'I've got Corellius to look after, Albia. Doesn't it matter a jot to you, that the poor man had a leg amputated?'

'He runs safe-houses for diplomats. He spies on sinister Parthians. Tell him to strap on his false limb, then get up to shout at the butcher.'

'You're a selfish cow, Flavia Albia!' My cousin never held back.

I listened to a song Glaphyra had taught the children. I planned meatless menus with Fornix while lying that Corellius would sort out our supply chain. I told Dromo he could come to the funeral that night, where his lantern skills would be absolutely essential to make sure nobody fell over a burial urn in the dark. 'I don't think your master and I would dare to attend, without you to look after us, Dromo . . .' *Cringe!*

'You're just saying that to shut me up.' *Yes, Dromo.*

Tiberius watched, smiling slightly. He had his own ideas about repair work: he took off into the builder's yard beside our house, where he made a clatter with materials. Only I knew why: he was looking at timber, nails, rope and, now, that piece of broken balustrade. All the clues had been delivered to us. I just had no idea where they led.

After lunch (cheese and eggs, no meat and, interestingly, no fish either) I had a bright idea. If the funeral was held across the river, the necropolis was some distance from the Aventine. The ceremony would traditionally take place at night. I had not been looking forward to it, especially in winter, with a long trek home afterwards when tired and depressed.

'I know! Let's have an expedition. Listen, Gaius and Lucius, how about we all pack luggage and go for a little stay at Falco's villa? It's right at the top of the Janiculan hill – you can look back over the river and see the whole city.' While Father was away at the coast, he would be grateful for me checking up on this long-term family property and geeing up its skeleton staff. The house also had its own private lane running down the hill, pretty well past the cemetery.

Dromo forgot to bring his lantern. Still, the villa had been fitted out by Falco's father Geminus. After his live-in girlfriend had given up and died (who could blame the woman?) he often rolled home in his litter at past midnight. He had bequeathed us a whole cupboardful of lamps and torches to borrow. Some were even valuable antiques.

32

The triumphal road into Rome entered the city at the big curve of the Tiber. It rolled in across gardens once owned by Marcus Agrippa, the same man whose monumental works dominated the top end of Campus Martius. Next to his bankside pleasure grounds, the highway passed alongside the Circus of Gaius and Nero, majestic and spectral. An empty stadium can hold suggestive shadows, particularly if you know the project was conceived by a pair of chaotic, chariot-loving emperors whose use of it was curtailed by their own early, violent deaths. This place had a bad history.

The red granite obelisk at the centre of the racetrack reached up into deceptive mist that made the Egyptian marker column seem to swim woozily. Echoes of old festivals had been replaced by troubled silence. Darkness was starting to infiltrate the road as it came along the circus's north side. Was it called the Via Cornelia? It hardly felt triumphal; it had the lonely aura of some long-abandoned route with no name.

At this wintry time of year, the river nearby made its presence felt, with chills that crept over the ground and numbed the feet of anyone standing motionless for too long – as we would have to do. Out here, the chosen burial place lay north of Rome's Fourteenth district, that mix of dubious foreigners and near-deserted parks. Lying beyond the civic boundary, the Circus seemed isolated. Separated from the Transtiberina habitations by the long, low ridge of the Janiculan Hill, this was open country.

The roadside necropolis remained an open area too, although it had been established on what people called the Vatican Plain a hundred years ago. All roads that lead out of cities are used for burials, but this had a grim heritage. After the Great Fire in Nero's reign had destroyed so much of Rome, Nero had used his circus to impose inventive punishments on some of the Christians he publicly blamed. He dressed them in animal skins, to be torn apart by savage dogs, or he covered them with bitumen, tied them to stakes and set them on fire as human torches. Those long-ago agonised victims were buried here. Yet more had died on a desperate row of crosses that Nero ordered to be set up along the *spina* at the centre of the track. His historic crucifixions were a sombre reminder for us: what had happened to Chremes was another unspeakable punishment, another imposition of cruelty and shame, clearly thought up by a desperate madman.

The necropolis contained dotted tombs, small brick or stone buildings with pediments. More have been built since then, lining a formal street of mausolea, but in the period when we gathered there for the actor-managers, the cremated bones of the general population, from miserably rich to desperately poor, with their children and slaves, were mainly interred in the ground, put straight into holes in glass jars and ceramic urns. Fortunately, winter had not been harsh, so the soil would not be too frozen for new graves.

Tiberius and I, with Dromo and a small group of guards, had slipped down from Father's villa early because I wanted to observe everyone who came. Near the unlit pyre we came upon a digger employed by Suedius, who was making slow efforts to prepare a small burial hole. 'Hello, hello, people! Come early for the comic interlude?' His spade smashed an urn, which he inspected, reading a plaque. 'Ebor-something – the rest is too broken. Who cares? Who knew him anyway?' Bits of glass and ceramic flew in all directions as the man burrowed further. He was smashing his way through old burials with no respect for previous incumbents. 'So, what happened to yours then?'

'One crucified, one gored by an aurochs,' I relayed crisply.

'Oh, you're a right comedian!' Tossing out a loose human skull, he speeded up crazily. 'Who's this? Alexander the Great? Or some child-molester, a creeper into closets – anyway, by now he's a humourless dead bundle of worms who brings no joy to anyone . . . And there's his dreary audience approaching!' A row of carrying chairs had come through the mist, from which emerged veiled figures, moving like ghosts to our meeting point.

To keep everyone entertained, the gravedigger maintained his slew of crass jokes. He harped on what had happened to our coming corpses: 'He's holding it together, hanging in there – death is the cross he has to bear – but she's in bits, they tell me!' Eventually my husband suggested he leave mourners in peace with their sad reveries. The digger looked rebellious.

I snapped, 'Button up your banter. This isn't a picnic.'

He opened his mouth to argue. I produced my crazy British druid stare. He threw down his shovel angrily, then left.

Tiberius chuckled. 'You know how to cut a comedian short!'

Dromo picked up the shovel; he started creating a toy fort, using ash and bits of bone.

We heard the funeral procession arriving. Usually, a flashy cortège tells the world someone wealthy and famous has passed away. This procession was impressive too. I recognised the actors who had worked with Chremes and Phrygia, along with strangers who must belong to the group Davos ran, plus acrobats, orchestra players and animal trainers who worked with Thalia. They must have combined to commemorate their friends in style, escorting them on their final journey here.

Suedius had hired professional mourners – wailers and hair-tearers – but tonight a crowd of genuinely grieving people made them superfluous. Processions would often include impersonators who carried ancestral masks of the dead while they performed an exaggerated version of their characters; instead, tonight we had our own actors. They had genuinely known the deceased couple. Their scurrilous satire was intimate and accurate; the masks they brandished were those of Tragedy and Comedy, with others used in plays that the actor-managers had produced. Two leading players in exotic robes strode beside the corpses, portraying their customary arguments: a mock Chremes on stilts made exaggerated gestures while a tottering fake Phrygia cursed him.

As the cortège reached the pyre, a shiver took me. The last procession in my own life had been for my wedding. That was the terrible evening of storms, when a lightning bolt nearly ended our marriage. The drizzle that now began to soak us insidiously reminded me, so I huddled against Tiberius, clutching his hand. He was standing next to his colleague Scribonius, both serious, both formal in their purple-decorated togas, heads veiled religiously. A phalanx of public slaves and other heavies surrounded them for protection.

Mucius and a detachment of vigiles had formed an honour guard for the procession – perhaps listening out for clues. After they arrived, they stood together on the edge of the gathering, looking awkward.

The bier, supervised by a croaking Suedius, had arrived amidst a cluster of torch-bearers. Nearby faces looked ghastly in the flickering light as bearers lurched to a stop. Chremes and Phrygia would be bedded together on their pyre, side by side, he in the clothes I had rescued for him, she in the rags of her own last outfit. For their journey out from the city, they had been placed upon the expensive couch I had seen before, with its heavily befringed cushions and coverlets. But Suedius quickly relieved the richer man's transport of our lesser persons, sending the borrowed bed out of sight with Sorgius before its return to its intended corpse. A much more basic board supported our bodies. With a wobble or two, they were raised onto the cold pyre. Extra wailing arose, while those who were nearest sprinkled sweet-scented oils upon them. Suedius began some complicated work with kindling.

It was a large funeral. This was a curse for me because it increased my circle of suspects. People I had never seen before had come; they were liable to do a flit before I could place them and ask questions. In the lull, I left Tiberius and kept busy, moving among the mourners, murmuring sympathy, while taking unobtrusive notes about who they were and whether they could suggest why the couple had met their dreadful end. No one could offer a reason. No one knew who might have hated them. People clearly felt normal grief and shock although, because of the terrible deaths, I saw much added anxiety.

In the past, grand funerals were accompanied by gladiatorial fights; we had theatre. Just as contributions were about to start, a woman arrived, causing a delay – veiled, not young, stout proportions. I assumed she was Sabina Gallitta, the play-loving, actor-loving wife of Scribonius Attica. She was handed onsite by a shortish man in a cloak, who patrolled her through the gathering until she reached her husband. The married couple exchanged cheek-kisses. The escort walked over to Davos and Thalia, who shook hands and embraced him. Then they all stood together.

Among the mourners, the Farcicals immediately stood out. Apparently they were to present a homage: they had come in their performing costumes. Maccus and Centunculus, the hook-nosed fool and the comic slave, were bare-chested in the outsize hairy loincloths of traditional farce, while the old man Pappus was covered up in a voluminous robe, and the soldier Dosennus wore a full curly suit of leggings, long sleeves and body tunic. All the males were hidden behind larger-than life theatrical masks, with grotesque mouths, hollow eyes, long curls, ringlet beards and disconcerting wild expressions. Each character looked startled, as if shocked by a terrible event.

I worked out which of the Farcicals was which, partly by build and partly from their characters' lewd dialogue. They honoured the dead with a short sketch they seemed to improvise, full of wordplay, horrible rustic humour and rowdy pranks. Ambrosia, presenting herself as a homespun wench under a chaplet of flowers, accompanied them with loud singing, hoarse ditties that sounded ancient and ethnic, punctuated by fierce bangs on a tambourine.

To me, the playlet was too simple and too crude. Even the way it was acted struck me as overdone. Ambrosia had announced it as *The Lupin Seed*. Thank goodness it was short. Towards the end, the characters of Maccus and

Centunculus, or Gnaeus and Megalo behind their masks, produced a rope and began to cavort in a comic tug-of-war.

At once, I saw Thalia stride across and sharply say something. It seemed a definite ticking off. She was angry. That cannot have been because the farce was so lewd. We were all used to impersonating and insulting the dead during funerals. Satire was supposed to be cathartic, with disrespect showing our loss in some weird Roman way. I was too far away to hear what Thalia said, though I guessed she was preventing rope horseplay, after a proposed tug-of-war had featured in troubles with Chremes and Phrygia. Was trying to perform it now a defiant Farcicals gesture? At any rate, they stopped and stood further off.

In their place, the professional actors took over. Pardicus still looked quite ill after being gored, but Atticus and Simo both gave speeches from tragedies. Atticus declaimed in a stately manner that was obviously a tribute to how Chremes would have performed: it was not a parody, but so recognisable of the dead man that some shed tears.

Davos was presiding as chief mourner. He gave a short personal eulogy, in tribute to his old friends. As Suedius formally handed him a torch to light the pyre, two tall young women, both dressed in fashionable white mourning as if they had planned it together, stepped forward like family members. I gathered they were the real and adoptive daughters of Phrygia: Thalia's musician, Sophrona, and Byrria, the well-known Roman actress. While flames started to take, Byrria gave a powerful speech from the play in which we knew Phrygia had always yearned to star. Against the sound of branches crackling below the bodies, she recited the terrible monologue from *Medea* in which the queen, betrayed by Jason, prepares to kill her children. It ended:

. . . My afflictions
Have conquered me; I now am well aware
What crimes I venture upon: but rage, the cause
Of woes most grievous to the human race,
Over my better reason has prevailed.

More people wept. The flames were lapping up around the corpses. Heat released scents of pine, cinnamon and myrrh.

Those words should have had resonance for whoever murdered Chremes and Phrygia. I glanced around to see how *rage, the cause of woes most grievous* might have affected the Farcicals. Too much?

I could not see them. They must have slipped away.

33

It takes a long time for fire to consume human bodies. If you give full respect to the departed and stay until they are reduced to fragments, then the ash and bone pieces cool down enough to be collected, it is a big commitment.

Out in the open, sounds carried from afar. Subdued, our group was now standing mainly in silence, or talking only in undertones. The night grew darker. We waited. The atmosphere was chill, our breath wreathing. People believed that until the dead were formally buried, their troubled shades lingered, hovering around their mourners, unable to find rest in the underworld. As flames consumed the bodies of Chremes and Phrygia, we could easily imagine it to be true.

I saw Mucius from the Seventh Cohort talking to Tiberius. They both looked towards me, so were probably discussing the Saepta Julia break-in. Dromo waved, as if we were all partying on a beach; he had no sense of occasion. I stayed where I was.

I sought out Sophrona for commiserations, since it was her birth-mother's funeral. She was a wonderful musician, I knew, but her instrument was the water organ: much too large to transport here. Sophrona had several small children, who were running around; I had heard that her husband, who had not come with her, was flighty.

She knew what I did. Calm and composed, the tall young woman declared that she would probably murder this husband over his next affair, but she had no time, energy or wish to kill anyone else. I never had her as a suspect. Sophrona, who seemed a gentle soul, only knew Chremes and Phrygia slightly; whenever she had met them, he had always been distant with her, she vague in her own way yet more kindly. Sophrona said she grieved their loss; she wanted me to discover who murdered them. As she grabbed at a mischievous infant, she sent regards to my parents, urging me on, saying they would want me to do my best. Among this group, many of whom had known Falco and Helena before I did, I felt overshadowed. It was hard work competing with their reputation.

In the loose amalgam of actors, backstage hands, acrobatic performers and animal trainers, no one else seemed to have any motive. I moved on from Sophrona to speak to Byrria. She said she had rarely seen Chremes and Phrygia in recent years; she had worked all through Saturnalia at Alba Longa, the Emperor's citadel – which I could check, though there was no reason to doubt it. Besides greeting Thalia, Byrria had barely talked to anyone, though that might have been because she was upset. With me, she, too, asked after Falco and Helena, speaking with affection about their travels in Syria. Apropos of that, she introduced me to Philocrates, another acquaintance from that time, then quickly moved off, as if to get away from him.

So: Philocrates. This star of the stage must once have been good-looking, though a broken nose had marred him. Sometimes that gives a victim's face interesting character, but he kept touching his schnozzle as if trying to straighten it, even though he must have lived with the disfigurement for years. He stood well. His voice was good. He carried his clothes handsomely; they were fine-napped garments, with expensive accessories. A very full cloak. Expensive fawn boots. He wore chunks of jewellery that women had probably bought for him and he was bothered about keeping his fine boots out of the dirt.

At first I could see him automatically checking whether I was interested in him. Despite that, the longer we talked, the less he seemed inclined to flirt. It might have been because his meal-ticket, Sabina Gallitta, was present. But like everyone who had met my parents, he spoke of them with sincere respect, my mother in particular. I suspected he had tried smooching Helena, but she had scorned him. Now he was wary of her daughter: clever fellow!

He was self-centred, I could tell. Not Mother's type. Not mine either. He never would be even if, like Sabina Gallitta, I turned one day into a bored wife looking to spend too much money on a hunk.

Despite the roué eyes, I could not object to his treatment of me. He was almost too polite. He must also be intelligent because he commented, 'I see Helena Justina has taught you to distrust men!'

'She and Marcus Didius taught me to doubt everything that moves,' I answered. The exchange was good-humoured, at least on the surface.

'I imagine they taught you a lot – if you are investigating this ghastly crime. They were pretty good at sleuthing, I recall. I can tell you at once, I do have an alibi.'

'So I heard. Perhaps you can help me even so.'

I discounted him as a suspect. Philocrates, though compact, had the hard body of a mature man who always kept in shape. He would have been physically able to overpower the taller, older actor-manager and haul him onto a cross, especially with someone else helping. But I accepted that he had been off in the hills with the aedile's wife.

He reminisced: 'Remember me to Falco and Helena. We had a good season out in the crazy east, before I came back for much bigger things.'

'I know they will take these tragedies to heart, though I have had no chance to give them the sad news yet. Tell me, Philocrates,' I said quietly, 'you had no quarrel with Chremes and Phrygia – they had assigned you the perfect part and, as you say,' I twinkled, 'your alibi holds up.' This was not the moment to sneer at his relationship. 'But you were there on that old tour. Recently someone was badgering them. Who else did they work with? Who might have met them again back in Rome, on more difficult terms?'

At first, Philocrates offered no suggestions, instead asking me what Davos and Thalia had to say. 'Davos himself is absolutely straight, of course.'

'I believe it. And he was too busy with his own group. He and Thalia had not managed to see Chremes and Phrygia on this visit.'

Philocrates frowned. 'He knew Phrygia for years, was a company stalwart at one time. Thalia went back with her even longer. We don't keep in touch much, but they were all good friends for a very long time. I dare say Thalia and Davos are kicking themselves for not meeting up.'

'They are, particularly Davos.'

I watched the actor puzzling to himself. 'I don't know . . .' I let him dwell on whatever he had on his mind, until eventually he said, 'There was someone unreliable on that old tour. He disgraced himself and he was left behind. I never cared for him. It was mutual. I cannot imagine he amounted to anything afterwards, though he was very conceited. I have not seen or heard of him since. When my career flourished, he certainly never turned up to pay me any compliments.' He made that sound as if failure to kneel in homage at the feet of the great Philocrates made anyone else a no-account. For him to accuse someone else of conceit was rich.

'Did he act? He may have acquired a different stage name,' I suggested.

'He will always be a punk!' snarled Philocrates, abruptly vicious. He lowered his voice. 'I can tell you the story. Not here.'

'Where, then?' I guessed: 'Are you staying at the aedile's house – Scribonius Attica?'

'I am often there,' Philocrates agreed, sounding off-hand. 'Patrons look after me very well these days. I move around between some exceedingly decent guest rooms. I don't have my own place. So, yes, try their house first.'

I said I would do so at the first opportunity. Then he moved off, as if unwilling to be questioned with public eyes on him.

I saw him bump into another man he seemed to know. They clasped hands then shook their heads towards the burning bodies, to deplore what had happened. A short conversation followed, during which I managed to drift closer. I cast scented oil, while I pretended to be rapt in contemplation of the pyre.

The two men were being rude about the Farcicals. Catching my eye, Philocrates called out, 'This man is Plotinus, a musician with the Chremes troupe.' I wondered how long he had been with them. Was he another leftover from Syria?

'It was damn good luck for them that they had me,' Plotinus exclaimed. Bald, olive-skinned and almost as short as his companion, he must be the man the actors had told me had 'gone off to buy a new lyre string'. I suspected a euphemism for having an affair. Plotinus kept speaking loudly and pompously: 'I orchestrate a play to a very different standard from those weaklings who just creaked through *The Lupin Seed.* Our appearance at the Games would have been a disaster, if it had had them plink-bonking their discords, like pig-farmers crashing sluice buckets! You want to hear class, you need me, me directing a decent ensemble who know how to play.' I disliked this boasting; I began to walk away.

Unfortunately, the Farcicals could not have left the scene, as I had earlier assumed. The flames were beginning to diminish. The cremation had reached its natural end. Mourners stretched their uncomfortable limbs. Unexpectedly, the amateurs came around the bier from behind, where they must have been standing, hidden by the tall construction and its blaze. Arriving back among the main group of us, they heard these insults.

Plotinus must have seen them. He did not stop or even drop his voice. 'Thank the gods Chremes came to his senses – I had warned him myself, if he opened our ranks to a cacophony of shrieking, clapped-out would-bes, I was going to push off. Phrygia had a go at him. She knew all our combo would have followed me.'

As they were still masked, it was impossible to see the male amateurs' reaction. Ambrosia had covered her mouth with one hand, looking troubled. Philocrates then had the grace to take Plotinus by the elbow, steering him elsewhere among the mourners.

Seeming subdued, the Farcicals nodded to Davos. Then they really did leave. They were going home early, before the ashes were collected, but the night was dark and they would be travelling on foot. It was the customary moment when only those with breaking hearts felt they had to stay. Indeed, I noticed Scribonius Attica and his wife also saying farewells. They retreated towards where their big carriage must be waiting on the road, followed by their guard party. No attempt on his life had taken place, though it would have been difficult among tonight's crowd. Tiberius came over to join me, hauling Dromo.

There was to be a feast. Dromo cheered up. Many people believed souls needed to be placated at one last formal meal, before they were set free of earthly ties. Sometimes the mourning period is delayed for several days, but since theatre people were transient, this would be at the graveside tonight, to involve as many as possible. The ritual would be our last farewell to Chremes and Phrygia.

Thalia's troupe was camped nearby where they always stayed, on the other side of the Circus of Gaius and Nero. They had planned for this, bringing along a large ox wagon, laden with equipment, amphorae and food. From their vehicle, which had to be left on the Via Cornelia because of its size, came trestle tables and long benches, platters and cauldrons. As this hospitable crowd tripped to and fro with stuff, they invited all the litter-bearers and drivers who had been having a long cold wait at the roadside.

With sumptuous eats coming out of warm hayboxes and a giant samovar providing hot water to take the edge off the wine, we all revived. The mood was quiet, yet as convivial as Chremes and Phrygia would have liked it; everyone said so, reminiscing. It was an occasion for half-forgotten memories and oft-told stories.

'Remember when Chremes decided he would leave her, taking all the cash? Phrygia said he was welcome to flit, because there wasn't anything to take. He never went, of course.'

'I do remember that dog I let her have,' Thalia mused, laughing. 'Old Anethum, poor arthritic pooch. He used to do tricks onstage for me but was getting well past it. When he played before the Emperor, I thought he was going to pee all down Vespasian's leg. After he really got too old, Phrygia had him off me as a pet. He tried to follow her everywhere, even though he was blind by then. But he could tell where she was by those silly platform shoes of hers, shuffling around every time she moved. She used to tease Chremes, saying she loved the dog more than him.'

'We all loved him. Anethum's stage act was playing dead, but one day he really did die on her,' Simo recalled. 'We thought Phrygia would go barmy with grief. Be fair to Chremes, he was good about it. Comforted her. They belonged together, really.'

We toasted the couple, as if they could hear us – until Suedius and his boy were ready to dismantle what remained of the pyre, first gathering up the cooled bone, teeth and ashes. The couple were gone now, body and spirit together.

A basic urn had been supplied, rough blackish pottery, egg-shaped, two thick handles, domed top with a round knob. I noticed Davos leave the table, go across and help with the ash collection.

The urn would simply be buried. No possessions would be included; in Rome that was not done: depositing grave goods would only encourage grave-robbers. There was no talk of any memorial plaque. Chremes and Phrygia had travelled to Hades, leaving us to carry on with life in the upper world. Tonight they would be remembered. Being realistic, it was unlikely any of their nomadic friends would return to this site to commune with their spirits.

The feast was ending. Helpful people were discreetly collecting dishes, so far leaving them in piles on the ends of tables. A few were anxious to leave, looking around to see if it seemed proper yet. Unless they had walked here, they needed to wait. Most of the men who carried or drove transport were still eating their free meal.

Philocrates, who must have arrived in his own classy two-wheeler, came to ask Thalia to say goodbye to Davos for him; he said he could perform a death scene better than anyone, but in real life people dying upset him too much. He beckoned his driver, then raised an arm to no one in particular as he slipped away on his own. I remember his short, square figure leaving the blur of torchlight where we sat, treading carefully in those soft leather boots as he walked over the rough ground into the deep darkness beyond.

A need to linger gripped the rest of us. High above, the skies must have cleared so the night became even colder, but we had the magical sense of dining under stars. Most people had stopped talking. Weariness and reluctance to break our last link with the dead couple held us there on the benches. Suedius stood holding a spade, while his boy just about managed to hold up the urn they would bury in the hole that had been dug for it. It was time for us to surround the final position, reverently place more flowers and perfumes, let the night's business reach its end.

Then, as we rose to our feet for that purpose, from the direction of the road came a tremendous noise. The night was rent by shouts, whinnies from troubled beasts and screaming wheels, all taking place in a confused sequence among a nightmare-sounding crash.

Horrified, Tiberius looked at me. 'Laius!'

'Scribonius!' I replied, in horror.

Laius is the father of Oedipus Rex. Before the play opens, Laius, in his carriage, had attempted to force a young stranger off the road. Oedipus refused to give way.

Road rage. Could happen anywhere: on any road, in any province, at any period. We have all been there. All those Greek travellers required to complete their misery was a flock of sheep being allowed to wander all over the place by a deliberately deaf shepherd.

It is fair to say that when the aedile received his notice, nobody had considered it referred to dangerous driving.

But in Sophocles's great drama, after their furious standoff, Oedipus killed his father.

34

By the time we reached the highway, whoever had stolen the big ox cart had fled. As some of us already expected, what had happened was no accident. It might not have been at a crossroads, as the play specified, but it was death on a road to a city – and it was ugly.

'Well, this is not where three roads meet in Phocis!' Tiberius complained.

I had been to Greece. We were scrambling along in a crowd of people running to give assistance and I had no spare breath, or I might have told him it was no Greek road at all: I remembered those horrible mountain tracks, each little better than a dry stream bed, all teetering above ravines and littered with boulders brought down in storms.

At night, there was little traffic. While we were all feasting, someone had slyly moved all the unattended chairs and litters. In the darkness, a short way past the necropolis, they were lined up unexpectedly. They now formed a substantial barrier, forcing anyone who was heading towards Rome to redirect abruptly to the other side of the road. Carrying poles and handles were wedged together to prevent easy separation and the elegant couch off Suedius's cart had been added to the makeshift barricade.

Everyone stopped at the accident site. Torches showed what we feared. The crash we had heard was not caused by a pothole. The road had no flaws. The Via Cornelia was a Roman tribunal highway, made for armies marching out to victory or returning home groaning with plunder. It was built to fortification standards: deep ditch levelled and rammed, stone foundation course, nine inches of rubble and lime, six more of broken potsherds, then polygonal hard-stones cut to hold fast into the layer below. Its surface was laid tight, on a camber that shed water into side gullies as successfully as tortoise scales. It was furnished with mile-stones, travel-lodges, occasional mounting blocks for horse-men, and regular troughs of drinking water. Although it was under guardianship of the curators of the nearby Via Aurelia, this road would last without maintenance for a hundred years. It took serious human guile to create a death trap here. But somebody had done it.

Before they had tampered with traffic management tonight, there would have been an eight-foot width for vehicles to pass: not generous, but adequate. The barrier had halved that. In the dark, it was lethal.

Philocrates and his driver had been relying on a dim lantern to find their way. He would have reclined inside, keen to escape the necropolis. I imagined the driver had originally been urged on by the actor, whose mood was darkened by the funeral. Stretched out within the vehicle, Philocrates must have been thinking of the past, while also looking ahead to the comfortable house of Scribonius Attica and Sabina Gallitta; they had gone ahead quite some time before, so there would be braziers and lamps, warmed wine, attentive slaves, a general feeling of duty done, relaxation and relief.

The *carruca*, with its spinning wheels, fine balance and gorgeous carriage work, must have been cracking along until it was sent aside by the narrowed traffic lane. Once the driver hit the blockage, he might have called out; if Philocrates knew what was happening, he probably cursed. While they slowed, and maybe even paused to investigate, some dark spirit had mysteriously driven up the funeral donkey and its vehicle close behind. The *carruca* had become trapped, unable to avoid whatever the road ahead now held. Then, out of the dark, the ox cart must suddenly have appeared, heading straight towards them.

35

I felt a breeze tugging my hair. The road strode on towards the Tiber. Though not as high as some I had seen in Britain, it was elevated above the surrounding countryside so the legions could spot marauders or simply feel like the lords of the world they were. Any traveller who was drunk, asleep, bemused in the dark or forced aside by malevolent plotters might find his vehicle plunging off, especially if he had been travelling fast. Even so, the drop was not large. A crash need not be fatal.

This trap had been intended to kill, however. The perpetrators had made sure of it. While we were feasting, without any of us noticing, the circus troupe's massive wagon had been taken from where it had been parked up; it was driven along the road towards Rome, then turned back. The wagon was two-beast transportation, suitable for moving giant barrels or even large animals in iron cages: four high wheels, a metal-reinforced frame, sturdy side-boards adding extra weight, a pulling-shaft like a battering ram, and huge draught animals that paused for nothing. This monster must have loomed out of the mist at the pinch-point of the diversion. Dead weight, it had swiped the actor's zippy *carruca* off the highway, so it muddled across a footpath and landed in a drainage ditch. Suedius's donkey cart had been stopped on the road in the wagon's path. So, the maniac driving the oxen had forced the heavy wagon off to the side too, ploughing down through the wreck of the *carruca*. Perhaps that was always the plan.

The oxen survived but they were bellowing their heads off and struggling in their harness. One mule was dead, the other had broken free; it was found on the road and put out of its misery by one of Thalia's menagerie hands. Others rushed to calm their own beasts.

When people hauled the *carruca* driver out from under the carnage, he was dead. So was Philocrates. Shockingly, he had not been killed in the accident. He must have crawled free. Now he was lying on his back close by. There, someone had bludgeoned his head, caving in his skull. A heavy wooden staff, wet with blood, lay abandoned, right beside the murdered actor.

The killers must have fled very fast. In the hushed winter night, they would have heard our reactions to the noise of the crash. If they were still close, they could probably hear us now. Suspecting they had no transport, Mucius sent vigiles running towards Rome in the hope of catching them. But if the fugitives, on foot but with a good head start, managed to cross the river, they could vanish into city boltholes, splitting up in all directions.

'It's those Farcicals! I should have arrested the whole bunch when I had the chance!'

'Why didn't you?' snarled somebody, one of the group who worked with Davos. They were all angry. Some must have known Philocrates. They may not have liked him, but they hated how he died.

'No proof, son.'

'It's the farce-fuddlers for sure,' Atticus ranted. 'Who had left the wake before them? Only the aedile and his wife. They never did this.'

'Who else?' Ariminius agreed. 'This was the hay-in-their hair mummers. They will look pretty obvious, even to a bunch of firemen – they still had their hairy loincloths on.'

They might have thrown away their masks as they escaped, but he was right about their distinctive costumes.

'I'll nab them.' Mucius had pent-up tension of his own. 'Rome will have no hiding place. I'll batter it out of them: what they had against Chremes and Phrygia and this poor swine, how they did it, why they did it—'

I had to interrupt. 'Mucius, my friend, I fear you are right. But be careful. No witness has ever seen any of the Farcicals carry out these murders. The so-called undertaker is clever. Even with this incident, those involved can argue, exactly as in the play they are referencing, that a group of robbers blocked the road, then ambushed and killed the traveller.'

'What play?'

'*Oedipus Rex*. Sophocles, Mucius. The first account of King Laius dying.'

Simo, the youthful red-haired actor, stepped up to reinforce me. 'Playwright's ruse,' he explained to the vigilis. 'Suspense. All seems a coincidence until more facts emerge, so Oedipus and the audience slowly absorb the grim truth of what he has done. Philocrates would have known the lines. I can't do it as well as him – I heard him, and the man was truly great – but this is it.'

Simo stood on the road above the two dead men: the actor, with his driver now laid alongside him. Raising his voice just enough, Simo pronounced from memory the plain speech when Oedipus confesses how an everyday travel incident went fatally wrong:

I met a herald and a horse-drawn carriage, with a man inside. The guide tried to force me off the road and the old man, too, involved himself in the argument. In a rage, I lashed out at the driver, who was shoving me aside. The old man, seeing me walking past his carriage, kept an eye on me; with his double whip he struck me on the head, right here on the crown. Well, I gave him back as good as I got; I hit him a rapid blow with my staff that knocked him from his carriage to the road. He lay there on his back. Then I killed them all.

For a moment we all stood in silence as if this were a solemn epitaph for Philocrates, right at the place where he had died.

'In the play, the robbery is just a tale,' Pardicus pointed out quietly. 'But things have been stolen here. Look at his feet.'

He was right. Those small, neat feet were bare. Even though they must have run a risk in delaying for it, his killers had taken the actor's soft, pale leather boots.

36

Exhausted and stunned, Tiberius and I decided to leave. There was nothing we could do, not at midnight, here on the wrong side of the river. Suedius was taking away the bodies, gloating over the extra work.

Everyone had arrived from the necropolis. Men began sorting out their transportation, rocking a big litter to free it, pulling apart chairs that had been locked together in the barricade. Thalia's people retrieved their wagon, easing the agitated beasts back onto the road. Beside the footpath, Mucius piled together the wrecked *carruca* parts, which he rapidly inspected for clues. Then, none found, he stomped off through the mist towards Rome.

Unless some major fire required his troops, they would keep searching all night. Mucius had told me he intended not only to find the Farcicals but to arrest everyone who had given them alibis. 'Bloody wives and mothers, lying for them – they'd better come clean now!' He was looking forward to a day of high-pressure 'interviews'. He spoke as if he intended to get physical.

We stumbled back up the hill to my family's villa, with Tiberius carrying the lantern that Dromo was too tired to lift. Next morning, we awoke in that quiet family home. Ancient slaves who had worked there for decades had crept in silently to leave us a brazier, warm water and towels, sweet drinks and titbits. Father had let staff stay on here after Geminus died; he said it was for security, but it gave them a home, and he kept a clear conscience.

The unhurried ambience distanced us from last night's funeral and its frenetic end, yet we felt sluggish. We grabbed the drinks and nibbles but huddled back under the bed-covers, talking. Although the farce-players seemed to have condemned themselves, we had no feeling that the case was closed. First, Mucius had to catch them. Then many questions still remained.

'I still cannot see them all being involved. Some, yes – but how much did the others know about?'

'Whether it's one or all,' mused Tiberius, 'these killings are hysterical in cause. The perpetrators won't stop.'

'Do we trust Mucius to find them?'

'I think he is doing all anyone can.'

I sighed. 'And I think the killers will be thrilled that he's their pursuer, not somebody with more resources and clout. If I was them, I'd have another attempt at once, to show I was laughing at him.'

Tiberius coughed, hoarse after spending last night outside. 'Yes, I can imagine you doing that!'

I dug him in the ribs. Teasing was good for me, but I had no time to enjoy it today. 'There are plenty of deadly plots from plays,' I pointed out. 'The average Roman audience is never squeamish.' I came up with a list: 'Hercules burned to death, Attis castrated – I can tell you, no one in my family ever goes to watch that. There's a Didius relative who is thought to have mimicked Attis in the Cybele cult! Uncle Fulvius – we don't talk about him. He lives in Alexandria.'

Tiberius winced. 'Castrated? Alexandria is probably the best place for him. A criminal named Meniscus had to dress up as Hercules,' he recalled. 'I don't know why ever he was set on fire. That's utterly wrong. Hercules died of a poisoned love potion.'

'Fine in a myth. Poison takes too long in theatre,' I explained cynically.

'Poison is good for an actor, though. Philocrates would have enjoyed himself, staggering about and groaning. Poor man.' Tiberius sounded sad, but went on considering ways in which somebody might die onstage. 'There's a play where a captured Sicilian bandit king called Selurus ends up on a fake Mount Etna. They make the volcano collapse, dropping him into a cage of real wild animals. Normally bears, I believe.'

'Give a crowd bears and blood, then they're happy! Wasn't there also an occasion when some condemned man had to impersonate Orpheus until bears got him?' It was my turn to criticise the adaptation: 'I suppose letting women tear Orpheus to pieces, like maenads in the original Greek, would have been too gross – you Roman men don't like even a suggestion that women might get so drunk they run wild.'

'I am totally opposed to unlicensed frenzy!' agreed Tiberius, faking piety. He had told me off once for drinking – though he had not known me well at the time. My story was that I was hoping for clues from my wine-buddies, just as he, recently, had become overwhelmed at a vigiles Saturnalia party and called it a public-relations effort.

'Stick with me, nervous husband. I shall teach you to enjoy Bacchic horror. Bears make decent substitutes. Horrible killing. Bloody. Very popular.'

'Very fast!'

'Regulars on the Roman stage – someone produced a play about Daedalus. They had him attempting to fly, until his costume wings broke and he, too, fell into a pit of bears. Is some gritty theatrical agent promoting a group of ursine clients? My father told a tasteless story about a previous Daedalus being dropped out of his harness so he landed very close to the Emperor Nero and splattered him with blood.'

Tiberius cringed. 'These are good myths being mangled by idiots. Historically, Daedalus survived. It was his heedless young son who flew too near the sun, so his wing-wax melted. The *Orpheus* production was an even worse travesty. I actually saw that. It was the opening of the Flavian Amphitheatre, where – good heavens – one would have expected higher adaptation standards!' Again he was only pretending to be pompous, though he was truly obsessed with accuracy. 'The whole point of Orpheus is that his exquisite music *tamed* wild beasts! Animals should have been sitting to listen. *That* would have been a real spectacle.'

'Hard to train them, love.'

'Yes, but any pointless skewing of a decent fable so annoys me.'

I chortled. 'I married a literalist! There were jokes about the amphitheatre's Orpheus being such a terrible musician he annoyed the bear. But I feel sorry for the man. If you were stuck on a stage atop a wobbling rocky outcrop, with thousands of spectators waiting to see you torn to pieces, your hand might well falter on your lyre. I suppose,' I mused, 'for a man who has been doomed to die, there can be no difference between a stylised death in a theatre or being chewed by arena lions. Why cooperate, though?' I myself supplied an answer: 'Hope of fame. We do know about Meniscus as Hercules and Selurus in the bear pit. You won't forget that Orpheus. People convince themselves that being remembered is important.'

'Do you think it is?' asked Tiberius.

'I'd rather be remembered for the life I'd led than an episode when I died.'

He nodded.

All the actions we had been discussing were deliberately sensational. To us, bloody representations onstage debased the intellectual purpose of drama.

The house remained quiet, so Tiberius and I made no haste to leave our bed. We grew even more serious as we discussed what Sophocles had meant in his *Oedipus* play. Even those two vigiles at the Theatre of Balbus had debated this, when they were talking about Phrygia: *'Our officer will say we have to find out whether this woman really had offended the gods. If so, what was her bad action, was it fated, or a tragic flaw in her character? And the key question, could she have avoided it?'*

In *Oedipus Rex*, by decree of the gods, humans faced undeserved suffering. The audience first had to decide if it was fair. Then, could the ancient characters avoid their prophesied fates? The play was clear: there was no point in trying. Attempts failed; they had no escape. Tragedy was inevitable. Nor was there any suggestion of participants being punished for a specific fault. What had Laius and Jocasta ever done to produce a son who, however hard everyone tried to prevent it, would destroy them all?

Tiberius felt it would be wrong to assume that no moral obligation follows. When Oedipus finally blinds himself with Jocasta's brooches, then sets off to wander the world, he takes responsibility for his unwitting patricide and incest. That is the hopeless pain of the human condition. His acceptance of what he has done makes him heroic; his tragedy feels greater to us because of his remorse.

None of that applied in the kind of brutal Roman theatre where the blood was real and punishment literal. Killers would feel no remorse for the deaths I was investigating; there was no justification for the madness behind them. None of this was prophesied by gods; humans devised it.

All three murders were shocking. They were clearly meant to have a harrowing effect on anyone who came to the scene, an effect that would linger with them. But the aim was not to engender understanding of the human condition. Chremes and Phrygia, and now Philocrates, had all aroused some entirely human jealousy. Their deaths were simple revenge. It came from moral emptiness. And Tiberius was right: now the grim pageant had begun, these perverted acts would continue until someone intervened.

Me.

It was time to rise. First scratching paws announced the arrival of Barley, who raced in and bounded onto our bed for licking and nudging activity. She was followed by Gaius and Lucius, running to find us, with cold faces and icy little hands and feet.

'We went outside. We went everywhere here – a man who tidies the garden showed us. They have a bath-house where a dead body of somebody murdered was once found under the floor! That's horrible. I'm not going in there. I'll stay dirty.'

'And we saw a tomb for a *dog*!'

'It's the memorial for an old man who lived here. He has his big stone that says you can't build on the ground, not ever, then a little notice says a dog is there too!'

I smiled. '*Nux, best and happiest of dogs, run with joy through all Elysium, dear friend.*' Family pet. My soppy father must finally have cracked and given her a plaque, after promising for a long time.

Tiny bone fragments of a stillborn baby were buried in the same place, but Falco had had his priorities: the lost child, who would have been my brother, had had his name there from the start. This was a house where my family had had happy times, but we brought our sorrows sometimes.

'You *know*!'

'Albia knows everything,' declared Tiberius, smiling.

'Did you know that dog, the dog called Nux?'

'Yes, I knew Nux.'

'He has a little picture carved, looking all cheerful and wagging his curly tail. And there are three stars. That must show he's running in the sky.'

Nux was a girl dog, in fact. Crazy, brave, devoted, fun-loving and bursting with character. To those of us who had loved her, even as a pet she deserved a memorial. I had often taken her for walks. I'd done a lot of thinking in the company of Nux. I liked to imagine she was racing around the heavens in perpetuity, cheekily nipping the extremities of any constellations she found in her way.

'It's just a dog.'

'No, Gaius. I won't have you say that, darling. She was precious to her family. Nux was never just a dog.'

37

Work then.

The aedile's wife was not at all as I expected. Seen from a distance at the funeral, with her head veiled religiously, she could have been any age. Up close in a salon – her domain, a more comfortable room than where we had dined with him – she was obviously older than her husband, if only by a few years. This is rare, except where money has a significant place in the arrangement. Her problem, I soon deduced, was that they both brought financial substance to the marriage, so he had no particular need to be grateful. It had left her floating spare.

I had the impression there were no children, so Sabina Gallitta would probably now have none. Yet she was bright-eyed and intelligent, not beautiful but well-kept, a pleasant, cultured woman who wanted something to do. In so far as she was an asset in a magistrate's portfolio, she deserved better than to be neglected while he led the public life. She had energy; she wanted interests to pursue. Hence Philocrates.

Sabina Gallitta presumably knew that her patronage of an actor had damned her socially. I felt that she had weighed up the situation then, whatever the cost in reputation, she doggedly went ahead. She did, genuinely, enjoy the theatre. Her husband was, frankly, not that way inclined.

Although a sexual element presumably featured, I decided it had not formed the core of her relationship with the actor. Dear gods, I had a horrible feeling she and he might have been proper friends. After all, that was what Scribonius had called Philocrates. So the scandalmongers must be wrong – which offered an interesting situation to an informer. Friendship, that luxury some of us treasure in secret, almost never features in cases.

It had fallen to me to bring the news that Philocrates was dead. I arrived with Tiberius, but he went to tell Scribonius in his study. We deliberately split up, to observe how each spouse reacted on their own.

After I met the wife, I was glad I had given her privacy for her first response to the news. Him too: having met him, I expected he would gloat when he realised the *Oedipus Rex* warning nailed to his door had not been aimed at him. To be fair, relief would be natural. Let him enjoy it, before he considered the tragedy's impact and how his wife might harbour mixed emotions. Her husband survived, but she had lost a friend. Perhaps the friend meant more to her.

I had suggested that Tiberius might urge his colleague to show understanding for his wife's loss. A tragedy can sometimes kick-start new possibilities in a marriage, even kindness. Tiberius was very willing; privately, although it was my own idea, I was more cynical. I suspected that Sabina grieving would more likely drive the couple further apart. *He* might think that, with Philocrates dead, she ought to have more time for him. *She* might ask that age-old question: what was the point of anything?

According to strict informing rites, I had to consider whether Scribonius Attica himself had wanted Philocrates removed from his domestic sphere. Might he have arranged the accident? To me, only a mindless purist would pursue this. Sometimes you don't bother. With the third death in a series that were so clearly part of a special pattern, I saw no point.

On arrival, I was led to the salon, where I broke the news without fuss. Sabina Gallitta had been waiting, already on edge. It was reminiscent of Phrygia wondering what had happened to Chremes. Philocrates had not come to their house last night, as Sabina had been expecting. Her position must have been rather tricky. I could tell that sometimes his attentions had been fickle and that she did not argue – perhaps she had never felt she *could* argue. She might have been anxious when he failed to show, but he led his own life. If he had met someone at the funeral after she and Scribonius left, Philocrates would have felt no obligation to visit that night, nor any need to explain. His absence might have been as simple as him going for a drink with the musician, Plotinus, or other old acquaintances – though on past form it might very likely have involved a woman.

Whatever she might have preferred, Sabina Gallitta had remained the wife of a magistrate. Now she was stuck with her role. Matronly status might provide some comfort; I suspected not. She had jewellery, fine gowns and stoles, properties to stay at – although I reckoned she might never return to that villa in the Alban hills. And would she ever want to go to the theatre again? Her future looked solitary, at best.

On being first told what had happened, she asked me to excuse her, then quickly left the room. I remained in the company of a set of maids who had been with her, all pretending to do nothing in particular. None of the chaperones followed Sabina. We sat in silence. I had a comfortable high-backed armchair, where I reflected on how I would not employ people simply to pretend to do nothing while occupying other comfortable chairs . . . Then it struck me that leaving the room abruptly like that was what my mother would have done.

Time passed. I was about to go in search of Sabina, when she quietly returned. Any tears had been dried. As we would have done with my mother, we all pretended not to know she was upset.

I explained again that I was here not only as wife to Manlius Faustus, her husband's colleague, but because I was investigating the deaths, all three of them. This soon led to Sabina telling me that as well as knowing Philocrates, at the time when plays for the Games had been under discussion, she had met Phrygia.

'Please tell me what you thought,' I said. 'I know only what I have been told by people who had worked with her, some for many years. They are all fiercely loyal.'

'I can believe it.' Sabina spoke calmly. I could see her working out how to give me a dependable portrait. 'Phrygia was colourful, very much so. Intelligent, realistic, extremely hardworking, one could see. Very knowledgeable about drama. We met only briefly but I enjoyed talking to her. I would have liked to talk with her again, had it been possible.'

'She had been a fine actress in her time, I believe. And Philocrates knew her?'

'Yes. That was how everything came about. He had heard the company was in Rome, auditioning for the Games. When he went to see them one evening, he took me along out of interest. Chremes was not there that night, but I met some of the actors. Phrygia told Philocrates they were thinking of offering *Rudens*, that play with the tug-of-war—'

'The script that does not have a tug-of-war!'

We laughed gently. She clearly knew the work.

Sabina went on, 'Philocrates immediately told Phrygia to drop that idea. If she could find something better, he would act in it. He would enjoy working with them again – at least, this once. He wasn't intending to rejoin the company permanently on their travels. He liked his life in Rome too much. If he was associated with the project, given his wonderful reputation, they might stand more chance of being chosen for the official programme. Together they came up with *Miles Gloriosus* to be the play, with Philocrates taking the main part.'

'Ah!' I said, in some surprise. 'I was under the impression it was you who made those suggestions?'

'Oh, no! I would never have presumed.' Though surprised, I thought Sabina sounded genuine.

'You did not try to influence your husband?'

Sabina looked even more shocked. 'Good heavens, no!'

'So, if you thought that would be improper, how did Scribonius Attica become involved?'

'He is an aedile. The aediles were supervising the programme.'

It would not have helped to insist that my Tiberius had been lumbered with most of the work, while his colleagues sat back. However, this was a bright woman. A sense of what I was thinking must have reached her. 'Oh, I am so sorry, Flavia Albia, I had forgotten you know all about that through Faustus. Anyway, later at dinner here, Philocrates put his suggestion to my husband – he gave a few lines of the blustering soldier to illustrate. Scribonius agreed it sounded marvellous. He did ask my opinion, although he committed himself of his own accord. My husband knows little about contemporary theatre but he has a very sharp eye for what will attract public recognition.'

Of course he did. He had put himself on a trajectory to become a consul. He was thirty-six; if he won the post 'in his year', that would be at forty. Not much time left for creating city-wide popularity and imperial interest. This must have looked ideal. The actor had wanted a chance to show off, while the politician would be linked to a public success at a key festival. It cannot have mattered to him that everyone assumed it was a set-up, because his wife had taken a lover and *she* was the pushy one. (If she really had been, might he have felt differently? I thought probably he would.)

I thanked her for clarifying. Then I wondered yet again who might have been so outraged by the choice of play that they wanted extreme, very violent revenge. 'Sabina, I hope it won't upset you if I mention a conversation I had with Philocrates yesterday.' It must have been one of the last conversations he had had with anyone. A feebler woman might have found that chilling. 'I had already learned from a witness that someone Chremes and Phrygia had previously worked with had caused trouble with them about the choice of play. Philocrates knew that person. He didn't want to discuss it at the funeral but promised me further words on the subject. Sadly, that cannot now happen.'

'Was he killed to stop him talking?' Sabina demanded at once.

'No. I believe he was killed in the same wicked plan that took Chremes and Phrygia. Starring in *Miles Gloriosus* was his downfall. Possibly the killers also know, as you have told me, that Philocrates had influenced the final choice of play.'

'If I had thought it would be the end of him, I would never have let him do it!'

'Could you really have stopped him? Don't blame yourself,' I warned her. 'Pyrgopolynices is a fabulous part for an actor of his standing.' I surprised myself by remembering the protagonist's name. 'Philocrates knew the play well and wanted to perform in it with his old colleagues. It was the correct choice, it was a successful event – anybody reasonable would accept that. No one could have foreseen where it would end.'

Sabina wrapped her stole around her shoulders more tightly. She seemed unable to gain any warmth; she was twisting the fine material so much it had dragged her bracelet, leaving a long red mark on her arm. 'Are the people who arranged these deaths completely mad?'

'Anyone normal must think so.' I sighed. 'Sadly, to such murderers, their crimes often seem reasonable. They are convinced they are victims of terrible injustice. Driven by that folly, they believe their actions are justified in return for pain they themselves have suffered. Unfortunately, they lack normal human sympathies. Their absence of feeling makes them capable of truly shocking acts. What choice do they have, they think. They feel nothing for their victims, who to them are less than human.'

'They are very arrogant and very dangerous.' Sabina Gallitta could listen to an argument, absorb its implications, then understand very quickly. 'My husband is sure to decide that if the *Oedipus* play was aimed at Philocrates, no risk threatens him. But is it true?'

She was too intelligent for bland reassurance, so I was blunt. 'The situation remains extremely volatile. Until the authorities have rounded up all their suspects, Scribonius Attica must take care.'

'He won't!'

'Then you must ensure precautions are taken for him.'

'Yes!' Sabina was firm. As a wife she was not downtrodden. In fairness to Scribonius, he probably would not have wanted her different. 'I shall keep him at home as much as possible. He will always have somebody with him.' She smiled ruefully. 'And, if I can, I shall even make him stop sounding off about the perpetrators' insane wickedness and how society must impose rigorous penalties.'

I answered her in similar wry terms. 'You understand! We are dealing with madmen, who are looking for excuses to do worse. Even while they are on the run, they will be clever and cruel enough to commit more crimes. They will feed off public comment. No one should be issuing challenges to them.'

'Try telling that to a magistrate!'

'I just treat mine as a husband,' I replied.

'You are very new to marriage,' commented Sabina Gallitta.

38

I returned to whether Philocrates had ever mentioned a potential trouble-maker. Sabina Gallitta said he was delighted with his part, and since the play was so successful, there had been no further conversation about the change to *Miles Gloriosus*. If someone had made complaints, Philocrates had never mentioned it.

She made me promise to find his killer; she would pay expenses. I told her where I would be if, once she had brooded about last night's events, she wanted to talk. She decided to take responsibility for Philocrates's funeral. She and her husband would normally patronise a different company, so she would send to have the body taken away from Suedius by their own mortician.

I mentioned that if Philocrates had left personal property at their house, Sabina should find boots for him to be buried in; I had to explain why. That was when Sabina broke down and, this time, cried openly in front of me. Apparently, he had loved the pair the murderers had stolen from his corpse; he wore those boots most of the time. I wondered whether Sabina had bought them for him, though she did not say so. I made no rash promise to find them, though if they had been taken as a trophy by his killers, those boots might eventually turn up.

As Tiberius and I left the house, we compared notes quickly. He said Scribonius had reacted as expected, telling the same story as Sabina about how the play was chosen. His acquaintance with Philocrates had been more distant than hers, so he had nothing to add about the actor's past contacts.

Tiberius was heading back to the villa on the Janiculan before any nervous little souls panicked again at our absence. I faced a long day of enquiries on my own. I wanted to speak to Davos and Thalia, and to Chremes and Phrygia's actors; I needed to pin down everyone from that old Syrian tour, starting with the musician Plotinus who had spoken with Philocrates last night. I had asked questions of some at the funeral, but now I must press much harder. Somebody knew who the killer was and I could see no reason for them to keep quiet. The shock of Philocrates's death might shake out more memories.

One situation niggled me: I could have written to my parents about all this. I was feeling reluctant, in case they crowded into my investigation. They would call my attitude childish. If you feel the same, don't bother saying so. Sometimes dodging parental interest is entirely justified. I hadn't mentioned men I passionately longed for when I was fifteen, and now I wasn't going to mention that I was working a case among people from their adventures before they met me.

On the other hand, I would look stupid and I would blame myself if as soon as Helena and Falco heard what had been happening they snapped back that the killer must be the grumbling one-armed pan pipes player who had always had it in for people. They would remember if some crack-brain with a grievance had been left behind in Syria, perhaps locked up at the time to prevent dangerous behaviour, ranting that he would be revenged on the whole pack of them . . .

I had a bad thought. Was it possible the undertaker killer had my own parents on his list of enemies? If so, what blood-stained play would he choose for Falco and Helena? If I saw any hint of danger to them, I would certainly contact them. If only they were not people who, the moment a dire warning was issued, immediately rushed towards the risk. My liberal mother would want to chastise and reform this killer, explaining how he was letting himself down. My hot-headed father would give him the works more physically.

I needed to tell them. First, however, I ducked the issue one more time and instead checked progress with the vigiles.

The Seventh Cohort's main barracks was the same as them all. It had courtyards crammed with equipment for dealing with fires: tools such as ropes, mats and buckets, which their part-time torturer could also use in inventive ways on prisoners who stubbornly claimed innocence of crimes. Some people in their sights got off. Master criminals wriggled out of trouble by not bothering to turn up. They sent their bribes instead, suitably matched to the scale of their lawbreaking, carried in neatly tied packages by fast-talking lawyers who arrived in fancy litters and later left smirking. Lower down the social order, landlords who failed to build regulation fire-porches were treated with jovial banter, because they always brought contributions for the widows' and orphans' fund.

I may have given the impression this barracks was a haven of corruption and cruelty. What else can be expected from a cohort of ex-slaves who are spat on while trying to rescue babies from house fires and jeered at as they extinguish conflagrations in the warehouses of rich men, who will only complain about having their valuables singed? Ex-slaves, moreover, who are led by ex-soldiers who have probably failed to win medals in the legions, plus flawed tribunes who daydream of becoming Praetorian Guards with double pay and really serious thrashing rights. Ex-slaves who risk serious injury every day.

The Seventh had a particularly bad reputation among people I knew. Since this cohort looked after all the monuments and swanky homes in the Ninth District, I could see why they were bitter. The Campus Martius must be a trial. On top of that, their outstation sat in the dangerous Transtiberina badlands, yet so long as the road down the north bank to the port was kept free-running, nobody in the city ever cared.

Their working term was six years. The potential reward was citizenship. Along the way some died, many broke bones, most acquired bad burns, one or two drowned in the river, were run over or had fatal falls from ladders, and a few went screwy with breakdowns. The fabled fund for widows was a cash conduit for their officers.

I dealt with the vigiles in my work and was used to entering their barracks, but I always did so very carefully.

Today, grey skies prophesied unhappiness. A cold wind and fine mizzle moulded my garments to me in a way I would have preferred to avoid as I banged on the great double gates and asked if Mucius was at home, please. After jokes about did I want his mother to let him out to play, I was told he was busy, so (leer) did I want to come inside? I should have brought a chaperone. It was too late by the time I thought of it. Still, if these men were going to assault me, they would assault a chaperone as well. Litter was bowling past. So much road dust was stinging me that I made a feeble attempt to pretend my husband was close on my heels, then scuttled in to take shelter. The Seventh were so impressed at capturing a lone woman they behaved quite nicely.

'That's a pretty necklace, Flavia Albia.'

'Not for sale, boys. Does Mucius keep his office in the left colonnade or the right? Or shall I just holler for him?'

They would escort me. It hardly required twelve of them jostling. I could have managed by myself. Nobody needs a roadmap in a station-house. They are all similarly laid out. I could have opened a few suitable doors and found the right place, though since this was the cohort's main barracks I was wary of accidentally picking the tribune's office. He was bound to be half asleep, while he ate a breakfast sausage and dictated the day's charge sheet to send to their duty praetor. He'd have me marched off the premises – if I was lucky.

It turned out I could not avoid him, because he and Mucius were together, talking tactics, or what passed for that here. They were in the investigator's bunk-hole so Mucius, with his tight porridge-coloured curls, had his bunions resting on the clerk's table. The browbeaten clerk was squatting on a stool, polishing Mucius's boots, which were off his feet. The tribune was eating Mucius's breakfast: more flatbreads, clearly the only thing he knew how to order.

'Must be where that woman did herself in – you know, the one who finished off her two snotty infants. Boyfriend had left her. What did she expect? That's what boyfriends do.'

'She should have got herself a pet goose for company,' Mucius agreed, staring at his vanishing snack with unhappy resignation. I could not tell whether he meant get a pet instead of a boyfriend or after he'd left.

The tribune was still having a go at her. 'I never understand why those stupid women have to kill the children too. It must be vindictive, so the man loses his heirs.'

'Suicide,' replied Mucius, shrugging off the whole affair. 'Passed me by. No case to answer, no one to punish. I don't get involved with crap like that. I heard about it – wasn't there a lot of blood? So, you think it's her place?'

'Could be. Better ask the lads who went after she croaked. They will remember – as you say, there was blood painted around everywhere. I had to give Hirtius a chit for the doc; he was a wreck.'

'Hyro,' Mucius corrected him.

The tribune ignored him. 'Check it out if you think it's relevant, though I don't see why the putrid fart it should be . . . Who the fart is this?'

Apart from a snappy haircut and the way he talked, there would have been no way to tell this was the tribune, except that I had seen him before. That stopped me asking who the fart *he* was. Restraint seemed a good idea. 'Morning, sir.' Always call them 'sir'. They will be nonplussed. 'My name is Albia, Flavia Albia. We met before. When Ursus, your man in the Transtiberina, arrested the mass murderer at the Trigeminal Gate,' I reminded him, as a courtesy. You have to look after them; all of them are inept.

He looked blank. That must have been the cohort's most significant collar for decades, and only happened a few weeks ago. Juno!

I helped him out again. 'The night he pinched your mule, sir.'

'Oh! That bloody night. That was you hanging about, was it?' Attending the arrest had seemed fair. It was me, after all, who had found the vital clue that, after we travelled to its hiding spot on the tribune's mule, finally led the other investigator, Ursus, to his arrest of a long-term killer. The tribune sniffed noisily, tucked the last flatbread into his belt, then left us. He swung out, saying to Mucius, 'I'll leave you to it. Don't let this woman near my bloody mule.'

I waited until he would be out of hearing. 'You've found yourselves a charmer there.'

'Pride of the tribunate,' agreed Mucius. He licked his middle finger and glumly picked up on its tip the few tiny crumbs his superior had left him.

'I noticed how his mother has taught him to speak nicely. Poor woman must have brought him up single-handed. I assume she never knew who his father was.'

Mucius eyed me thoughtfully as he admired the demure way in which I had called the pride of the tribunate a bastard.

39

He gave up on the crumbs. He looked so dispirited, I wished I had brought him in a stuffed vine leaf. 'I'm glad you've come, Flavia. I'm being buggered around by women, who act as if it's all a big joke. I'll let you take a shot at them, while I'm planning strategy.'

Strategy sounded sophisticated. I gathered he did not look forward to quizzing a bunch of local women.

'Mucius, you old-fashioned turnip, you suppose they will respond to a female?'

'Just help me out, now you're here, will you? They came in giggling like shrimp girls. Tell them it's serious. If they won't talk to you, it will have to be the usual persuasion – and I'm not meaning thumbscrews.'

He was not meaning a glass of borage tea and an almond tart either. If it came to a hardcore interrogation, I would not stay to watch – and I could see even he was nervous. He caught my expression. 'There's enough horrible acts already, in our causes of death! Crucifixion, heavyweight goring, traffic rage – what's next?'

'Mucius, I hope we never find out.'

'Too right. Grab me some clues then. Wring these chickens' necks if you have to, but make the ditsy darlings tell us something.'

Mucius took me to the witnesses, or suspects, as he was

calling them. As we emerged, the men who first admitted me reappeared in the colonnades, eager to carry out more jostling. Seeing Mucius, they evaporated.

The barracks was cold. I had the impression its grey walls ran with moisture. I could have imagined old cries of suspects' pain, though at mid-morning it was almost silent. The dayshift were out annoying the public, while any men from the nightshift who were upstairs in the crude dormitories would be dead asleep.

'You never pinched his mule?' marvelled Mucius, as we walked along to the end of a dank cloister.

'Not me. I wasn't to know it existed. Ursus borrowed it. I just went along on a ride to a shrine and back.'

'I didn't know Ursus was religious! The tribune loves that mule. Really loves it!'

'Don't tell me any more, Mucius. I've had enough bestiality with the aurochs.'

'Was that bestiality? I thought he raped her.'

'Now you're being surreal.'

'What?'

'Never mind. So, what prizes have your fellows picked up?'

'Three stroppy wives – two legit, one adulterous – one mouthy mother.'

'Any of the Farcicals?'

'Just that red-faced lump who thwacks the tambourine. She won't know anything.'

I thought she might know everything, but I kept that to myself.

Before he let them out of the cold, unlit cell that was supposed to make them submissive, Mucius collected a large long-handled mallet. He picked it out carefully from a store. It might have been more effective to let the victims watch his sinister choice-making, but his grip on the implement offered plenty of threat.

'You'd better not use that thing.'

'Watch me, girl!' Mucius bared his teeth and abruptly swung the mallet. He was practising what in butchery would have been a stun blow.

He had the far-from-contrite women pulled out into the courtyard by the men acting as guards. Scruff-of-the-neck methodology: it reminded me of porters grabbing at sheep in a cattle auction.

Their cell had been a small one. They had been there half the night and most of the morning with no facilities. They all tumbled into the light and air, stridently complaining. The barracks must have a latrine but, not being offered it, the five women found a fire bucket for themselves then formed a modesty circle while they desperately used it. Hot pee, expelled at force, zinged into the metalwork. Passing vigiles cheered. The women chose who had next turn, using a sisterly regard for age and other causes of urgency.

Once every bladder was empty, they milled around Mucius, demanding breakfast; he said to forget it. He tried to round them up for interrogation, but none of them listened. One cooed derisively, 'What a lovely mallet!' I hid a grin.

They walked off and took drinks from a fountain basin. All washed their faces, for which they organised a different bucket, afterwards drying themselves on their drapery while loudly deploring the fact the vigiles produced no towels. They seemed to view the station-house as a travellers' mansio, one they would not recommend to friends.

While they went on with their ablutions, apparently with no idea that a harrowing probe was imminent, I watched. I was assessing how well they knew one another and what mood they were in. They had certainly known intimate facts about each other's waterworks.

I could detect no anxiety that their men were suspected of murder. I saw little fear for themselves. These women looked tough but had probably never been in a station-house before, not even to report a lost kitten. If someone stole their purse in a market mêlée, they must either regard it as life's unavoidable misery or, if they recognised the thief, they would send a large cousin to duff him up and get the money back. Might they act for themselves? If they noticed a crime in process, I thought them all capable of thumping the side of a thief's head so hard they burst his eardrum.

'Can we talk to them singly, Mucius? Any chance of segregation?'

'This is a fire-station. We don't have an audience chamber.'

'What about your office? Can't that be a grilling box?'

'My scribe's in there.'

'Chuck him out, then!'

'No fear. He's got his work to do. I wouldn't dare to stop him. He's a terror – he runs this place. And don't say let's use the tribune's nook.'

'Why not?'

'He doesn't let anybody in. When he goes out, he locks it.'

'Juno and Minerva! Where did you get such a weird one?'

'We think he's shy.'

'Sounds like he's picking his nose in there.' Or worse, I thought. 'Fix them up with a bench,' I told Mucius, quietly despairing. 'This is chaotic. I can't have them drifting all over the place.'

The women were taking the opportunity to look around, freely going in and out of storerooms and picking up tools. I could see a couple over by the siphon engine; any moment now they would be climbing aboard and pretending to spray water around. Other prisoners called out to them, crude invitations. Vigiles in the vicinity came to stare, as if they had never met a female before. Once they plucked up courage to speak to these beauties, all hope of control would be lost.

In an ideal world, you avoid a group interrogation. If it must be done, you are organised. You gather your suspects in a room of modest proportions, where there is carefully spaced furniture upon which they can install themselves in casual poses. You place yourself at the focal point. An antique candelabrum illuminates your noble countenance. They fall silent. You speak without notes. You run through events, astounding these stunned people with your detailed research into past incidents, your keen observation of the murder scene, your insider knowledge of how incidents have been carried out, your understanding of human nature and your compassion for people who must have been under intolerable strain. Even the wily culprit now accepts your talent. Beneath your guise of modesty, you have a will of steel and cannot be misled.

This process has customary blips. You may cause a false confession, someone fainting as a distraction, someone else nervously picking at a necklace until the Hercules knot parts so priceless elements spill everywhere. Through this, you steadily proceed. You slap down evidence on a marble-topped demi-lune. Your eager (less intelligent) sidekick puts in a few comments – then the climax: you demonstrate that every baffling clue has clunked into place. You have solved it.

This was not like that. This was real life.

* * *

I pulled out my note-tablet, with its previous list, to help me decide who they all were. Mucius, the nearest I had to a wacky sidekick, stabbed with a finger at my list, then identified individuals, grunting.

'Ambrosia, Ambrosia's mother.' Where Ambrosia was stocky, broad-featured, rosy-cheeked and self-confident, her mother was stocky, broad-featured, rosy-cheeked, self-confident and thirty years older. Wearing similar green gowns, shawls knotted around their midriffs, and end-of-life sandals, they were side by side on the same bench, arms folded. Ignoring Mucius and me, they chuntered away to each other most of the time, as if nothing was happening.

'Megalo's wife.' I had put down Megalo as creaky and surly, but bold. The crone Mucius indicated was the same, peering about intently, though I could tell she was short-sighted. As the oldest in the group, she had been allowed first go with the fire bucket. Of them all, this frowning granny seemed most likely to cause trouble. My notes said that Megalo himself was bald with a long bushy beard. She had a thin, tight topknot and a nasty expression.

'Wife of Questus and his mistress.' The pair? The surprise here was that both women had been brought in, sticking together like old friends. Perhaps they were. I guessed their husbands knew one another. Why should a man go out searching for love among strangers if there is a willing volunteer in his own circle? Grey-clad, sinewy and middle-aged, the two women looked as if they had long working lives behind them. They were probably younger than they looked but would die before their time.

'Septimus is a widower, who lives with two young children,' I called out to the group at large. 'Who has his infants at the moment? And when he goes to rehearsals, who looks after them?'

'He drops them off at our house,' offered the official wife of Questus.

'Did you have them last night?'

'Yes, he was going to a funeral.'

'I know that. We'll come to it. Who is minding them now?'

'Him, it must be. He picked them up again yesterday evening. Same as always.'

'He picked them up?' I was startled. 'When everyone was on the run? Didn't the Farcicals tell you that they were being chased by the vigiles and had to hide from arrest?'

Everyone, even Ambrosia who had been there, looked amazed by this news. Why had she not gone into hiding too? And if Septimus ran to a bolt-hole, did he take his children with him?

Could these women's bafflement be true or was it an act? I pressed for more. I learned that when the Farcicals came back across the river, Septimus had simply picked up his children, a boy and girl, then gone off as if taking them home. Then, although Questus himself failed to appear at home with Septimus, his luckless wife had merely supposed her two-timer had gone off to his other woman. Meanwhile the mistress assumed he was with his wife. 'For once!' Her own husband was becoming a handful about their relationship, so not being lumbered with Questus had been a convenient relief.

'Do you know where's he got to, Flavia Albia?'

'I do not. I want you to suggest what rat-runs these missing men have scampered down.'

No ideas were forthcoming, even though Questus had two women who could have snitched on him. Ought to have dumped him in it, in my opinion. But they were colluding merrily, both keeping him out of trouble.

I moved along the line. Megalo's elderly wife told me she had gone to bed last night at her usual time; she never realised her man had failed to come home from the funeral until she was roused by the vigiles. 'No point bringing me here. I never know where he is. He goes off and doesn't show his face.'

Don't they all? seemed to be the common view.

'There is one woman missing.' I consulted Mucius, turning away and speaking in an undertone. 'Gnaeus had an alibi – what's happened to her? The night Chremes was killed, he said he was at home with his wife.'

Mucius muffled his explanation: 'Gave us a false address. We never found her.'

'Why didn't you tell me before?'

'Happens all the time.' Mucius spoke without prevarication, as far as I could tell. Witnesses giving false information were as much of a trial for him as they were for me. He maundered on dourly: 'We are never sure if the lads have tried the proper address. "By a fountain at the crossroads" could mean any damned fountain and a completely different crossroads. I admit my lads don't use much nous. Half the time while they are knocking like hell on the wrong door, if they just turned around through ninety degrees, they would realise the next fountain along looks a lot more promising. Odds on, the person they have come for is right there, staring off a balcony to see what all the racket is.'

'You paint such a pretty picture of Roman district life! Didn't they ask among the neighbours?'

'As best they could. The house was boarded up with nobody living there. People nearby had heard of this individual, Gnaeus, but he was gone from the address.'

'When?'

'Months ago. Then his wife died. Nobody could say where he did a flit to.'

'To a new wife! He did own up to a second marriage. I seem to remember the others sniggering. The shifty slug will probably pretend he gave his old address automatically, but I bet it wasn't an accident. He is too sharp,' I said. 'He seemed quiet, but that was a front. He has that air of being too clever.'

'Arrogant,' Mucius agreed. 'So he lied. People do that, Flavia Albia.'

'Oh, really?' I took my decision. 'I nominate Gnaeus as top suspect. Others must have helped him carry out the killings, though. It looks as if his helpers are from the drama group. But he will be the mover. He has the significant mind. Cracked, and very, very clever.'

'Prime suspect,' confirmed Mucius. 'Now we only have to find him!'

With one accord, we turned back to our last witness, Ambrosia: the only one present who would know what had happened at the funeral last night, and afterwards when Philocrates was killed. I beckoned her off the bench. Her mother made a move to follow but Mucius stopped her, holding up his hand, palm out. The older woman subsided. I half expected her to shout, 'Don't you tell them nothing!' but she left her daughter to it.

Mucius and I led Ambrosia away to stand beside one of the big water basins. They tended to be in constant use, but at that moment they were deserted. It would have to be our makeshift private spot. I hoped no one started a fire, so the vigiles needed to push us aside and fill buckets.

We settled either side of her and prepared to extract everything she knew.

40

'Now, you be a good girl and tell us the story,' ordered Mucius. He must have thought he was being avuncular. If an uncle like this ever turned up at our house, my mother would send any young children out to play. 'Come clean and be quick about it. Otherwise, I'm going to send your ma to my torturer.'

It was not how I would have begun. 'The officer means,' I told her more gently, 'we know you want to help us, Ambrosia. Your mother isn't implicated, so don't worry about her. But we do think you must know about the dangerous members of your little group.'

Surprisingly, this drew no interest from Ambrosia. Mucius and his threats had at least made her look nervous. She stared back at us, round-mouthed, as if watching acrobatics at a circus.

'Who's your boyfriend?' barked Mucius, abruptly.

'I don't have one,' she answered straight back. The daft woman seemed happier with his crudity than my understanding. She worked on a market stall, after all. She expected aggression.

'Who do you flirt with?' he growled. 'Whose filthy knee have you sat on with his hand up your skirt?'

Before I could protest, Ambrosia supplied details of her past love-life. She had had a short fling with Septimus before his wife died; she had stopped contact rather than become an unpaid nurse for his children. She had tangled with Questus, before he had taken up with his current ladyfriend. He was a nightmare, too indecisive and constantly scared that his wife would find out – which was stupid because she always knew what he was up to. Gnaeus had once made overtures, but Ambrosia had not trusted him. He knew a lot about drama but was too snooty and he could be quite nasty. 'I don't take the men seriously in any case. I only want to sing and dance.'

'Gnaeus!' Mucius, immune to her sweet ambitions, homed in. 'Now you are talking. Give us the gen. How long has this Gnaeus been in your group?'

'About three years.'

'Where did he appear from?'

'I think he met Megalo in a bar. They go in the Winkle sometimes. He's been around; he's been abroad and all. He always says he once acted professionally.'

Pricking up my ears, I checked my notes. 'He told us he now works as a house painter and carries refreshments at the races.'

Ambrosia shrugged. 'You have to take what you can get. The same goes for all of us.'

'Is Gnaeus unhappy with the level of work he has?'

'He moans sometimes.'

'He thinks he deserves better?'

'Oh, he's very sure what he deserves!' exclaimed Ambrosia, tellingly.

Mucius folded his arms and stood off as I took over. 'I know you were all disappointed, but was Gnaeus very upset when Chremes and Phrygia let you down?'

'He was furious.'

'Did he utter threats against them?'

'He said there was no justice. They were half-baked, jumped-up old has-beens who had no consideration for the little man who was struggling to survive. No respect for talent. And no loyalty.'

'What did that mean?'

'Couldn't tell you.'

'Did Gnaeus already know them?'

'He never said so.'

'What did he have to say about Philocrates?'

'Called him an overblown lecher, living off a pretty face that wasn't even pretty any more.'

'No, he looked as if he'd had a broken nose. So Gnaeus did know Philocrates?'

'Well, Philocrates was famous, wasn't he?'

Mucius broke in on my questioning: 'Gnaeus, Septimus, Megalo, Questus . . . Any of them do carpentry?'

'Carpentry?'

'Joinery. Making things with wood.'

Ambrosia was looking vague. I seized back the initiative. 'Tell us about yesterday's funeral. Who suggested the Farcicals should go?'

'Well, you did, Albia.'

'What?' barked Mucius. He glared at me.

I glared right back. 'You mean, Ambrosia, I mentioned where and when the burial was, in case your group wanted to pay respects?'

'Yes, that.'

Mucius careered on at me: 'You told them? Don't you have any idea of procedure, Flavia? You must have led the maniac right to his next location and his next victim.'

'Cobnuts! Mucius, anyone could have found out where the funeral was. That procession crossed the Campus

Martius all the way to the Neronian Bridge. They had actors and musicians prancing, with flutes, trumpets and drums. The whole Ninth District must have come out to watch. Back off, you idiot. I am not your suspect. Now, Ambrosia, I want you to tell me everything. What discussions did you have beforehand? Who supported the idea of performing your scene at the funeral?'

Ambrosia looked defensive. 'After you told us, we just thought going was a good idea. We do funerals. People like a laugh to ease the tension. We often give *The Lupin Seed* – it's highly popular.'

'Was Gnaeus keen?'

'Yes, he liked the idea pretty much.'

'What did he say?'

'He told us it was one way to make Chremes and Phrygia hear us performing.' She had the grace to look embarrassed. 'Even if they had to be dead first. Besides, he said it would look as if we could take a knockback nicely. That we bore no grudges.'

'Really! And what else?'

'This time they couldn't stop us.'

'Sounds as if he did bear a grudge. Anything more?'

'Not that I recall.'

'What did he say about that actor?' Mucius barged in again. 'The one who got the big part because he was whizzling the magistrate's wife?'

'Nothing.' Ambrosia paused. 'Well, that was until we overheard Philocrates and that other man saying horrible things about us. We knew they were doing it deliberately – they wanted us to be upset. Then Gnaeus said it was typical. The actor had always been the same, and it was time somebody dealt with him, the . . . Well, he used a word that isn't nice.'

'I heard the comments,' I told her. 'As you say, they were definitely meant to sting. So Gnaeus did dislike Philocrates? But don't you think driving him off the road and then beating in his brains was overreacting?'

Ambrosia looked shocked, and I suddenly realised no one had given these witnesses any details of what had happened last night. 'Get that,' Mucius said to her. 'Philocrates is dead in an organised road crash. Now the Farcicals are our suspects for it – which lines you all up on my charge sheet for the murders of Chremes and Phrygia as well.'

'We never did that! None of it.'

'Well, let's try to find out.' I struggled to reassert my leadership. 'Describe what happened when you all left the pyre.'

'We had had enough of them all. We went home.'

Mucius gripped my arm painfully. He intended me to give way. He addressed Ambrosia with patronising emphasis: 'Now, listen, darling. In my business, we like to use even the tiniest details. Little facts that don't look important to you will give us the full picture. So I'm going to walk you through this, Ambrosia, my dearie, nice and slowly.'

I shook off his grip though I let him ask his questions.

'You were together by the burning bodies, then you all walked from the burial place to the road – yes?'

'Yes.' Ambrosia looked puzzled.

'You and the men in hairy suits and masks.'

'Yes.'

'You reached the road all together?'

'Yes, of course.'

'Then what? You began walking along the highway towards Rome?'

'Yes. I told you, we were coming home.'

'All of you?'

Ambrosia stared at him for a moment, then understanding came. She squeaked, 'Oh!'

'Oh what, darling?' Mucius asked, cocking his curly head on one side.

'Oh, I see!'

'You see what I mean?'

'Yes, I see what you mean.'

'Spit it out, then.'

'Should I?'

'Best to.' Mucius was now surprisingly patient. 'Come on, woman, let's squeeze some truth out of you!'

'I walked back to Rome with Septimus and Questus. We were together all the way, but just us. Because at the necropolis, Gnaeus and Megalo had hung back. They said they would wait for a fellow they knew, who was still at the funeral. They'd probably go to a bar with him, to end the night with a warm-up drink. For old times.'

'Who was this fellow?'

'They didn't say.'

'No,' said the vigilis. 'I don't suppose they would have done.'

41

To double-check, Mucius asked whether the group Ambrosia walked with had first been involved in moving the litters or the ox cart; she said no. She seemed genuinely surprised to be told about the roadblock. She had not seen it. It must have been created after she and the two men with her had gone up the road. Afterwards, Gnaeus and Megalo, with a third party if they really did intend to meet someone, had killed Philocrates.

'Which of these madmen dabbles in undertaking?' demanded Mucius of Ambrosia.

'I never heard of anybody in our group who does that.' She looked prim. 'It's not a nice job. Wiping corpses' bums and dabbing on their eyeshadow.' Glancing again at my list, I thought scraping the sludge out of catering pots or rat-catching in the Emporium might be worse, but I said nothing.

'Anybody overtake you, Ambrosia?'

'No, the road was deserted all the way. I didn't like it. It felt eerie, especially after a funeral. I was listening out for ghosts screeching after us.'

'Why would they come after you?'

'That necropolis is full of dead Christians. Victims of Nero go screaming about the Vatican Plain, reliving their horrible agonies when he killed them.'

'You think? Do Christians like to haunt people?'

'They have weird ideas. They meet in secret houses and drink blood. One lives near us. She's always talking about peace and love.'

Mucius shivered. 'Peace and love? Good gods, that's outrageous! Give me her address and I'll get on to her . . . Now, forget about those blood-drinking, peace-pushing eastern bastards. Tell us what you did.'

Unassailed by spirits, Ambrosia and her companions had crossed the river into Rome at a steady pace, then gone to the Charybdis. They left their costumes in a chest the landlord always let them use, after they changed back into normal clothes. Septimus rushed off to pick up his children. She went home to Mother.

'What about Questus?' I put in. 'Neither his wife nor his fancy woman ever saw him last night. Where was he? If the infants belonging to Septimus were being minded at his house, wasn't it odd for Questus not to return home at the same time as Septimus?'

Not really, said Ambrosia. Nobody was surprised. There was a waitress at the Charybdis that Questus was also sweet on. The group knew, but not his womenfolk. He had disappeared upstairs with this girl, who was filthy but willing, so rather than face harsh words from both of his other women this morning, most likely he was still up there.

To relieve his feelings, Mucius started making jokes about my notes. 'Questus? What a cheat! You were correct about this individual: "tired" and "jumpy"? I bet he is! Mind you, "bruised from his work" probably means bruised from something else, if he puts his back into bonking! But "scrawny"? I'd say anyone who picks up dinners from three different women is more at risk of running to fat.' He settled down. He was probably jealous.

'Maybe,' I suggested, with nothing to lose from banter, 'Questus is such a dynamic lover that as soon as he comes in through the door they all rip off his tunic and have him on the mattress with no time to eat.'

Mucius looked admiring. 'No dinners, only hectic screwing! You have a fine imagination, Flavia.'

'It's Albia.'

'Who says?'

'I do!'

Flavia was a late addition for bureaucratic reasons when I was being fitted up with formal citizenship. I had always harboured a faint hope that Albia was how my birth-parents in Londinium had known me, a link to them. Of course it was impossible. 'Albia' really came from the cabbage-sellers who picked up a crying baby from the smoking ruins after the Iceni swept through Londinium. If I was wearing a dear little tunic with an embroidered label, the greengrocers dumped it. If I had an amulet around my chubby neck, they sold it. At puberty they would have sold me too, but I ran away. I took nothing of theirs, but I kept my name.

'Don't call me Flavia. I don't need validation from purple-paunched imperial upstarts.'

'Whoa! Hold the treason in my barracks!'

'Mucius, if you haven't even picked up what your collaborator is called, how are you ever going to catch ingeniously devious suspects?'

He gave me a dirty look, while ordering that Ambrosia be locked back in the windowless cell on her own. First, she was to provide any details she knew about where Gnaeus and Megalo had jobs—

'I don't know nothing!'

'Yes, you do.' I was terse, no sympathy now. 'You knew how to find them when I asked for a group meeting.'

Places would be searched, and work colleagues required to provide suggestions of where the fugitives might be hiding. Men were to revisit where Septimus lived. They were to pick up Questus from the Charybdis but, smirked Mucius, no need to bring in the waitress if she was really filthy. He did not want his station-house defiled.

'And what about Gnaeus?' I insisted. 'Where does he hang out with his second wife?'

Ambrosia shook her head; she muttered that Gnaeus was secretive. That fitted. Show me a man with a string of violent deaths behind him, and I'll show you all his acquaintances who admiringly claim, 'He likes to guard his privacy.' You bet he does. It would not surprise me if this man had spent his life moving on whenever he came under threat of discovery. Gnaeus would have a new identity by next week now. If he fitted my pattern, it would be in a new town, maybe a new province.

Mucius must have agreed with me because he went off to knock on the tribune's door to ask permission to send to all the city gates to order soldiers to watch for Gnaeus. Good thinking, although nothing would come of it. As a part-time performer, Gnaeus would not even have to hide in the back of a wagon: he would be capable of disguising his appearance and acting a new part convincingly. Besides, what soldiers at town gates ever bother to read their daily alerts? Even if they do, people trying to enter Rome are the ones they scrutinise. Anyone can leave. Vicious killer, was he? Run him out of town quick. Let some other community suffer him.

'Ambrosia, what was the story with the new wife anyway?' I asked. 'I did notice you all looking sideways at each other, when the subject came up.'

'Oh, it was just sad.' Ambrosia spoke reluctantly. 'When Gnaeus left the first wife, she went and died. It happened not long afterwards. He came in for criticism, that was all.'

'What kind of criticism?'

'Oh, the second woman had a father with money, so people believed her old man paid Gnaeus to live with her after she fell pregnant – at least, she said she was. Gnaeus was moving up in the world, he thought. Trust him to enjoy that. He had been painting their house when he got to know her. Usual thing, you know painters. He would ask for a pannikin of water for colour mixing, then start chatting her up – he did have all the gab. The first wife was very upset when he told her he was going because she had always been good to him. We heard she could be pretty fierce.'

'The first? Who said she was fierce?'

'Well, he did. But we know that when he came to Rome, she gave him a place to live and helped him to find jobs. She supported him when he was down on his luck and destitute. So,' said Ambrosia sadly, 'people thought it was unfair, what he did to that first one, poor woman, leaving her.'

'Did the Farcicals rag him about it?'

'We gave him some banter at first. After the wife died, we dropped that. You have to show pity, don't you? It was his turn to be upset, even if it was his own fault. Mind you,' scoffed Ambrosia, 'Gnaeus is not one to ever take the blame. He is more likely to talk himself out of it. Everything he does is right, according to him. It's other people who do all the wrong. They are the ones who need punishing.'

If Gnaeus really was the undertaker killer, he had demonstrated how he believed punishments should be carried out.

42

While Mucius went to whisper sweet nothings if his tribune was in, I found myself alone. I assumed nothing more would be required of me unless the troops brought in the missing men. I wanted to see that, though I was not prepared to waste all day in this chilly place on the off-chance. I still intended to find Thalia and Davos. Could Davos recall this character, Gnaeus, from his past years of acting with Chremes and Phrygia? Was the man abnormal? Obsessive? Did he bear grudges? Did he have sufficient intelligence and energy to arrange complicated deaths?

I wrapped my cloak tighter and readied myself to leave.

As I looked back across the exercise courtyard, I noticed someone in a patch of dank shadow, halfway along a colonnade. Whoever was there could have been listening for some time. When I stared, they suddenly came into the open. It was Ambrosia's mother, in a bustling strop. 'What is going on about my girl? Why is she being locked up again, all by herself? If anything is done to her, I'll have you – I shall have you all!'

I beckoned her over. Closer to, she reeked of fish pickle and indignation. A potent mix that informers know well. I didn't waste time shuddering. 'Your girl has been involved with some very nasty people. Until it's sorted out, the vigiles want to be sure they know where she is.'

'I heard all about those deaths. The man on the cross and that poor woman with the bull. It was nothing to do with my girl.'

Although she kept calling Ambrosia a girl, by my reckoning she was in her thirties. Time she broke away, I'd say. I was a similar age and I wouldn't want my mother weighing in on my life.

'Well, don't worry. What's your name?'

'Lana.'

'Just be patient, Lana. This is about some terrible crimes. Another man was killed, last night, and the Farcicals were there. That's why you were all brought in this morning. Some of the group may be innocent, but no one is taking any chances. If your daughter knows who the killer is, she may even be safest here.'

'Among a bunch of nasty men? I don't think so!' The mother went into an exaggerated act, gesturing and mouthing her words like a very poor farceur herself: 'Is somebody coming after her? Why would they? She's never done anything to upset him, whoever he is!' Under the posturing, Lana was actually shocked and frightened. 'Why does that stupid man with the curls want to know about all the fellows she has been with?'

'It is no reflection on Ambrosia's character, I am sure,' I said, not believing it. 'But Mucius is convinced she does know the members of her group very well.'

'He's a stupid pervert.' For once, I disagreed. To me, Mucius was far from daft, and he was doing his job. But Ambrosia's mother stuck by what she thought. 'He should leave her alone. That group is her hobby and her life. She is a lovely singer. And she dances beautifully.'

'Of course. Lana, Mucius simply thought she could shed light on the killer's motives, or perhaps help us find the men who ran away last night.' As her mother still looked unconvinced, I added, 'Ambrosia did help. From what she said, we believe that the perpetrators are Gnaeus and Megalo from her group.'

Then Lana surprised me: 'Oh, I hope it's not old Megalo. I had a little fling with him myself!'

I concealed my astonishment. Age is no barrier, or so the elderly tell themselves before their spines lock into spasm. 'How did that come about, Lana?'

'He did a few bits for me, around the house.'

Now I was interested. That suggested hammers and nails. 'A handyman?'

'I've got quite a nice bed that had collapsed. It's the one I use myself – it came when things were easier, years ago. Ambrosia just sleeps on a pallet. I won't have her top and tailing with me. That Megalo put all the pieces of bed back together for me.'

I joked, 'And then you had to test it out?'

'Oh, yes, he thought his luck was in. I knew his game. He had his eye on a bit of money he had heard I kept under the mattress – but, of course, when I knew he was coming, I moved it.'

'Well done, you! Is the bed wooden?' I stuck with my case: 'Did Megalo wear a carpenter's tool-belt while he was mending it?'

Lana was no help. 'Oh, I don't know. Why should I notice where he kept his gadgets? I think he brought a few things in a basket. I didn't stand over him. He had enough ideas in his horrible head, without me showing too much interest.'

I tried a new approach: 'Didn't you like him?'

'He was all right. I acted friendly to him for a time – I had a window shutter that had come off its hinges and a few other little jobs I reckoned he could do for me around the house. Once he finished those, I never had to invite him back. I didn't cry when he stopped coming. I don't like that big hairy beard and he's not exactly agile. You want somebody flexible if you're having a fling. Get it over quick. I was sorry I ever bothered, really. Old Megalo is knackered. He hurt his back about ten years ago, falling off a scaffold.'

Perhaps by some slow meander we were getting somewhere. 'What was he doing on a scaffold?' I asked.

'Putting it up, I think. He was working at the new amphitheatre, when they built that big old thing for the Emperor. They had those prisoners-of-war from abroad doing most of it, but some locals were taken on, especially when they wanted something important to be done properly. You can't really trust foreigners, can you?'

'I was brought up not to trust anyone!' I quipped, wearily holding back that I was a foreigner myself. 'Megalo did tell me he has done heavy work.'

'Well, that would have been it.'

A man who could help erect the mighty scaffold to build a three-storey imperial arena would be perfectly capable of fixing together two beams for a crucifixion. 'Was his work any good? Was he a good carpenter?' I was thinking of the fake-cow frame someone had made to contain Phrygia, its professional alignment marks cut with a specialist tool that Tiberius had called a race.

'No, he was hopeless!' scoffed Lana. 'Left to him, it would have ended up with only three legs and me tipped on the floor.'

'So how is your bed now?'

'Oh the bed is fine. But he had to bring in a mate to help him fix it.'

Hello! Hello! 'A mate! Who was this?'

'Don't ask me. Megalo just trotted out and fetched him from somewhere. Then they went at it together. Nobody introduced me. I kept back and didn't say anything, in case with two people they wanted more money – or more of something else.'

She was wearing me out, but I smiled. 'And did they? Ask for money or anything else?'

'No fear! I bet they could tell I was ready to slap down that kind of merriment. Well, not with two at a time. What would people take me for?'

'Indeed! So did the other man have a proper tool-belt?'

'Probably. He seemed to be fully equipped!' smirked Lana. 'I wasn't looking at his hammers and chisels. I might have tested out his functions, but he wasn't having it.'

'Shame! So what did he look like?'

'Ordinary. All right, but nothing special.'

'What was he like otherwise?'

'Unhappy. When they were talking together, he was rude about everything they mentioned. Mind you, in between, when the bed parts were going back together well, I heard him humming to himself, under his breath. He could hold a tune, when he wasn't moaning about old Megalo holding the nails for him. They had cross words. He called Megalo a dud apprentice.'

'Aren't all apprentices useless? So is the other man one of the Farcicals?'

'Ambrosia's crew? No, she didn't know him. I caught her giving him the eye as if he was a brand new gammon on a hook. I sent her out quick to get parsley. It was the wrong time of year, so I knew it would take her a long time to find any.'

'You are very protective,' I commented, though I suspected this woman's true motives.

'Well! You have to look after your own.' Lana was cackling. 'Besides, when the other man went off back where he came from, I wanted another tickle on the bed with Megalo. I thought he might try a bit harder, without her there watching.'

'And did he?'

'No, he had to go home for his dinner. That wife – we met her here – she keeps him on a short leash. Still, I had a nice comfy nap before Ambrosia came cantering back with nothing in her shopping trug.'

43

Good grief, I meet some characters!

While talking to Lana, I had been aware of movement in the colonnades. On extracting myself from the scheming mother, I was then stopped at the gate by two more familiar figures. A couple of short, rotund vigiles had positioned themselves where I had to pass on my way out of the station-house. They were waiting for me. Until I made a move, they had been in deep discussion, which they broke off regretfully in order to pull me over. This time they introduced themselves. They were the bonded pair who liked discussing drama, a couple called Hyro and Milo. They had been ordered to escort me everywhere. I would have no choice.

'What new plot is this? Why is Mucius assigning bodyguards?'

'Health and safety.' Milo was their official spokesman. 'Magistrate's wife, supervision of by operatives, full-time duty, unspecified time scale. Can't take chances. We're calling you the Girl from the Aventine.'

'Code?'

'Cipher.'

'Experts!'

'He said to tell you not to lure us into bad habits.'

'I shall try to avoid that. Where is he?' The cultured couple revealed that their tribune had been sent an official message, after which the tribune had sent Mucius off somewhere by himself. I was alarmed: 'Messengers are always significant in plays.'

'Can't tell you,' they chorused.

'Oh, come on, lads. Be my omniscient chorus. Has some plot twist happened offstage?'

'Oh, Flavia Albia! What makes you ask that?' Hyro threw back at me, looking implausibly innocent.

'Intuition. Now, I have interviews to do. Are you tailing me in the one-and-two formation?' I put to them. 'Or are you acting as deterrent muscle, shoulder-to-shoulder for wider coverage?' They squared up, keen to engage in this technical blather. I stopped them. 'I'm going. Walk one each side of me nicely.'

We regrouped. I felt more like a prisoner than a protected person. I have heard important persons with security staff say this is normal. 'At least lictors march in front and clear a space through the crowd.'

'We need to be told where you are going, Flavia. Risk assessment.'

'Don't call me Flavia.'

'Mucius said—'

'Mucius can jump down a well. It's Albia – or I shall show you how I cut out flowers with my fruit knife, using human flesh.' They blinked. Looking after me was more of a thriller than they had been told to expect. 'Hyro, I am visiting a couple of bars called the Halcyon and the Golden Cup, where I am hoping to find the professional actors. Milo, the worst hazard is their stale snacks. Now walk on, boys.'

They became oddly acquiescent. I thought this must be how an expert charioteer feels, when he harnesses up an untried team of horses, then finds them responsive to his lightest touch.

The actors were not there.

Instead I found Davos sitting in the Golden Cup, staring into space, not even with a drink. He was very depressed. He said Thalia had taken the Chremes and Phrygia troupe to the dead couple's lodgings where, now the funeral was over, she would divide up their personal belongings among the company. She had appointed herself executor. She and Davos were determined not to let Eucolpus get his greasy landlord's hands on anything. She would find keepsakes for Sophrona and Byrria. Davos would be brought something from his old friends: he told me he could not bear to visit the apartment.

'I'm glad you're here instead. I must talk to you.' I seated myself, flanked by my vigiles minders. 'My rules, boys: don't fidget and don't talk. Ignore them, Davos.'

'Do we get a drink?' asked Hyro, smacking his lips hopefully.

'No. I never asked for you, so you are stuck with your usual entertainment allowance.' That would be none. 'My budget is too tight for treats.'

They took it well enough, but I noticed Milo went off anyway to find the landlord or a waiter. Hyro asked politely if they could fetch anything for Davos and me, but we were too startled by the offer to accept.

Davos seemed to cheer up slightly, watching this scene with amusement. That put him in a better mood for answering my questions about the past. The grey-haired actor-manager looked more haggard than when we had first met at the Saepta. Shaken by events, he nevertheless began of his own accord: 'Thalia says there are things I should tell you.'

'Lead on. I want to know about when you were working with Chremes and Phrygia, but I won't interrupt.'

So, in an off-season, mid-afternoon bar in the Tiber hinterland on the Field of Mars, I heard about life on the road, travelling in a caravan through the eastern deserts. Chremes and Phrygia had collected an interesting group of fine actors and musicians, many of whom stayed with them, but including Byrria and Philocrates, who went on to make substantial names independently in Rome.

Davos himself had been with the couple for some years, acting main parts in a variety of plays at far-flung provincial theatres. He had known Phrygia since she was starting out and Chremes since he married her. How close to Phrygia Davos had ever been remained unspoken. It was clear he had tolerated Chremes for a long time, but eventually preferred to leave their group and set up his own, perhaps because of friction. However, once his own relationship with Thalia began, that had been a natural reason to return to Italy with her, ahead of the others. Then he formed his own company.

Towards the end of his time in Syria, there had been a memorable season when the company encountered my parents. They had met in a spectacular wadi in Nabataea, joining forces while making fast exits from a tricky situation with the local administration. 'Sounds typical of Falco and Helena!' I chortled.

'And us too. Actors are often unwelcome. We all fled hot-foot, then we spent many weeks together. We went from Bostra to Damascus, via all the towns in the Decapolis, then on across the wilderness to Palmyra, where the Silk Road arrives. There was trouble on the journey. It turned out our group contained a lunatic who attacked people he held grudges against, and he drowned them.'

'In a desert?' I raised my eyebrows.

'Deserts necessarily have water saved in pools and cisterns.'

'Ugh, I'll never drink the water again when I'm travelling. You don't know who's been drowned in it. I suppose my crafty elders soon worked out who was dunking victims?'

'You know those two.'

'Do I! My parents have a habit of solving mysteries when nobody has even noticed that a mystery is there. What happened to your fanatical lunatic? I am wondering if he has found his way to Rome.'

'Oh, no. Things came to a head in Palmyra. Thalia came galloping out of a sandstorm – glorious sight! She happened to bring a vicious Egyptian cobra, which, in the middle of a mêlée onstage, conveniently bit him.'

I thought I recalled Thalia mentioning this. 'He died?'

'Same day.'

'Saves holding a trial!'

'You are your parents' daughter.' Of course I was not. Still, never mind. 'Thalia got rid of that particular snake, thank you, omnipotent Jove.'

The killer had been jealous and obsessive, a man without a conscience. It sounded nastily familiar.

He had also been one of a pair. Davos described a couple of young actors everyone called the Twins, although they were not related. Someone had mentioned them to me before: their stage names were Tranio and Grumio. In plays requiring twins, they acted the mix-up characters. They told ghastly jokes, raced about, performed monologues, played with the trick dog and fell off ladders.

Offstage, they always shared rooms in deadbeat lodgings or tents in the outdoors. The one who became the cobra's victim was rougher, harder and crazier; he only thought about himself. The other had greater sophistication and a quicker intelligence; he had made a study of the history and aims of drama. Both light-hearted yet spiteful, the pranksters drank heavily, gambled hard, promiscuously womanised, and engaged in mischief by design.

My parents had eventually exposed them. It was Grumio who killed people. Tranio took no part, but he had known what was happening. He failed to report his friend's violence; he told lies to provide an alibi. His collusion was so bad that he was left behind when everyone else moved on from Palmyra.

'Was he under arrest?'

'Yes and no,' answered Davos, with a shrug of his shoulders. 'Rome had a military base there, on watch at the remote frontier. The commander locked up Tranio for hindering justice, though I believe he was never charged formally. I have heard that either he escaped or was eventually set free. I suppose he made his way back to Italy, but he would have had no money and no friends to help him. Of course he was finished in regular theatre.'

'Might he have asked Chremes and Phrygia to take him back?'

Davos looked thoughtful. 'He had enough brass neck to approach them. They would have considered him too big a risk, I'm sure. Besides, they had a full company – you've met them, Albia. Simo, Atticus, Pardicus – they are fine performers. Tranio must be over fifteen years older now, like us all. Who would want a washed-up has-been, by that time broken by harsh experiences?'

'Did you recognise him at the funeral?'

'No, but the farce-players were all masked. It's been years, and I wasn't looking for him. Thalia had known Tranio. She remembered him as a youngster, doing low-grade stand-up at the Circus of Gaius and Nero where her team always camps, as you know.'

'Did she spot him yesterday?'

'She can't be sure.'

'So,' I suggested slowly, 'if this Tranio is now calling himself Gnaeus – which I suppose may be the name he was born with – his grudge against your old friends may have been very personal, not simply that they let down the Farcicals over the Games?'

Davos nodded. Point agreed. He was not a man who would exclaim and elaborate. As a witness I found him refreshing.

'And what about Philocrates?' I asked next.

'Philocrates? The Twins never got on with him. He was better-looking and a much more successful flirt – always at it. Wherever we went, he would run through the local skirts in days. Women who thought they were respectable especially appealed to him – he loved the challenge. He boasted about it too, aiming to annoy the rest of us, and the Twins resented that.'

'So from what you say, Tranio hated him?'

'I remember some aggression,' Davos agreed, a measured response. 'Of course, even then Philocrates was a more significant stage performer than the Twins. Effortless talent. I could hold my own, but he put that pair very much in the shade.'

'Who did Philocrates mix with?'

'No one really. He kept to himself,' Davos remembered. 'Well, he was too busy with his love-life, off on his own at every stop. He kept aloof from the rest of us. To be honest, I was quite surprised to hear he had looked up Chremes and

Phrygia again – though I suppose we all get older and more nostalgic.'

'You never met him in Rome?'

Davos pulled a face. 'No.'

'Not enough in common?' He let that pass. 'Davos, if your Tranio really is the Farcicals' Gnaeus, he is now struggling to survive on meanly paid jobs. Plus, he can only use his acting skills among rag-tag, part-time amateurs. I guess he won't be too happy about any of that. Their being bumped from the Games would have been a bitter blow, too. I can see why he might attack Chremes and Phrygia for what felt like a heartless decision, though his methods have been vile. Then to be pushed aside so that Philocrates could have a plum part will have rekindled animosity.'

I was wondering whether, if so, Gnaeus had always intended to attack his old rival at the funeral. I mentioned to Davos how last night I had overheard Philocrates and Plotinus being brutally rude about the Farcicals. That could have led to the subsequent attack on the Via Cornelia. 'Though it seemed to be Plotinus who was propounding the most objectionable bile. He sees himself as the lead company musician – a prickly, foul-mouthed character. Do you know him, Davos? Was he there in your time?'

Davos thought the name was familiar, but if Plotinus had been in Syria, it must have been in only a junior capacity. He said the actors had not mingled too much with their accompanists. 'Well, apart from the girls who played pan pipes and tambourines. They were always available for a snuggle with anybody under the desert stars.'

One of the free-and-easy girl musicians had been killed. It led to a threatened strike by stagehands and the orchestra, who were so afraid for their own safety they downed instruments and agitated to go home. My father, their temporary playwright, had attempted to act as a peacemaker – according to Davos with muted success. So would Falco remember Plotinus in his younger years? Had he pleaded with Plotinus not to leave the company? *Hard luck, Flavia Albia: the only way to find this out is to tell Falco what is going on* . . . Never mind that.

I still wanted to solve the case myself and present the parents with a fait accompli. I was able to stop wrestling with my conscience because Thalia and the others turned up. They were all bearing colourful objects, vases, bags, clothing and furnishing accessories, some of which I recognised from when I was waiting for Phrygia. They looked more cheerful. As in so many bereavements, a share-out of valuables after the funeral had gone a long way to helping their spirits recover.

MEDEA

44

As soon as the company trickled back, they split up and vanished. I should have known. People always pretend they want no heirlooms: it is all too painful, they are too high-minded. Even so, they will jealously inspect whatever comes to them in the share-out, desperate to be sure their acquisitions are better than anyone else's. From a beaded purse to an olive grove, it's easier to think fondly of your donor if you like their bequest.

This lot were no different. They all dived off to their rooms, to check they had no cracks or chips in their vases or to pull open the seams of woven bags in case any forgotten coin was hidden there.

Thalia had taken over Phrygia's colourful wardrobe. She was sending a vibrant tunic and cloak to my mother. 'Helena's a tall girl. These are a bit ordinary for me. I'm giving Davos all the play scripts because his troupe can use them. Don't tell your pa, I found one of his old ones.' She slid a ring into my palm, lookalike gold with an Athena owl. 'That will fit your little fingers – Phrygia would have wanted you to have something, for tracking down the killers.' That assumed I could manage to do so. And that I hadn't already acquired my own souvenirs from Athens. What does a teenage girl bring home? A ring with an Athena owl.

'What's the play, Davos?'

'*Rudens*. His version with the tug-of-war.'

'Will you ever perform it?'

'No bloody chance!'

Thalia and Davos were heading back over the river to their own people, but I managed to extract a few more details from Thalia. She had known that the comedian they called Tranio was back in Rome. 'I used to see Phrygia. We met up to dream stupidly about old times we ought to have forgotten. One time when our paths crossed, she told me she had met Tranio a few times, but she sent the despicable runt packing.'

'Her words?'

'Her very words to him, I think.'

'I suppose he would not have liked that! Did he want Chremes and Phrygia to take him back into their company?'

'Never. She wouldn't have allowed it – he was too edgy and unreliable.'

'That will have upset him again,' I commented. 'Especially if he broods.'

'He was bright,' Davos put in. 'He ought to have understood. His professional career had ended. It was all his own fault. Covering like that for Grumio in Syria, the clown had done for himself.'

If he was a psychopathic killer, they never blame themselves for anything.

'Thalia, Davos didn't recognise him among the farce players at the funeral. I don't suppose you noticed him?'

'Never knew him that well.'

'I think in the farce he was called Maccus, pretending to be a hunchback.'

'Possible. When I first met him in Rome,' said Thalia, 'he was a gangly stand-up with lousy patter, but he's bound to have changed. It must be twenty years since Phrygia hired him for her eastern tour, and I'd met him here before that. Under those beaky masks, who knows? Look, we need to be going . . .' I could see she and Davos were anxious; they wanted to check on her animals. 'We've just heard a rumour that troublemakers got into the imperial menagerie a few days ago. Animals were stolen. I need to make sure no one is playing silly beggars over where we are.'

'Don't worry, the menagerie is on the far side of town from you.' It was a huge, horrific site where beasts intended for the arena were crowded in sordid conditions, outside the Praenestina Gate on the city's south side. 'People wouldn't do anything dangerous?'

Thalia growled. 'Risk only attracts them. Whether they are drunk or merely idiots, lads-about-town love rattling cages to find out if lions really bite. I'm going to put up a notice: *Don't bother trying, they really will eat you.* Anyone tries claiming compensation – it's been known! – they can take a hike up the Apennines.'

After they left, there was more disappointment for me, because I had wanted to talk to Plotinus, the musician. Most of the group had scattered before I realised he was not there. I managed to grab Ariminius, the older scene-shifter, to ask where the band-leader was. 'I have the impression you all think Plotinus is keeping a woman somewhere.'

Ariminius smiled. 'That's a tease. He comes from Rome, that's all it is. There are friends he has a drink with, I believe, but when we're here for a play he goes to see his granny.'

'His grandmother? That's what he says?'

'That's what he actually does. She's real, and a lively character. Some of us have met her, Flavia Albia.'

I had to accept it, though Plotinus had not struck me as a dutiful family type.

'What's he like, Ariminius? As good a musician as he claims?'

'Not really. He does a bit of everything, most fairly well. He came from a smart background, but he was a wastrel nephew doing odd jobs in a renovation workshop, furniture mending, before he joined us. Phrygia only gave him a job because he owned his own lyre. His family must have paid for it. Now, I'd love to talk, but I must go . . .'

I was left alone. That is, apart from my two minders. Well, they were interesting.

Hyro and Milo had watched and listened eagerly, drinking in these stories of theatrical life. They offered me mint tea. I declined. I wanted strong drink, and plenty of it, but so far in our acquaintance I was playing the nice lady, not the depressed informer. I sat with a straight back, hands linked on a table edge. If they stuck around, there would be plenty of time for the Girl from the Aventine to show her true self.

While one half of my brain was absorbing what I had heard, I used the free element to ask about them. By definition, vigiles were ex-slaves. Most came from labouring backgrounds, but these two had been house-born attendants to a cultured man, who took them along whenever he went to the theatre. Afterwards, he discussed whatever plays they had seen. He had taught them a great deal about the principles of drama, the written word and even philosophy. They loved it. Under his tutelage they had become intense critics. After he died, they obtained their freedom as a kindly bequest in his will, although most of his cash was left to friends and family. With minimal funds to support them in future, they were attracted by vigiles' pay, which they could stretch to allow their interest in drama while working their way to full citizenship. Besides, they enjoyed fire-fighting.

'Mucius decided we should be assigned to you,' Milo told me, with a shy grin, 'because we have shown bravery in fires.'

'I'm that dangerous?' They blushed.

They were somewhat alike, with wide faces. Milo was the one with the wicked twinkle while his partner had a mole and looked more serious. They both had hefty girths, so as they sat on stools at the Golden Cup, with large cups of what looked to be porridge, their posteriors overhung all round.

'Milo, I take it you are the one who enjoys comedies – while you,' I challenged Hyro, 'have to be given a tribune's note for the doctor, if you are called out to any tragedies?'

They stared in silence.

'Something he let drop,' I explained quietly. Earlier, when I encountered the cohort's top man talking to Mucius, I took in more than he may have intended. 'I understand this Gnaeus we're looking at for the murders had a wife who died. She killed herself? Various people have alluded to the incident. Dead children have been mentioned. And according to your tribune – what's his name, incidentally?'

'Caunus.' It was Milo who supplied this, while Hyro remained immobile, set-faced.

'Caunus said there was a lot of blood. That would have been distressing to sensitive men.'

'Hyro had a little boy,' Milo murmured to me, quickly filling in, using as much of an undertone as he could. 'Poor scrap had gone to the gods, natural causes, but it gave Hyro a great deal of sadness. He was the one who found the children. The incident got to him. He suffered flashbacks and he still has nightmares.' He paused. 'It is true there was blood smeared everywhere – but that had nothing to do with what happened.'

'The whole set-up was wrong!' Hyro finally spoke up. He sounded angry. 'I don't care what Caunus says. He wasn't there.' Milo patted his arm, after which Hyro reverted to staring fixedly ahead in silence.

'Tell me, Milo. I am sorry if this is difficult.'

'But you need to know?'

'Correct.'

'All right.'

Without more ado, Milo related what had occurred. Gnaeus had announced to his first wife, who was mother to two young children, that he was leaving her for the second woman. He did go off, though he returned from time to time to see his young sons – or, Hyro and Milo thought, *not* seeing them but arguing about parental access, which the mother was forbidding. 'That went on for some months. Neighbours said he was the type who ignored the boys after they were born, until his faithlessness came out and he was told to get lost. Then he decided the children were his property.'

'Legally true,' I murmured. 'It's time they changed that law!'

One day, Gnaeus came back and found everyone dead. Deranged by her situation, the abandoned mother had smothered her children, then hanged herself. No knives or other sharps were used. However, to ensure Gnaeus received the most hideous shock when he discovered the bodies, she had painted the apartment with great swathes of blood, though it was blood she had fetched from the meat market. 'We can say that for certain. We found the bucket.'

For a moment we all sat without speaking.

'You can see what it was supposed to be,' Milo said quietly.

'Sadly, I think I do.'

'From what Davos said about him, if he is that Tranio, he was interested in much more than farces. He knew a lot about mainstream plays. While they were together, he had probably talked about it to the wife. So she punished him by using a play to impart her message.'

'*Medea.*'

'*Medea,*' agreed Milo. I had the impression Hyro wanted to say more, but a warning glance from his colleague stopped him.

I asked the professional question. 'Did *she* say that? Did she leave a note?'

They shook their heads.

'Suicides leave messages,' I insisted. 'You are the vigiles, you know that. Who made the connection with *Medea*? Was it you two?'

'Not us,' Milo answered quickly. 'Him.'

'Ah!'

'Yes!' said Hyro, heavily.

They were first on the scene after neighbours raised an alarm. They had found Gnaeus sitting on the tenement stairs, with his head in his hands, sobbing. Milo described that: 'The sobs sounded real. I'm not so sure about the tears. It was him who said it: "She has played Medea – she has killed herself and taken my innocent babies with her. This is all to spite me." He said that to us, as we squeezed up the steps past him to go into the apartment. Then we found the bodies and apparently it all made sense.'

I looked at Hyro. He was shaking his head slowly, side to side, as if deploring what had happened. But he could have been disagreeing with how it looked.

'Where had Gnaeus been earlier that day?' I demanded. 'Was he interviewed? Did anybody ask him to account for his movements?'

'With the second wife,' stated Milo.

'Really?'

'She said so.'

'Oh, it must be true, then!'

'Our tribune signed it off,' said Hyro, his voice dull. 'That was obviously what happened. He agreed—'

'So Caunus ordered you not to waste any more time on the incident?'

Neither replied.

'I get it, lads. Caunus took the sensitivity option: People were suffering. It would be wrong to harass them with questions nobody needed. You were to stop investigating – and you were not to talk about it to anyone? Case closed, job done.' They pulled rueful faces. I still had to persuade them they could be fully open with me. 'You had doubts. Did you argue with Caunus, Hyro?'

He looked uneasy but answered with care: 'I explained that the situation worried me. I had feelings about how the scene had been presented. Our tribune is always approachable. He takes an interest.'

'I'll take it you know your Sophocles and Aristophanes, so that is classic irony! Tribunes mostly take an interest in closing down anything awkward. And then?'

'Caunus said I had had an upsetting day, with which he fully sympathised. That is the kind of officer he is. He wrote a chit for the cohort doc to prescribe me a break. Mental strain. I was to recover at home all the rest of the week, and when I came back, things would have moved on. He was right. We had other jobs to do.'

I gazed at them. 'Some murderous bastard has got away with it.'

'We are troops, Albia, we serve Rome. We cannot engage in public speculation.'

'No. Stick with the official line.' I adjusted bangles along my arm, like a respectable woman, before I gave the pair a stern professional talk. 'Your fart-arsed tribune thinks he knows! I understand you are not allowed to comment, so please don't get into trouble, but he doesn't govern me.'

'Right!' murmured Hyro, obviously startled.

'Let me venture to propose the two possibilities. One as Caunus reckons, this Gnaeus lost his family in terrible circumstances, when his first wife had an unfortunate breakdown. He is a tragic hero, who could not avoid his fate.' The theatre-loving troops nodded, though narrowing their eyes sceptically as they followed my argument. 'This unforeseen disaster then unhinged him. He erupted into a jealous mania that he could not help, so he started attacking people he imagined had offended him, even many years before. When she killed herself and the little boys, the wife's use of a play provided his inspiration for using scenes from drama. It was her idea. What is happening now exonerates him. It is all her fault.' I breathed in sadly, pausing.

'Or?' asked Hyro.

'Or, two Caunus, your farting wonderful tribune, wouldn't recognise the truth if he hit it face on.'

I had made them nervous. I let them settle down.

'You and I do see it. This only looks like *Medea*. You felt the scene had been staged. You – two experienced men with an eye for detail who ought to be listened to – are entirely right. This is a basic domestic murder, carried out for the usual crass reasons, yet it has been shockingly covered up. No one committed suicide. The abandoned wife and her little ones are innocents, *all* murdered. Gnaeus didn't need to be shocked into bad behaviour: he had learned that in Syria. He was already unbalanced. Either because the woman had dared to stand up to him, or simply to get them out of the way, that man killed his family himself.'

45

The two vigiles pushed aside their beakers, not bothering to lick their porridge spoons. They pounded the table with their fists. They were angry at being right all along, dispirited that a culprit had got away with his crimes, troubled about what they could do next. I preferred not to stir up cohort problems. I told them I could understand why the tribune had acted that way, since there were only gut feelings not proof. Besides, he would have wanted to avoid filling out a praetor's report. That they understood.

'Things will change,' I reassured them. 'Now Gnaeus has committed other murders, Caunus will adjust his stance. Given the more recent deaths, he will not object to adding back the wife-and-children incident – you'll see. Since Gnaeus killed the theatre people, it won't need further resources for a reinvestigation. Caunus benefits: he acquires a bigger closed-case list.'

'You seem to understand procedure, Albia!'

'I've been at it a long time.'

I said Mucius seemed reasonable. I could tell he was determined to wrap up the theatre killings with a full rota of charges, so it should be easy to gain his support. I might be pushing my luck, but Hyro and Milo wanted to hear that.

This pair were beginning to ally themselves with me. As Mucius ought to have known, it is always a risk with bodyguards: once they start a conversation with the person they are protecting, neutrality is lost. I had already learned their past histories, that Hyro had had a child once, which also suggested a girlfriend, how they reacted to a crisis emotionally, that senior officers could be a source of tension. My protectors were forgetting their assigned role and being caught up in my schemes. It made me smile.

'What next?' challenged Hyro.

'Well, clearly,' I replied drily, 'I am heading for my descent from the clouds in a chariot, to impose a rational solution on the madness we are facing.'

'A classical goddess?'

'Free-flowing drapery and, if it's to be had, a rainbow.'

'You are supposed to be a druid,' Milo informed me, sharing what must be the barracks whisper.

I winced. 'No talk of illegal practices, please! I am an informer. I charge too much and I talk too much, but I have nothing to do with severed heads polluting the water supply.'

'How much *do* you charge?' asked Hyro, sounding interested. After their six-year stint with the cohort, these two would be wanting some other paid activity to fund their theatre outings.

'Not as much as you think.' I stood up. They hauled themselves off their wooden stools, groaning and pulling at their red tunics. 'Come on, we have to find the Farcicals, particularly Gnaeus.'

'All our lads are out on a seek-and-find. They will bring them in.'

'They may bring in some,' I concurred, setting off from the bar anyway, 'but the bright ones will hear them coming. I, aided by you, if you are up for it, am going to tiptoe along to where I believe Gnaeus may be hiding.'

'His second wife's house?' Milo guessed, as I set off.

'No. He will know Mucius must have discovered where that is so, of course, your lads are going to turn up there with leg-irons. Mucius will think that, after once being given the wrong address, the right one is a sure thing.'

'No?'

'No.'

'Where, then?'

'How can you know where to look when Mucius doesn't, Albia?'

'Because I listen,' I said patiently.

I kept them walking.

'Where are we going, Albia?'

They were like two excitable five-year-olds. If I gave them a packet of nuts, they would eat them in one go and be sick.

As we walked, heading away from the actors' lodgings and towards the Tiber, I explained that we were about to investigate the rougher, dirtier shacks that huddled by the riverbank. 'When Mucius was questioning Ambrosia with me, she gave up an intriguing clue. She said about Gnaeus, "I think he met Megalo in a bar. They go in the Winkle sometimes." Heard of it?'

The vigiles shook their heads.

'So you don't drink anywhere nasty! The Farcicals hold their rehearsal meetings in a horrible place called the Charybdis. The Winkle is straight across the road. Be brave, lads,' I told my trusty guards. 'None of these thermopolia can be called hygienic. Never touch the serving counter, and certainly don't manhandle customers. You are out with an informer now. It's going to be rough but I'm not taking you drinking. So don't you go telling Mucius that I led you into bad habits.'

Hyro and Milo looked disappointed.

'Sorry!' I said kind-heartedly.

46

Hyro and Milo had had practice in catching villains and thought they knew how. As soon as we arrived, Hyro decided he would go into the other bar, the Infant Hercules, where he would pretend to the hairy waiter that he intended to order a drink but, first, was desperate for a leak. He would leave by the rear exit, then come into the Winkle 'accidentally' by its own back door, blocking anyone's escape if they saw us arrive.

'Tight tactics!' I approved, though I felt nervous that these keen lads might be taking over.

We paused to brace ourselves. We had come by the good straight ceremonial road. It runs across the Field of Mars from the Vicus Pallacinae up to Nero's Bridge where it crosses the river into open country becoming the Via Cornelia, where the funeral was held yesterday. The Farcicals must have come back into Rome along this road. Somewhere around here, if we knew where to look, we would probably discover all of them, hugging rafters in roof spaces or fighting spiders for space in broom cupboards.

The longest section of the southern bank is where the Tiber takes a big curve around the Field of Mars, which was once swampy and still floods regularly. In theory there is no habitation, only public monuments. Between the fancy stuff and the water there are still spaces. The river has landing spots, even if it lacks the wharves that line the embankment that I knew better, down below Tiber Island. Smallish boats can navigate as far up as this, though they have to avoid the dangerous shoals caused by the narrowing piers of bridges.

There was a reason why the Circus of Gaius and Nero had been built across the river immediately beyond the Campus: the stables. We were in a district that reeked of horses, fodder and stalls. Strange flies zoomed in to bite us. Beasts could be exercised right here, when it wasn't too spongy, or taken across one of the bridges to firmer going below the Janiculan. Miss a step, even on the paved roads, and you ended up with dung in your shoes. The area even had an old racetrack called the Trigarium, perhaps because three-horse chariots raced there. More importantly, it housed the big stables of the modern four-horse factions: the legendary Blues and Greens, plus the inferior Reds and Whites, and the more recently established Golds and Purples. Drivers and jockeys, farriers and vets abounded, all full of their own importance because chariots were Rome's best-loved sport.

No district with so many river and stable workers would ever lack bars. Those were inevitably crude shacks, frequented by hard-faced, bent-legged men who hated strangers. I was glad to have back-up . The bars all smelt of yesterday's fried fish and all-winter garlic. Importers were beginning to build fine-wine warehouses across the river, but no one has ever sold an amphora of sleek Falernian here. In this haunt of nameless vintages, they never list their house-wines on the wall: you have what is served in rough-cast jugs. It will sear your throat. Take what you get. Have the raw red. Don't dare to ask for white, let alone amber.

These cramped cabins did not feature on the grand map in Agrippa's Porticus, but many existed. Once the lads and I had left behind the Theatre of Pompey and moved onto what remained of the old military training ground, everything opened up, so the grey sky yawned above and cold breezes made us shiver. This empty quarter was populated yet desolate. We had come to narrow, skulking double-backs that were lined with small catering places, not movable stalls; their low huts seemed rooted in the wet ground where they had probably been sucked into the squelch since Romulus had come to review troops. Somewhere around here the city founder had been taken up in a cloud of mist to become the god Quirinus, or so it was said. If, on the other hand, old Romulus had offended someone and was bashed on the head, his corpse could have disappeared into the back storeroom of one of these desultory bars and nobody any the wiser that a skeleton lived there. This riverside hole made a far from promising take-off point for a new god ascending to the stars.

I had pointed out the Charybdis to Milo and Hyro. A woman who must have been the famously filthy-but-willing waitress leaned there, staring out with vacant eyes. That place at least had its backyard behind, plus a counter of sorts in front. At the Infant Hercules and the Winkle, waiters served off little more than planks. Most customers took away what they bought, back to their warm horse-stalls or their rowing skiffs.

The Winkle's waiter with the slicked-back hair was not offering free gherkins today. All he had was a barrel of wine that looked as if it had been made in a shed by his cousin, plus a cauldron of gluey gloop that he would ladle into lentil bowls for people who had had enough of life. Although he wore an apron tied with strings around his midriff, half of it must have been missing for the past five years. I reckoned he used cooking oil as his hair pomade.

As soon as they saw the vigiles, his few customers scrammed. I said to Milo, 'They are probably honest men rushing off to vital appointments with their business advisers . . . Where the hell has your Hyro got to?'

'Probably did decide to have a wee while he was out the back.'

'Well, come on. I'm going to start without him.'

There was one roadside stool. Nobody got a look-in, because the caupona cat was sitting on it. Licking his whiskers, he looked a plump, happy, orange-stripy beast, which, around there, must have had plenty of rats in his diet. Much-loved among customers, his name was Rheon. Milo found out. Everyone called him Cleopatra, even though he was male, because the Winkle's cats had always been called that. They had had about nine so far . . .

Juno.

While my backing group were otherwise engaged, I started a solo search for our fugitives. I tackled the waiter. I could have asked whether anyone was there, but I took the simple attitude that we all knew for certain that they were: 'Own up! Where have you put them, Greaseball?'

He feigned ignorance. They always do. I marched around, looking for myself. Greasy began to yell loudly, no doubt as a warning. That told me someone was definitely there. I ordered Milo to stop stroking the damned cat and help.

Hyro appeared through a curtain at the back. He had found Megalo hiding in a lean-to outside.

The oldest of the Farcicals was looking bedraggled. A day after they performed at the funeral, he was still wearing his costume, the big hairy loincloth, though he no longer had his mask. His beard looked wet as it straggled down his bare chest; his bald head was dirty. 'This,' I told the boys, 'is

Megalo, who plays "Centunculus", the comic slave. He's not very comedic now!'

Megalo said nothing, looking tragic. He was not acting.

Milo (still holding the caupona cat in his arms despite my orders) and Hyro (leering with mock-friendly menace) stood either side of the older man, leaning inwards, crowding him. Neither was particularly tall, yet both were solid lads; that must be the porridge they ate. This looked to be their signature move. For them, persuading suspects involved extracting breath from lungs at high pressure. The presence of a heavy cat would not, I presumed, be standard.

'Where's your pal Maccus hiding?'

'Come on, Centunculus! Who's a cheeky slave, then? Show us your wisecracks, while you give up Gnaeus.'

'Don't hurt him,' I said, my voice telling the captive I did not mean it.

'We never hurt people, Flavia,' Hyro assured me.

'Well, only a little bit,' murmured Milo.

'Like this . . .'

I don't know what they did. They were vigiles. They must have methods that were mythically efficacious. Theirs focused on bending back the little bones in suspects' fingers or even wrists. I may have heard something snap.

Megalo yelped horribly. Even so, he shook his head: he would not be talking.

Milo sighed, then took things further. Still carrying the cat, he walked over unhurriedly to a bucket of water that must be used for general purposes. Turning back to the waiter, he smiled brightly, miming his intentions with dandling movements.

Milo firmly suspended the big bundle of tawny fur that everybody loved so much. Cleopatra the Ninth was about to be put in the bucket and held there by large hands until he stopped squirming. Unless the puss had fathered Cleo the Tenth, this was the end of his historic line.

The oily-haired waiter let out a groan of disgust. His eyes obediently went to a stained trapdoor in the dusty floor.

Hyro still grasped Megalo, with his arms pinioned painfully behind him. I, feeling superfluous, simply tried taking an intelligent interest.

Milo placed Cleo on the dirty floor, with one last friendly tickle between his pointy ears. 'Thanks, Rheon. Nice co-operation. Off you go now, pussy.'

He inspected the floor stains. 'Could this old dirt be dried blood?'

'In that case, can we be at the crime scene where Chremes was beaten up?' I wondered. Mind you, around here there could have been any number of past incidents of violence. They probably counted an evening lost if no blood was shed.

'Let's ask. I'm going to haul out the man who knows.'

Milo pulled up the trap by a loop of rope and slung the heavy wooden cover so it crashed on end. Cleopatra had a brief squint in over the edge, lost interest, then took a walk elsewhere.

'Come out!' cooed Milo, alluringly, down into the dark underground space. No one would think he might be addressing a dangerous multiple murderer. 'Come out for air, my son, don't give us any trouble. Surrender will be so much better than if I have to climb in there to fetch you!'

Gnaeus came up of his own accord.

47

Murderers never look much.

I had forgotten that he and Megalo must be the oldest two of the Farcicals. His behaviour had always seemed youthful, with that nervous, trying giggle. He giggled again, acting innocent, as he climbed up through the hatch. Now that I knew he was probably our killer, it grated worse than ever.

Gnaeus must have been approaching fifty. In his acting role as Maccus, the greedy fool with a hooked nose and hunched back, this would work well, but his daytime jobs as a house painter and arena snack-carrier would be starting to tax him. Like Megalo, he had dumped his mask somewhere, but had had no opportunity to change out of his over-large shaggy underpants. Whereas the other man's torso was naturally hairy all over, this one's chest was almost completely smooth; it looked natural, not plucked or pumiced. From what I had heard of his acting career he had plenty of agility: he had fallen off ladders and used his muscle in tugs-of-war. I should have thought about that.

Things had been going well. From the moment Gnaeus climbed out through the hatch that ended. Once up on his feet, he immediately took action. When Milo stepped towards him, his right hand flashed out. He poked Milo hard, straight into one eye. He had aimed for both – at least he had missed the other.

Milo yelled with pain. As he clutched his eye, bending over, blinding tears streamed. Hyro shouted. He let go of Megalo, who fled out through the curtained back exit. Milo turned after him, was caught in a whiplash from the curtain, and had clearly lost his prisoner.

Gnaeus, meanwhile, took a flying leap over the rough plank that served as a bar counter. Cleopatra the cat streaked out of his way, yowling. I was shoved aside by the waiter. It might have been accidental, if you believe in magic. Hyro spun back from the exit, ripping down the leather curtain. He punched Greaseball so hard he fell on his back screaming. Perhaps his nose was broken. Perhaps none of us cared. We three barged into one another as we left the bar, which held us up. Another time I must pre-plan an exit strategy.

Gnaeus had gone haring away, full pelt, towards the river. Across the road, we saw a group of other vigiles emerging from the Charybdis. Mucius was with them. They must have just extracted the two-timer Questus from the filthy waitress's upstairs bower. She was watching his departure in custody with a bored lack of interest. I sympathised with her lifestyle, if it had been forced on her, but she really was a girl my grandmother would have taken briskly in hand.

Milo let out a loud whistle. Hyro gestured. Some of the vigiles followed us as we chased up the road after Gnaeus. Customers who had earlier fled from the Winkle were now standing outside other bars, drinks in hand. They had obviously alerted people to the fact that excitement was expected. Unpleasant men watched us running by. At least no one interfered in the chase, but nor had anybody tried to stop Gnaeus as he escaped.

He went west. Heading into town. He ran parallel with a long, straight part of the river. This took him through bankside gardens that had once belonged to Marcus Agrippa, along paths that were open enough for us to glimpse him ahead of us. He could have jumped onto a boat and rowed out, but we would only have commandeered others to follow him. The few people in the vicinity took little notice as a man in a low-waisted hairy loincloth raced by. Only one old vagrant, wildly drunk, pretended to be thunderstruck. A couple of women with baskets of fish stopped their gossip momentarily but picked up their thread before our stream of vigiles had gone by.

If he had turned left, he could have lost himself among Pompey's Theatre and the old temples around it. He turned right. This brought him onto Agrippa's Bridge. It was a four-pier structure that joined gardens on both sides of the river, taking people across to a generous old villa that I presumed had once belonged to Agrippa himself.

Gnaeus did not cross. The first pier was almost on the riverbank this side. He passed that. We saw him climb athletically onto the second. He stood for a moment at baluster height, looking back towards us. It was as if he was waiting to gather enough of an audience. His timing was excellent. Just before we reached him, he turned away to look down. Then he held his nose and plunged off.

At the spot, there was no sign of him. All of us leaned over the parapet. A few men were sculling bumboats; they were shouted to, but waved back negatives. We waited for Gnaeus to reappear in the racing currents caused by the bridge as they flowed angrily downstream. He never came up.

'That's it, then!' muttered Mucius. 'Goodbye to the undertaker.'

I continued to stare at the water below, yellowish with silt as usual. Goodbye? However it looked, I did not think so.

48

Some of us continued staring down into the river until we could persuade ourselves no one could possibly hold his breath any longer. Either he had to desperately break the surface, or he must be gone.

We were all depressed by the melancholy feeling that follows a waste of life – let alone a lost hope of justice. Gnaeus must have known what he was doing. His look of triumph as he jumped had said it: no hope now of a confession or an explanation. No certainty of anything. Even if we managed to recapture Megalo, the old fellow was likely to claim that all the choices had been made by Gnaeus; all the ideas for killing came from him.

Mucius reacted, tight with annoyance, not bothering to curse or complain. He sent troops along the banks on both sides to watch the water. Some were to tramp down as far as Tiber Island. A watchman was to be stationed nearest to us, on the boat-shaped island's prow in mid-river, scanning for a body. Just in case Gnaeus did magically survive, vigiles were to visit the Temple of Æsculapeus at the other end, with the hospital where they took in dying slaves and gave funerals to the destitute. 'Never mind any fart-arse medical aid. Tell them what he's done. They should pin him down with a hayfork. No sympathetic nursing orderlies are to start wiping his brow with lavender water. If he turns up, I want him.'

Mucius took Milo and Hyro to task for their bungled arrest of two wanted men. They looked chastened. I stood out of earshot, to spare them embarrassment, but I waited in case they were still detailed to escort me.

More vigiles were turning up, as if sucked from lazy afternoons elsewhere into the vortex of Mucius's desperate busyness. Most of those present told the new arrivals it was all over. Only I seemed to believe that Gnaeus would eventually reappear. That meant only I thought there was still a large risk of danger.

Eventually Mucius turned to me. Before he could start barracking, I said in a low voice, 'You know it's not over.'

He paused. To my surprise, he was matter-of-fact in agreement: 'No. That bum is going to turn up somehow.' When I gave him a questioning look, he added, 'He had more plans. He can't have been ready to drown himself.'

Whatever he had meant to tell me about plans, he gestured instead to a litter that was being brought along by huffing bearers. The conveyance was substantial in size though its decoration was faded, in so far as mock-gilding had ever existed. If there were cushions inside, they must have been thin and hard. The two sweat-shiny slaves were struggling after they had rushed all through Agrippa's Gardens; they were too old for the job and had not been fed the right diet for heavy lifting. Reaching us, they dumped the litter on the pavement with relief, then leaned on it to recover.

Out tumbled a man who had convinced himself he was a canny entrepreneur. For that he ought to have hailed from the eastern end of the Mediterranean, where men of business cheat foreigners without remorse, as they have skilfully done in their Greek-speaking milieu for so many centuries. (Apart from the fact Rome is packed with them, I had been there, so I knew.) This character approaching us had failed to win the nationality lottery. He was born in the wrong place: I could see he was a native Gaul. His features looked right for that, while his spiky hair proved it. All he needed was a torque.

That background must have put him at a disadvantage, commercially. Where he came from, people are only perfidious to other Gallic tribes; they don't know anybody else, not since Rome came along to contain them securely in their villages and very kindly prevent invaders turning up to bother them. While he seemed to think he had no reason to disguise his origins, I could see his heritage affected him. He had the look of someone whose ancestors had been beaten to a pulp by Julius Caesar, someone who expected here in Rome to be downtrodden again. The tip of his nose was red; he felt the cold. His Latin was barely up to it.

However, he had an interesting job. He could be proud of this, because he had invented it himself. Like all the best jobs, it was one that had never existed before he came along, and really it did not need doing.

'Cintugnatus!' exclaimed Mucius. The man's name proved he was Gallic, though he could easily have done something about that. Actors were not the only people who might assume appropriate pseudonyms. Any good businessman decides early in his career what will sound best in whatever market he plans to dominate. Think of Augustus, once merely Octavian. What an operator. Shady as Hades, yet grabbed himself a brilliant honorific. Never looked back.

I had assumed Cintugnatus was a loser. I was wrong. The job he had invented made him a winner in Rome.

'Where is the bastard who took them?' he cried, clearly in anguish, staring around.

'Jumped in the Tiber,' answered Mucius, heartlessly.

'Did he tell you where he put them?'

'He never said a word.'

'Oh, no!'

'Took whom?' I interjected.

'His clients,' said Mucius.

'My clients!' the Gaul confirmed, wailing. 'Gnaeus stole my clients.'

'What kind of clients?' I asked, trying to imagine what part of any workforce Gnaeus could possibly have poached – and why. 'Are you an informer like myself?'

'I am an agent.'

'Who do you work for?'

'I am freelance,' he answered proudly.

'What's your line?'

'The theatre.'

'In what capacity?' Our conversation was circular but I had deduced that the vigiles thought this character had a vital contribution to make, so I was persistent. I wanted to find out for myself, too, not have to rely on Mucius. (He was smirking as he listened.)

Given his poor Latin, it was not surprising Cintugnatus had taught himself a formal declaration: 'I supply specialist acts for performance in popular stage drama.'

'*Io!*' I tried a new angle: 'Would I have heard of them?'

Cintugnatus looked pitying. 'But who has not?'

'Names?'

Finally I screwed something out of him: 'Patursus, Matursa and Ursulinus.'

Oh, no. In my head I could suddenly hear Thalia's voice: *There's a rumour that troublemakers have got into the imperial menagerie . . .*

'Bellerophon's balls, Cintugnatus.' My plea was desperate. 'I do hope you are not telling me your "clients" are three bears?'

'But of course!' he exclaimed, with a Gallic shrug, as if I should have realised all along.

49

His 'clients' were a brave choice: they were Caledonian brown bears. Two enormous parents, he told us, and their second-year cub, who had grown almost as big as his mummy and daddy. Their main job was killing either people or other big animals in the arena. They carried out criminal executions, rampaged in mock-hunts, or were pitted against wild beast opponents. Occasionally they would fight a bull – and win.

Cintugnatus was someone's freedman, released from slavery but cast out into the world; without means, he might well have starved. Only poets tend to be more desperate for dinners. He had looked around and hit on a hole in the skills market. He convinced someone at the Porta Praenestina menagerie that arranging for the bears to appear in plays exceeded their remit and skills since they were little more than primitive zoo-keepers. Performance in drama, he pointed out, required firm dates, contracts, terms, and consideration of safety needs, both to protect the public and for the bears' own welfare. They carried value. They should not be put at risk unnecessarily. Nor should their bloodthirsty talents be wasted on inferior scripts.

Cintugnatus was more affable than most Gauls and as shrewd as a Greek squid-seller. He was soon negotiating with theatre producers, splitting the profits with the menagerie keepers. I guessed this was all unofficial; public auditors never saw any evidence. He would not specify to us the going rate on appearance fees, a subject he claimed was commercial-in-confidence and even private to his clients; whatever the base rate, his percentage was visibly adequate. He owned his litter. It needed paint; it was second-hand; but few people had them. He owned the slaves who lugged him around as well. He was thin, but maybe he liked salad.

The imperial keepers provided all practical care. Cintugnatus was not burdened with feeding, housing or generally looking after the bears. He need never sweep his clients' enclosure, let alone check their teeth and gums, inspect their faeces or keep notes on parasitic infestations. For him, this was ideal. It went without saying, they were extremely fierce. Handling them was so dangerous, it was next to impossible. Their diet might include grass, nuts, roots, and fish, but their first choice was raw meat, in large quantities. An idealistic keeper once tried to engage Patursus with the notion of vegetarianism, feeding him seeds and berries. All went well for a while.

'And then?'

'Then he ate the keeper.'

Two nights ago, somebody had broken in and stolen all three imperial bears. Each had his personal travel-cage on wheels for being transported to places of entertainment; the thief had stolen those too. One alert keeper spotted the abduction in process. He was knocked unconscious, but survived. When he came round, he was able to croak that he had recognised one of the thieves, a man who regularly delivered snacks and engaged in conversation during their engagements at the new amphitheatre. His name was Gnaeus.

Before he whacked the keeper, this Gnaeus had crowed that the bears were all about to play parts in special dramas.

'Dramas plural?' I asked anxiously. Mucius nodded. Remembering the conversation I had had only that morning, in bed with Tiberius, I knew there were various dramatisations of myths that had featured characters who were despatched by wild animals, generally bears. Cintugnatus told us that Patursus, Matursa and even the young Ursulinus knew what they were supposed to do. So long as they were hungry – which would easily have been achieved by not feeding them since they were taken – they would kill and eat anyone they could get hold of.

'Daedalus spooks them in a performance, when he suddenly drops in on them,' Cintugnatus informed us. Like all the best agents, his outlook was ruthless. 'But he tends to be splatted by the fall, so they soon rip his wings off and start feasting.'

'This is all gory! Did you represent the animal that tore Orpheus apart when Vespasian's amphitheatre was opened?' I asked, feeling depressed.

'Oh, yes, that was one of mine. No ear for music. He trashed the harp too. That was a bit of a waste. I didn't get paid for his amphitheatre outing – it was imperial business – but I soon picked up other events for him. Bit of a grumpy character, though hard-working and a valued client. Gone to the gods now, but I am still living off his fame.'

I was trying to find a feel for the general situation, but Mucius had had enough chat. 'The thing is now,' he decided, 'we need to find where Gnaeus has stashed your bears.' He must have been thinking about it, because he then added, 'I'm going to send my lads out searching for advertisements for plays.' He was signalling a bunch of vigiles to gather for instructions.

'What you need to look out for,' I pre-empted, 'are either titles or named characters called Selurus, Orpheus or Daedalus.'

'Or any mention of appearances by bears,' Cintugnatus insisted. To Mucius and me he explained, 'In all contracts I sign, I always insist that the bears have full billing in publicity material.'

'Very professional!' scoffed Mucius. I detected that entrepreneurs were not his favourite members of the public. I also guessed that, as a rule of thumb, he despised Gauls. In ancient times a Gallic horde once swept down Italy and nearly climbed the walls of Rome; Romans had long memories. Besides, Gauls, who had now been allowed over the doorstep and even into the Senate, were easier to hate than tribes outside the Empire because here they were, face to face, ready to be sneered at.

'Don't be like that,' whined Cintugnatus, routinely.

'Like what? What I want you to do, Cintugnatus, is very quickly organise some experienced handlers who can be kept near here. Then, if we find your furry, friendly clients, men who know what to do can be called up in time to stop a tragedy. That Gnaeus likes to stage his horrors here in the Field of Mars. We had an episode with a ferocious bull that was far from nice . . .' He tailed off. Rallying, he finished, 'Sit yourself where I can find you. There's a bar called the Abyss of Tartarus where they will look after you until needed.'

'On expenses?' demanded the agent.

'Sorry!' Mucius disillusioned him. 'Public duties. Entertainment claims are not allowed.'

Viewing me as a reasonable woman, who understood rules, he beckoned me somewhat apart. Milo and Hyro followed and stood close. 'Now then, Flavia!'

'Call me Albia.'

'Don't mess about, this is serious. I am doing my best. I've flooded the area with troops. They are searching all the auditoria: the Marcellus, the Pompey, the Balbus – again – all the circuses, the stadium – again – and the Odeum. I've even sent a lad to warn the staff at the Flavian Amphitheatre and the Circus Max, even though I don't feel this individual is interested in going so far afield. That Davos is going to make me aware of anything suspicious over at the Gaius and Nero. Now, about him: he's got a theory, which could be a bit worrying, so you and I have got to have a talk, Flavia Albia.'

I now understood what message had sent Mucius haring off on his own: acting on a report of the bear-theft, he had rushed to the menagerie. That was when he had assigned me my minders. Later, this had become even more urgent. He received a visit from Davos. While Thalia had gone off to check her own beasts at her encampment, Davos had been sent back with a warning. What he had said did not surprise me.

Now they were sure that 'Tranio' and Gnaeus were one person, Davos and Thalia were afraid he had a list of further victims. If what had happened all those years ago in Syria had fuelled his anger against Cremes and Phrygia, and coloured his antagonism to Philocrates, his next move was bound to be against the people who had exposed his crony. That had led to personal hardship for Tranio, all the worse when he must consider himself broadly innocent.

Which two informers had exposed the other 'Twin', Grumio? Who had caused Tranio to lose his position and be taken into custody? Davos had told Mucius that on his list of victims were certain to be my parents, Falco and Helena.

'They are out of Rome,' I said quickly.

'Right! Then what is he going to do, girl? He doesn't know where they are. If he cannot lay hands on them, Albia, he can still cause them heartbreak. He can do it by attacking you. I reckon he tried it once already, that night at the Saepta.' I feared he was right. 'Be reasonable,' Mucius pleaded. 'Until we round up these beasts from the zoo, and catch the man himself, if he is still alive, I want you to go back to the Aventine. This pair can come and stay with you, Hyro and Milo. They will help that decent man you married to guard your house as tight as Titus until we give you the all-clear.'

I listened with more patience than he might have expected. Even so, I saw he knew already that I found this idea unacceptable.

He sighed.

I did not even bother telling him no.

SELURUS
THE BANDIT KING OF SICILY

50

Mucius dumped Cintugnatus at the Abyss of Tartarus. The agent hounded us with questions on the way, demanding why a 'respectable' bar should be named for a primordial god and a dungeon he kept where wicked souls were tortured after they died.

'It's called that because it's surrounded by a flaming river to keep out timewasters who never buy much. Plus they keep a filthy hydra there to stop you leaving without paying.' This was a new satirical side to Mucius, though he told jokes with a dismal expression.

Encouraged by his officer, Hyro warned the Gaul: 'Don't venture down into the cellar. It's so deep seven bronze hammers could be thrown in one after another yet would never reach the bottom.'

'Besides,' Milo backed him up with that twinkle of his, 'it's full of Titans, all furious about having been locked up.'

Cintugnatus believed none of this, which showed he was not entirely dumb.

Mucius repaired to the Winkle. I followed him; the two lads followed me.

Mucius decided he had to have privacy. People were standing about in the street, discussing how the fugitives had been found and what excitements might come next. Mucius brusquely ordered them all to move on. Looking offended, most at least edged out of sight. Once the place was quieter, he felt comfortable enough to question the oily-haired waiter.

To my surprise, this involved neither shouting nor physical violence. Mucius might have felt shy about interrogating women, but he was relaxed and easy-going with a male witness. There was no suggestion of dragging him off to the station-house. Mucius simply leaned on the wooden bar counter and talked to him.

I perched on the cat's stool. Cleo stalked off, waving an orange tail at me in complaint.

Hyro and Milo squatted on what would have been the edge of the kerb, if this muddy back lane had had any such thing. Mucius told them to get up and stop dirtying their tunics. He would keep an eye on me; they were to make themselves useful for once and go into the Infant Hercules for a background chat with the waiter there. I stayed put, saying nothing. I didn't suppose I was welcome, but I was not ordered to leave.

The session began with classic softening up, as the investigator asked simple questions about the waiter's origins, past life, daily routine. Was he married? No? Very wise! What was the bar owner like to work for? Did they have a lot of customers?

'And what's your name, son?'

'Crispinus.'

'Good man! Nice and Latin, none of your damned Greek! Now, Crispinus—'

And so Mucius worked his way into discussing Gnaeus and Megalo. Crispinus, who must have known what to expect if the vigiles dragged him to their barracks for a going-over, answered everything he asked. At least, at the time we thought he did.

He knew that Gnaeus and Megalo went to the Charybdis across the road every week, meeting the other Farcicals. The wine there was terrible so Megalo had always liked a drink at the Winkle. Gnaeus had taken to joining Megalo; they also hobnobbed with another man, who was not one of the acting crowd. Short fellow, balding, vicious tongue on him. He and Gnaeus were old cronies. He and Megalo seemed to know each other, too, but more from occasional piecework they did together in theatres. Employment tended to be patchy because the third man was often away for long periods. He must have some other job that took him elsewhere, though Crispinus believed his home base was in Rome.

'So where does he travel?'

'Down south. Neapolis sometimes.'

'What's in Neapolis? Sea, and a bloody horrendous volcano!'

'Gladiating?' Crispinus suggested, shrugging vaguely.

'Theatres,' I piped up, since it was relevant. Mucius flicked a glance across, then indicated with a raised finger that I should pipe down again.

'Doesn't Megalo go?'

'His wife won't let him. While he's left behind, that Megalo does shit-shifting for extra money,' Crispinus volunteered.

'Shit? He told us he washes out *dolia*.'

'Pot-washing too, yes. He'll do anything that comes along.' Crispinus glanced at me, phrased it delicately: 'Mucks out stables and such.'

'Stables?' Mucius queried, sceptically.

'Under the amphitheatre.'

'You mean he scrapes up the stinking lion poo?'

'Lions, rhinoceroses—'

'Bears?'

'I suppose.'

'Bears!' Mucius threw at me, with heavy meaning.

'Bears,' I returned quietly. So Megalo had some relationship with arena bears. I had noted him as 'surly but bold'. He probably thought he knew enough to handle the beasts.

Mucius continued to grill the waiter. The third man had appeared quite frequently this autumn, here for his family, for the winter festivals. Yes, they had all been holding deep discussions in recent weeks. Crispinus did not know what. He had his work, serving people. Besides, sensible waiters did not eavesdrop on regulars' schemes. They could always go off in a huff and drink at the Hercules instead. Well, they could if they wanted to be insulted by old Hairy-arms, the useless twat. Actually, he was all right really.

What, Mucius asked (ignoring Hairy-arms), did Gnaeus and Megalo say when they turned up in their sheepskin loincloths, wanting to hide?

'Just that. We have to hide up. Don't let on. Anyone asks, you haven't seen us.'

'Did they threaten you?'

'Why? They know me, I know them.'

'All lovey-dovey! Tearaways often use your bar as a place of concealment, do they?'

It had been known, Crispinus admitted.

Mucius then showed he had missed nothing earlier: 'So! What is this work old Megalo does in theatres with the third man?'

'Scenery, I think.'

'What scenery?'

Crispinus said they built special features. He couldn't say what; he didn't understand that kind of thing. Anyway, he was not interested. He never went to the theatre. He'd rather sit here, earn a crust, stroke the cat. He did know the men had been hard at work yesterday on some very big platform that had to be made so it would collapse.

'Yesterday? I thought Megalo was hiding in your back shed?'

'The other fellow came and got him. Gnaeus went as well.'

'What – they went out, then came back again?'

'The Winkle was a kind of base for them.'

'Where's the platform job?'

'No idea.'

'The three men are doing it?'

'Knocked up working drawings right here in my bar.'

'See the drawings?'

'I told you I don't do eavesdropping.Didn't want me to look, in any case. They always made stuff in a workshop somewhere. Mind you, I heard Megalo was often kicked off the job.'

Megalo was not much use – it was often remarked on: he could no longer climb ladders because of his bad back, couldn't hammer a nail in straight. He only carried things. According to Crispinus, Megalo had grown very tired of all the criticism; out in the Winkle's shed, he had grumbled to the waiter that he was ready to give up on the other two.

'Think he'll tell me what's been going on?'

'You'll have to ask him.'

'I shall do that, son, if I catch him! So tell me more about these projects.'

Most of the work, Crispinus said, was carried out by the third man, who was more skilful. He was a sad lot, always unhappy at everything, a complete misery. He had been trained as a carpenter, worked for a fancy firm in his youth, had a professional belt with all his tools hung on it.

Oh, really!

He had made the counter, this one right here. We all looked at it: not such a crude plank, but extremely well-planed wood, wood so smooth I was amazed to realise I had acquired no splinters from leaning on it. I peered underneath and found a good dove-tailed joint that I guessed Tiberius would approve. I kept my hands in my lap afterwards, not wanting to lean on something made by the man who had created the Pasiphaë cow.

So, asked Mucius, hardly altering the casual tone he had used throughout, was there any chance Crispinus knew this clever chippy's name?

'I should bloody well think so,' scoffed Crispinus, hotly, as if his social skills as a waiter were being maligned. 'He's been coming here long enough! He's Plotinus, isn't he?'

Sharp intake of breath!

Then Mucius surprised me again, because he produced from the hidden depths of his inner tunic a four-tablet memo booklet. Flipping it open between his hands, he searched with a stubby finger, then found a note. He half turned to me. 'So, Albia! What have you got? I've put Plotinus down with the professional actors.'

'He is their chief musician.' I did not need to look him up. 'Seems to have done it since they were in Syria.'

Mucius finally gave me a straight look, as we both faced a reassessment. Plotinus? The self-satisfied orchestra-leader, who might have a woman somewhere in Rome, but more often went to see his grandmother? Plotinus who, Ariminius had told me, had joined the company as a feckless youth who had been working for a furniture restorer. Someone had given him his own lyre. The loving grandmother?

If he had served a long time with Chremes and Phrygia, Plotinus could well have developed a loathing for them. They had favoured their actors over musicians. He could be unpleasant. I had heard him at the funeral: foul-mouthed and brutally sure he was right about everything. He must have known Gnaeus in Syria, when he was calling himself Tranio. They had picked up again, back in Rome. Plotinus could also have met Philocrates. There might have been woman-trouble between them, trouble that still grated with a man who bore grudges.

As if to ram home this new, very different situation, Crispinus assumed the look of apologetic mock-honesty that waiters use – I mean when they have taken your order for grilled red mullet, but come back to say they have just been told by the chef that mullet, though still chalked on the menu board, is now off. At which point, you slowly realise that mullet is always on the board, but never actually available.

Mucius and I had to accept we had allowed ourselves to be misled, or had even over-eagerly misled ourselves. Crispinus assured us: 'Of course when they are doing all that plotting of theirs, the man in charge of all their clever pranks is that Plotinus. He is the one you want.'

I wondered. The accusation felt wrong, especially since the waiter claimed he never listened in on customers. This sounded like something he had been told to say. But we had hardly time to absorb it when a member of the vigiles ran up, breathless, shouting that they thought they had found where the bears were.

51

The Theatre of Pompey was always extraordinary. He had built it as a gesture, a victory monument to himself. Romans in public life do not see modesty as a virtue. Pompey grandly donated his monument to Rome. Father calls him a flash bastard.

It was still the largest theatre complex anywhere in the world. In order to create a permanent stone structure for performances, Pompey Magnus had had to build outside the ancient walls, which at that time formed the city boundary. So he chose the Field of Mars. He dedicated everything to Venus Victrix, his personal deity, and, to circumvent other regulations, made out that he was building not a theatre but a temple to the goddess, as the rules allowed. A dominating shrine was perched right above the semi-circle of seats, to look as if they were the temple steps. The main message was that he was a very successful general and, in granting his many victories, Venus had made Pompey her favourite.

The other message was: Sucks to you, Julius Caesar.

I could not remember ever being in the theatre, and certainly not the temple. I knew the complex best from the large, attached enclosure, where audience members stretched their legs during intervals. The general public came here too. The colonnaded garden, with lavish fountains and sculptures, was a favourite assignation place. Hopefuls could also cruise the arcades, which had rooms dedicated to art and other works that had been collected by Pompey on his eastern campaigns. There were fine female representations of no less than fourteen countries he had conquered; a famous painting of Alexander the Great brazenly invited comparisons. Statues of artists and actors featured too, but the monument had been planned to focus on Pompey's war booty. Golden curtains from Pergamum gleamed in all the colonnades. To my mind, after a hundred years, they were rather bedraggled, but at least moths had avoided the gold thread.

Somewhat lesser art was sold in one of the colonnades during auctions held by my family's business. We treated that corner of the porticus as ours. It was very close to the Saepta Julia, handy for bringing sale goods. Pleasure gardens full of plausible adulterers are ideal places to offer showy trinkets. We sold a lot of jewellery. Most was not quite as good as its sparkle promised, but you may think that's typical of sex itself.

At the opposite end of the garden from the theatre and temple, near what we regarded as our site, stood a curia for political meetings. The senate sometimes met there, which my grandfather and father always regarded as a personal slight, messing up their auction calendar. No ordinary buyers would come while the place was cluttered with poshos in their wide purple stripes, and senators rarely bid on anything. If ever they did, it was impossible to screw the cash out of them so our podium rule was to pretend never to see them gesturing.

If one of Pompey's aims had been to outdo his rival, it became a spectacular irony that Julius Caesar was assassinated, ostensibly for his own unpalatable ambitions, while attending his enemy's curia. The murder of the divine Julius should have meant the complex was untouchable. However,

Augustus felt he was entitled to perform radical remodelling – a cynical move to play down the political overtones of Pompey's work. Famously, he created a huge public lavatory on the blighted spot where Caesar collapsed at the foot of Pompey's statue. Somewhere so evil should be used only for filthy purposes. Fine by us. This latrine was useful during auctions, especially now our head porter was a very old man with a bladder problem.

Due to its splendour and size, the Theatre of Pompey continued to be Rome's main location for plays. Its presence had drawn others, forming a theatre district. Given its prominence, it had been inevitable the undertaker killer would choose the place for some new expression of his mania. Even before we could get there, we had a good idea what horrors he might have left for us on the famous old stage.

As we hurried along, Hyro felt called to expound drama history: 'When the theatre first opened, they brought a famous tragic actor called Clodius Aesopus out of retirement, especially for the dedication show.'

'And they had gladiators,' Milo contributed, also able to talk while running, though he was slightly more puffed. 'Exotic beasts. Five hundred lions – and elephants. Fair dos to the public, people were so upset by the beast-killings, they rose up, all complaining about Pompey—'

'Never mind Pompey's heart-rending bloody lions!' Mucius ordered, once more exasperated by this pair. 'Concentrate on that Gaul's three bears. Shut up and move yourselves!'

The entrance to the theatre complex had always been tightly controlled, using doors at either side of the curia. This was to direct the fresh visitor's gaze down the inner garden area towards the theatre and temple of Venus Victrix. The central axis must be almost a thousand feet long. Its planting design incorporated topiary rectangles with overlapping circles, a geometric delight that was shaded by enormous plane trees. Viewed through a double avenue of greenery, the intended sightline had perhaps been finer originally, but was permanently blocked when the spoilsport Augustus had a stone scaenae frons built in the theatre. Its back wall now hid the fine temple view. Even so, for patrons, the long walk through the plane tree groves was a crucial part of their play-going experience.

It was less good for us.

Coming away from the river, to enter the grounds we had had to hurry along the Hall of a Thousand Columns. I felt I was counting them all. That walkway ran the entire length of the enclosure on the outside; it must have seemed a grand idea to some old Republican designer who was not rushing to find a bunch of stolen bears. Rounding the end at last, we came into the Sacred Area, a piazza where a group of carefully preserved, small, age-old temples was incorporated into the overall development; reverence for the pious past was to elevate attending a play as a religious experience. The piety was probably missed by those of the public who used the gardens as a pick-up point.

There were four little temples. A marble and bronze statue of Fortune lived in one smart round shrine, which was dedicated to Today's Good Luck. This happy concept probably meant more to skulking lovers than to whoever was awaiting us at the theatre today. Somebody there was definitely out of luck. Unfortunately, by the time we raced down through the elegant garden and entered the beautiful theatre to find him, we could not tell who he had been.

Bears are messy eaters.

52

We walked straight in. No one was asking to see tickets.

The building was almost deserted. It seemed that the theatre had been out of use during the recent holiday. Curators were nowhere to be found and any maintenance slaves had run away. They must have been so terrified they had told no one what was happening. Inevitably, slaves would believe they would get the blame. Generally, it would be true. They were not to know we already had prime suspects. The suspects were not here, but their instrument of death was: the heavy-duty Caledonian bear Patursus.

The stage and scaenae sections of Pompey's Theatre were attached directly to the auditorium, making a single structure, whereas Greek theatres slightly separate the two. This, according to Hyro and Milo, created acoustic issues that called for specialist acting techniques. Such demands did not bother Patursus. While the vigiles speculated in undertones, he grunted a loud warning that carried as far as the top seats, right in front of the temple. Either someone had taught the huge beast how to project his growl or making threats came naturally.

We had known we were likely to find at least one animal here, because what had alerted the vigiles was a wheeled transportation cage they had discovered, empty and with its door open, outside the theatre entrance. Deep ruts suggested two other cages had been there earlier, though they were now missing. The group who discovered the transport had waited for Mucius, before looking inside the theatre. The men had reasoned it was now too late to prevent anything horrible.

It was. Onstage stood a representation of Mount Etna. A big, battered sandal, perhaps stolen from outside a shoemaker's shop, portrayed Empedocles's footwear when spat up by the volcano in the old myth; hung on a pole, this served as a scenery board. Some torches, no longer lit, had been positioned around, perhaps to flicker like lava flames. A large platform had been piled with fake rocks. The three bears must have been kept ready below the stage; when a trapdoor was opened in the floor, they emerged. The victim, arms bound, was unable to escape. He had somehow been made to climb the volcano's rocks, which had been to collapse, pitching him down onstage, helpless, into the bears' reach.

Patursus was still onstage. He was by himself. If the others had been with him, someone had taken them away. We reckoned he had been there all morning, having a fine time. He must have been hungry to begin with, though this no longer applied. He and his companions had either eaten most of the victim or hidden body parts for later as bears do. The remains we could see scattered around him were nauseating.

'Oh, Jupiter! That is so disgusting!'

'Who is it?'

'*Was* it . . . Who can tell? They've had his head.'

'Oh, Jupiter!

Patursus stood up. He was tall. He was taller than us, when he reared on his hind legs, though fortunately at that point he made no move to come and introduce himself. None of us dared to approach. We looked at him, trying not to catch his eye. He was brown, shaggy-furred, long snout, mean eyes, strong claws, fierce and unpredictable. Standing, he gazed around the theatre. The atmosphere was tense, though so far more thoughtful than panicking. What was going to happen next?

Nobody moved any more than necessary. We all tried not to contemplate what was scattered around the stage: those bloody pieces of bone, intestines, brains and flesh that must once have been a human being. Patursus was still holding what looked like a part of a man's arm.

Mucius told men to fetch the menagerie keepers he had called up to the Campus. Others were to start pushing in the wheeled cage. He instructed me to close my eyes and get out. For once, I complied. Milo came with me, to wait in the fresh air until the situation had been made safe.

I sat on a low garden wall outside, trying not to think about what I had seen. Once the vigiles had arrived, by the usual social magic a crowd soon collected, though curious onlookers were now being held back in the garden. Some troops were inspecting the ruts and confirming that other cages had been there before.

I told Milo, 'Someone must have managed to recapture Matursa and Ursulinus, but not the bigger animal. There could only be one reason why they would bother—'

'They are planning to use the other bears again!'

The menagerie keepers arrived at a run, hurrying straight into the theatre. A vigilis came out and called to Milo as he passed us, saying he had to fetch Suedius and the funeral cart. 'Nobody's going to make a death mask, that's certain!'

The joker loped off, while I controlled myself. I think I have a strong stomach, but today all my strength-of-will was tested.

'Want to go and watch them catch the bear?' asked Milo.

'No, thanks. You go, if you want to.'

Milo decided he would rather guard me. He, too, had a novel pallor.

Hyro joined us. He said the bear had been successfully lured into his cage. As soon as Patursus saw the familiar contraption, he had wandered straight over, climbed in meekly, lain down on his bed-straw and immediately fallen asleep. The keepers would send for a mule to pull his cage home eventually, but for the time being Patursus would stay here. Nobody yet knew where the other two bears were. Once they were found, their big patriarch might be needed as a decoy.

'They've managed to get that arm off him. Mucius has it.' Hyro fell silent.

Mucius came out. Thank goodness he was not carrying the dead man's arm. Hyro stepped to one side, nodding for Milo to follow. Out of the corner of my eye I saw them muttering shiftily, while they looked anywhere except at me.

Mucius was carrying a short length of bloody rope. He seemed exhausted by horror. 'Oh, gods, I can't take much more of this! We managed to retrieve that limb. It's his left arm. This rope was trailing off it. Poor fellow must have been tied up. Maybe your husband can say if the rope matches the other stuff.'

'I shall ask him, if we need to.'

'I'll get it cleaned up, put it in a bag. You don't have to touch it . . . Now, listen, there's two points.' Mucius seemed embarrassed. I demanded to be told these points. Mucius was making efforts at kindness, which was troubling.

'The lads have found a notice. Charcoal. Same as before, you won't be surprised. This one is announcing *Selurus, the Bandit King of Sicily*, which it says is having an extra performance, with an exciting conclusion – King Selurus executed by bears, "by special permission of the aediles".'

He stopped.

'Aediles' special licence. Right. Get on!' I told him. *Aediles? This bear has killed an aedile?*

Mucius was holding one fist tightly closed. 'We found some items. Cloth – can't tell if it's toga or tunic, but with purple banding. Magistrates' width. And there was this I've got here. Still on his hand. I had to wrench it off myself, can't wait for Suedius . . .' He was stalling. 'Albia, I am very sorry to be asking—'

'What?' I could hardly breathe.

'Your husband, Faustus: does your husband, the aedile, wear a seal ring?'

Without waiting for me to answer, he opened his hand to show me. A small gold object, probably wiped roughly before he brought it out to me, yet still showing a red smear of blood, lay upon his palm.

I was still sitting on the low garden wall, or I would probably have fainted.

53

I could not even look. I had lost a husband once. At least when they brought his body home to me, it was still recognisably Lentullus. He only looked to be asleep.

I had buried my face in my hands. I managed to gasp out that Tiberius signed with a hippocampus. Mucius quickly told me this had a classic helmeted head.

Finally, I looked. We both gulped in air. For a moment, my head swam even more.

'Not his.'

'You are absolutely sure?' He spoke gently.

'Certain.' Waves of sheer relief were making me queasy. 'His ring is a thrashing seahorse. Not that.'

'Good. Some other poor bastard copped for it then . . . You all right?'

'Yes.' I was sensible again. Not his. Not him. An aedile was dead, murdered, but not mine.

The ring in the investigator's hand was gold, incised with a warrior, side on, right-facing, crested helm. The design is so common, it's a cliché. It comes on gold, silver and iron, or hardstones, obsidian, carnelian, sardonyx, even more easily carved jet and amber. At auction, Father just chucks them into mixed lots among necklaces with broken clasps. To me, and presumably Tiberius, that overused pictogram was useless as proof of signature. As long as I had known him,

Tiberius had worn and used a seal ring with his much less common wave-romping hippocamp: half horse, half scaly, curly-tailed fish.

Mucius signalled to Hyro and Milo. 'Flavia Albia wants to be taken to her man. Hire her a chair – you should find one out in the Sacred Area. Go with her.'

I made a feeble protest.

'Don't be daft. Come back tomorrow,' chided Mucius.

He was right about my need to be with Tiberius. I said my family were over on the Janiculan, in Father's house. That was good, decided Mucius. Nobody would look for me there. Dusk was starting to draw in now. Though full of questions, I could not wait to have my arms around my man, to feel his living warmth.

'I last saw Faustus this morning, at the Scribonius house. Is that—'

'Must be,' said Mucius. He was bleak. 'I'll have to go.'

He was not even ruling me out of the inquiry, as I might have expected. He seemed to share his plans with me while he was making them: 'We'll finish up here once the undertaker comes. It's too late to do much. Tomorrow we start back here, try to find those two missing cages. I'm going to call in the Urbans to help with searches. I hate doing it – I'll have to get Caunus to put his name to the request, he's a fart-arse – but this nightmare has gone too far now. A magistrate – that's going to count. All bloody Rome will be looking at us. We need more resources. We need men who are armed . . .'

He had been talking to me and the two vigiles (who stood to attention, looking quelled). When he stopped, he rubbed his empty hand through those tight, pale curls, as if consoling himself.

His final remarks were quieter, spoken directly to me: 'Trust me. I can be sympathetic. I'll say, shall I, you will be there tomorrow? Give her a night to sleep on her trouble, then you go to comfort her.'

'She has lost everyone—'

'I know. This is my duty, Albia, not yours. Jove knows, it won't be the first time. You see your Faustus now and be very glad you've got him. Then you get some rest. Leave this with me. I'm going now. I'm going to inform the wife.'

We had an identity for the dead man, so we understood the motive. This was his punishment for changing the play and for his patronage of Philocrates. The bears had killed Scribonius Attica.

54

Everything did feel a little better once I reached the Janiculan villa. Once I had held Tiberius tightly, I relaxed as much as was possible, stroked the dog, let our little nephews climb all over me. I felt better – yet also worse, because I still had all this warmth to come home to, while over on the Pincian, alone now in the ways that would matter, was Sabina Gallitta. She had staff, but I had already seen that she did not show her feelings in front of them. She would have no comfort tonight.

Tiberius was terse. 'How? How could the bastards get to him?'

That would be an urgent question for next day. I had others. The still-missing bears. The missing men. Who else might be lined up for attack? When? Where? Could more tragedies be prevented?

We dined, though I had no idea what the meal was. My thoughts were churning.

Hyro and Milo had been welcomed. They quickly made themselves at home in the kitchen. Tiberius went to speak to them. He did not tarry; he wanted to be close to me. He knew I had been shaken by my fears for him; he was also afraid for me. On some evenings, after our fosterlings Gaius and Lucius had been told stories and tucked into bed, we two would sit together, chewing over events and discussing plans. Not tonight. There was a deep silence between us, followed by an early night. We held each other close, in further silence.

I did sleep. Sometimes you manage, when your brain and body know they need to be fit and fired up for a long day.

Tiberius was taking the family back home. He had to go to the Aventine: he wanted to visit the aediles' office at the Temple of Ceres. The fatal loss of a magistrate meant a bureaucratic crisis.

As soon as anyone dies during his term of duty, great wheels of officialdom begin turning. By tradition there are four aediles looking after Rome. Freedmen would be panicking, though managing the situation. There had to be four aediles. Be reasonable: something might come up that three intelligent men with a year's experience behind them could not handle on their own.

A report must be flashed to the Palace; someone with the appropriate level of authority must keep the Emperor up to speed. Never mind the human loss – grief would be formally acknowledged, of course, standard condolence despatched to the wife (or better still, since this was Rome, to male relatives of the deceased) but with no delay. A rule book must exist – Hades, there must be one after centuries of city administration. The top-flight secretariats would not need to consult it: a scroll was already on a desk, listing who was to be considered next and contacted. A wise head. Safe hands. A man with a sound record, who had never annoyed Domitian.

This substitute would be approved, confirmed, summoned from his holiday villa, inaugurated, inducted, added to rolls of honour, congratulated by his serving colleagues, booked in for working lunches with the consuls, perhaps introduced to the Emperor, assigned his curule chair, advised of his rights to a fringed toga and ancestral masks, and notified as to which sector of the city was under his authority until New Year. On the Kalends of January he would be decommissioned and packed off back to his villa. If he was lucky, they would thank him for his term of service.

Tiberius said he had best go along to the office at the Temple of Ceres to try to impose common sense. I would take his deep sympathy to Sabina Gallitta. He and Scribonius might not have been close, but she was his colleague's widow; we had dined at their house. As more than a matter of protocol, I was to urge her to say whether he could assist her in any way. He would call on her when he could.

Even to this decent man, there was a slight sense that, as his wife, I was going to see her as his representative. Of course, my view was differently skewed.

It turned out I did not have to visit the house. This was lucky. Up on the Pincian, it was inconveniently placed for anything I needed to do later.

I was travelling in a chair borrowed from my grandfather's stable, borne by two of his slaves, ancient but moderately keen for adventure. We were flanked by Hyro and Milo. As they brought me over Nero's Bridge into Rome, we were stopped by a man I recognised as the Scribonius chamberlain. He had been chosen by his mistress because he would recognise me and I would remember him.

'As she is busy away from home, Sabina Gallitta asked me to meet you here at the bridge, to save you a wasted journey.'

'How is she?'

'I believe Domina Sabina wept all night, but now she wishes to be active.'

'I see.' She was coping by being sensible. I wondered whether it was a natural response for Sabina, or if making herself busy masked inner hysteria. 'So where can I find her? What will she be doing?'

'She went at first light to reclaim our master's remains from that person, Suedius.' The chamberlain had sneered; seeing my expression, he added quickly that she would take with her the mortician the family preferred to use. *He* would collect the ghastly bones and flesh; she would not have to do it herself. 'We shall cremate Scribonius tonight, along with her good friend, Philocrates.' I wondered how that would please the aedile's fancy relatives. With any luck, they were all away, with no time to travel back to Rome. 'My mistress intends to visit the professional actors to invite them to the funeral.'

'Where will it be?'

'The garden of our house, followed by a private interment of the two urns in the family mausoleum.' Philocrates as well? Juno! 'Meanwhile, I believe she would feel more comfortable if you can join her when she speaks to the company members.'

'Certainly.'

I decided I could skip trying to find her with Suedius, 'that person', whom the flunkey and I both despised. I went straight to the actors' lodgings.

As we parked outside the Halcyon, I noticed straight away that a private litter was waiting there too. The widow had not come in the cumbersome carriage that I knew the couple owned. I was to learn why.

The actors had stationed Sabina at a table with a glass of mint tea. They surrounded her respectfully, all with sombre expressions. I could see that she had indeed spent the night crying, though she had now bravely pushed back her veil to face the world with dry eyes. On my arrival she stood up. We embraced. I put both hands to her shoulders and kissed her forehead. She re-seated herself quietly. I waved away the offer of similar refreshment. I had never been a devotee of herbal liquors. Bitter green water never helps my concentration.

Most of the people I had met were there: Simo, with his pale skin and receding red hair, Atticus in his hat, Pardicus with his bandaged wound from Buculus and his pigtail, Ariminius the scene-shifter and occasional bit-player, Crispa and Philotera, the women who hated roles where they had to take their clothes off. A big podgy lad must be Porrus, who was sent up ladders as an eavesdropping slave. Needless to say, one person failed to put in an appearance.

'I see Plotinus has gone off again! Another visit to his gran?'

Nobody seemed to think it untoward.

I would not discuss suspects in front of Sabina in her fragile state. Before I turned up, she must already have invited the actors to the cremation. When I arrived, Simo had been telling her they would be here for that, but afterwards everyone would leave Rome.

'So you are parting company? Where will you all go?' asked Sabina, as she sat down after greeting me.

'We expect to stick together for the time being. We had a prior booking for early spring on the Bay of Neapolis. Most of us are still intending to travel down there, in case we can pull something together, even without Chremes and Phrygia.'

'You need a patron,' she said quietly. I stopped her discreetly. I asked the actors to give us a few moments alone.

'I understand what you were saying, just then. I assume you will be a wealthy woman once your husband's will is read? You love the theatre, so you might consider giving this troupe support. But my advice to new widows is to take no major decisions for at least a year.'

'Some things cannot wait,' she answered. 'Those poor people need security. The company will fragment otherwise. Flavia Albia, I can help them and I think I shall.' However, she made no further attempt to speak on the subject.

She must have been thinking through a lot of things already: 'I shall never marry again.'

'Perhaps.'

'But I need to be occupied.'

'Of course.'

In an instant of clarity, Sabina gave me a direct look. 'I suppose I will be shunned, because of the manner of my husband's death.'

I confirmed the truth as I saw it too. 'People will turn away. More even than they did over your friendship with the actor. *Eaten by bears?* There will be members of your social circle you will never see again.'

'One woman called straight away this morning – but her interest was prurient. She wanted to be thrilled by hearing of agony and blood. I told her nothing. I do not suppose she will be back.'

'No. I apologise for the human race, Sabina. Tell your staff always to send them away, saying you are too distressed. Have their names taken. Then, if you want, you can visit the truly kind ones.' If there are any, I thought.

'Or not!' she replied tersely, in agreement.

I changed the subject. 'Sabina Gallitta, if you can endure it, there are some urgent matters. I don't expect you had much discussion with Mucius, when he brought your sad news, but please be brave and talk to me. It is very important to know how your husband was drawn away from home yesterday.'

She made no objection. She spoke calmly. It was simple enough. The oldest trick in the world. A note had been brought to Scribonius: it said Megalo had had enough of murder; he was offering to confess to the authorities. Terrified of what might be done to him by his confederates if he squealed, he was hiding in a bar near the river, afraid to come out. He offered to surrender to the aedile if he came in person with suitable assurances.

'Protection for Megalo? I think he is too deeply implicated to save! Whether or not the message came from him, it was a trick. Who brought this bogus note to your house?'

Someone anonymous had handed it in at the front door. Since the person immediately scuttled off, the porter took no further notice. The only description was 'furtive'. That applied to half of Rome.

'Do you have the note? May I see it?'

Fate so regularly snaffles clues. Scribonius took it with him because it contained directions to where Megalo supposedly was. It had not been found since.

Whoever had brought this trickery arrived after lunch. Scribonius was in a cheery mood: the idea that he might personally collar a key witness when the authorities had failed to do so greatly appealed to a man of his character. Within minutes, he was calling for the carriage. Sabina saw it disappear down the drive; a slave had been told to explain to his wife.

He was not stupid. Conscious of potential danger, he took armed guards. He went in that lumbering carriage of theirs – now impounded by the vigiles, said Sabina. Scribonius had bodyguards, highly visible, marching in front. It was how lictors would guard other important persons in Rome, yet not a wise arrangement. For one thing, unlike lictors, these guards failed to clear a passage ahead. The big carriage was held up in traffic. As soon as Sabina said this, I guessed another roadblock had been organised by the criminals.

The vehicle stopped. The hold-up mysteriously cleared, so the carriage moved on – until passers-by alerted the driver that one of the passenger doors was swinging open. The driver pulled up and jumped down. By then, he was too late. The guards ran back too, but there was nobody inside to help. Scribonius had gone, disappeared. Somebody must have leaped inside while the carriage was stationary; they stifled him, pulled him out and rushed him away. It could only have taken moments. He was a fit man, in his prime. It undoubtedly needed two of them, two at least. They must have caught him by surprise, instantly gagged him and bound his arms.

Passers-by claimed not to have noticed anything. It is very sad how many people on the streets of Rome suffer from total blindness. Most are deaf as well, apparently. Then they all go out to buy blind, deaf slaves to lead them around . . .

I confined myself to asking, 'Where did it happen?'

'They had driven along the Via Lata, following the directions sent. They had to turn where that road goes off alongside the Circus Flaminius.' The Vicus Pallacinae. It was featuring a lot in this case. Scribonius had been driven right outside the Halcyon and the Golden Cup, then past the premises of Suedius.

The stoppage occurred by the Temple of Bellona. That was well thought out. The abductors could bundle their victim straight off the main road, down an alley around the temple, into that piazza called Area Sacra. There, they could dive through the four ancient small temples, and when the coast was clear, rush into the Porticus of Pompey. If my family had had an auction yesterday, we could have waved to them as they stumbled past.

Of course we were not there. On a dark winter's day, the place must have been deserted.

I knew the rest: the abductors would have frogmarched Scribonius down one side of the garden. They could rely on being unobserved due to wintry weather having its deterrent effect on strollers. Anyone who had braved the complex at all would be sheltering under cover in the arcades, pretending to admire art. Nobody would have been gardening. Even the slaves with brooms who normally tried to overhear scandal and sell it to informers would not have bothered to be there.

When they reached the far end and hauled him into the theatre, he would have seen Mount Etna all set up onstage, with its demountable rocks. Below was the cage that would drop open with a flip of a string, to release the starved bears. The scene was waiting for this hated aedile to act as Selurus, the Bandit King of Sicily.

Perhaps the perpetrators gloated, telling him why he was doomed. They likened him to an establishment bandit, a ruling oppressor maybe. Now his reign was over. They probably warned him of what was about to happen. He was forced up the stage volcano. A lever was pulled; the rocks collapsed. A string-tug opened the bear-pit's trapdoor. Down he went. Up they came. Bears swipe and bite to kill their prey. They are powerful and horrible.

At some point after Scribonius was dead, the mother and the young bear must have been lured back into their travelling cages. Patursus refused to comply. He stayed there until we found him.

55

Retelling what Mucius and her staff had described about yesterday's event left Sabina Gallitta badly shaken. She was imagining far too much detail. I helped her out to the litter, where Hyro and Milo stationed themselves in the street, looking up and down.

I did offer to go with Sabina, but she refused. She wanted me to concentrate on pursuit. She had more faith in me than in the vigiles. 'Call me a client. Send me a bill. Do your best for the dead.'

I closed the half-door for her, quietly nodding. This was not a situation for spelling out my daily rates and expenses. I felt confident she would be generous.

As the chairmen lifted the shafts, she put out her head: 'A praetor came.'

'But did not stay long?' I prophesied. 'I believe his name is Corvinus.'

'That's correct. He is mobilising the Urban Cohorts. Is this good?'

'Well, it's something!' I spoke drily. The last thing we wanted was the riot squad galumphing around. Still, sometimes it helps the bereaved to know action is being taken. Sabina seemed reassured. The praetor would feel self-satisfied. The Urbans would give the public something to stare at.

Under cover of this madness, a decent search could quietly continue.

I went back inside the Halcyon, trailed by my minders.

The actors had disappeared. I sent Milo and Hyro to roust them out, and they crept back in dribs and drabs. I waited, with my arms folded. Perhaps they looked apprehensive, though nothing prepared me for what I was to learn from them.

I began by demanding the truth about the missing Plotinus. Despite their previous nonchalance, they had been expecting questions and, for the first time, they seemed apprehensive when talking to me. Ariminius looked hangdog. Simo was rebellious, as if he had had a disagreement with the rest.

I gave them the ice treatment: I was disappointed in them. I had been sympathetic all along, yet they had withheld a vital clue. It looked like a conspiracy. If they had any loyalty to Chremes and Phrygia, any respect for Philocrates, any compassion for the aedile and his wife, now was the time to be honest. Surely they were not covering for him?

'We just thought he knew the wrong people. We didn't want to get him into trouble,' whined Pardicus.

'What? Not even after he and his pals got Buculus to gore you? How is your wound, by the way? I don't imagine Plotinus has sent you a flagon and a bunch of grapes, with an apology!'

As Pardicus hung his pigtailed head, Philotera, always the stroppier of the girls, tried self-justification: 'In a group like ours, we stick together. Half the world treats us like a bad smell. Anyway, we had no idea how deeply involved he was.'

'It was obvious at the funeral!' Simo was arguing with the rest now. 'For Heaven's sake, it was clear enough! He went off afterwards, saying he had arranged to have a drink with old friends. Bloody dangerous ones, it turns out.'

'We never knew who his drinking mates were,' Ariminius muttered defensively.

I scoffed. 'Nothing like a swift beaker with a gaggle of murderers!'

'Enough of the sarcasm, Albia! She's right, though.' Simo was still annoyed with his comrades. 'He took himself off just before we heard the crash on the road. I worked out that it was suspicious. Didn't any of you?'

Even if the others had stupidly avoided the truth, Simo could have confided in me, I thought. And he ought to have warned the vigiles. 'Have you asked Plotinus about it?'

'We haven't seen him since.'

'He was very rude about the Farcicals,' I reminded everyone. 'He made it deliberately cruel, the way he insulted them. And in their hearing, even though Gnaeus and Megalo were his fellow conspirators. Mind you, that could have been a front. Right! Let's have the real story at last, shall we? Plotinus has known Gnaeus since Syria. Did he bear some kind of personal grudge against Chremes and Phrygia?'

'He hated how they only cared about acting,' replied Atticus, taking off his woolly hat for once and twisting it in his hands as if to help him play humble. 'He always said they saw musicians as throwaway accessories.'

'And Philocrates? Did Plotinus remember him?'

'After Philocrates arrived to play the boasting soldier, Plotinus muttered all the time,' Simo agreed. 'He called him Titch, and to his face. Philocrates told Chremes to sack him, but Phrygia took the opposite line from Chremes as usual, so she never did.'

'He doesn't seem to have been grateful!' I exclaimed.

'Oh, he thought *they* should be grateful to *him* over the room,' Philotera scoffed. I raised my eyebrows. I saw Crispa give her a push, though it was not clear whether it was encouragement or to shut her up. Either way, Philotera carried on: 'Whenever they were in Rome, he got them in at that really nice place. They had to pay rent, but normally people weren't put up in that house at all. He used his influence.'

'Their genteel lodging was fixed up by Plotinus? How?' I was already guessing. 'Oh, Juno! Not family connections?'

'Right,' said Simo tersely. 'Uncle's house.'

'*Uncle's?*' I was with it now, careering into appalled recognition. 'So that's where Plotinus goes to stay. That's where he visits his grandmother. She exists – she's a spiky old lady. I even met her. She dotes on him? His uncle is Eucolpus, who probably doesn't adore him so much. And his granny is Naia Nerania!'

I would have a few strong words for her next time we met.

56

It was stupid to go there by myself. All right, I had Milo with me and the two chair-carrying slaves. I sent Hyro running to find Mucius, who had said he would begin work this morning back at the theatre. Simo had gone too, because he knew where the house was.

I should have waited. No chance of that. I am Flavia Albia: I never hang about waiting for back-up. I have to get in there pronto.

We hauled up the Via Lata as best my creaky bearers could manage. They did what they could, but Grandfather's poor old souls were struggling these days. In the end I jumped out, so they could patter along faster without my weight. I hurried alongside the chair; Milo marched beside me, grinning at the daft situation.

We passed the station-house of the First Cohort of Vigiles but I did not summon help. There was no time to explain, even if they would listen. Anyway, Mucius, of the Seventh, would curse.

We did notice a large Urban Cohort presence all along the main road. I didn't invite them along either. I'd sooner eat almond fancies with the ladies of the Good Goddess cult. In any case, if Plotinus was hiding up at his uncle's house, bringing the riot squad would hardly achieve a quiet arrest. In my view they are called the riot squad because when they shove the public around it causes riots.

Yes, they were barging into shops until sales staff ran out screaming abuse. They were kicking at dogs, or if the dogs looked too fierce, they kicked old ladies instead. That was foolish: the shrunken grannies grabbed anything to hand and fought back. I hoped the Urbans found the missing bears. No, I hoped Matursa and Ursulinus saw them first and attacked.

When we came to Agrippa's Park and the Porticus Vipsaniae, I climbed aboard the chair again for a few last moments of repose and planning. I told Milo to wait at the front of the house, ready to liaise with Mucius – unless he heard a commotion, in which case he had better burst in quick. Meanwhile, I was taken around to the back quietly for a sly look around.

I managed to open the gate by the waggling procedure. I left it open. We took the chair inside – why not? I told the two ancients to have a rest but to be ready to run like hell if I came back in a hurry. Everywhere seemed quiet – a domestic haven where you would not expect to come across a psychopathic killer.

We were in the service yard. No one was about. I had not taken much notice of this area before. No outbuildings were locked. I looked inside. They seemed to be normal storerooms. Broken furniture. Sacks of vegetables. Old amphorae, mainly empty. Finally, I came upon a familiar smell. A deep breath confirmed it: the pleasant aroma of clean new wood dust. I eased open the door of what turned out to be a workshop. I was ready to run away; fortunately it had no human occupants.

Everything else was there. All the questions Tiberius had asked were answered. Immediately inside stood a trestle that must be brought out into the yard when someone was working. Against it leaned a short ladder. The space beyond was crammed to the roof with heavy timbers, like those used to make the cross, and with other miscellaneous planks of wood. Many tools – sharp-bladed saws, planes, chisels, and smaller gadgets for fine working – were hung neatly on one wall, amongst coils of rope and twine. A pottery jar on a ledge contained charcoal. A bucket was full of different nails, some the long military type. There were even off-cuts of cowhide.

I paused, feeling that patter of the heart when you finally turn up the clue you need. Then my heart turned over more heavily, so I felt queasy. Lying on a workbench, a project was under construction. It had a long willow bough, which would be for easy flexion, though it had broken midway, so the piece was either abandoned or left for repair. It was a wing. Straps were attached, for fixing onto human arms. A row of long feathers was in process of being added all along the bough. Quills were everywhere.

There was only one. Had a pair of wings been completed already, and taken away to be flown?

So here we were. Myth again. Back to Crete: the king eventually quarrelled with his inventor, long after he had created the fake cow and the labyrinth. Suspecting that Daedalus had helped Theseus kill the Minotaur, Minos imprisoned him and his son Icarus in a heavily guarded tower. The only way out was by air. Daedalus and his son escaped on home-made wings. Despite warnings, Icarus flew too near the sun, so the wax attachments melted; he plunged into the sea where he drowned.

Romans loved seeing that onstage. Drowning, though perfectly feasible in a custom-made *naumachia* or flooded amphitheatre, was too wet and long-winded to arrange on a stage. Whoever plunged groundwards after flying above a theatre audience – it tended to be Daedalus because, as my husband so bitterly complained, accuracy never mattered – would instead drop into a pen of bears.

Oh, hell. The killers must be planning to have Matursa and Ursulinus savage Daedalus or Icarus.

57

I took a moment, considering what to do. My brain decided that whoever had originally led the undertaker killings, if Gnaeus had genuinely drowned in the Tiber, Plotinus was now the most dangerous; maybe he had been the leader all along. That waiter at the Winkle said so, not that I placed faith in him.

Caution would have been advised. As you grow older, you reluctantly learn that. I ought to wait for the vigiles. Too late! I had no time for standing about employing wisdom: I heard voices. I could have hidden in the workshop, but that was a bad idea. If Plotinus was coming to tinker with death machines, I did not want to be trapped in that small, crowded space with him.

I strolled out, acting confident. I ran into a couple of the slaves of the house, but I had summed them up before as lackadaisical. I assumed the air of a person with an appointment, asked them to give a drink of water to my carrying slaves, perhaps with a cinnamon biscuit if the kitchen could run to that, and confidently walked past them, heading for the interior. Never assume that actors are the only people who can act.

In the main courtyard, I ran into Eucolpus. Same as before: shiny pate, neat beard, bright eyes. Same underlying shiftiness, although I now understood the reason. Either he had known the truth all along, or when I met him he was beginning to suspect that Plotinus bore a grudge against Chremes and Phrygia and was planning them harm.

He realised I had grasped the situation. I wasted no time on exclamation or a full interrogation. I demanded curtly, 'Is Plotinus around?'

'He is not here.'

I lowered my tone, staring him straight in the eye. 'Your nephew, I believe.'

'My nephew,' he agreed. 'His father, my brother, died young.'

'I gather he left a child who is the light in his grandmother's eye – though perhaps not yours!'

'She loves him to play his music for her . . .' The man was dodging the issue.

'I have heard him. You can be sure,' I said, 'I have not come to ask him to provide music for me now. Do you know where he is?'

'No.'

As Eucolpus writhed with discomfort, I squared up to him. 'You once said to me, "This is a very quiet district. Nothing like murder happens around here." Did you know even then how ironic that was?'

No answer. Which gave me my answer.

I moved past him, heading for the stairs to his mother's room.

'Please do not disturb my mother.' It was the same request he had made last time. It made more sense now. Once again, I ignored the plea.

She was there, with her maid. Here was the tiny old lady, with her bolsters, plaster plaques and finch in a cage. She had the same small table with its silver cup and wine-flagon.

This time, an extremely beautiful cithara was leaning against a cupboard. I didn't remember him having it with him at the funeral, but Tiberius and I had heard him playing that night we stayed here.

How much of the grandson's behaviour was because his grandmother had indulged him all his life, I wondered.

'Naia Nerania!'

'Don't shout. Who's that?'

'Flavia Albia. I need to know where your grandson has gone.'

'What does she want?'

'Your grandson,' said Assia, patiently.

'What's that?'

'Your grandson!' yelled Assia, more angrily.

'Don't shout. I won't be shouted at by you.'

'Let the girl shout if she wants to,' I chastised the old lady unfeelingly. 'After all, she is mindlessly loyal! You can't buy that.' Assia could see my arrival meant the game was up. 'I am disappointed in you!' I threw at the maid, through gritted teeth. 'I gave you all my trust and you repaid me by lying. You lied to me, girl. I was bound to find out. You *did* recognise Plotinus when he was taking poor Phrygia out to her death. Had you realised how dangerous he was? What he had just done to Chremes?'

Assia shook her head wordlessly.

I remembered how Naia Nerania had seemed merely a bored, inquisitive, shameless old lady, yet before I left last time, she made me tell her all about the crucifixion. Had she known her grandson made the cross? I hated the way she had relished the details of how Chremes died. The way I had let her persuade me to share the ghastly facts now gave me a foul feeling. Was she proud of Plotinus? Had she known all he was doing? Dear gods, had she perhaps actively encouraged him?

Assia had listened to my story, expressionless, at the time. She must have been warned not to say anything.

She was a slave. She relied on the old lady and her family for everything, bed and board, safety and security; she needed whatever legacy they intended, to give her a future. I was furious, yet I understood. I despised her – yet still I understood. If you have ever been poor and hopeless, you know how the poor and hopeless have to think and act.

Eucolpus rushed into the room in high agitation.

'Troops are here. We had to let them in . . . It's over!' he yelled at his mother. Even Assia cowered. 'You always let him do exactly what he wanted. He was the useless son of a useless father, but you never saw it, did you? There was a perfectly good family business where he could have earned a decent living, but he had to turn his back on it. He was bright enough. He went from job to job, and you helped him.'

'He always had bad luck,' quavered his mother: the old excuse. 'He was perfectly fine on that contract for the big water display. You can't blame him because the Emperor built a *naumachia* after his year's hard work. He was badly let down when they cancelled the *Argo* project.'

'Stop covering,' snarled Eucolpus. He was taut with irritation as they replayed tired old arguments. 'You know the project manager complained. So what if the display never happened? Plotinus would have been sacked from the shipbuilding in any case.'

The grandmother, besotted, kept maundering: 'Those people could never appreciate him. He went back to his music. He is sticking to it this time—'

'No, he is killing people.' Eucolpus lost all patience. 'Face it, Mother! He is responsible for horrible things. Nothing we can do can stop him or save him. He is lost.'

Naia Nerania began weeping.

Eucolpus miserably carried on: 'We have soldiers in the house. All the neighbours are standing in the street, staring. The gods know where he got it from, but Plotinus has turned into a monster. He is not coming back, so you may as well say where these people should look for him. They are bound to find him anyway. He is your darling, Mother, but you have to give him up!'

'Get out!' screeched his mother, in equal distress. 'All of you, get out of here! Leave me alone. I'm a helpless old woman, only waiting here to die.'

It was probably true now.

Unable to watch the family disintegration, I walked out onto the balcony. Down in the courtyard I could see the red-tunics throwing open doors and lining up the slaves. I looked into the room Chremes and Phrygia had rented: it was empty, the bed stripped. I went on to the next, which showed signs of occupation, but nobody was there.

Assia ran out after me, causing agitated wails from her mistress. 'I know something, Albia.' Perhaps she hoped telling me would redeem her for her previous lies. Or perhaps she was so afraid of Plotinus she wanted him caught so he could not come back. 'He told the old woman he was going to make a machine for flying.'

'For Daedalus?' I asked, thinking of the broken wing I had seen.

Assia looked surprised. 'No. He said it was for Orpheus.'

Tiberius would roar, *Orpheus does not fly!* Orpheus, the

sublime musician, only leaves the earth when he is searching for his dead wife in the bowels of Hades. He famously bungles that by looking back at Eurydice, against instructions. Maybe he could change his animal-charming position from sitting on a rock to sitting on a cloud . . .

'I don't care if he's going to fly, swim, or wear snowshoes for crossing the Alps. I need to find him and the two bears!' I raged.

Assia had decided to whisper all she knew: 'Plotinus told his gran last night. He and the others have locked away the bears until they are needed. They are waiting in the Diribitorium.'

ORPHEUS

OR POSSIBLY

DÆDALUS

58

Mucius had arrived at the house; he was directing the troops he had brought with him to search. The bawling was as lively as a cut-price bazaar: 'Give every room in the place an intimate search. Turn this building inside out. Ask even the bloody spiders on the ceilings whether they've seen the pervert.'

I managed to interrupt, passing on where Assia had told me the bears were being held. Mucius scratched his curls. He snarled that if they were just sitting in the Diri, they would have to wait. First things first: he only had the day duty but he wasn't going to let the Urban Cohorts in on his case. I asked very politely whether he would mind if I went along myself – with my security escort – and took a quiet peek in advance? Mucius said, 'Don't interfere, just get out of my damned way, woman.'

I decided that merely looking would not be interference. So I got out of his way.

'Come on, boys!'

Hyro and Milo were extremely excited. The Campus Martius was their beat: they knew how to get around rapidly. They put me back into my chair and directed the bearers. Once across the Via Lata, we cut along the north end of the Saepta and down its quieter western side, using the narrow passageway beside the Pantheon. This whipped us through the long Porticus Argonautorum. The chair was jerking too much for me to admire the giant artworks of Jason's seaborne adventures, but it set me thinking.

No time for that. We all believed we were homing in on the end of the case.

The Diribitorium stood at the end of the Saepta. In the era of Agrippa and Augustus, it had been designed as a hall for counting election votes. That was before emperors made elections superfluous. Now the huge space, with its divisions for sectioning off the different Roman tribes' ballots, only served as a memorial for redundant democracy. To lovers of liberty, it had a mournful air.

The vast interior was most famous for having once possessed the largest roof span in the world. Poets and historians – not normally experts in construction methods, Tiberius would grate – spoke with reverence of those hundred-foot trunks of larch. After everything here burned down, Domitian rebuilt the hall, though the astounding roof was lost. It could not be reconstructed; it had gone for ever.

I had been inside the Diribitorium not so long before, when floats for the Emperor's Triumph were being created and painted inside. All that had been cleared away since, apart from a couple of huge representations of supposedly conquered lands that had proved too bulky to be loaded onto carts. That's the trouble with conquering: you tend to end up with more than you can handle. One shoddy bit of measuring, then say goodbye to your enterprise. Countries or carnivals, the risks were all the same.

Mostly, there was no reason for anyone to be in this great open-air interior. The Diribitorium sat empty. For sure, nothing was going on today. The redundant building would have made a good overnight hiding-place for the bears, out of public sight and hearing, but they weren't here now.

Hyro and Milo puffed their cheeks in disappointment. Milo then sniffed and pronounced that wild creatures had been there very recently. Although I could not smell them, Hyro told me, apparently sincerely, that identifying animals by nasal observation was a popular section in the vigiles' training manual. I chortled. These two oddly cultured lads had worked out what kind of jokes I liked.

'Mother and Baby were here all right. Those murderous bastards have been back and moved them,' Milo complained grumpily, still sniffing.

'Moved them on,' I agreed. 'To carry out their next horrible work at their next ill-fated venue.'

Where, though?

Heads on one side, Hyro and Milo looked at me, awaiting some great thought.

This is the problem with staff. Big expectations, yet they leave you to do all the work.

Simple faith can work as a catalyst. Everything was down to me and, let's face it, that is how I really liked it. I was a true informer: if I couldn't be solo, I wanted to be in charge.

A true *woman*. Tiberius would smile. Wrong, darling – given my experience of the wider Roman sisterhood. Most of them are feeble.

Not girls on the Aventine, Father would retaliate. Then it would be Mother's turn to smile.

How would the killers be thinking now? Their shocking acts had invariably taken place on the Campus Martius. I could come up with only one big performance space there that remained untouched by their ghastly genius. The Theatre of Marcellus, almost level with Tiber Island, was the largest in the city. It was named for the nephew of Augustus, once the young hope of Rome. A grandiose Republican construction a hundred feet high, the handsome venue was clothed in recently cleaned white travertine. I had attended a concert inside prior to my wedding, so was familiar with its refurbished stage. Also I knew (from my fact-checking younger brother) that it possessed underground corridors and trapdoors to use in performances. Beasts could definitely be deployed.

It was too central. Not the Marcellus. It snuggled up to the Capitol, was close to the Palatine, and you could pretty well see the Aventine. It neighboured the main forum, the Forum Romanum. Almost next door on the riverbank were the busy Trigeminal Porticus, the bustle of the meat market and then all the waterborne commerce along the Marble Embankment. Crowds were constantly moving between those heavily used places, cursing the great lump of the theatre as it forced them to walk further to get around it.

No, not the Marcellus. There were simply too many people nearby. Arranging an elaborate charade in the Marcellus now that everyone was keyed up for more violence would draw attention. At least, anybody who appeared with two cages of bears would be beset by eager theatregoers wanting to know what play was coming up and how could they get hold of free tickets? Forget that.

Where then? Where was more secluded? Much less frequently in use because it was so much newer? Quiet: intended for music, which fails to hold its own against the bloody allure of gladiating or the crowd's roar at the racetrack? A suitable building, only a step from the Diribitorium, just beyond the placid water of Agrippa's Lake?

My two minders gazed at me, waiting.

'She's got it!'

'Where, Albia?'

I knew better than to be too definite. But I suggested thoughtfully, 'Maybe we should take a look at Domitian's concert hall.'

'The Odeum?'

'That's it – the Odeum!'

59

We walked. I told the chairmen to leave me and go to the Saepta Julia, which they knew well from Grandpa's time. They would wait however long it took before I could return to my family on the Janiculan, hopefully tonight. Terrible things would probably be discovered before then.

Back I came to Agrippa's Lake, around which I had walked with Davos and Tiberius the day we found Chremes crucified. Now I had Hyro and Milo either side of me. Walking around the lonely Stagnum under a wide grey Campus sky gave us time for reflection. We could only hope the nightmare series of deaths would soon end.

A low wall surrounded the basin, with the water lapping gently some three feet below. Marble steps led down for swimming or boating access. The safety wall had never been much of a deterrent; people larking about could jump or be pushed in by prankster companions.

Today the expanse of silent water had a chilly atmosphere. Few people came here nowadays, especially in winter. The pool had lost its charm, after Domitian cleared all the houses and workshops when the Campus was burned out. Locals had once spent leisure time on the sunlit banks, picnicking or jumping in with shrieks and happy laughter all day during hot weather. Long gone, too, was the louche partying Nero had brought by night, when fancy boats with gold and ivory fittings were rowed to and fro by male prostitutes; exotic sea creatures taken from afar gambolled (and died in the fresh water); strange, imported birds swooped overhead (and flew away); brothels were stocked with sex-workers who were 'women of high birth' (supposedly). The Stagnum then must have rung with music and the wine-fuelled hum of voices, everywhere alive with glowing lamps, while naked figures cavorted as partygoers disappeared into stern Agrippa's Grove for sinful conjunctions of flesh.

Now it lay silent, all torchlit glitter gone. A severe censor monitored the area. Flavian morality had taken over from Julio-Claudian excess. Vespasian never bothered, but well done, Domitian, father of your people, devotee of solitude, coldly unloved self-appointed god. You know what is good for us, Master: decent entertainment in beautiful buildings that all carry your august name, venues where the standards are classical and there is no mucky behaviour. Men running very fast, like healthy Greeks, in your elegant stadium. Demure audiences (rather small ones) enjoying refined recitals in your fabulous Odeum.

Until today, maybe. Today the tone may be about to sink. Someone on the Campus Martius plans a different kind of party, as blood-soaked and merciless as anything in Roman history. O Master, I suspect these crazed ogres have got themselves into your bijou concert hall.

In fact, if they were there, there was no sign of them. We ourselves could not get in.

Architecturally, the Odeum could have been placed with its straight side facing the Stadium, so the hemisphere of its seating banks formed a match to the delta end of the athletics track. Instead, its plan had been turned through ninety degrees; this echoed Pompey's Theatre, which stood next door. It made an odd right angle with the Stadium, but only on the map. On the ground, they were so close together you were simply taken aback by the white, column-coated beauty of Flavian architecture, distilled to greater perfection than ever in this exquisite building gem.

From the Stagnum we had arrived at the back, the blank wall behind the scaenae. We walked around one corner to an entrance, which was locked, then kept going around the whole curve to the opposite side, which was locked also. Where they always advertised performances we came upon a neat sign, in charcoal: a presentation of Orpheus, to include charming of live wild animals with the power of music, and his own tragic fate; it would be held here today. We saw no animal cages, although they might have been inside.

Mucius arrived, despite having claimed it would have to wait. He was heading up a jostling charivaria: his men, their tribune Caunus, various other troops in the legionary-style uniform of the Urban Cohorts, and a praetor, who was reclining on a litter, fronted by two hefty lictors with bundles of rods, and accompanied by a smart secretary with a ready-opened note-tablet. They marched in noisily as if to scare off culprits, cutting between the Pantheon and the Baths of Nero to where we were disconsolately standing. They had omitted the Diribitorium because Mucius had already been told about the charcoal message I had just discovered. Vigiles had spotted it earlier.

Word had spread. From other directions appeared the bears' professional agent Cintugnatus (stressed), menagerie keepers with tridents (impassive), and the mortician Suedius (slapdash and nonchalant), with his boy and funeral cart. There were few members of the public, since concert halls never counted for much in Rome. Those who did venture near in the hope of scandal quickly disappeared when they saw the Urbans.

The praetor's secretary sidled up to me. Someone must have told him who the lone woman was. He had ridiculous red shoes and a haircut that must have taken a meticulous barber hours, yet his eyes were bright with intelligence. 'You are Falco's daughter?' When I nodded, he murmured in a significant tone, 'I am Lusius. Tell your father we had a good life, but my wife died of natural causes. Assure him I am still safely here.'

'Will it mean something?' I had been given odd messages for Father on other occasions. He usually brushed them off, before flashing his most evil grin.

'It will if you tell him that I never needed to access the haemorrhoid lozenge.' Mention of intimate medicaments did make me blink, though I knew better than to raise a query when an associate of Falco's was being mysterious. 'I am here,' repeated Lusius, who seemed a pleasant character, despite what must have been a colourful past. 'Unfortunately, so is the useless vile old menace I still work for. Must go. The praetorian lump may wish me to disfigure my tablet with some pointless aide memoire.' He sidled away, back to attending Corvinus. I filed his message mentally.

A considerable crowd of men were standing about, all baffled by the situation with the locked doors. They were, they told each other, taking stock.

'Where is the curator?'

'Dead of a seizure. Misadventure with an amphora.'

'Hit on the head?'

'No, he drank it.'

'Who has the key?'

'Nobody knows.'

The praetor decided to take charge. To my right, Lusius rolled his eyes. To my left, Mucius covered his.

Corvinus had climbed out of his litter, the better to impose his presence on the scene. He was an overweight figure in the full broad purple, defending against the winter cold with a huge pseudo-military cloak. Since nobody had come up with an idea to deter him, the big-bellied pomposity struck a pose like a general on a rostrum, lictors either side of him. Then he bellowed, as if shouting down hecklers in the senate: 'Nothing for it, men. I have made my decision. Break down that portal!'

I groaned. Tiberius would loathe this. Any public entrance to a new building in fine materials that bore the Emperor's name was bound to be furnished with stunningly gorgeous, absolutely enormous, wincingly expensive doors.

Even Mucius cringed. 'That's a corking set of bronzes he thinks he'll shatter.'

Lusius heard. 'I imagine there is a budget for accidental damage!' Casual humour seemed to be his trademark, at least when he came across people he liked. I found out later his relationship with my father went back even more years than the actors'. He must have liked Falco. 'But will the reserves be sufficient?'

'Your man is going to pay for this?' Mucius tried.

'Oh, no. He presumes that yours will cough up.'

In that case, the praetor was an idiot. Nevertheless, the vigiles had to answer formally to magistrates of all mental capacities. A praetor was at the top of their command chain. This man had turned up here because it would be his job to sign the trial warrants if we caught anyone. So, even though it would mean no new equipment for the next five years and permanent cancellation of all festive drinks, Caunus politely began making preparations to smash in these tall, ornate, fabulously patinated doors. He eyed up a battering point. He told men to run and find a ram.

At least in the pause while this search party went off to the vigiles station-house, the Seventh's tribune did suggest that what was to follow could be highly dangerous, so – matter of health and security, your honour – Corvinus might prefer to absent his valuable person until the premises had been declared safe. Of course, Caunus was an ex-legionary, indeed an ex-centurion: he was tall, broad, nasty, and even when he was talking through his fundament he could speak with an air of rugged experience. The praetor took his advice. That interfering coward was soon vanishing at speed, with his litter, lictors, and unperturbed rascal secretary, Lusius.

Once he had gone, Caunus talked to no one. He began digging into his arm purse. From among his small change he retrieved a gadget. It might have been a manicure spike, but he was not cleaning his nails. Watched by grinning vigiles, he sauntered right up to the entrance doors, where he stood with his back to the rest of us. After a few moments, he raised an arm, a signal to his men. The vigiles immediately began moving up to him. They must have known what he was up to.

Caunus leaned one shoulder to a mighty door, which swung gently inwards. Someone cheered quietly. Catching my eye, Mucius gave me a huge wink. The Seventh smirked at the Urbans. Their tribune was still despised by all, of course, but the lovely bastard had his good points: Caunus had gained access to the Odeum without damage to the doors. He had picked the lock.

I supposed I could now understand why Mucius always let him pinch his flatbreads.

60

Regular free breakfasts had not made the tribune grateful to his junior officer. Despite the imminent danger, Caunus made Mucius enter first.

Almost at once, Mucius shouted that there were abandoned cages just inside the doors. Caunus ordered the Urbans, who had no officer present to overrule him, that they should round up all civilians, move them back on safety grounds, then wait outside on crowd control. They might like to send off for weapons, since they were allowed them and legally the vigiles were not. Otherwise, he pronounced, this would be his cohort's show.

I managed to scramble in with the first group. Those heading up the party were far too intent on the risks to themselves to bother with me. Tension gripped us all.

At first we could hear nothing. After shoving through an entrance lobby, past the two empty travel cages, the vigiles nervously fanned out. Some edged into the orchestra; some climbed the seating rows. I made sure I stayed near the exit. Informers have a motto: when in doubt, make sure you can get out.

The Odeum followed a familiar layout, on a reduced scale: raised stage with a tall back scaenae, above a decorated podium with statue niches at ground level. A flat semi-circular orchestra space. A perfect half-circle of seats above an imperial box, centred, and fine front-row nobility thrones. Domitian knew how to spend money. Travertine slathered everything. It all had a sleek finish, buffed to a light gloss, with oodles of gilding.

I wouldn't want it. Travertine is hell to clean. It absorbs your dirty water all the time you are scrubbing it. Still, here they must have a lot of slaves. Not that any were visible today.

This was the kind of venue where an elite young man could suitably bring a fiancée, or a rich aunt might treat nieces and nephews. Genuine music-lovers would demand season tickets and their usual seats. It still smelt new. No one had left crumbs in the aisles. It was intimate, the better to allow appreciation of the quieter concert instruments as they pinged and tweedled, but it would also work for drama if uplifting plays were produced. It must be equipped with first-class apparatus for special effects. The acoustics were excellent. That allowed us at last to hear muffled grunts from below an open trapdoor on the stage.

It was tempting to relax, because nobody was dead or even wounded. Not yet.

They were here. Mother and Baby Bear, plus two men we had been searching for, both perpetrators of past crimes, both now surprise victims. This time, whatever happened, the scene was to have an audience.

'Double feature!' commented Milo. My guards were standing close to me.

'Never before attempted,' marvelled Hyro.

'Waste!' Milo disagreed, more of a purist. He added, 'Nice set-up they have here. I'd love a go on their thunder-sheet!'

The optimists trotted off to see if they could find it. Everything seemed safe enough to let them go wandering. The staging was the same as at the Theatre of Pompey, only this time the two bears were still secure, down in a holding cage. The trapdoor onstage was open, however, so they could be seen from above, and heard growling.

Megalo had been made to act as Orpheus. A wreath, which had slipped, had been plonked on his bald head; his big beard looked incongruous. A very basic stage cithara was leaning against his rather badly painted rock. The old fellow would not be playing unless somebody freed him. Still wearing his big hairy performance pants, he was roped up so he could not move, gagged, and positioned in a cleft of the fake rock. This put him looking straight down into the hole in the stage – and a ramp up which the two bears would run if they were released. This thought was naturally dominating his attention. He was sweating badly.

On hearing our voices, the animals' underground growling became much more urgent. The heavy ursines were seeking to escape. Occasionally they threw themselves against the cage down in the bowels, trying to burst it open.

Plotinus was acting Daedalus. We did not spot him at first, until a vigilis pointed upwards. Despite what I had seen at his workshop, he did not have wings, but was suspended horizontally, arms and legs akimbo, in a harness. This was attached to an overhead mechanism, worked by a pulley, which could be used to allow gods to descend from the clouds. They would usually be in chariots, which might give descending actors or singers some sense of security. Plotinus lacked that. He was not gagged, yet he was trying not to move a muscle, or even to speak, because if he even breathed hard, the flying harness lurched. The movable trolley in the roof must have had something wrong with it. Plotinus hovered in mid-air not quite above Megalo, as if poised to watch him die.

On the other end of the stage a bloated orange sun with wonky rays hung limply from the flats. 'Don't fly too near it!' someone called up helpfully.

Mucius told men to find a way down to where the bears were. Others had to search for any controls that made the flying apparatus work. 'Better not touch anything, lads. Just call me when you find any interesting levers.'

Plotinus managed a few frantic gurgles, pleading to be let down.

Caunus and Mucius were standing in the orchestra together, looking up at the victims, arms folded. They had powerful voices, with parade-ground projection as they heartlessly joked: 'Him on the rock has shat himself. Him in the sky seems desperate – we could try catching him in an esparto mat—'

'Too long a drop. He'd miss – and be nastily splattered.'

'Would you say, Mucius, we can organise a little accident here to save ourselves paperwork?'

Mucius only sucked his teeth, shaking his head in sorrow.

Braving the open orchestra, I skulked up beside the two officers. Despite their banter, they were grim. I felt anger myself. None of us were in any hurry for rescue attempts.

Some Urbans came into the concert hall, armed with javelins. Keepers were with them, holding poles and large studded collars. Mucius gestured for them all to wait outside the entrance.

I had a sense of dark vigiles' motives. Some grim drama was to happen. Mention of 'a little accident' meant something.

Troops clustered onstage now. They looked over to colleagues down below the trapdoor, who shouted up that they had found Matursa and Ursulinus. The holding pen made creaking sounds as the animals threw themselves around, audibly growing more agitated.

'That one on the rock,' Mucius called up to the stage. 'Cut his ropes and give him his harp to play. See if he can soothe bears.'

'What about his gag?'

'Leave it on. I don't want to hear any sickening pleas for mercy.'

Once Megalo was free, a vigilis thrust the cithara into his arms. It was out of tune, but he was prodded into using it. As one of the Farcicals, he must play instruments, though Plotinus had been right about his lack of accomplishment.

'Do better!' yelled Mucius, brutally. 'Let's have the music of the spheres.'

Megalo improved, giving us the uplifting tug of popular music from farces, catchy in its ancient ethnic way.

Other troops shouted that they had found how the overhead machinery functioned. I heard manly talk of counterweights. Caunus and Mucius climbed steps into the wings. This time I stayed below.

From the stage a vigilis called up, 'Butterfly, how should this lever work?'

'Towards you!' Plotinus screeched, causing his tethered body to swoop around in wild parabolas; I could hardly bear to look up at him. 'To you – not the other way! Get me down! Get me back, for the gods' sake!'

'How are you liking the suspense?' asked the vigilis, wittily.

'Right, lads!' Mucius bellowed. 'At my signal! Let's have some action. Heave away!' All the troops then scampered into the wings, leaving only Megalo onstage, with Plotinus stuck above.

'Heave' was enough of a signal to his men. We heard a

crash below, as if metal sides to the holding pen had opened. Immediately, the trained bears knew they should belt out at a run, heading up the ramp for the light, ready to attack.

Megalo stopped harping. Someone over on the other side called, 'Now!' A rope snaked, then went taut. The fake rock dropped apart. Pieces fell onto the stage floor. Megalo tumbled; though hurt, he began hastily crawling away. He would be too late.

Hyro and Milo must have found the thunder-sheet they wanted. Rattling waves of metallic cacophony rolled around the stage. Having the time of their lives, both big strong men, fuelled by porridge, seemed ready to vibrate the deafening percussion indefinitely.

As I covered my ears, I noticed the officers standing together by the deus-ex-machina control. Plotinus also saw what must be coming next: he screamed.

Caunus made an exaggerated bow, almost as if amateur dramatics were his own spare-time hobby. With this courteous flourish, he gave way to his investigator, whose case it was.

Mucius grasped the lever. Two-handed, he leaned into it and pushed away. 'Oops! Silly me. Wrong way . . .'

High above, the tackle jerked out further. Then, with a grating racket, it jammed. The counterbalance weights should have smoothly moved it on, but snaggled ropes refused to pull. Still pinioned, the hanging man looped around awkwardly. Straps broke under his weight. He flailed an arm, then more leather gave way. Down he dropped.

Cintugnatus had been right that a plunging Daedalus would spook his clients. Ursulinus was crying in panic; the big youngster wanted to turn back. But his huge fierce mother was running first up the ramp, and she kept coming.

Bears, when they attack somebody, move extremely fast.

Aeschylus

61

I did not see what happened next. I spun and fled from the Odeum into the open. Hyro and Milo soon joined me; they had abandoned the thunder-sheet, too squeamish to watch.

I had brought the ineradicable memory of the mother bear Matursa's slow, wide-legged walk as she took command of the stage. I had seen her long snout with its lighter fur, the dark stripe running down her back. She crouched on all fours, prior to running at Megalo, the moving prey. Ursulinus, now emboldened, was coming out too. After that I did not look.

I felt I should wait, so I stayed in the area between the Odeum and the Theatre of Pompey. We heard occasional noises from inside. Most were of a distressing nature. Eventually Caunus emerged, bringing Mucius.

'That's all over. I'll leave you to finish. Writing this up will be easy: *they killed an aedile and three victims from the performing arts, then killed themselves, suicide by beasts. No further action.* I'm going back to the station-house.'

I started to protest that there was still a killer on the loose, but he ignored me. Satisfied the case was a wrap, he marched from the scene like a victorious general.

Mucius was wearing a no-comment face; instead of backing me up, he signalled to Suedius, who began fiddling with his funeral cart.

'That's that, then?' I raged. 'You've played your games with the men who were left for you like free gifts – and you're finished?'

'Apparently!' Mucius was terse.

'Well, it was fine working with you. I thought we cooperated pretty well. Thank you for the protection.' I assumed Hyro and Milo would now be returning to regular work.

'See her home,' the officer told them.

'Save it. I can manage, as I always do. Thanks, and farewell, boys.'

I was furious. Mucius had an uptight air as well because he was intelligent. The difference was, he would accept the establishment line. Do what he had been told to do. Accept the easy decision. Go along with the wrong verdict.

I refused to let him get away with this. 'It seems the Seventh never change! Skivers and shirkers, with an indolent tribune who vanishes when the demands of the job are too much. I hope you can invent enough, in your *no action* report for him.' Mucius pretended to look puzzled, though he knew what I meant. Even so, I spelled it out angrily: 'Who pulled the lever originally, to fix Plotinus over the stage, Mucius? Who had snagged the ropes so he was stuck? Then, after it was all set up, *who turned the key on the Odeum to lock the doors behind him when he left?*'

He answered, 'Oh, sod off, Flavia! He drowned. He's dead.'

I turned on my heel, ready to strike off alone, back around the lake to the Saepta where my transport would be. Over one shoulder I threw back with a sneer: 'You're behaving like your farting half-wit tribune – but, Mucius, you are an honest man at heart, and you know Gnaeus is not dead!'

* * *

That might have been the end. I would certainly have stormed off in a cloud of discontent. But I had to pass where Suedius had parked his cart. He had left the boy there, holding the donkey's reins.

Despite my fury, I made myself find a smile for Sorgius, because ten-year-olds who do their best are rare. Besides, I thought he led a lonely life. I had old reasons to sympathise with that. His work was foul. He might not have witnessed the horrible deeds just now, but he would soon be aware of the beasts' leavings. People might say he was used to it, but one day I envisaged him suffering for the horrors he had known.

Sorgius wanted a chat.

He glanced over at the Odeum, as if to make sure Suedius was out of sight and hearing. I walked up; I patted the donkey, which ignored me. 'What is it, Sorgius?'

He spoke quietly. He reminded me how I had asked about the dead woman who had said 'the undertaker' did it. He wondered if I had ever found out who she meant.

'Unhappily no, Sorgius.'

Then the boy shyly confided: whatever I had been told before by Suedius, Phrygia did once come to their premises. She had wanted someone to perform an unusual funeral. Suedius refused. She was very upset. In the end, to get rid of her, Suedius referred her to a man who sometimes helped him out when they had too much work. This man never did anything expert, he just shifted wood for pyres.

'Who was he?' I asked gently.

'Gnaeus. His name is Gnaeus.'

'I know who that is. He helped her? And do you know, Sorgius, who Phrygia had wanted the unusual funeral for?'

'It was a dog.'

'Oh! A special one?'

'He was very old. Phrygia had been very fond of him. He used to act onstage when he was younger. He had performed clever tricks in front of the Emperor.'

'Ah!' Anethum.

'She kept saying that her wonderful dog was not going on some rubbish pile for scavengers to gnaw him, he deserved a proper burial.'

Anethum, another character pet. *Best and happiest of dogs, run with joy through all Elysium, dear friend* . . . I never knew this particular creature, though my parents had once seen his act, which was famous. Thalia trained him. He pretended to be poisoned, played dead very convincingly, then jumped up and delighted the audience by coming back to life. He loved the applause. After he became too old to perform, Thalia had given him to Phrygia. *She used to tease Chremes, saying she loved the dog more than him. One day he really did die on her. We thought she would go barmy with grief.*

'So Gnaeus helped her?'

'After that,' said Sorgius, 'if ever he came for log-loading to earn himself a bit of cash, he always told us about how he buried her dog for her. Whenever Phrygia saw him afterwards, said Gnaeus, she still called him "the undertaker" because of it.'

62

The Saepta Julia.

I had known this place, popularly called the Sheep Pens, ever since I was brought to Rome. Designed to contain the whole male population while voting, it was an enormous rectangular quadrangle, on two levels. Forming the two long sides were colonnades, each forty strides wide, as they needed to be, to suit the scale of their staggering half-mile length. The side facing the Shrine of Isis and Serapis was broken midway by a huge four-cornered arch, the dramatic, most frequently used entrance.

When my father was in fanciful mood, he would say the long porticoes were tributes to staples of Roman commerce: wine and wool. (What about oil? cry the oil-producers.) (No good: no myths.) The porticus with the arch contained frescos depicting Meleager leading heroic cronies in their hunt for the enormous Calydonian boar. Released by a slighted goddess, this mad-eyed critter ravaged the countryside, tearing up vines. A heroine, Atalanta, won first blood by wounding the giant oinker. Being beaten by a woman caused outrage among the nude Greek muscle-men with their big spears, lively hounds and carefully slung hunting-cloaks. In defence of Atalanta, I could easily have thrown paint at the frescos in the cursed Meleager Porticus.

The opposite arcade, a project of Marcus Agrippa's, displayed grand pictures, plaques and statues that showed Jason's adventures with the Argonauts. This was a cracker: clashing rocks, fire-breathing oxen, dragon's teeth, iron man, Circe, the Sirens, ghosts, gods, the mouth of Hades, the Gardens of the Hesperides and, of course, help with magic from Medea so they were able to seize the Golden Fleece. In the manner of every lying, heart-breaking hero, Jason would then promise to make Medea famous, to marry her in gratitude and to love her for ever – thereafter not doing so, since a hero's vow is worth less than a shake of dried beans.

Everything had happened in the Saepta Julia: electioneering and balloting, troop musters, gladiators, flooding for mock sea battles, one meeting of the Senate (years ago; the old codgers we had nowadays would think it too far to walk out here), political jockeying, conspiracies. A slang word '*columnarii*' had grown out of so many agitators clustering to plot behind its multiplicity of columns, which stood tall in massive lines of elegant travertine.

Now it was a showplace for luxury. Everyone who had anything expensive to buy or to sell came: slave-dealers, jewellers, merchants with furniture, statues, bronzes or ivory, then, happily for them, crowds of customers. The place often reeked with perfumes and incense, not all of that perfumery contained in glass bottles, but much of it slopped by masseurs and hairdressers onto the idlers, time-wasters, flaunters and *flâneurs* who strolled in the arcades. Too many were there only to be noticed: ants, criss-crossing the vast space with their 'Here I am! Look at me!' trails of toadies, cronies and slaves.

Informers worked out of the Saepta. Auctioneers and goldsmiths made fortunes. So did shop-lifters, barrow-raiders and pickpockets.

I had entered from the Porticus Argonautarum. Far across on the Porticus Meleagris side, my chair was standing unattended outside the family warehouse, below my father's office. The ancient bearers must be waiting for me indoors. On a winter's afternoon close to New Year, with cold weather, few people were about. My eyes are good, but I had to cross all of the huge central area before I made out that a flyer had been nailed to the warehouse door.

It was part of the frontispiece of an old scroll. Everything useful had been ripped away. All it said was: *Aeschylus*.

On the alert for anything to do with plays, I stood there. Aeschylus is called the father of tragedy; he introduced characters interacting with each other, not simply with a chorus. A fluent producer, he wrote scores of titles in his native Greek, some in trilogies, many not recently performed in Rome and most never seen by me. If this was a message, it was as oblique as a Pictish riddle. Without a title, I was stumped.

I peered along at the nearest premises to ours, none of which had the same bill-posting. We did get flyers, advertising fake medicines or urging people to join restrictive cults. One person we called Uncle Umbonius consistently claimed a typhoon was bringing the end of the world – so before it struck, buy his lupins for your mule.

If this *was* a message it was specifically aimed at the Falco auction house. Threatening my father – or me? Perhaps threatening Falco *through* me?

I soon learned. Irritated, I whisked about abruptly, intending to bounce in to demand why none of the staff had seen this put here, or why nobody had removed it. At that moment, a missile crashed alongside me. Solid and heavy, more than a foot long, it flew down from right above, onto the spot where I had just stood.

I yelled. I stepped back, to look up. A male figure went running along the balcony, half hidden by its safety barrier.

The missile was a tortoise shell. I bent but dropped it and left it, choosing to go after the man instead. I shouted again, in the hope of alerting our staff; they stayed cosily indoors. Too used to wild cries from revellers or wrong-doers, they tended to go conveniently deaf.

I could not wait. Gathering skirt in hand, I started running along at ground level; I followed below the route the fugitive had taken. When I saw anyone else, I called out, but everybody only stared. Even those who knew me clearly thought, *Falco's strange daughter: what's she up to now?* They probably supposed I was chasing a thief who had snatched a goblet or necklace from stock; this was so common at the Saepta they just left me to it. Those who had shops turned back into them, to double-check on any loiterers inside. Potential customers, strolling and looking at trinkets gormlessly, only showed vague curiosity. Anyone whose eye I caught directly pretended to be foreign.

I came to a staircase, which I climbed breathlessly, losing more time and letting him get further ahead of me. Although this colonnade was broken by the dramatic quadrifons entrance halfway along, a quarter of a mile of enticing nooks and crannies still filled my end of the upper storey. Up here, it was traditional to assume no regulations about blocking pavements applied. It was a haven of fine wares, furniture, giant urns and statues, all piled outside on the balcony to attract interest. Wizened jewellers perched on stools, braving the weather in the hope of nabbing customers, but too stiff to move rapidly out of my way. 'How's your mother?' an old man asked kindly. I could only flash a smile as I carried on as fast as possible. Falco's daughter: the crazy British one, the bloody rude one.

I lost him. Spit! I stood still for a moment, in case he made the mistake of emerging from a hiding spot. No luck. He was mad, but by no means stupid.

He could have gone in anywhere or run down another staircase to meld in with passers-by. I stared around but failed to identify him. I had only glimpsed him anyway. All I could do next was to limp slowly back along the walkway to our office, check that it was safely locked, then go down to the warehouse.

At ground level I found Hyro and Milo. With various staff members, they had formed an anxious cluster. Hyro was examining the Aeschylus notice; Milo was holding the tortoise shell. There was no reptile in it: this was an object of interest for people with spare desk space. The shell was whole, both carapace and plastron still fused despite the violent fall. It was large for a Mediterranean tortoise. This missile might not have killed me, but on the other hand, it could have done.

'We came to look after you, Girl from the Aventine. Just in case of trouble, Mucius said.'

'Oh, thank you, Mucius!' Everyone went on arguing about the tortoise's potential as a weapon, though I chose not to join in. 'Hyro, Milo, what is the theatrical point of this, do you know?' I interrupted.

It was the kind of question they loved. They knew, of course: Aeschylus was an active playwright, a citizen soldier who had fought at Salamis and Marathon. With the Greeks expanding their territory, they had colonised southern Italy, including Sicily. There on a visit, Aeschylus was warned that one day he would be killed by a falling object; he stayed out of doors to avoid his fate. Fate never works that way. While he was sitting in a wheatfield, an eagle flying overhead mistook his bald head for a rock. To smash open a tortoise, the bird dropped its prey on him, and the playwright died.

'Barely feasible!' I claimed the shell as mine now. I put it into the carrying chair, to take for my little nephews. I would probably not mention the danger of killing people, or Gaius and Lucius would run straight up onto a balcony, to see if it worked.

I was tired. I wanted to see Tiberius. Hunching in my cloak, I gave the old bearers a quiet nod. While everyone else stood around jabbering, we set off to go home to the Janiculan.

We were heading for an exit near the Pantheon. Outside the Saepta, we would take the road to Nero's Bridge. Only as we neared the far corner, still inside, did I see something that made me signal. They put down the chair. I climbed out. Hyro and Milo came scurrying up.

'Wait for us!'

'Get a move on, then.' I held up a hand to stop their protests. I laid a finger to my lips. 'Less noise, shall we?'

'Hello! What are you thinking? What is this place, Albia?'

For once, it was not a stage, not even a building. This was a wooden hoarding erected some years ago around a piece of ground. In the vastness of the Saepta Julia, it was dwarfed; not even busybodies questioned why the authorities allowed such an eyesore to remain. It formed an open invitation to vagrants although, like the rest of us, they seemed to ignore the call. People simply never saw it. It had never been damaged or obviously broken into. It just stood there.

A long-forgotten project, reputedly imperial, had once been abandoned. Everyone was vaguely aware the storage space perhaps contained building materials. It was bigger than a site-hut, better constructed than a cover for rubbish. Somehow the disfiguring huddle remained invisible to visitors and to locals who saw it every day. I never thought twice about it. Like everyone, I assumed that one day, without explanation, it would all be cleared away.

Rome under the Flavian emperors, especially Domitian, was covered with new building works. Signs advising 'Danger, keep out' were everywhere. Familiar places would suddenly acquire closed gates and notices about restoration, as our city was glorified and beautified, knocked down and redesigned again, year after year. Often they hit a problem. The site would be closed; the tradesmen went away. Sometimes the scheme restarted, occasionally not. Whatever this had been meant to become, it had been left half finished, abandoned, boarded up: a pigeon perch and rats' nest.

When I thought about it, I did know. Most Romans would have had no idea, but I was the Girl from Londinium: I took an interest in this complicated city. Not long after Domitian gained the throne, he wanted to hold a *naumachia*, nautical manoeuvres on a man-made lake. He wanted it here in Rome, but not in the Flavian Amphitheatre because his brother had used that. Ditto the purpose-built *naumachia* in the Transtiberina. Domitian had to be different. He might have used Agrippa's Stagnum, but it was thought not deep enough. He therefore suggested flooding the Saepta Julia. It had been done in the past. Agrippa's aqueduct, the Virgo, ended right outside the Pantheon as if put there for filling purposes.

The proposal caused an outcry. Occupants of ground-floor premises were furious at the prospect of trade being stopped for a long period, then wetted rooms growing mouldy, with no hope of compensation; those upstairs complained about crowds who would certainly disrupt custom and might break in to steal stock. My father, who rented at both levels, became colourfully incandescent, which was how I heard about it. I also knew that Domitian eventually created a purpose-built *naumachia* beyond the Tiber instead.

When the Saepta project was cancelled, materials remained here. 'Temporary' wooden partitions, several times taller than me, concealed the long-forgotten store. Whatever it contained was much, much bigger than a shrouded statue. Something inside was too cumbersome for a clerk-of-works simply to order it to be loaded onto a cart. The contents must be related to a show they had once planned, a show I had heard mentioned only today: complementing the Porticus Argonautica, the idea had been to replicate Jason and his crew on their search for the Golden Fleece. This naturally would have called for a spectacular boat.

'So, Milo and Hyro, what is this? I think it is a ship-shed. Now you go around the back as usual to catch anyone who runs out that way. I am going in there to find Gnaeus.'

JASON

63

Incredible. Even though I was expecting it, I felt stunned. Dry-docked in that palace of luxury, the Saepta, stood the bare bones of an almost full-size deserted ship.

Supported on a wooden cradle with keel blocks and side blocks, the ghostly shape towering above me must have sat there in secret solitude for nearly ten years. When I squeezed in through two wobbly hoardings that had clearly been forced on other occasions, I was next to the supports, almost under the hull. For a moment I could barely comprehend what I was seeing: a usable model of the *Argo*. She had a great eye painted on her prow, and her name.

The ship virtually filled the interior. Also in storage were construction materials, their once-neat heaps now crumpled lopsidedly: timber for the most part, but I spotted pieces of balustrade, like the one the intruder had left at our warehouse when he came after me.

As I had believed, he was not dead. Since we had captured and lost him at the Winkle, Gnaeus had been nesting under the ship's cradle here. I took three steps and found him. He must have heard me coming in. He appeared to be reading, like someone who had been doing so all afternoon. It was a pose.

'So this is where you're hiding! I wouldn't stay here myself. It's a hazard. They say the ship is cantilevered over air.'

He had positioned himself outstretched at ease, with his feet up. He wore an ordinary brown tunic, not his Atellan costume from the Farcicals' play. The way he was lolling with his ankles crossed, I could see his footwear: enviably soft fawn-coloured leather, which I recognised. 'Dead man's boots, Gnaeus?'

'How he would hate that!' gloated his murderer, suspiciously bright-eyed.

I hated it myself. Philocrates had not been my kind of man, but whatever he was, it was honest. 'Father Tiber failed to drown you! How did you escape?'

'Practice. A theatre trick. Held my nose and hoped. Popped up by a bumboat and nobody spotted me.'

He raised his eyes from the scroll he was pretending to read, assessing me.

I assessed him too. Easily fifty, tall if he stood up, lean, more athletic than I wanted if this came to a chase. Brown eyes that seemed more untrustworthy than mad. Like all crazy killers, he looked moderately normal – or would do, until someone riled him. Then, if he was caught on the raw, his true nature might show.

'Flavia Albia, Falco and Helena's daughter. You lied to me!'

'You know my parents. You knew them in Syria, when you were called Tranio.'

'How wonderful it was, up into the small hours, discussing the principles of comedy with the brilliant Falco, under the desert stars.'

'While my mother was alone in a tent, half dead of a scorpion bite!'

'Your mother?' The man sounded irritated, flushed with real anger. 'You were not there in Syria. They were childless.

And you told me, "I met him and his wife abroad, some years ago." That was a lie,' he complained again, as if obstructing him was an outrage.

'It was true,' I replied calmly. I noted that he had harboured my words, brooding on them malevolently as such criminals do. 'I met them later. They adopted me. I see it as special, a child chosen because she was wanted, rather than inflicted upon them by nature.'

Something had made a muffled sound, as if the materials in store were settling. I ignored it. Gnaeus seemed part distracted, but he failed to give it proper attention, too intent on his demands of me. 'Did they force you to do the same work as them?'

'Informing? No, of course not. That choice was all mine.'

'Ha!' I could see his excitement. 'So have you come to ask questions?'

'Would you answer?'

'Why should I? I have done nothing wrong.'

He was a monster with no human empathy, emotionless, self-obsessed, vicious. Even so, he was somehow able to believe all he said. 'Gnaeus, you have destroyed lives with unbelievable cruelty. Those were the most terrible sights I have ever encountered. Were family friends not affected, I would have abandoned the case.'

'They all deserved it, their punishment for my sufferings.'

'Sufferings?' Outrage burned in me, but I kept my voice level. I needed to stay in control. 'Your life may have been harsh, but much of that was your own fault. Nothing you experienced ever called for such merciless violence. Your victims have endured torture. And you even killed your own family. I know the man who discovered your murdered children. He was devastated. He still has nightmares.'

'You know nothing. Ask your questions, Flavia Albia.' Gnaeus thought he was goading, but I knew he was desperate for an opportunity to boast about his crimes.

'Not me,' I said. 'What is there to ask? I see your motives. I understand what was done. Your set-pieces were clever, but your justification was false. I don't want to hear what you say had been done to you. I know what you did to the victims. That's enough.'

He sniggered with that arrogant mischief of his. 'Not even the teensiest curiosity?'

Playing for time, I threw at him suddenly, 'Where did the timber for the crucifix come from?'

He blinked, startled. Then he immediately answered me: 'Repurposed scaffolding. Off the big amphitheatre. Tons of wood is available. Anyone can have it. You should tell your husband. Megalo got hold of it for nothing – he knew someone.'

'Megalo? He, I presume, really did threaten to go to the authorities – not that they needed a confession. Nor would they have given him a plea bargain. But I suspect he was just weary of brutality and blood, so he wanted to stop.'

'And Plotinus?' demanded Gnaeus, intently. 'What did you make of him?'

'Apart from the fact you have broken his old grandmother's heart? Crispinus, the waiter, tried to convince us Plotinus was your ring-leader, but waiters are liars – it comes with the job. I suppose you put him up to it. Perhaps there was some truth: Plotinus believed he was the brains, purely because of his skills with wood and rope. But you are the expert on drama, and I am sure you provided all the creative input.'

'I am very intelligent.'

'You could be. You pervert your intellect. Where did the rope come from?' I shot in again.

'Here. Intended for rigging. We found mounds of it . . . What did you make of the Odeum?' asked Gnaeus, abruptly, as if he genuinely wanted a critique. 'Wasn't that brilliant?'

'Devious and cruel even to your own. You and Plotinus bluffed Megalo into going there, as if to arrange some different death, then you jumped him. You must have suggested that killing him would be even better if Plotinus was to fly overhead, watching. What made Plotinus hate Megalo?'

'Thwarted love! That woman who snuffles around the Farcicals—'

'Ambrosia? She truly loves performing.'

'If you say so. All rosy cheeks and misplaced enthusiasm. When she was showing an interest in Plotinus, Megalo warned her off.'

'Her mother was doing a good enough job of that! Why did you decide to be rid of Plotinus?'

'Because I could. Plotinus is so dumb he fell for the flying trick. I strapped him in, then whoops!'

'One final spectacle? You had fixed the rope so he was stuck. I was surprised you left them both there alive.'

'I enjoyed the scare it gave them. And even if they were rescued, Megalo and Plotinus were going to the beasts.'

'What about you?'

'Oh, I shall escape! Did those bears actually get them?'

I refused to answer. I still could not think about it.

'Not freed by the vigiles?'

'Megalo and Plotinus?' My voice sounded cold. 'The vigiles dealt with them in their own way. All that remains is to deal with you.'

Gnaeus let out a high burst of that irritating giggle, completely at ease with it. He was proud of what he had done and saw no reason to fear condemnation. Accusation left him untouched. 'I am not as bad as you make out.'

'You are worse than I could ever say.'

'Oh, come now, Flavia! Isn't the job you do, the ideal your parents handed down to you, supposed to be based on high-minded restraint? Don't get emotional! What would Falco say?'

I replied coolly, 'Falco would say as I do: given your crimes, restraint would be an obscenity.'

'They will be sorry when you are gone.'

'If they ever lose me.'

Gnaeus stood up. He had rocked easily to his feet, a man who performed athletic feats onstage, still active and still desperately dangerous. 'My only regret,' he said, clearly intending to distract me, 'is how I wish we had put on Falco's version of *Rudens*!'

I stepped away, to put space between us. I unbrooched my cloak, as if I felt too warm. 'His script has been found, if you'd like to know. His tug-of-war makes the play, I believe.'

'No!' Gnaeus flashed hotly. He was stepping after me. 'The tug-of-war is all about the "business", only that. The triumph comes from the moves, and the comic acting talent that makes those moves work, not some half-baked hack's tiresome lines. I – *I*, Tranio the sophisticated city clown – I myself blocked out the tug-of-war. The result was superlative theatre.'

'What an artist dies in you!' I mocked him quietly.

I mocked him, then I had to make a run for it. First, I flung my cloak right at his head, temporarily blinding him.

When I jumped, I scrambled around and under the prow of the abandoned ship. Gnaeus followed, swinging himself after me, two-handed from a beam on the tall supporting cradle. I heard it creak, which might have made him hesitate. I ducked fast, under the hull to the opposite side, out into the arms of Milo. As my pursuer saw my back-up, he exclaimed. Stumbling, he sought to retreat, but he fell foul of Hyro – Hyro, the vigilis who had been distraught when he found those two suffocated children.

It was Hyro who yanked the first rigging rope they had been fixing around poorly positioned side blocks. He quickly moved to others. Milo had pushed me to safety, then flung himself against one side of the cradle where the wood used had a giant split.

They were strong, tough lads, trained in pulling down buildings to create hurried firebreaks to stop huge blazes. They did not need ocean rot and barnacles, though woodworm in the cradle helped. When those two decided to demolish some old, decaying wreck that had been given flawed construction, and never any maintenance, it worked. We had had no plan. While I was talking to Gnaeus, my team had prepared. Hyro and Milo, lovers of theatre yet famous for acts of bravery, had created a perfect dramatic trap.

The incongruous pair had known, of course, about the end of Jason's life. The world-weary hero had supposedly died beneath the hull of his old ship: the *Argo* collapsed onto him. So this *Argo*, too, groaned in its death throes. It, too, broke apart and fell. The blocks flew in all directions. Cradling collapsed. The ship crashed, foundered, crashed some more. A hail of planks formed a split and splintered mound, covering Gnaeus.

The vigiles observed and waited, then made sure that this time he would not crawl out to freedom. He made no sound. Under the weight he had stood no chance.

I shared the watch. I stayed until we knew for certain, everything was over.

All performances on the Campus had ceased now. It was time for a mentally shattered audience to gather themselves. We must creep out to the December twilight, in these last days of the year, ready to go home. There we would find lamps, welcoming faces, and warm hearths. In repose, we could absorb the truths of tragedy and comedy, however harrowed or uplifted we had found ourselves while they were put before us onstage. Eventually, the players who had given their all would become like ghosts to us. Night would fall. The passion would dissolve. Reflection, peace, and then sleep would come. Tomorrow we would feel refreshed, more alive for this experience.

All pain would dissipate. Because, after all, whatever you see at the theatre, any play is just a story, a story retold, and now a story ended.

THE GIRL FROM LONDINIUM

To M. Didius Falco and Helena Justina, at their Laurentian villa, by the hand of Paris the runabout, two days before the Kalends of January, when the Consuls are about to be Imp Caes Domitianus Augustus (For the fifteenth bloody time, haven't we suffered enough? moans Father) *and M. Cocceius Nerva* (a somewhat decrepit has-been). (Be fair; he might surprise us, offers Mother):[1]

1 Your mother was prescient – archive scribe's marginal comment, seven years afterwards in the third consulship of Imp Nerva Caesar Augustus

Dear ones,

I know you will complain that I ought to have written this letter earlier. No point raging: this is how it is. I have news for you now, involving terrible sadness that befell past friends of yours. I must tell you in person. I could come out to the seaside, but I know you will want to talk to Thalia and Davos, because this story affects them.

I could say there is no need to worry or to rush here. That would bring you speeding straight away. So I say very simply, it is time for you to come home, please.

Don't break an axle. There is nothing to do.

Happy New Year to everybody, from Tiberius Manlius and me. Any moment now, if I can prise his reluctant fingers off the baton, the most excellent Manlius will shed his official duties; we are both looking forward to a new phase of our lives, with

only the pleasures of business and the hard work of domesticity. You, I suspect, are looking forward to watching us grapple with it.

First, we invite you to welcome in the New Year with us. I am anxious to see you.

Your loving daughter, Albia. Don't call me Flavia.

PS to Father: whatever was the story of the praetor's clerk and the piles lozenge?

RECEIVE THE LATEST NEWS FROM LINDSEY DAVIS

Go to
https://www.hodder.co.uk/contributor/lindsey-davis/
to sign up to Lindsey's email newsletter

Visit Lindsey's website at www.lindseydavis.co.uk

Or head over to the official Facebook page
/lindseydavisauthor